SING TO
SILENT STONES

FRANK'S WAR

David Snell

Hornet Books

Sing to Silent Stones: Frank's War

First published 2017 by Hornet Books

Previously published as the second half of one edition in 2011

Text © David Snell

This work © Hornet Books Ltd

Paperback ISBN 978-0-9957658-0-1

Editor: David Roberts

Proof-readers: Matthew White, John White

Hornet Books

Ground Floor, 2B Vantage Park, Washingley Road, Huntingdon, PE29 6SR

www.hornetbooks.com

info@hornetbooks.com

For Frank Balfour, who perished in the Great War. For his son Frank, my father-in-law, who fought behind the lines in the Second World War, and for his mother, Violet, who I came to think of as my own granny. For my brave and beautiful mother, Pat, who ferried bombers in the war and trained bomb aimers. Most of all for my dear father, Eric, who served three tours in Bomber Command, and was in the skies over wartime Berlin at just 19 years of age.

For the men and women of the French Resistance who perished in that senseless massacre in the Forest of Orleans, days before the end of hostilities. For the men, women, boys and girls who fought in all those wars. They were not, in the main, soldiers. They were people from all walks of life, all religions and all races who did their duty and got caught up in events of their time, beyond their control.

The title for 'Sing to Silent Stones' comes from the lines of silent gravestones in northern France, with the larks singing down at them from the sky.

David Snell
byohsnell@yahoo.co.uk

Special thanks to:-
Linda Snell, Naomi Snell, Cynthia Scott, Pauline Holsgrove, Mark Neeter, Jacqui Freeman, Gisela Hunting, Naomi Handford-Jones, Moira Houghton, Birgit Muller and Michel et Annie Fouilleul for all their help and encouragement. Very special thanks to Joan McConnell-Wood for her enthusiastic support and for her insights into just what life was like in the period.

SING TO SILENT STONES

The cast list so far . . .

Frank Balfour ....*Illegitimate son of Violet and Frank Balfour Snr who died in the Great War*

Violet .... *Frank's mother*

Ernest Matthews .... *Violet's father*

Elsie Matthews .... *Violet's mother (deceased)*

Alice .... *Housekeeper to Violet's parents, then married to Ernest*

Jim Slater .... *Violet's second husband*

Ian and George .... *Violet's twin boys by Slater*

Maxwell .... *Slater's solicitor*

Armand Taillefer .... *Deceased. French landowner and Violet's first husband, who made Frank his heir*

Philippe .... *Armand's and later Frank's driver*

Leclerc .... *Manager at the factory*

Nicole and Henri........... *Armand's sister and her husband*

Marie .... *Housekeeper at the chateau*

Jean-Claude .... *Marie's husband and handyman at the chateau*

Father René .... *Priest in Chateauneuf-sur-Loire. Armand and Frank's friend*

The two sisters .... *Daughters of one of Armand's tenant farmers*

Pierre-Luc Cabal .... *Frank's boyhood friend*

Marcel Fleisch ....*Frank's boyhood friend*

Cast List continued

Jesse Long .... *Frank Snr's aunt, who raised him after the death of his parents*

Rosie .... *Nurse who served with Violet in France*

Doris............... *Nurse who served with Violet in France*

Keith .... *School chum and Great War comrade of Frank Snr*

Florrie Pope .... *Young Frank's foster mother*

Joe Pope .... *Young Frank's foster father*

Lizzie Pope .... *Florrie and Joe's daughter*

George .... *Lizzie's cousin*

Kate .... *Florrie's sister and George's mother*

Dieter Schmidt .... *German soldier, murdered in front of Violet's eyes*

Gisela Schmidt .... *Dieter's widow*

Gunther Schmidt .... *Dieter and Gisela's son and Frank's best friend*

SING TO
SILENT STONES

The story so far . . .

In David Snell's opening novel, *Sing to Silent Stones: Violet's War*, Frank Balfour, the illegitimate son of Violet Matthews and Frank Balfour Snr, was fostered out to the Pope family in Devon, where he lived oblivious and happy until his mother came to reclaim him just after the end of World War I.

Violet, having reluctantly given up her baby son following the death of her lover, had bravely gone to war in France as a nurse, experiencing all the horrors that entails. Amidst the chaos and dangers of war, she met and eventually married a wounded French soldier, Armand Taillefer. A man of means, with farms, factories and a large chateau, Armand provided a new happy family home in the Loire Valley for young Frank, who formed deep and lasting friendships with three boys; Gunther, the son of a German soldier, whose murder Violet unfortunately witnessed, Pierre-Luc, the son of a nearby farmer, and Marcel, a Jewish boy from a nearby village.

With Armand's untimely death, Frank inherited his much-loved stepfather's estate in France.

Unhappy and still mourning Armand, Violet attempted to re-make her life back in England and inadvisably married Jim Slater, one of her father's acquaintances. Despised by Frank, Slater turned out to be a bully and a bore, who was full of contempt for Frank's illegitimacy.

The uneasy family division grew, prompting Frank to renew contact and find solace with Florrie and Joe Pope, still living in Devon with daughter Lizzie, now a precocious 11-year-old.

Meanwhile, the death of Violet's ailing mother, Elsie, enabled her father Ernest to find love and companionship with the family's housekeeper Alice, which further fuelled Slater's contempt and anger.

The not unwelcome early death of Slater left Violet in straightened circumstances but rid her and the twins she bore him, Ian and George, of his suffocating presence.

As Frank reaches maturity, he takes charge of his stepfather's estate in France, provides for his mother, and his life looks set fair. But the storm clouds of another World War are approaching.

How will the 24-year-old Frank fare with split loyalties between France and England? How will his fellowship with Gunther, Pierre-Luc and Marcel, encapsulated in the name of their boyhood playground, 'Allemanceterre', withstand the divisions of race, religion and nationality?

This, then, is David Snell's telling of Frank's War.

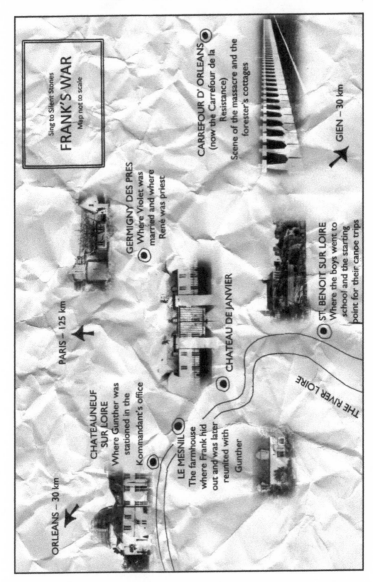

Sing to Silent Stones
FRANK'S WAR
Map not to scale

CARREFOUR D' ORLEANS
(now the Carrefour de la Resistance)
Scene of the massacre and the forester's cottages

GIEN – 30 km

GERMIGNY DES PRES
Where Violet was married and where René was priest

ST. BENOIT SUR LOIRE
Where the boys went to school and the starting point for their canoe trips

PARIS – 125 km

CHATEAU DE JANVIER

THE RIVER LOIRE

CHATEAUNEUF SUR LOIRE
Where Gunther was stationed in the Kommandant's office

ORLEANS – 30 km

LE MESNIL
The farmhouse where Frank hid out and was later reunited with Gunther

SING TO SILENT STONES

Volume Two:

FRANK'S WAR

September 1939

Frank sat up in the canoe and dipped the paddle to take him closer to the bank, beneath the shade of the overhanging willows. A strong smell of fish made him wrinkle his nose, and he could see now that the bank and branches above were coated with white from the night-time roosts of the flocks of cormorant that wheeled and dived in the wide waters of the Loire. He grimaced in disgust and guided the canoe back out into the current.

He settled back, the paddle across his lap, his face up to the sun to let the world slip by. My, what a week it had been! Gunther and Lizzie had only left this time last week, but it felt as if it were ages ago.

On the Monday he had restarted work at the factory, expecting that after the summer recess things would be relatively quiet, but at the gate he had been met by an excited Leclerc, waving a piece of paper in his hands.

"Look Monsieur Frank! Look at this, we have got it."

Frank had waited for the man to reach him before taking the papers from him. "What have we got Monsieur Leclerc?"

"The order for the new railings for the Mairie and park in Chateauneuf."

Frank had looked at him, his mouth falling open. He glanced down at the papers and quickly ran his eyes over them. "We got that? But that's... that's just wonderful." He handed the papers back to Leclerc. "That's a massive order, isn't it?"

Leclerc beamed. "It most certainly is my dear fellow. It most certainly is, and it means that with the confirmation of the new gun-carriage wheels we have now fulfilled our targets for the next two years."

Frank put his hand out and Leclerc took it. "It is your victory, Monsieur Leclerc," said Frank. "We... all of us owe you so much."

Leclerc bristled with pride. He drew himself erect as he shook Frank's hand. "Thank you Monsieur Frank... thank you very much. I do my best."

"As you always have Monsieur Leclerc. As you always have." He had let go of the man's hand and transferred his arm to his shoulders, turning him back in the direction of the gates. "Now how can I help? What have we to do?"

Lying back in the boat, Frank smiled to himself. What a silly question. How can I help? Well, he'd found out alright! And the result had been a week of non-stop activity. Late into each evening, right up until the Saturday night, they'd been in the offices poring over plans and designs. The factory floor had to be rearranged to accommodate the new lines. Castings and moulds had to be perfected and duplicated, and while Frank had busied himself with these in-house tasks, Leclerc had got on with the ordering of materials.

The activity in the factory throughout that momentous week had all but blotted out what was happening in the big wide world. Oh, Philippe had tried to keep him abreast of what was going on, but, to be truthful, by the time he got back to the chateau each night, he'd been so tired that he could barely comprehend what the man was trying to tell him.

The war clouds were looming once again over Europe. Ultimatums were being bandied back and forth, and only the day before had come the rumour that Hitler had finally invaded Poland. Frank had sighed to himself as he listened. The consequences of that were tremendous. A German invasion of Poland would, almost certainly, mean that Britain would declare war on Germany, and France was sure to follow, and where on earth would that lead?

"Tell me it won't happen," he'd said to Gunther in August.

"It won't happen," Gunther had said. "Our two peoples will never fight each other again."

"Which two peoples, Gunther?" Frank had asked. "Are you talking of France or of England?"

Lizzie had leant forward eagerly. "Yes Gunther, surely you could not contemplate being at war with any of your friends?"

Frank had watched Gunther's face as she spoke. It was funny. Gunther had never before exhibited any real feeling for women, but on meeting Lizzie all that had changed. He had danced attendance on her as if she were the most beautiful woman in the world. He had, Frank laughed to himself at the memory, really worn his heart on his sleeve for the vivacious English girl he had met for the first time that summer.

At times, Frank had felt something almost akin to jealousy. This was his Lizzie, and although he had always thought of her as a little sister, something was different this time. Perhaps it was the fact that for the first time they were away from Devon. Perhaps it was just the joy of having her here at the chateau at last.

Frank opened his eyes and squinted along the bow. He steadied the canoe's passage and then lay back to think once more.

More likely, it was that, for the first time, he had really appreciated just how beautiful Lizzie was and that she was definitely, most definitely, no longer a little girl.

"Show me your river, Frank," she had said mischievously the week before. "Show me your secret places."

Her eyes danced with wickedness, and Frank's mind had raced back to that spring day in Devon, the cold waters and the white of her body.

"Yes, let's go for a swim," Gunther had said, jumping in, clearly excited at the prospect.

"Yes let's," said Pierre-Luc and Marcel, almost together. Frank had looked across at Lizzie, a resigned smile on his face. She had smiled back sympathetically, knowing, he had no doubt of this, where his thoughts had been, and when they had all got to the river's bank, no swimsuit could ever hide the fact that the child's body he recalled was miraculously changed.

His friends' faces as Lizzie emerged from changing in the bushes!

Admiration would be a polite word, but from three... no, to be fair, four boys, the looks she had received amounted to a lot more than that. God, she had looked wonderful! Slim legs and waist. Full bosom, scarcely concealed in her costume. Her hair, long, dark and shining... flying free. Frank shook his head at the memory.

The day after that, Marcel and Pierre-Luc had left to re-join their regiment and Frank, along with Gunther and Lizzie, had gone to the station to wish them goodbye. Lizzie had remarked how smart the two young men had looked... how handsome. Gunther had merited a frown of disapproval when he had tried to say that, in his opinion, the uniform of the German army was considerably smarter. "How could you say that?" Lizzie had complained.

"Yes, explain yourself man," Frank had interjected, slightly amused at his friend's obvious discomfiture... at his suddenly finding himself at odds with Lizzie when he had tried so hard for weeks to impress her.

Gunther floundered. "Well... well it's just that... well... oh alright, have it your own way."

"I think all men in uniform look wonderful," said Lizzie lightly. Frank and probably Gunther too, at that moment, had earnestly wished that they too were in uniform. Frank had even toyed with the idea of dressing up in his when they got back to the chateau but decided, in the end, that it would be a little silly... and very, very obvious.

He had elected to do his Service a couple of years before, as he had not wished to bother with higher education. "Go to university, you'll love it," Violet had pleaded. Love it? Why should he love it? What he loved was right here in Germigny and Chateauneuf. No amount of schooling or university would change that. Why should he waste time on higher education when what he really wanted to do was to learn how the factory worked and be ready to take it on full-time when Leclerc finally retired. Leclerc had been his teacher, his friend, and in the years since he had finally returned full-time to France, he had listened and learnt from the older man. What more could he ever aspire to?

He rounded a bend in the river and drew near to the old quayside at Saint-Benoit. This was one of his favourite places. Gone now were the quays and berths that trading gabare of old had tied up to, and in their stead the stately willows held the bank and tickled both sky and waters with their silvery green. What had once been a place of noise and activity now slept quietly in the summer sun. A small circle of houses and cottages lay back up to the top of the levee, and from them, half hidden now in the long grass, you could still discern the steps leading down to the water's edge.

The river ran straight for a while and then curved gently to the left before running on down past the road leading back to the chateau. As it turned, the waters slowed and deposited sand and silt to form the chain of islands to the right-hand side of the river, culminating in their boyhood island of Allemanceterre. Frank drifted quietly by these, staring intently up the banks for signs of life. Terns roosting on the shingle rose into the sky, protesting as they wheeled around his head, before settling again as he passed.

The river now ran faster as it drew level to where he had arranged to meet the ever-faithful Philippe, and Frank scanned the bank for sight of him. The glint of well-polished paintwork caught his eye and he powered the canoe to the edge and beached it. He got out, calling Philippe's name as he did so, and then lay back on the grass, his eyes closed, savouring the sounds and smells of this river that he loved so dearly. A footfall beside him told him that his friend had arrived. "That was lovely," he said without opening his eyes. "I've waited all week for that."

There was no reply. Philippe sat on his haunches, gripping his knees and staring out across the waters. For a few moments there was silence between the two of them, but then the older man spoke, slowly and quietly. "The British have declared war on Germany."

Frank sat up slowly. He didn't look at Philippe. Rather, the two of them just sat quietly, staring out across the moving waters. They must have sat like that for five to ten minutes, each locked in his own thoughts, before Frank finally spoke. "And France?"

"Today, maybe this evening... but for certain."

"It begins again."

"It begins."

The silence resumed. Frank thought of his father, the rows upon rows of silent white stones. Was this now his destiny? Philippe stared straight ahead, lost in his own world of memories. At length Frank turned, and resting on one elbow touched his companion. "What should I do?"

"Do?"

"Yes, what should I do? Should I go to England and enlist or should I stay here?"

Philippe sat back on the grass and stretched his legs out before him, leaning back on his hands. "Do you want to go to England?"

"Not particularly, but I can't just sit and do nothing, can I?"

"You are not doing nothing. The factory is making parts for the guns of the French army. That is important, no?"

Frank thought for a moment. "It is important, but is it all I can do?"

"I think," said Philippe, turning to face Frank at last, "that you are already a reservist in the French army and that you should wait for orders if they come. If you went to England would you enlist?"

"Yes... yes I would."

"And you'd be sent to France to fight?"

Frank smiled. "Yes, I suppose you're right."

"Then why waste the journey?"

Frank laughed now. The clever old fox. He got to his feet and dragged the canoe further out of the water. "Here, give me a hand to pull this to the top," he called, "and then we'd better get back home." The two of them dragged the canoe up the steep bank and tied it to a tree at the top. "I'll come back for it later," said Frank, walking off to the motor car. "I know you wouldn't want it near this thing."

"Certainly not," agreed Philippe. He paused as he noticed Frank going to the driver's side, then shrugged his shoulders and got in the other side at the front.

Frank reversed the great car away from the top of the levee and did a three-point turn behind the willow tree, with Philippe watching anxiously to check that his beloved vehicle was not scratched. Frank smiled at him in recognition of his fears. "Don't worry old man," he said, laughing as he slipped into forward gear. "I know how to do it you know."

They rode back to the chateau in silence, each deep in his own thoughts. As they pulled into the driveway, Jean-Claude came down the steps, his face serious, the traces of tears still showing on his cheeks. He waved his hands in the air, shaking his head silently.

"I know Jean-Claude, I know," said Frank. He reached up and pulled down the older man's hand and held it. "Let's wait and see shall we?" Jean-Claude nodded. He glanced up at Philippe coming around the motor car to join them, and the three of them retired to the house.

All Europe held its breath for the next few weeks in the general expectation that the Blitzkrieg that had destroyed Poland would be repeated throughout the continent. When it did not come, a semblance of normality crept back into life in the French countryside and towns, despite the restrictions which were gradually being imposed. The order for the new railings, so joyfully gained, was cancelled at short notice but was replaced by a larger one for gun-carriage carcasses, and Frank and Leclerc were kept extremely busy reorganising the factory for this new production.

Pierre-Luc and Marcel, finding themselves in uniform at the outbreak of war, were confirmed in their regiments and posted north of Paris, but Frank received a letter telling him that he was in a reserved occupation and that he should stand by to receive further orders if the necessity arose.

As expected, there was a long letter from Violet agonising over whether he should stay in France or come back to the safety of England. Frank could scarcely resist a smile as he read the letter. Poor Violet. In spite of the fact that she had lived for so long in Germigny, she still clung to the idea that it was a foreign land and that the only real safety lay in England. She had been to the chateau only twice since he had finally moved back there permanently, and although she and the children had enjoyed themselves immensely, she had been quite happy to go home. For Violet, the chateau could never be separated from the memory of her beloved late husband Armand. All the time she was there she half expected him to come through the door, and when he didn't the disappointment built up to such a degree that eventually she felt that she just had to go.

Frank understood her feelings. He had loved having her there and had revelled in his twin half-brothers. What characters they had become and how amazing it was that two, so alike in looks, could be so different in every other respect. George was loud and jolly... always the first up in the morning, always the keenest to get out and get on with whatever activity had been arranged for him. If nothing special had been laid on, then he would sulk and moan until, eventually, by dint of his sheer determination, either something would be organised or he would end up in some sort of trouble, which served to enlighten his day just as well.

Happily, even though the driving forces in his make-up quite obviously sprang from Slater's tree, there were subtle differences in character brought about by environment. Whereas Slater's personality had been honed by loneliness and an unrequited craving for the love of his mother, George was surrounded by affection. If Violet was not available then, at home, there was always Alice and, if they visited, it was to Jesse in England or Marie in France.

Ian, on the other hand, was a quiet and gentle boy who one day would aspire to all things learned, but for now was content to bask in the company of his brother and the love they felt for each other.

When Frank had first taken them down to the river, George had rushed straight down to the water's edge, shouting out his joy. He had picked up stones and hurled them as far out as he could, whooping as they splashed into the current. Ian, however, had stood quietly for a moment at the top of the bank, taking in the view. He had smiled up at Frank, and although no words had passed between them, Frank had understood that the little boy was telling him that he liked this place as much as he did. After that, and only then, he had run down to the water's edge to join his brother in their game.

As the phoney war continued and the autumn wore on, Frank wished that he could go to England and visit them, but it simply wasn't possible. The work at the factory continued apace, and as the year drew to a close, increasingly he was called upon to don his uniform and report for duty at weekends.

He received several letters from Lizzie. In the first she thanked him profusely for the wonderful holiday she had spent with him at the chateau, and in the subsequent letters she went on to bemoan the division of the friendships she had so obviously enjoyed. She passed on her love to Pierre-Luc and Marcel and hoped that they were safe. Most especially she mentioned Gunther and expressed the same fears that had been growing in Frank's mind.

How could he regard his boyhood friend as an enemy? Yet that is what he now was, and the possibility remained that they might well find themselves pitted against each other in the future. How could he cope with that? They all knew that Gunther had gone home in August with the specific intention of joining his regiment, and the thought that he was somewhere out there, in the uniform of the enemy, was a terrible one. Night after night Frank ran all the various scenarios around in his mind, and when Pierre-Luc or Marcel visited on leave they discussed the problem endlessly.

But it was the other part of her letter that disturbed him the most. George, cousin George, that lumpen yokel, had proposed to Lizzie just before he had enlisted. She wrote quite candidly to Frank that she didn't... couldn't ever love the man, but that she had not felt able to turn him down and send him off to war grieving. 'Oh she hadn't accepted, thank God for that,' Frank thought, but she had left the matter open and George was expecting an answer when he got back from initial training. "What should I do?" she had wailed in her letter. "I can't hurt him and I can't hurt Auntie Kate. He's told her... and mum and dad... and it really has put me on the spot. Auntie Kate is so excited, you'd think it was all arranged."

Frank tried to analyse his own feelings. Were they those of a concerned brother, or was there something more? Even though he had noted how beautiful she was... even though he had revelled in her company and delighted in her friendship... there was nothing else between them... was there? How could there be, they were practically brother and sister. But George? Why him? If she had to be married, then surely to God she could do better than that.

Frank determined to write to Lizzie, urging her not to throw herself away. He sat down one evening, tired after a hard day at the factory, and started the letter. Four times he got half way down the page before he tore it up and threw it in the waste paper basket. Sometimes he thought he was being too patronising. Another time he read what he'd written and decided that if George ever came across the letter, it would be impossible for them ever to be in the same place. And on another occasion he realised that what he had written could be upsetting to either Kate or Florrie or both and that was something he could not... would not risk.

Eventually he nodded off in his chair and put off the letter until another day, but as he did he wished with all his heart that he could write in a completely different vein. 'Oh, don't be silly Frank,' he thought, as he drifted into sleep, 'she'd think you a fool and just where would that leave you?'

He never really wrote the letter that he wanted to... felt he should have written. In the end he combined the simple message, "Think carefully", with his letter of Christmas greetings, and that in turn was put in the same envelope as his greetings to the rest of the Devon family. No mention, in turn, was made by Lizzie of any decision having been reached, and Frank finally put the matter to the back of his mind to concentrate on the tasks in hand, namely the constantly increasing orders for arms-related fabrications from the factory.

Leclerc was cock-a-hoop. "If this is what the threat of war brings then it's not so bad," he said jovially.

Frank wasn't so sure. The fact that no actual hostilities had, as yet, taken place on French soil did not convince him that Leclerc could possibly be right in his theory that the Germans would never actually dare to attack the might of the French army. A theory that was certainly weakened when the Germans invaded and conquered first Denmark and then Norway. "It's coming," he insisted to Leclerc.

"Nonsense my boy," the older man had replied, clapping him on the back. "They'll never get through, and if they did try it then our chaps and the British would crucify them."

"I do hope you're right," Frank had replied without enthusiasm, but all the while a feeling of dread was growing within him.

On the 10th of May, the Germans invaded Belgium and Holland, and for Frank that sealed his convictions. As he received the news from a stunned and clearly upset Leclerc, he felt no sense of vindication. Instead he felt a profound sense of sadness and, something he could, of course, never tell anybody else, a distinct fear for Gunther. The thought of his best friend lying dead and mutilated in some field haunted him, and he remembered how Violet had recounted the story of Dieter's death. Could that same fate await the son? That evening he made a point of visiting Gisela's grave in the family plot behind the chateau and placed a bunch of flowers upon it.

In the days that followed, the news from the north got grimmer and grimmer, culminating in the invasion of France, with the German army driving a wedge between the British and French forces.

"The British are trapped on the beaches," Philippe informed Frank. "The channel ports are lost."

Pierre-Luc and Marcel had last been heard of with their regiment north of Paris, and increasingly Frank found that he now had all his friends to worry about. He visited their parents and shared with them the hope and expectation that the two young men would soon be home. Marcel's parents could not bring themselves to believe that the French army, the greatest army the world had ever seen, could possibly be defeated. Pierre-Luc's parents, on the other hand, were a little more realistic. They knew of the Blitzkrieg tactics that had overwhelmed country after country and saw no reason why France, alone, should be immune to such warfare.

As the British and French armies scrambled off the beaches at Dunkirk, in the last days of May and the early days of June, Frank reported to army headquarters in Orleans. He was assigned to the 57th Regiment, who were preparing to move north in company with the 4th Regiment and a battalion of the 17th Senegalais.

***

Frank opened his eyes to a chattering sound and for a moment lay there trying to remember where he was. Above him the magpie hopped along the branch of the pine tree and flapped off in search of its morning meal. Frank shifted his position and winced as the hard earth dug into his complaining bones. Around him now he could hear the sound of men stirring and orders being barked. Montargis. They were on the road to Montargis, where they had stopped and bedded down for the night.

Frank shook the life back into his legs and rubbed his right arm to rid it of the pins and needles, which for the moment rendered his right hand useless. He flung aside the thin blanket, rolled over on his stomach and jack-knifed to his knees. Another strange sound came to him. A long moaning wail that rose and fell. What was it? He stood and looked around.

Across, at the edge of the wood where they had slept separately from the rest of the men, the Senegalais were lined up in long rows bowed down to the east. They rose in unison, their hands in the air and then, as one, prostrated themselves. Frank watched fascinated as they completed their devotions. Tall, fierce men in their mustard-coloured uniforms offset by white turbans. Men far from their homes, preparing to fight for France. Cold in the early June morning, they silently now gathered their possessions and arms and prepared to resume the day's journey. Frank smiled to himself. He was glad they were on his side. He would hate to come up against one of these strange, proud warriors in combat.

Along the road, the five lorries they had travelled in were parked in a line on the verge, and beside each one its contingent of men were moving around packing their things and heaving them up into the trucks. The engines started with great roars, and clouds of silver-blue smoke rose into the cool morning air.

The refugees who had clogged the road the day before seemed to have gone; indeed, as the day had worn on their numbers had dwindled. Sad, silent people with hollow, vacant faces trudging to who-knows-where. 'Probably,' Frank thought, 'the north-south road will be full of them, whereas here... God what a mess.' He turned and made his way up the bank, through the trees at the verge and into a thicket. As he squatted down he could hear the sound of other men in the bushes nearby, obviously engaged in the same task.

The sound of aircraft overhead made him look upwards inquisitively.

High in the sky, through the trees, he could see three aeroplanes circling. They peeled off and stooped down towards the convoy, crooked wings howling as their dive steepened. Quickly he stood, pulling violently at his trousers.

He stumbled forward and tripped, falling flat on his face in the leaf litter as a tremendous explosion rent the air and the lorry he had travelled in disintegrated in a ball of flame. Instinctively he buried his head in the litter and clapped his hands over his ears as shards of white-hot metal scythed through the trees. A strangled scream came from behind him but he kept his head down, his face pressed deep into the dirt.

Even as he dared to raise his head slightly, the second aircraft stooped and a cluster of bombs exploded in a patterned line along the road and through the next two trucks. Behind, from the direction of Montargis, the third aeroplane swept along the road, its guns chattering, sending spurts of tarmac and dirt into the air and making men reel about like drunken puppets before they fell broken. Frank watched, appalled, as the forward truck tried to pull out of the mayhem, its engine roaring above even the din of men's screams and the sound of exploding ammunition. The driver tried desperately to turn the vehicle in the road but the lock was not sufficient. Gears crunched and wheels span as he threw the vehicle into reverse.

As the lorry came into the third point of its turn, Frank could clearly see the driver's panic- stricken face as he struggled vainly to find the forward gear. Behind him, a dot in the sky that grew and grew with menacing speed, the aeroplane screamed in for its prey. Frank stood and stumbled forward a pace before the trousers, still around his ankles, tripped him once more. As his head hit the fallen log in front of him and his hands grasped its rough surface, he heard the stuttering fire of the guns. He raised his head to peer over the top of the log as the driver half stood in his seat before crashing, bloody and broken, through the shattered windscreen. The lorry swerved away from Frank's side of the road and careered wildly into the ditch opposite before rolling over on its side, its wheels still spinning. There was a dull thud as the petrol tank exploded, and Frank buried his face behind the log as the super-heated air rushed over him.

And then they were gone, and the only sounds were those of the crackling fires from the burning vehicles. He lay for a moment listening to them and then stood up to survey the scene. He glanced up into the sky apprehensively and was rewarded with no sign of the enemy. Slowly he bent down and pulled up his trousers, buttoning the belt. He stepped over the log and started as his trouser leg caught on a projection. He bent down to free the garment and burnt his hand on the still-hot shard of metal embedded within the wood. This had been meant for him. If he had not stumbled... He shook himself, refusing to contemplate the unthinkable, and stepped forward to the edge of the trees.

As he reached the verge he could see that four of the lorries were completely destroyed, but one miraculously stood intact, its engine still running. Bodies and parts of bodies lay everywhere, strewn around like so many discarded toys. How strange that a picture of early morning army domesticity could be transformed in minutes to that of the charnel house. Was he really part of this? How strange it was to walk amongst it as men stood up and others filtered out from the trees.

A Sergeant sat on the grass by the unbroken lorry. Frank crossed to him. "Are you alright?" he asked.

The man sat staring into space humming a tune! Frank shook him. "Are you alright Sergeant? We've got to get out of here. They could come back." The man just sat there wide- eyed. Frank looked around desperately. Twenty or so Senegalais rose mysteriously from the earth, where before there had been no sign of them. They began picking over the bodies of their fallen comrades, placing them all in a line facing east whilst one of them wailed some prayer or other. Frank watched in spellbound horror as two of them knelt down beside a wounded comrade. Briefly perfunctorily, they examined him. One bent forward and whispered in the stricken man's ear, and then he rose. A flash of bright steel, a slight shudder, but no sound before they stood and carried the fresh corpse to place it in line with the others.

Frank stepped forward, raising his hand and opening his mouth to speak. A hand on his shoulder restrained him and he turned to the face of a veteran. The question was answered before it was uttered. "Leave them to their business soldier. They are a long way from home."

"Yes, but surely?"

The older soldier held up his hand. "Let's see what we've got here and then we'd better decide what to do."

There seemed to be no officer left alive, and the Sergeant still sat humming his own tune. A group of about twenty able-bodied men gradually assembled on the verge, and they began to check amongst the fallen for survivors. Frank went from bloody corpse to corpse, turning them over, prodding them for signs of life. One young soldier lay crumpled up on the grass and, as Frank approached, he turned his head to him, revealing the tears in his eyes. He knelt down beside him and cradled his head. "Where are you hurt?"

"I don't know," the boy replied weakly. "I can't feel anything."

Frank let go of his head and bent forward to examine him. He felt down his torso until his hands encountered a stickiness. Lifting the torn remains of his jacket he could see that a long thin fragment of casing had driven into his side. He felt around its cruel entry, feeling the lifeblood oozing. "You've got a piece of metal in your side," he whispered gently.

The boy turned his head, licked his lips and coughed. "Pull it out," he breathed. "Take this thing from me please."

Frank sat back on his haunches. "Well I'm not..."

"Please," he begged. "Take it from me."

Frank leant forward and seized the still-hot end of the shard. He watched the boy's face for a moment as he gazed up into the clear blue morning sky. A bird began to sing in the trees behind them and the boy tilted his head back in an effort to see it. Frank yanked at the metal and it slid surprisingly easily from the wound, followed by a rush of dark, almost blue-black blood, which flowed over Frank's hands as the life drained from the body. Frank stood and flung the metal shard away, wiping his hands down his hips, desperate to rid himself of the sticky gore.

Then he reeled away to the bank's edge, sank to his knees and vomited.

"That one over there!" A voice broke into his misery and he turned to it. "That one over there. See if he's alright."

Frank's eyes followed the man's outstretched hand. A young soldier was crawling away from the wreckage of the middle lorry, his elbows digging frantically into the turf as he pulled himself forward. Frank stood and ran across to him. "It's alright soldier," he said as he reached the boy.

He looked up, relief on his face. "I've broken my bloody leg," he cried.

Frank knelt down beside him. "Keep still, let's have a look. Which one?"

"The right-hand one."

Frank felt down the leg. The thigh seemed alright, but as he passed the knee he could feel through the trousers that the lower leg was crooked in an unnatural way. He looked into the boy's face. "You weren't going dancing tonight were you?"

The soldier smiled through his pain. "Funny you should say that... it's just what I was planning."

Frank grinned back at him. He felt the horror draining from him. This broken boy, although he didn't realise it, was helping him as much as he was him. He turned and called back to the others. "Here, give me a hand with this fellow. He's broken his leg."

One of the other able-bodied came across. "Fetch me some stout sticks," said Frank, "and I'll pinch the belts off some of these poor chaps that won't be needing them anymore."

Between the two of them they quickly splinted the leg and then half carried, half dragged the boy across to where the other injured had been placed, amongst them the Sergeant who still persisted in humming his tune.

The veteran soldier called them all over and proceeded to count how many remained. Fifteen wounded, twenty-two able-bodied, plus about thirty Senegalais and one lorry between them all. Some of the wounded would not last the day and nearly all of them obviously needed better attention than the rough field dressings the rest of the soldiers had performed.

The sound of an engine had all of the fit men rushing to pick up their rifles and they stared up into the sky, ready to run. "Look!" called one of the men, and they all turned in the direction of his pointed finger. Down the road came two motorcycles.

"Germans!" yelled the man standing next to Frank, and they all threw themselves prone on the ground and took up firing positions.

"Hold your fire," screamed the veteran. "Wait until we're sure."

Frank, lying there in the grass peering down his rifle, called across. "Don't the Germans usually have sidecars?"

"Not always, but you may be right. Hold your fire men, they may be French."

The two motorcycles weaved past the burning trucks and halted about thirty metres from their group. The riders slid up their goggles and looked around at the scene of devastation laid out before them. "What's gone on here?" one of them yelled across in French.

A collective sigh ran through the prostrate men, and those who could stood up and ran across to surround the newcomers. "Air strike," Frank explained. "We've got near enough seventy men, including fifteen wounded, and one lorry."

"What's happening up ahead?" asked the veteran.

"The motorcyclist looked at him. "Haven't you heard?"

"Heard what?"

"General Weygand has ordered a general retreat. Paris has probably fallen by now."

"General retreat!" came the murmur on many lips.

Frank stepped forward. "Why, what's gone on?"

The man turned to him. "The British have scarpered and the government moved first to Tours and now to Bordeaux."

"Bordeaux?"

"Bordeaux."

"Jesus," said the soldier standing next to Frank. "If they go any further we'll all be Spaniards." A titter of nervous laughter ran through the company.

"The British will fight on surely," Frank mused.

"Yeah," said a soldier. "The British will always fight to the last Frenchman."

Frank went to reply but thought better of it.

There was no doubt at all that the French felt that they had been dragged into this war by the accident of failed diplomacy. Why, even he had been reluctant to do anything positive until recently, feeling, as most French did, that something would be worked out to avoid actual combat.

"Well," said the motorcyclist. "We're going to get going and I suggest you do the same." He kicked his starter and his companion did the same.

"Where do we go?" Frank asked.

The motorcyclist pulled down his goggles and waved his handlebars to clear a way through the throng. "Get yourselves across the Loire before they blow the bridges, or back to Chateauneuf where General Frere has taken control."

"Blow the bridges?" said the veteran. "When will they do that?"

"Search me, but I suggest you get across as quickly as you can." He revved the engine, let out the clutch, and the two of them rode off down the road towards Bellegarde.

"Well we are in a mess," said the veteran. "Nearly seventy men and one lorry."

"Seventy? How do you make that out?" said a soldier standing at the back of the group. "I only see twenty odd of us."

Frank craned his neck to see the face of the man who had spoken. "What about the fifteen wounded and those chaps over there?" He indicated the group of Senegalais.

"What about them? The wounded will have to take their chances, and I'm damned if I'm getting caught for a bunch of blackies."

Frank felt the rage rise within him. "Those blackies, as you call them, have left their homes to fight for France..." He paused as the older soldier put his arm out to him.

"Whatever the rights and wrongs of it we can't get everybody in that one lorry, can we?" Who knows this area?" the man asked.

Frank raised his hand. "I do. I live near Chateauneuf."

"Where's the nearest bridge?"

Frank thought for a moment. "Gien is a straight road from here or..."

"How far is that?"

"About fifty kilometres."

"Right, in the absence of a senior I'm taking charge of this outfit," announced the veteran. "Any objections?" He looked around at the group of soldiers. The one who had made the racist comment raised his hand and went to speak, but was silenced by a look of pure menace. "Right, get the wounded into the lorry now."

They loaded the injured as gently as possible into the back of the lorry, but even so, despite their care, some of them screamed out in pain as they were handed up and dragged to the front. Eventually they were all on board and the veteran stepped forward to look into the back. He jumped up onto the tailgate, looking down on the faces of his expectant audience. "I reckon there's room for maybe three plus the driver in the front and maybe ten of you in the back."

Frank looked across at the Senegalais. No room would be made for them and they knew it. They sat on their haunches looking impassively at the French men preparing to desert them.

"Right, get on board," shouted the veteran as he jumped down. "Take your weapons and mind out for the wounded. Don't go stepping all over the poor buggers."

He crossed to stand next to Frank as the men scrambled about, picking up their rifles and clambering up and into the lorry. Frank held back. Something nagged at him. He felt that the last place he wanted to be right now was trapped in the rear of a speeding lorry on the open road, at the mercy of the next enemy aircraft. The lorry filled quickly and the men in front began to call out that they were being pushed on to the wounded.

The veteran held his hand up. "That's enough." He turned to Frank, and in a low voice said, "You didn't want to go?" Frank shook his head and the man nodded his understanding. He turned to the three others that were left. "Looks like we'll be staying together lads." Then, taking Frank's arm, he guided him around to the driver's side of the vehicle. "Do you know where to go?" he asked the driver.

"Sort of," came the reply.

"Tell him," said the veteran to Frank.

"Go towards Montargis, and then at Villemandeur take the road to the right... that's the south, and that leads through to Gien."

The driver signalled his understanding and slipped the vehicle into gear. Frank and his companion stepped back as it jerked forward, bumping over the rough ground and onto the road. As it passed, Frank glanced back to where they had left the other three soldiers. They weren't there, and as the end of the lorry came past they could be seen hanging over the rear tailgate. "Come back here you bastards," the veteran shouted in vain, but all he got for his pains was a cheery wave.

Frank laughed out loud. "I hope they make it. I don't think I'd want to be crammed in that with German aircraft roaming the skies."

"Me neither," growled the other man, "but that was wrong of them."

"My name's Frank, Frank Balfoure," said Frank, holding out his hand.

"Pierre Charie," the other man growled. "Pleased to meet you." He looked over at the group of Senegalais. "Looks like we're now in the colonial army."

"Yes," agreed Frank, waving them across. They got up and joined the two Frenchmen.

One that the others obviously looked up to stepped forward. "Where we go?" he asked simply.

Pierre turned to Frank. "What do you reckon Frank? Do we follow that lorry?"

Frank thought for a few moments. "No. No I think that the road to Gien will be very open and that it may be clogged with refugees. I think... I think that we should head back from here and turn off towards Lorris and then go through the forest to either Sully or Chateauneuf."

"Sounds good to me." Pierre looked at the Senegalais. "Sound alright to you?"

"Trees good. Can hide in trees," said the man.

"Then that's settled," said Pierre. "Let's get going. What time is it?"

Frank looked at his watch. "Nearly midday. God, where has all the time gone?"

"Midday, and how far did you say it was to the bridge?"

"About the same, fifty kilometres, a bit more to Chateauneuf. Why?"

"Nothing, it's just that we're not going to make it in one go are we?" Frank shook his head. "So we should get there by midday tomorrow. or a bit before if we march through part of the night." Frank again nodded his agreement. "Well we'd better get moving then."

The Senegalais shouldered their weapons and Frank went across to retrieve his bag. For the first time he noticed that it was riddled with dark holes and that the contents had exploded from them. He kicked it and turned away. Nothing in it was of too much use to him now in this predicament. He searched around and collected as many water bottles as he could carry, as well as a few extra magazines. Then he joined Pierre and they set off.

"What's the date today?" Pierre asked.

"The sixteenth of June. Why?"

"Oh nothing. I just wondered."

The date held little real significance for them but, had they known it, the days immediately preceding that one and the following few days were to prove some of the most momentous in the history of the French nation. On the 10th of June the Italians had declared war; on the 11th the government in Paris had fled to Tours, only to move on the next day to Bordeaux whilst ordering a general retreat. This much they knew. What they didn't know was that on the 14th of June Paris had fallen, and on the very day that Frank, Pierre and their band of Senegalais commenced their march back to the Loire, Premier Ministre Paul Reynaud had resigned and Philippe Petain had taken power. Even as they finally camped that night, the news was spreading through the country that the hero had returned and that now the humiliations of the past weeks would be reversed.

As Frank and his party prepared to set off from Lorris early the next morning, they could hear the bombardment of Gien and see the smoke from the shattered town rising in the distance. It confirmed them in their decision to head for Chateauneuf instead of Sully, so as to be able to spend more of the journey in the shade and safety of the forest.

"Where exactly do you live?" asked Pierre as they marched through Vieilles-Maisons, heading out towards Bouzy-la-Foret.

"Just outside Chateauneuf."

"In a village?"

"In a... well sort of, I suppose."

"Sort of?"

Frank faced him without missing step. "I live in a chateau I inherited from my stepfather."

"Stepfather? I thought all stepfathers were bastards."

Frank laughed. "Not this one. He was wonderful."

"Did he die in the Great War?"

"No," he was badly wounded but he died in an accident when I was a young boy."

"I'm sorry. I was just trying to make conversation to pass the time."

Frank smiled. "It's alright. Really I don't mind."

They walked in silence for a while before Pierre started again. "What happened to your real father?"

"He was killed in the war."

"Yeah... what regiment was he in?"

"Oh you wouldn't know. He was English."

"English? Oh then you're half English?"

Frank marched on, thinking, remembering. "No. No I'm all English. My mother was... is English. I also have French citizenship by adoption."

"You won't have liked the comments of our friend back there then, will you?"

Frank grinned. "The English side of me didn't, but the French side might have agreed."

They marched on through the morning, aware now of increasing air traffic above them and the sounds of battle ever closer to the east and the north behind them. Several times they had to leave the road and take cover under the trees, but each time either the aeroplanes were too busy or they failed to spot them.

As midday approached they reached Saint-Martin-d'Abbat, joining the main road to the east of the village just as a convoy of French military traffic sped through, heading towards Chateauneuf. Frank attempted to flag them down, but the drivers merely swerved, honking their horns. "Damn you!" Frank yelled as the last vehicle trundled by, crammed full of grim- faced soldiers.

Pierre grabbed Frank's arm and pulled him back onto the pavement. "How far now?"

"Not far at all," said Frank, still clearly annoyed at their betrayal. "We could make the bridge in about half to three-quarters of an hour." The crump of exploding ordinance reverberated across the fields, and glancing up into the sky over what would be Chateauneuf they could clearly see aeroplanes circling and diving in succession. "Listen," said Frank, tugging Pierre's arm. "If it's all the same to you I'd rather cut down from here to my home."

Pierre looked at him. "What about the bridge?"

Frank thought for a moment. "I have a motor car there. We could make the bridge and then have transport. They won't blow the bridge today will they, not with all this traffic still trying to cross?"

Pierre rubbed his chin. "No... No, perhaps not. Depends on how far into the town the Germans have got." His eyes lit up. "Besides, I bet there's some good grub at your home, isn't there?"

"You bet," said Frank, slapping him on the back. He called across to the leader of the Senegalais. "We're going to divert to my house to collect some things. If you keep on this road you'll make the bridge in about half an hour if you hurry."

The dark-skinned man nodded his understanding. He turned and shouted orders to his band of men and they picked up their gear and set off at a lope. "Good luck," Frank called after them. "See you on the other side of the river." The man waved an acknowledgement as Pierre and Frank cut across the road and down the hill towards Germigny.

The sounds of battle were by now awfully close and, looking up and across towards Chateauneuf, they could see palls of smoke rising. "Looks like we might just have made a mistake here," said Pierre ruefully.

Frank looked over to where his new-found friend was pointing. "You might be right," he agreed, "but now we're here we might just as well push on." They broke into a jog and soon entered Germigny, passing by the church on their left, where Violet and Armand had married all those years ago. "Then again, there is the car," Frank panted.

"I hope there's still a bridge by the time we get there," Pierre laughed. "Otherwise we'll have to swim it I suppose."

About ten minutes later they reached the outer walls of the farm buildings leading to the chateau. Frank led the way through and under the towered arch, past Philippe's rooms. As they passed he banged on the door. "Philippe! Philippe, it's Frank! Come to the house!" It half registered on his mind that the large motor car was not in its usual daytime place under the arch, but he assumed that perhaps in view of all that was going on Philippe had locked it up in the barn.

They got to the back door of the kitchen and Frank burst in. "Jean-Claude! Marie! Where are you?" he called as he ran through the scullery and up the stairs, followed by a breathless and slightly overawed Pierre.

Marie appeared at the kitchen door, her hands held to her mouth. "Oh Monsieur Frank, it's you," she cried, as Jean-Claude joined her.

"Marie. Thank goodness you're still here." He turned and indicated his companion. "This is Pierre. We're very hungry and we only have a few minutes. Can you please throw some food in a bag... anything, we're not fussy."

Frank turned to Jean-Claude. "Jean-Claude, where's Philippe?"

"I think... I'm not quite sure Monsieur Frank. He went out in the motor car."

"In the car? Where to?" Jean-Claude shrugged his shoulders and grimaced.

Marie bustled into the larder and started gathering food, laying it out on the table. Frank saw Pierre's look and jerked his head towards it to indicate that he was free to take some there and then. Pierre grabbed a hunk of bread and cut off a wedge of cheese. Marie looked up at Frank, enquiring. "It's alright Marie, we haven't eaten properly for a while. I could do with some myself if you could make me a sandwich quickly." Pierre looked up briefly from his food, aware that his lack of manners had probably caused some offence. Frank shot him a reassuring look and he continued eating.

"I'll take the small car Jean-Claude, if you can get it out for me whilst I hunt up a few things," said Frank as he ran over to the door to the passageway. "See if you can find a bag to put that lot in Marie," he yelled as he went through the door. He ran upstairs to his room, Armand's old room, glancing briefly out through the tall windows and across the lawns down to the lake. 'God I love this place,' he thought. 'Will I ever see it again?' He turned to busy himself with collecting some fresh underwear, which he stuffed into his jacket pocket. The old stuff he was wearing would definitely be thrown away at the first opportunity. 'Anything else I need,' he thought quickly.

He looked around the room.

His eye alighted on the small bedside cabinet and the framed picture of Armand and Violet. He rushed over and quickly removed the photograph from the frame, tearing the corner in the process. Damn, he really didn't want to lose that photograph. He opened the small drawer in the cabinet and threw in the frame and the corner of the photograph. As he did, his British passport caught his eye. All he had on him in the way of documentation was his identity card and his army details. If he needed to get to England then he'd need this. He took it from the drawer and put it in his inside jacket pocket with the photograph.

One last look and he ran from the room.

Frank burst into the kitchen just as Jean-Claude came in by the back door. "All ready?" he yelled.

"The car's running and ready for you Monsieur Frank," replied Jean-Claude. "Is there anything more you need?"

Frank thought for a moment. "No... No I don't think so, leastwise there's not really time to think. I expect there's something, but for now food is all we really need." He glanced at Pierre. "Ready?"

"Yes," said Pierre. "I'll see you in the car, but hurry now." He picked up the bag of food and made for the door.

"Yes, one second. Let me just say goodbye and I'll be with you." Frank turned to Marie and held his arms open. She slipped into his embrace, the tears coursing down her face.

"Where will you go Frank?" she sobbed.

"South, maybe to England, but I'll be back don't you worry. I'll be back." He hugged her tight as Jean-Claude joined them, tight-lipped, struggling to control his emotions.

"Where shall we go?" sobbed Marie.

Frank looked down into her face. "You must stay here and keep the place for when this is all over. Can you please do that for me?"

"Oh Monsieur Frank," she cried. "Of course."

Frank gently released himself from her grasp, took off his jacket and guided her over towards the door. "Now I must go." He turned from her and faced Jean-Claude, standing there, his eyes glazed, his lip trembling. "Goodbye old friend... for now," said Frank as he embraced him. He felt the man's lips brush his cheek. He stood away from him, still gripping his elbows, and they stared into each other's eyes. "Stay safe old friend," he mouthed.

"And you too Monsieur Frank." Jean-Claude swallowed hard. "Come back to us safely, please."

The sound of aeroplanes could be heard above, screaming through the sky along with other ominous sounds of battle. Pierre leant across and hooted the horn impatiently just as Frank ran from the room and out into the yard, with Jean-Claude and Marie following. "Go to the cellars, you'll be safe there," Frank called out to them as he jumped into the driving seat, chucked his jacket into the back and slipped the motor car into gear. "And look after Philippe when he gets back, tell him to keep his head low." His words were lost to the tearful couple as they waved.

Frank drove out through the main gates and turned towards Le Mesnil. As they passed through the hamlet they could see that all the houses had their doors and shutters firmly closed. They passed the farm where the two sisters lived, alone now since their mother had died. Frank smiled as he glanced quickly into the yard. It looked no different now than it ever had. Ownership had made no difference to their life whatsoever. But what difference would that which was coming bring?

They drove on through to the memorial and turned right, out into open country, with Frank bent low over the wheel, squinting through the windscreen at the skies above. "Keep a look-out for aeroplanes Pierre," he called to his companion.

"I'm doing so," replied Pierre, craning his neck in all directions at the sky.

"Did Marie give you that sandwich for me?" said Frank. "I'm famished."

"She did." Pierre rummaged in the canvas bag and produced the rough sandwich, which he handed to Frank, who ate it as they drove, not knowing when there would be another opportunity.

"Not as good as she usually does, but good nevertheless."

Pierre looked at him. "How can you bear to just leave all that to the Germans?"

Frank laughed as he put the sandwich on his lap in order to negotiate the double bend over the bridge. "What do you expect me to do, stand there and tell the naughty Hun to go away and leave me alone?"

Pierre laughed, but it was cut short as they both heard the sound of an aircraft across the field to their right. Machine gun fire spurted from its wings as it swooped across at them. "Out!" screamed Frank as he slammed on the brakes and opened the door. He rolled free of the motor car and down the small bank into the duckweed-covered waters of the old river. Behind him Pierre dived across his vacant seat and out onto the verge, slithering headfirst into the waters.

The aeroplane swept over them, its guns blazing. Then it was gone, sweeping low over the fields in the direction of Chateauneuf.

For a while the two of them lay there in the filthy water, waiting to see if the aeroplane returned, Frank immersed up to his waist lying up the steep bank, Pierre belly down gripping the weeds at the water's edge. Then Frank raised himself and crawled out and up the bank. He turned and held out his hand to Pierre, as he too topped the bank. "Are you alright?"

"I think so," said Pierre, feeling down his sticky, wet body. "Bit difficult to tell beneath all this, but nothing hurts."

Frank laughed despite the hollow feeling in his belly and the dry taste of fear in his mouth. "Well at least if they come back again all we'll have to do is stand still. They'll never see us with all this camouflage."

A hissing sound and the crump of a small explosion made them both wheel around to look at the motor car. As they watched, it seemed to settle on itself. Steam bellowed from its bonnet in a rising cloud. Flames licked from beneath its rear end and ran along the stream of petrol forming at the road's edge, setting the dry grasses of the verge alight.

"Get the stuff out quick!" yelled Frank as he dived at the open door. He reached inside and grabbed his jacket, the rifles and the small canvas bag with the food in and passed them back to Pierre standing just behind him. "Where's our kit?"

"In the boot, but leave it Frank it's too dangerous." There was another whoosh and flames burst through the rear seat. Frank felt the heat scorch his face. He pulled clear. "Get away," yelled Pierre as he ran up the road. "Get away Frank. Now!"

Frank needed no further urging. He turned and ran from the vehicle, pulling his jacket up over his head to shield himself from the blast he knew was coming. It came as a dull thud and he felt the heat on the exposed flesh of his hands. He ran on, joined by Pierre, who handed him one rifle as they went. At the main road they paused. Frank doubled up, trying to catch his breath. "That was a close one," he panted.

"I'll say, and now we're on foot again."

Frank glanced at his watch. "Look, if we hurry we can cut along by that hedge, over the footbridge and down through La Ronce to the bridge, avoiding the town."

Pierre slung his rifle over his shoulder. "Well lead on then. Let's get there."

They left the road after the canal bridge and cut along the edge of the fields, heading towards the river and the town beyond. Behind them and away now to their right they could see enemy traffic on the road they had left, and as soon as they could Frank led them through to the other side of the hedge, where they ran doubled up as far as the river. Here a small narrow footbridge led over a spur of the main river and a footpath ran on to the outskirts of the town.

"Quick! Hurry up," Frank cried as he ran on ahead. "I think we're being outflanked." The footpath merged with the Rue de la Ronce at the river's edge, and ahead of them they could see the bridge and the Quai de Penthievre.

Frank paused as the bridge came into view, shielding his eyes as he scanned for signs of movement upon it. He opened his mouth to urge Pierre forward again, but then stopped as a series of huge explosions rent the air.

As the smoke quickly cleared the bridge stood alone above the haze, but then it seemed to fold in on itself, its huge metal struts tearing and wrenching apart. "Oh my God," said Frank dejectedly, lowering his hand.

"What time is it?" Pierre asked quietly.

Frank looked at his watch. "One o'clock. We missed it by a few minutes." He turned to Pierre. "I'm very sorry my friend, I seem to have landed you right in it."

"Nonsense," said Pierre, clapping him on the back. "If it hadn't been for that bloody aeroplane we'd have been here a while ago. It wasn't your fault at all."

"I do hope our coloured friends got across." Frank rolled his eyes. "Maybe if we'd stuck with them we'd have made it." For the first time in his life he felt a long way from home, from England and from his family.

He looked towards the bridge. Could they still cross? The first section had dropped onto the quay before lurching broken-backed up to the toppled stone pier. From there the next section dropped down into the water before rising again to half climb the next pier. They could get as far as there for sure, but after that the stone walls of the second pier itself presented an impenetrable barrier and the subsequent sections were almost completely submersed.

"It looks shallow enough to cross," said Pierre. "Apart from that centre section. How deep is that?"

"Too deep I think."

"Let's get there anyway."

Without further ado the two of them picked up and ran, beneath the huge protective trees of Le Chastaing towards the bridge, arriving at the end of the Rue Saint-Nicolas. For an instant Frank gazed at the ruined bridge, the currents rushing and swirling through its twisted steel. But then the urge to find shelter drove him on and they ran on past and up the Grande Rue du Port before cutting right to join the Grande Rue, ominously aware of the sounds of battle all around them.

A strange, almost expectant calm hung over the town centre. Every door and window was firmly closed, the shutters bolted in place. If there were occupants within or below, then they were giving no hint of their presence and they were certainly not going to willingly open the doors to men in uniform of any description. The signs of flight were all around. Pavements and roads littered with discarded clothing, bags stuffed with household goods that had obviously been dropped in the panic to make the bridge before it was blown. Even a child's rag doll was lying in the gutter, its blonde tresses draped up the kerb, its once cared-for dress torn open.

They reached the main street and Frank gasped as they saw the ruined church, its southern wall blown out, its rubble blocking the road. In front of it the houses and shops had disappeared, and in their place was a smoking crater festooned with the fragments of the lives that had gone on within their walls. Blackened timbers reached vainly for the summer skies from piles of rubble, like the bones of some flenched leviathan.

Frank stood stock, still trying to take in this scene of devastation, which seemed so incongruous in his beloved town. How could the gentle peace he had known for so long be transformed to this evil? He stared into the hole seeking to make sense, but could make none of it. He had known these people. Were they still here, lying broken and bleeding beneath this awful mess? Had they escaped, leaving all that they had known to lie here exposed? A hand touched his shoulder and he turned to look once more into Pierre's concerned face. "It... I cannot..."

"We have to go," said Pierre quietly but firmly. "Which way?"

Frank looked at him, his mind racing, a dull pit in his stomach. "I don't know Pierre. West and we run into the fighting you can hear and... east and..." He stopped, staring down the road towards the new market. "Philippe!" he cried. He pointed towards the large black motor car parked diagonally across the road, partially blocking it. "It's Philippe! He's come for us!"

He scrambled over the rubble and ran off down the road. Pierre tried to stop him, seeing from the car's position that all was not well, but Frank was by now at full stretch, running for all his worth. He dropped the bag to the floor and ran after him, calling for him to wait.

Frank came up to the familiar black motor car. "Philippe," he called as he approached. "Philippe it's me, Frank. Where are you?"

He stopped as he saw the open driver's door, its sheen disturbed by jagged holes that ran in lines across its width, onto and across the proud bonnet. Beneath the door he could just see Philippe lying across the running board, his head buried within the vehicle, his legs lying out on the pavement. What was he doing? Was he trying to fix the damage? Silly Philippe, even he could surely see that this was one breakdown he couldn't fix. "Philippe, what are you doing?" he said as he swung the door further open. "It's dangerous here, you can't..." He stopped, transfixed with horror.

Philippe lay still, his jacket torn and shredded, his once neat hair matted with the drying blood from the wounds that had taken his life. Frank sank to his knees beside the body as he discarded his rifle and gently turned it over. The eyes stared sightless. A hand flopped down and brushed Frank's thigh, resting in his lap as he caressed the beloved face. A glint of brightness distracted him for a second and he fingered the row of medals wonderingly, lovingly. He had never spoken of his service.

Had he been looking for him? Had he hoped to meet him and fly with him to safety? Had he hoped to transport him there? "You have found me now old friend," Frank whispered. "I'm here." He stroked the hair back from his forehead and pulled shut the eyelids.

Pierre coughed. "Frank we have to go. We can't stay here."

"Where Pierre? Where do we go?" said Frank, looking up into the anxious face of his companion. "If we go east, west or north you'll run into them. South is where we need to go and..."

He stopped and stared behind him. Pierre followed his look. A troop of about ten French soldiers came running past the church, carrying their weapons, and made off down the Rue du Mouton towards the bridge. As they caught sight of Pierre they waved and shouted. Neither Pierre nor Frank could pick up what they were saying, but from their urgent signals it was obvious that they were urging them to join them.

Pierre looked from them to Frank and back again. "Frank," he pleaded. "Come on. There's nothing more you can do for your friend."

"I can't just leave him here in the street like a bit of dog's dirt to be cleaned up later."

Pierre looked around quickly. He looked back at the motor car. "Put him in the motor car!"

"The motor car?"

"Yes, put him in the driver's seat and then when they clear up this mess they'll know who he is."

Frank looked from him back into the car, his mind working. "Everybody knows who Philippe is."

"It may not be Frenchmen who clear it up Frank."

As if to reinforce his point, they heard the sound of rapidly approaching vehicles. Frank suddenly pulled himself together.

"Quick," he agreed. "Help me get him in." Pierre needed no further urging. He leant his rifle against the front wing, bent down and grabbed hold of Philippe's feet. Frank stood and held the body under the arms as they shuffled and heaved him into the driver's seat. The head flopped forward, leaning on the steering wheel. Frank tried to position it so that he leant back in the seat, but the body only fell sideways.

"Leave him Frank!" Pierre yelled, looking urgently down the road. He pointed past the car. "Quick or we'll be caught, they're nearly here." Frank popped his head up and looked through the rear window. Two motorcycles and sidecars swept into view at the end of the main street. They screeched to a halt by the new market, then accelerated up past it and out of sight. Behind them, cruising more slowly down the road, came a line of half-tracks with soldiers walking alongside.

Frank ducked down and crawled around to the front of the motor car, keeping out of sight. "Keep the motor car between us and them and back up to the rubble," he said to Pierre.

Pierre needed no guidance as the two of them backed away from the vehicle, bent double, their eyes fixed on the street. Pierre's heel caught on the first large stones of the fallen church wall. He crouched as Frank retrieved the discarded bag and joined him. "Right, let's get out of here," he whispered, and the two of them turned and scuttled across the ruins, on to the open street and on down towards the bridge.

A shot rang out as they ran into the open space of the Place du Port, normally a place of peace and contemplation lined by neatly polled lime trees, where the only hint of activity was the daily game of boules played on the sandy surface. Above Frank's head a chunk of stone split off from the wall of the house behind him. "Don't shoot! We're French," Pierre yelled.

"We're the ones you saw as you went past the church," Frank shouted.

"Sorry. Come on in" called a voice, and a soldier stepped from the ruins of the bridge's landing. "Have you seen the Germans?"

"Yes, they're just at the top on the main street by the market," said Frank as they joined them, the soldiers acknowledging their arrival with tired nods and mumbled greetings. Frank and Pierre slithered down the slope of the Quai.

"Bugger," said the first soldier. "That means they're coming in from both ends of town."

"What are you planning?" asked Pierre.

A Sergeant who they had not noticed until then stepped forward. "We're going to try and get across on the ruins of the bridge."

Frank looked at the man, and from him down into the swirling brown waters. "Then what are you waiting for? They'll be here in a few minutes."

"We thought you were them."

"Well we're not, and if you're going you'd better go now," said Frank. He cocked an ear in the direction of the town. Distinctly they could all now hear the sound of armoured vehicles coming down the Rue Saint-Nicolas and the shouts of men. Frank and Pierre rushed back from the river's edge and crouched against the sloping stones of the Quai. The Sergeant followed them and the three of them edged up the stones to the level platform. "Too late for the bridge," Frank whispered.

"Where then?" murmured the Sergeant.

Frank ducked and slithered back down the slope, motioning the other two to follow him, which they did. The other soldiers grouped around them, dazed and confused with fright. Frank pointed west along the river bank. "The Mairie, the Hotel de Ville."

"Right," said the Sergeant, "lead on." Frank needed no further urging. He picked up and ran, with Pierre and the Sergeant running beside him. Two of the other soldiers also joined them, but the rest stood still for a moment, undecided. The Sergeant stopped and turned briefly to them, waving at them to follow but afraid to raise his voice for fear of attracting attention. For a moment they looked at him, but then they turned and ran up the slope of the broken bridge to the apex of the first pier. For a moment they were silhouetted against the sky, but then a burst of gunfire from the bank caught them and sent several of them spinning over the edge.

Frank and the others started to run once more, staring back whenever they dared as they hared up the rise before pausing briefly at the end of the Quai Barrault to look back at the bridge. They could see that several of their comrades had in fact made it over the apex unscathed, and even now they were running down the next section, into the water and up to the second pier. Here they stopped, unable to proceed, and Frank could just make them out as they swung down into the waters on the upstream side, seeking to negotiate and cross to the third section.

Pierre grabbed Frank's arm and directed his attention back to the first section of the bridge. A lone figure was crawling on his belly up the ramp of the bridge, like some dark, black salamander outlined against the grey of the road. A group of German soldiers rushed out from cover and knelt, firing over at the men, trying to negotiate the second pier, whilst one of their number almost casually walked onto the stricken bridge and up to the crawling figure. Frank heard the deep intake of breath his companions made and felt his own as they watched the German raise his bayoneted rifle and bear down on the helpless figure. He turned away in horror as the Sergeant whispered. "Come on lads, or we'll end up the same way."

They ran down the road, turning away from the river and through the stone pillars into the grounds of the old chateau. A straight track, lined on both sides with ancient polled limes, ran along between the sunken vegetable gardens to the right and the open parkland to the left, stretching back to the Loire. Above and beside them, beyond the gardens, the town rose in terraces, its grey stone houses clinging to the escarpment. Ahead lay the old moat beneath the high stone walls of the old chateau. Pigeons fluttered from nooks and crannies in the stones, flying out and over the running men before returning to their lairs. Ripples disturbed the still, opaque surface of the waters and a large fish broke the surface with a loud splash. "Where now?" panted the Sergeant.

Frank pointed ahead, speechless from shortage of breath, at the stone flights of steps leading up to the arched open bridge. They brushed past the ancient yews and ran up the steps, over the bridge and on up the next flight to the level lawns below the Mairie. For a moment they all stopped, bent double in the shelter of the low wall as they fought to regain their breath, but then, below them, they could see and hear approaching German soldiers as they rounded the bend at the end of the lime walk and the pigeons were, once more, disturbed.

"Quick," panted the Sergeant. "Up those steps." He pointed ahead to the steps leading up to the top level and sprinted across the lawns towards them. As he broke cover, the troops below saw him and several dropped to their knees and took aim. Bullets smacked into the stone steps ahead of him and whined back up into the trees. He dropped to his belly and turned, crawling back to where Frank, Pierre and the other two crouched against the wall. Frank pointed along the side of the Mairie at the level they were on and, bent double, they ran to the edge of the building and around the corner at the basement level.

They were funnelled now into a narrowing sunken area leading on to steps leading up to the rear of the Mairie and the open space in front of the orangerie. At the foot of the steps to their right a door opened into the basement area and Frank, as the first to reach it, grabbed the handle and turned, more in hope than in expectation. It was locked. "Break it," shouted Pierre.

Frank stood back and kicked hard at the oak door but it held. The Sergeant pushed Frank aside and hurled himself at it, shoulder first, but still it held and he reeled away clutching his arm. Shouts on the steps leading up from the bridge over the moat alarmed them and they all turned to see the first German soldiers reach the top and take up firing positions, whilst those behind them ran past and over the lawns, out of sight against the bank and the entrance to the caves.

Frank turned away from the door and sprinted up the stairs, followed by the rest. His breath came in gasps now, racking his chest with pain as he forced the air in and out. Behind him he heard the stuttering of rifle fire. He ducked and the bullets whined over his head. A strangled scream behind him made him momentarily glance back to see Pierre, who was immediately behind him, throw his arms in the air and fall back. He crashed into the Sergeant, following on behind, who side-swerved to let the body fall on past to crumple at the feet of the soldier following.

The poor man missed his footing as the body tangled up in his legs and he too fell back, knocking the last of their small group off balance. For a split second Frank hesitated, staring down at Pierre's lifeless body, but then the Sergeant came on up the steps, his outstretched arms pushing Frank onwards. Behind them the two other soldiers struggled over the body. Frank reached the top step and dived into a crouch beyond it, seeking to remove himself from the line of vision of the enemy below, and the Sergeant joined him. The other two soldiers breasted the top.

"Down!" screamed Frank. "Get dow..." A burst of gunfire from below caught the two soldiers, sending them spinning and jerking. One fell towards Frank, his gaze fixed on Frank's face, seeking to hold eye contact, before finally crashing down into the sand. The other sank to his knees slowly, turning as he did so, on the top step before diving head first out of Frank's sight.

"Where now?" shouted the Sergeant. Frank looked around desperately, a hunted animal at bay. Panic rose in his chest as he forced himself to exhale within the strange silence that seemed to be closing in on him. He turned wild eyes up to his companion, who shook him, breaking into his thoughts. "Come on! This way then." He grabbed Frank's jacket by the shoulder and hauled him to his feet, away from the steps and across the open space, towards the old stables in the direction of the main gates and the dry upper moat. As they cleared the end of the building, they saw to their horror that the enemy was now ahead and to the right of them, having sprinted up the flight of steps leading directly up from the lawns below, and at any moment they knew that the others would appear at the top of the steps behind them.

For a second they paused in their flight, uncertain about what to do next, and for a moment the soldiers ahead of them also paused to regain their breath. In that moment Frank, followed by the Sergeant, vaulted over the parapet wall and tumbled down the four-metre drop into the sunken gardens of the old moat, landing on all fours. He struggled to his feet to see German soldiers take up firing positions on the parapet of the bridge ahead of him. To the side, on the right, more appeared, looking down into the pit. He wheeled back, spinning in his panic, and his rifle spun from his grip and fell softly onto the manicured turf. 'I'm dead,' he thought. His mind raced and his eyes darted from the unyielding stone walls to the lines of pointed rifles aimed at him from above. Laughter? He could hear laughter. Would they now mock him even as he died, trapped here for all the world like a beast in a Roman amphitheatre? He raised his hands in surrender, expecting no mercy, and beside him the Sergeant, whose name he still did not know, raised his also. They would die here together, comrades of only a few minutes, unknown in life yet together in death.

"Auf die knie! Schnell! Schnell!"

The Sergeant looked at Frank, an inquiring look on his face.

"Get on your knees. They want us to kneel down," said Frank as he slowly knelt back down onto the turf, grateful almost for the relief it gave his aching legs. The Sergeant looked around for a moment as if trying to decide what to do. "Down," Frank hissed. The Sergeant dropped to one knee. "So they can shoot us," he whispered, "or bayonet us to save ammunition?"

"We have no choice." The Sergeant muttered something and bent the other leg.

Three German soldiers climbed over the parapet wall and scaled down to their level. They walked up to Frank and his companion with rifles pointed all the while at them, the wicked bayonets aiming directly at their hearts. One stood back whilst the other two went behind them. Frank looked up into the face of a young man about four years his junior, whose fixed stare of wariness must have matched Frank's returning one of fear. The soldier behind the Sergeant placed his boot in the small of his back and pushed down viciously, forcing him to the floor. Instinctively Frank tried to rise, but was felled by a blow to the side of his head from the rifle butt of the man behind him.

For a moment he was aware of the blow, although he felt no particular pain, then his head seemed to explode in flashes of light. Sound magnified, vision faded and then, just as quickly, the sound too disappeared and he fell headlong into blackness.

***

"Is that you daddy?" Violet called out as she heard the front door. She walked from the kitchen out into the hall, wiping her hands on her apron. "Ah it is you. Tired?"

Ernest took off his helmet and hung it on the hat stand. He turned to the wall and shrugged the coat off his shoulders. Violet took it and hung it up on the coat hook. "I'll say." He turned around and kissed her. "Any news?"

Her face dropped. "None I'm afraid. They say that up to forty percent of the soldiers who got back here were French, but that they're going back to France."

Ernest embraced his daughter. "If Frank was with them then he'll telephone I'm sure, and if not..."

"If not, is he dead or injured back there on the beaches..." She wiped her eyes with her apron. "Oh I wish he hadn't stayed in France. I wish I'd insisted..."

Ernest put his hands on Violet's shoulders and shook her slightly. She looked up into his face. "Violet, there's no point in torturing yourself with these thoughts. Frank's an adult now. I'm sure he'll be fine, and in the meantime there's certainly no point in blaming yourself." He smiled and wiped away a tear from the corner of her eye. "Now come on. I'm tired and I'm hungry and I could murder a cup of tea."

Violet smiled wanly back at her father. "Sorry daddy, it's just that... oh well, you know."

"Yes I know my darling. Now where's that cup of tea?" He put his arm around her shoulder and the two of them walked across to the kitchen door. "Where's Alice?"

"She had to go to the hospital. Apparently they're bringing in some of the wounded from other hospitals." She looked into her father's face. "Sometimes..."

"Sometimes you feel that you should be there as well." He chucked her playfully under the chin. "Violet, you did your bit and more in the Great War. Now you've children to raise and a household to keep."

"I know but..."

"...but I'm starving hungry and dying of thirst," he grinned. "Damn it woman, you can't even manage one job properly let alone two."

Violet laughed. "Oh daddy I'm sorry. You go and wash up and I'll get you something to eat."

"Bacon, egg and mushrooms?"

"Yes sir, coming up sir, only if you don't mind they will be disguised as toast and margarine."

"That'd be lovely," said Ernest as he disappeared out into the rear scullery to wash his hands. "Where are the boys?" he called back.

"Alice dropped them off at Mrs Sykes' house. School's there today."

"Have you given any more thought to what we were talking about?" said Ernest as he came back into the kitchen.

Violet turned from pouring the water into the teapot. "Well yes... yes I have daddy... but... do you really think it's necessary?"

Ernest sat down at the kitchen table. "Yes I do Violet. This thing's going to get a lot worse now. I mean the Jerrys are just the other side of the channel and they could launch an attack on London at any time."

"But they've already done so a few times and it didn't really affect us did it?"

Ernest looked up at his daughter. "That was nothing darling. What I'm talking about is the wholesale bombing of London, the like of which you've never seen." He stopped and sniffed, looking past Violet in alarm. "The toast!"

Violet spun around. "Oh bother. She grabbed the toast pan handle and yanked it out from under the gas, flicking the blackened toast onto the draining board. "Oh I'm sorry daddy, I wasn't paying attention."

"My fault," said Ernest. "I expect it'll scrape, we can't afford to waste it."

Violet reached into a drawer, took out a knife and started scraping the toast into the sink. "Where do you think they should go... Jesse's?"

"Jesse's would be one place, but she's very near the coast and there could be trouble down there."

Violet put the now just dark brown toast into a rack and put it on the table in front of her father. He reached out for a piece and thoughtfully spread it with the thick, lumpy margarine. "Daddy," Violet wheedled. "Most of the children that went away have now come home. Do you really think it's going to be as bad as you say?"

Ernest looked up. He waited until he had swallowed his mouthful before answering. "Worse darling, believe me. If you heard what they say they're preparing us for you'd not hesitate."

Violet picked up the teapot with its knitted cosy and placed it on the table.

She turned to get two cups and saucers from the sideboard. "I've no sugar I'm afraid," she said as she went out to the larder to fetch the milk jug. "Oh, I have got some blackberry jam, would you like that with your toast?"

"Yes please," said Ernest, laughing. "I'm having a bit of difficulty swallowing this."

"Sorry I wasn't thinking," said Violet as she returned carrying the jug and a pot of home-made jam, which she put before him. "I'll pour." She sat and sorted the cups onto the saucers and poured the tea. She handed Ernest his cup. "Where to then?"

Ernest took his cup. He took a long swallow and sat back a little in his chair, relishing the warmth flowing into his body. He put the cup down on the saucer and looked across at his daughter. He took a deep breath. "The Popes'?"

Violet put her cup down quickly. "Oh no! No not that far... not... oh daddy I can't keep dumping my children on Florrie." She put her hands on the table, fists clenched.

"Is that all there is to it?"

Violet looked up at him, her eyes guarded. "What do you mean?"

"I mean, is that all there is to it?" He stood and walked around to behind Violet's chair. He bent down and put his arms around her shoulders, kissing her on the cheek. "You've not lost a child to another woman yet. Frank was not lost to you, however much he loves Florrie."

Violet turned into her father's embrace, weeping now. "I don't want to be apart from my children."

"Then go with them."

She pulled back, looking up into his face. "Go... go with them?"

"Go with them. Go with them to Florrie's, stay down there until things seem better."

"But what about..."

"Me and Alice? We'll be fine here. I've got my ARP work and Alice is busy at the hospital and... and you can send us up some fresh food from time to time. Honestly darling, it's for the best." He let go of her and resumed his seat, helping himself to some more toast. "Think about it."

"What will we do for money? I've no income now that Hitler has stolen it."

"All the more reason to go to Florrie's. You can help out there I'm sure, and you'll still get the children's allowance after all."

Violet giggled. "What about Maxwell?"

"What about him?"

"He won't take kindly to the house being occupied by just you and Alice, will he?"

"I think that we should go and see him and tell him that you are going to take the children to the country for their own safety and that I'm going to look after the house whilst you're away. He can't possibly object to that, can he?"

"You don't know Maxwell."

"Well," said Ernest thoughtfully. "If he objects then what can he really do about it, after all, for all he knows the house may be requisitioned for needy people anyway and then what would he do?"

Violet thought for a moment. "You have your sleep when you've finished breakfast and I'll go and see him later this morning. She paused. "What about Frank?"

"What about him?"

He won't know where to contact me."

Ernest sighed with exasperation. "Violet. Really Violet, I'll still be here and we'll let Jesse know where you've gone and… well if he couldn't find you through one of those, then he's not looking is he?"

Violet looked sheepish. "Yes. Yes I'm sorry daddy, I'm being silly. It's just that… well it's just that it all seems a bit… well a bit unnecessary."

Ernest stood up, placed the chair carefully back under the table and dusted the crumbs of his shirt front onto the cover. "Violet, you'll have to make your own mind up, I can only advise."

She caught the note of admonishment in his voice and crossed to him as he made for the door. "Oh daddy don't be cross... it's just that it's such a big move to make."

Ernest looked down into her upturned face. "You think about it Violet and let me know what you decide, but don't leave it all too late, don't risk the lives of my grandsons." He kissed her and opened the door. "I'm going to bed now, I'll see you later darling."

Violet watched him go, watched the door close, heard his footsteps on the first steps. She got up quickly, reached for the handle and opened the door. "Daddy!"

The footsteps stopped. "Yes."

"I'll go and see Maxwell."

"Thank you darling. Goodnight."

"Goodnight daddy, see you after lunch. Sleep well."

***

Frank stirred. He squinted into the light. His forehead creased as the pain shot through his head. God this was the mother of all headaches! He tried to raise his arm to stroke his head but it seemed so heavy. Voices! There were voices. People were speaking around him. He listened for a moment as nausea swept through him and once again the pain shot through his head. He forced his hand up and felt his temple. Wet! Sticky. He peered at his fingers through one eye. Blood! The memory of what had happened came flooding back. The voices started again and he turned wearily to their source.

"Auf! Schnell, schnell!"

Could he? 'Am I able to stand?' he thought. He turned over onto his knees, his hands flat on the ground, his head hanging down, the pain throbbing through it. "Auf!" A boot crashed into his backside and he jerked upright and struggled to his feet, turning to face his tormentor.

A boy about a couple of years younger than he was stood facing him, his face grim and set beneath a hard, steel helmet. His hands gripped his rifle with its fixed bayonet and he jerked it at Frank, causing him to retreat backwards. The rifle jerked again. "Schnell!" Frank turned and faced the direction that the soldier was forcing him to go. His head swam and his vision became cloudy, but he could see a group of familiar uniforms standing in a disconsolate group and he stumbled over to join them, falling to his knees as he did so. One of the French soldiers stepped forward to assist him and tried to hold him up. "Lassen sie ihn fallen," shouted their captor, and the man stepped back as Frank fell forward onto the hard cobbles.

Shots and the sound of more shouting made the soldiers guarding the group turn to see what was going on, and Frank dragged himself to within the group and sat up, leaning against the wall.

More shouts, and a group of German soldiers appeared prodding a French soldier in front of them, his hands raised in surrender. Frank raised his head and looked through the legs of his compatriots at the face of the approaching man, who he recognised as one of the men who had elected to try the bridge. He came up to join them, his uniform dripping and wet, his boots still draped around his neck where he had hung them. Murmured greetings met him as he joined their band and slumped to his knees on the edge of the pavement. He looked across at Frank, nodded his recognition and shuffled across to sit beside him.

Blood dripped down Frank's face and splashed onto his clenched hands. He felt his head, felt the sticky ooze from the wounds across his temple and up into his hairline. "You need a bandage," said a voice. Frank turned, and his heart leapt with joy as he recognised the Sergeant he had been captured with. "Here, any of you fellows got a dressing?"

One was handed to him and he knelt beside Frank. "Got a handkerchief?" he asked. Frank nodded and reached painfully into his jacket pocket, handing one to him, noticing as he did that it was still wet from the ducking he had had with Pierre. The Sergeant took it and folded it into a pad, which he then bound into position, with a great swathe of dressings circling Frank's head and partially obscuring one eye. "There, that'll do for now," he announced as he finished. He sat back beside Frank, his back to the wall.

"Thank you," whispered Frank.

"It's nothing."

"Stehen sie auf 'raus!" screamed a voice from the road. "Stehen sie auf! Schnell!" The French soldiers shuffled to the side, prompted by jerks and thrusts, exposing Frank and the Sergeant sitting with their backs against the wall. "Auf!" their captors screamed.

Frank struggled to rise to his feet. The Sergeant bent down to help. "Here you," he said to one of the other captives, "give me a hand with this fellow." The other chap slung Frank's other arm around his shoulders and between them they supported him as they were marched off towards the town centre.

Frank tried to help as much as possible, and as they continued he began to regain his faculties, despite the pain in his head and the swirling vision. He was aware that they were passing by the church and Philippe's car, and he strained to see if his friend was still there. But they swept by too quickly for him. His feet dragged and his body slumped as the concussion lured him back. "Hold up," whispered the Sergeant, and Frank raised his head and forced himself to concentrate.

As they approached the old school house the order was given to "Halt!" and the ragged bunch stopped. The doors were flung open and they were forced in by pushes, prods and much shouting. Frank looked around at the familiar interior. He had not attended this school, but had visited it on many occasions in the past. Now its grey walls became his prison as the doors were slammed shut, with an armed sentry standing just inside each exit.

The Sergeant looked around. "You're best off over there mate," he indicated as he guided Frank over to the far wall. He bent down as Frank gratefully sought the floor and closed his eyes. "Have a sleep and I'll see about some water," he said. Frank mumbled his thanks and relaxed, sliding back into unconsciousness as the Sergeant folded up a jacket and placed it under his head.

He was woken when it was dark by a gentle shaking. "Soldier. Soldier. Water, drink some of this. It'll make you feel better, and if you can manage it they've brought us bread."

Frank struggled back into consciousness and sat up. His head cleared and he remembered where he was. "Thank you," he said to the Sergeant. "My name's Frank. Frank Balfoure."

"Victor. Victor Picard from Le Mans."

"Pleased to meet you Victor Picard from Le Mans," said Frank, smiling.

Victor handed him a mug of water. "Do you want the bread?"

"Yes please," said Frank, putting the mug down on the floor and reaching out to take it. "How many of us are there in here?"

"Well they've been pushing chaps in here every so often... I reckon there's about forty of us in here now."

Frank chewed on the stale bread, which for all that made strength surge back into his body. "How come you missed the bridge?"

"Us? Oh we were up at the north end of the town by the railway crossing."

"And they left you there?"

"No. No not really. We had them pinned down from about six o'clock this morning, but then we realised that they were coming in behind us. We tried to get back to the bridge but..." He smiled. "...well it didn't work out. We heard the bridge go..."

"We saw it."

Victor grinned in the darkness and Frank could hear the smile in his voice. "Oh well, I doubt it'll make a lot of difference in the end, the way things are going. I reckon the end result is going to be the same." He laughed. "Least we'll get to choose the best bunks where we're going."

"Where are we going?" said Frank.

"Search me. I expect they've organised prisoner of war camps.

They seem to have thought of everything else. I should get some sleep, if I were you, we may have a bit of a journey ahead of us."

Frank murmured his agreement and lay down again. His head felt better, apart from a nagging headache and a stinging in the actual wound. At least he no longer felt nauseous. Sleep returned surprisingly quickly, despite the hard stone.

"'raus! 'raus!" The calls woke Frank with a start and he sat up quickly. The doors were open and, already, at a moment's notice, the prisoners were being herded and pushed into two lines. Four soldiers entered carrying two desks between them, which they set up at the head. Victor stood and held out his hand to Frank to haul him to his feet. "You alright?"

"Yes. Thanks."

"Silence!" came a shout from the rear of the hall and the whispered conversation died. Orders were barked out and a line of schoolchildren's chairs was set up across and down the hall, creating a funnelled area leading away from the desks, which was in turn garrisoned by a line of armed soldiers.

More orders were shouted and both lines moved forward one step. As each man gave his particulars to the men behind the desks, everything was noted down meticulously until eventually he was directed through into the area cordoned off by the chairs. For an hour or more Frank slowly moved forward, until at last he stood in front of the desk. He stared at the men sitting behind it. One, a young blonde soldier, his uniform pressed and clean, his hair neatly combed, glanced up at Frank briefly before taking up his pen and preparing to write down the details. Tiredness and hunger dulled Frank's wits as he stood expectantly in front of the desk.

The cold, grey eyes of the senior man looked up at Frank. "Name and documents," he demanded in a thin, cold voice, speaking in French and holding out his hand, palm up.

"Frank Balfoure," said Frank as he simultaneously reached into his inside jacket pocket for his Identity Card. The German reached out for the papers as Frank withdrew his hand. Too late he realised that amongst them was his British passport. He tried to withdraw the documents, but the German had his grasp on the whole sheaf and he shouted to the soldier standing beside the desk, who moved forward and grabbed Frank's arm, twisting it until he was forced to let go.

Slowly and deliberately the officer spread open the damp papers on the desk in front of him. A long silence seemed to follow. Frank looked back at Victor standing behind him. Victor looked puzzled as Frank shrugged his shoulders and smiled wanly. The soldier prodded Frank with the muzzle of his rifle and Frank turned back to look straight into the eyes of the officer.

"So what do we have to call you?" the man hissed menacingly. Frank opened his mouth to speak, but he held up his hand to silence him. "Balfoure it says here," he said, holding up the Identity Card. "Balfoure it says here," he repeated, holding up Frank's army documents. "But here..." He held up the passport. "...here it says Balfour."

"I..." The rifle thudded into Frank's stomach and he doubled up, his face level with the top of the desk.

"Silence!" shrieked the officer. "You are a British spy are you not?"

"No sir I..." The rifle was reversed and the soldier brought the butt end round and clubbed Frank across the neck. Pain shot through his already injured head and tore down his back as he jerked forward and fell to his knees in front of the desk. Victor made as if to step forward to assist him, but immediately two other soldiers stepped between him and Frank's kneeling figure, their rifles pointing straight at him. Victor held up his hands in submission as the soldiers pushed him and the line of men behind him back.

Frank's head whirled with pain and fear. His stomach churned as he knelt on the floor. Rough hands hauled him to his feet. Orders were shouted and he felt himself being half dragged, half carried towards the back of the hall. Shocked faces from the prisoners in the line stared down at him as he was dragged past them, and a hum of conversation arose as all wondered aloud what it was that had singled out this treatment and whether they too would be subjected to it. The doors were flung open and Frank was carried out into the street. He looked up at the sky, convinced that these were his last moments on earth.

The sun shone and the birds sang. He raised his head and glanced down the road to the east towards his home and wished himself there. He looked sideways at first one and then the other of his executioners. Men of his own age who maybe in different circumstances could have been friends of his, friends of Gunther, maybe even Gunther's school chums. Now they were going to kill him and there was nothing he could do or say.

An engine started as they frogmarched him across to a lorry, his arms pinioned up his back, forcing his head down. The tailgate crashed down in front of him and he felt himself lifted bodily and hurled into the back. For a moment he lay there in the well, but then the two soldiers joined him and once more he felt himself being hauled to his knees. They flung him back against the tarpaulin and sat down either side of him as he subsided onto the bench.

Frank's mind was a numb void. The lorry moved off with a jerk and he braced himself back against the side, trying not to crash into either of the soldiers. The familiar street rolled by like the flickering scene from a newsreel. The market, right, left, left again, then hard right, throwing him against one of the Germans. "Scheiße!" the man yelled as he hefted his rifle and prepared to club Frank with the butt. His friend muttered something to him and he relaxed a little, grumbling as he looked away out of the rear.

The park and then the town slipped past and Frank felt as if his life itself was ebbing away with the road behind him. Where were they taking him? What would they do to him? He reached up to his head. The soldier beside him grunted in alarm, but Frank smiled and pointed to his head, slowly raising his hand until it touched the bandage. He pushed it up from his eye and felt gingerly through it for the wound below. It seemed to span his temple and run on into his hairline. In places it felt hard, but closer to the centre he could feel it swollen and soft to the touch, stinging as his fingers gently grazed the surface of the dressing.

The soldier leant against Frank as he reached into his pocket for a packet of cigarettes. He shook one out and put it in his mouth before stretching across Frank to offer his companion one. The other soldier took it and leant away from Frank as he searched for his matches. He lit his own cigarette and then leant heavily across Frank to offer the light to the other man. As he did so the lorry hit a pothole and his arm flew up, dropping the match and hitting Frank under the chin. Frank's head rocked back against the tarpaulin and scraped across the canvas. The bandage lifted from the unhurt side and rode up to the top of his head, stuck on only by the dried blood from the wound itself.

The German started to laugh, pointing at Frank sitting there with his head throbbing once more, the bandages perched on top like a lop-sided crown of dirty white. Frank closed his eyes. He tried to imagine the chateau, and when that was interrupted with pictures of Philippe's broken body he switched to Florrie's and then Violet's face. He felt the soldier pass the matches across to the other, heard the strike and smelt the familiar first exhalation of new smoke, but he kept his eyes closed, desperately trying to conjure up thoughts of happier days.

For about an hour the lorry rumbled along as Frank leant back on the bench, his eyes firmly closed, seeking to keep as low a profile as possible with his obviously volatile captors. They chatted amongst themselves in raucous and jocular fashion, rocking with laughter whenever some shared memory prompted. Frank tried to listen, tried to understand, but the speed of their delivery, the guttural tones and the frequent shouts sounded nothing like the measured speech that Gunther had taught him.

Gunther! Where was Gunther? Could he help him? No, of course not. If anything, Gunther's knowing him could mean curtains for them both, and anyway how many Gunther Schmidts would there be in the German army? The lorry slowed down and Frank opened his eyes as it swung through some gates, past armed sentries and through into a walled courtyard before screeching to a halt. Doors banged and the two soldiers stood and hauled Frank to his feet. Marching, booted feet rang out on the hard stones of the yard and three uniformed soldiers appeared behind the lorry. Two stood silent whilst one of them reached up and undid the catches on the tailgate. He pulled and stepped back as it crashed open, swinging and banging on the chassis. The soldier furthest in pushed Frank towards the rear of the lorry as the other jumped down and stood aside. Frank paused briefly on the edge of the lorry to see where he was, but a boot in his back sent him flying to land crouched on the hard stone. He felt the sharp pain of the smaller stones as they penetrated his palms, felt the jarring in his wrists and the shock running on up and into his head. For a moment he knelt, head hanging, as the world once more span around him, then rough arms grabbed him and yanked him to his feet. "Stehen sie auf! Auf! Auf! Schnell!"

Frank peered at his captors. The two soldiers who had accompanied him, after exchanging a few words with the others, climbed back into the lorry. One moved forward and banged through the canvas on the rear of the cab and the lorry started off, swinging around in a wide arc as it headed for the gates. Frank watched it go, wishing perversely that he could go with it, could return with it to where it had brought him from. He felt totally and utterly alone in the world. Nobody he knew would know that he was here, and now the last umbilical link with his world, an enemy lorry filled with rough and brutal men, was disappearing from his life. Despair and terror filled him and he instinctively took a step towards the gate.

A soldier, his face set and grim, his eyes cruel, stepped in front of him, reversing his rifle and raising it muzzle-first over his shoulder to strike. Frank stepped back and felt his arms pinioned by the two behind. They pushed him forward and he stumbled, but recovered himself. 'Don't fall Frank,' he thought. 'Stay on your feet. If you fall you will be kicked until you rise again.'

He was marched across the courtyard and in through the wide entrance of what had obviously once been an imposing hall. Now it was decorated with Swastika flags in garish red, black and white, and a large picture of Adolf Hitler, mounted on the half landing of the staircase in front of him, stared down pitilessly. A rifle at his right side prodded Frank into turning left, and he was forced down the long corridor running across the front of the building. At the end they turned right again and stopped before a door, in front of which stood a sentry.

Orders were barked as the door was flung open. Amidst shouts and prods from the soldiers behind him, Frank was forced through. He found no footing and fell freely down the hard stone steps into the blackness beyond. Coarse laughter rang in his ears, cutting through his pain and humiliation before his head finally struck the floor below and darkness swallowed him up.

***

"Mummy! Mummy! Can't we go up the front nearer to the engine?" George tugged at Violet's arm, pulling her down the platform.

"Now then George, stop pulling your mother about like that, this is quite far enough," said Ernest. "These cases are heavy."

"Oh daddy, I do wish you'd looked for a trolley," said Violet. Ernest smiled apologetically as he put the cases down.

"Oh come on mummy, please," urged George, tugging with one hand whilst he held on to his wildly swinging gas mask box.

Alice and Ian joined the little group. "What's the problem?" Alice asked.

"I want to go up to the front of the train near to the engine!" cried George.

"And I don't want to carry these suitcases any further," laughed Ernest.

Ian stood back, looking up the platform and then back again. He coughed. "Here's best George," he said quietly.

"No. No Ian. Up by the engine, then we can see it."

"We'll see it better from here."

George stopped. He looked down the platform at the engine, longing to be beside its gushing, pulsating life. He looked back into his brother's serious face. "Ian," he whined.

"We'll see it better from the middle of the train. Each time we go round a bend we'll see it. If we go closer to it, it will always be hidden from view."

The adults looked at each other, eyebrows raised, then back at the two boys standing facing each other, one serious and patient, the other shuffling from foot to foot as he stared into his brother's face seeking confirmation. Ian nodded his head. George looked up at his mother. "Here. We'll go here."

Violet smiled. "In you go then boys and find a seat. Wait! Say goodbye to grandfather and Alice please George."

George turned from dashing towards the open carriage door. He ran back to Ernest. "Bye grandfather," he said, stopping barely long enough to receive the hug and kiss before rushing over to Alice. "Bye Alice." Alice bent down and hugged him close, planting a kiss on his cheek, but almost as the lips touched he was off and across to the door. Violet caught the amused look her father gave and shrugged her shoulders at Alice's knowing wink.

Ernest picked up the suitcases and heaved them across the platform and into the open door. "Leave them on the floor daddy," Violet called. "If you put them in the rack we'd never get them down."

"Well I hope there's a porter at the other end," said her father.

"If there's not, I expect Joe will meet us anyway."

Ian stepped forward. "Goodbye gramps." He held out both arms, looking up into his grandfather's face. Ernest squatted stiffly, his hands on each of the small boy's shoulders.

"You take care of your mummy now and that brother of yours." He drew the boy to him and kissed him on the forehead.

Ian hugged him close. "And you take care gramps."

"I will," said Ernest, standing, his hands still on the boy's shoulders. He looked at Violet as Ian walked calmly across to Alice and was swept up into her embrace. Violet saw the tears in the old man's eyes and held out her arms for him.

"I'll miss you daddy," she sobbed into his chest as they held each other tight.

"Me too. Me too my darling." He pulled away from her so that he could look down into her eyes. "But it's for the best, believe me."

"I know but..."

"...but nothing. You go and be safe and we'll be here waiting for you when you all come home." Violet nodded, reaching into her pocket for a handkerchief. She drew one out and Ernest took it from her and opened it to dab her eyes. The monogrammed 'V' stood out in the corner and he sucked in his breath. "Still... after all these years?"

She realised what he meant and nodded. "Still after all these years."

Ernest looked softly at her. "He was a good man, wasn't he?" Violet nodded again and Ernest shook his head sadly. "I wish... I wish I'd known him... allowed myself to know him better."

Violet smiled her understanding as Ian re-joined her with Alice in tow. Ernest stood back as Alice embraced Violet and then came to his side and slipped her hand into his. "Take care you two," said Violet. "Come on Ian, let's join that brother of yours." She held the boy's hand as he stepped up and took a seat by the window, looking forward. Violet walked across the compartment and looked down the corridor. George was looking out of a window trying to see forward to the engine. "George, shut the window and come back here. We'll get smuts everywhere."

George turned from the window, his eyes gleaming with excitement. He pushed the glass up and ran back to their compartment. Violet could see that nothing would please him more than to have his face covered in smuts. She smiled, to herself more than anything, and indicated the seat opposite Ian. His face fell. "I won't be able to see the engine."

"It's just until we go George," said Violet as she squatted on the edge of the seat looking out of the still-open door. "You want to wave goodbye to gramps and Alice, don't you?"

George pulled a face. "S'pose so." He flopped into the seat and pressed his nose to the window.

"Are you sure you can manage with the cases there on the floor?" asked Ernest. "What if other people want to get in?"

Violet looked at the luggage and then back at her father. "Perhaps you're right. Here, I'll give you a hand and we can both lift them up onto the rack."

Ernest climbed into the compartment and shuffled past the two cases. The two of them heaved and pushed the heavy things up onto the rack. A whistle blew and there was the sound of slamming carriage doors. Violet looked at her father. He embraced her once more. "Best be off daddy," she said, turning around so that he was closer to the door. He mumbled something, hugged her tight again and then dismounted. Alice stepped forward to take his arm as the guard arrived.

"Close the doors. Trains leavin'," the man said as he swung their door shut and walked on to the next. Violet slid down the window and leant out as far as she could, her hands outstretched. Ernest took one and Alice the other, and the three of them stayed transfixed, looking at each other, fighting back the tears that threatened to obscure their final sight of each other. Ian and George looked out of their windows, Ian waving serenely whilst George pressed his nose to the glass, both hands framing his distorted face.

The train jerked forward. George stood on the seat, pushing at his mother to get near the open window. Ernest and Alice moved along the platform as the train jerked again and started to move steadily away. Alice let go and stood waving with both hands, but Ernest continued holding on to Violet's hands, running along. "Bye bye my darling," he gasped as he was finally forced to let go. He stood waving.

George squeezed his head under his mother's arm and out, looking forwards towards the engine, marvelling at the clouds of steam and smoke that rose up into the broad canopy. The end of the platform slid by and Violet stood back. George immediately jumped down to the floor, intent on leaning right out of the window, but Violet pulled him back, sliding the window up as she waved her hands to clear the smoke that had come in. "Oh," said George, disappointed. He sat back in his seat and idly picked at the taping on the windows.

"Leave the tape alone George, there's a good boy." He persisted and she leant forward and smacked his hand. "George, you know you mustn't touch the tape, it's there for our safety. I've told you at home."

George pouted. His bottom lip stuck out, and for a brief moment he looked like his father. "'snot fair, I can't see anything."

"Here, change with me George," said Ian. "I'll sit with mummy." George looked up. The pout vanished and the excitement came back into his face as he jumped across and into Ian's seat, barely giving his brother time to vacate it. Violet smiled at Ian and patted the seat beside her.

***

Harsh light burst into Frank's thoughts and he willed himself towards it. A blow to his head made him reel, and for a moment the light receded. He fought to move his arms to ward off the unseen attacker but was powerless.

Suddenly he was in the light, he could hear voices. His senses swam, his vision clouded. Gradually he could make out blurred figures in front of him and voices... commanding guttural voices.

Another blow to the head. He turned to face his attacker but could only make out a dark shape. Instinctively he drew back as he detected an incoming hand, jerking his head to soften the expected blow. None came, and instead the hand grabbed hold of the bandages that obscured his sight and tore them from his head. He screamed as skin and scab were torn from his flesh and struggled to stand up, only to find that his arms and legs were pinioned to a chair.

"Bonjour monsieur," said a smooth voice. "Ca va?"

"Ca va b..." His reply was cut short by another blow to the side of his head. He slumped forward in the chair, staring at the crumpled bandages on the floor in front of him. Dark black dried blood rimmed with fresh red framed the yellow-green of the wound-covering itself.

"Or should I say, 'good morning'?" Frank raised his head and looked at the man in front of him. He wasn't in uniform and, instead, wore a dark suit with a black tie. Frank detected movement from the soldier standing beside his chair and tensed. Almost imperceptibly the suited man shook his head and the blow never came. "Come now Mr Balfour," he continued in English, "you are among friends. We all know that you are a British spy, don't we? Oh, dressed in the uniform of the French army... but a British spy nonetheless."

"I am not..." The blow fell. Again Frank's head flew forward onto his chest. He forced himself to look up, to look directly into the eyes of his accuser. "I am a French soldier... I..." He sensed the next blow coming and instinctively flinched, his eyes flickering in anticipation of the pain.

The man in front of him held his hand up and the blow was stayed. He turned and walked across to the desk underneath the high window. He reached down and picked up a chair, which he carried across and set, back first, before Frank, who watched as he took off his suit jacket and laid it carefully across the desk. He rolled up his elegant white shirtsleeves as he walked back to the chair, which he straddled, leaning on his elbows, to study him intently. Frank returned his gaze, taking in the details of this man who seemed to have his whole life in his control. He was dark-haired with penetrating grey eyes. His features were aquiline... patrician almost, with a hint of sensual cruelty accentuated by the thin-lipped mouth, which now smiled at him from a distance of no more than one metre. "What are you then Frank?" he asked in a quiet, polite voice, which nevertheless served to carry with it more menace than Frank had ever yet met. Frank glanced up at the man beside him and then back at the man in the chair, who followed his look and smiled even more broadly. "Oh don't worry about him, he won't hurt you... not if you give me the correct answers."

"I've tried to give..."

The man raised his hand, motioning Frank to silence and staying the threatening blow. "Frank. Frank. No more silly stories. Please do not insult my intelligence." He stood and crossed to the desk, picking up a file and opening it before turning to Frank. "I have your British passport, which lists you as one Frank Balfour, born in..." For the first time since the conversation had begun, he faltered in the pronunciation. "Glough... Glowcest..."

"Gloucestershire."

"Gloucestershire, thank you Frank. There we are... proof of your impeccable British credentials. Frank Balfour born in Gloucestershire." He raised the passport on high in his left hand. "And yet here we have documents, army paybooks..." He crossed to the desk and put the passport down so that he could leaf through the other documents with both hands. "Even an Identity Card... and your wrist tags, all of which describe you as Frank Balfoure. That's Balfoure with an 'e', of Germigny-des-Pres, near Chateauneuf-sur-Loire." He tossed the papers onto the desk top and returned to the chair, leaning forward, staring intently into Frank's face. "Interesting, don't you think Frank?"

"I..." Frank stopped as the man held up his hand once more.

"You see my problem, don't you Frank? On the one hand I have documentation which shows you to be a French soldier and citizen, and on the other, I have a passport... oh, and a rather charming photograph of some people I take to be your family."

"My mother and my stepfather."

"Your mother and your stepfather. How nice." The grey eyes narrowed. "And are these... these imaginary parents of yours supposed to be French or British?"

"One of each."

"One of each?"

"Yes."

Frank looked the man straight in the eye, but his interrogator broke off the eye contact. He stood and walked across to the desk, his back to Frank. For a moment he stood drumming his fingers on the desk top, then, without turning, he picked up his jacket and banged his fist down. The uniformed man beside Frank stepped forward to stand directly in front of him. He swiped at Frank but Frank, seeing the blow coming, recoiled, throwing his pinioned body backwards. The blow missed, and for a moment Frank's chair teetered on its rear two legs before crashing back to the floor. He felt the chair back hit the ground and stiffened his neck muscles as hard as he could. For a split second he thought he could hold it, but then his head snapped back onto the hard stone floor.

Pain cracked through his brain and once more his senses threatened to slip from his control.

"Scheiße!" he heard the soldier hiss as he kicked into the base of the chair.

"Halt," cried the other man. Frank slipped in and out of consciousness, squinting against the pain that seared through him. He rocked his head from side to side, feeling the blood that now flowed freely from the wound in his temple. Vaguely he heard the voices of his captors as if listening through a towel. Rough hands grabbed at the chair and stood it upright where he sat slumped, his head hanging down on his chest. He waited for the next blows, knowing that any more to his head would render him senseless.

None came, and instead he heard their departing footsteps on the stone floor. A door slammed shut, and he realised with a sense half way between elation and despair that they had left the room. He was alone. Blearily he raised his head, wincing at the pain, and looked around. Cold stone walls greeted him, throwing back their bleak message of hopeless captivity in his face. He raised his head to the light of the high window beyond the desk and concentrated his thoughts on the world beyond. He thought of fields and smiled as he recalled his run down the hill with Lizzie all those years ago. Thank God Lizzie was safe in England... even if she was with that shit George. The image of her slim, white, naked body swam before him and he grinned up at it. How strange that after all these years his memory still clung to the image that he knew was long since supplanted by the reality of her full-grown beauty. He frowned, thinking hard, trying to rationalise the absurd. The wild, free spirit that floated in his mind personified by her white body and the river transported him from this prison. He closed his eyes and hummed softly to himself as sleep of a sorts overcame him.

He started as the door opened once more, and raised his head slowly as footsteps came up behind him. The German in civilian clothing walked past him and up to the desk. Frank didn't turn but was aware that another now stood behind him. "Feeling better Frank?" Frank looked up at him. "Good. Good. I'm so glad. Perhaps now we can continue our little chat and... perhaps this time we can get to the truth. Eh?"

Frank tried to speak but found now that his lips had begun to swell. The words dribbled out, making no sense, and he stopped and concentrated hard. "I... I am English," he slurred.

"Ahhh, now we have it... you are English. I am so sorry I called you British. For one silly moment I forgot how you cling to your separate races in that island." The man stopped. He raised his hands to his mouth. "Oh forgive me Frank, I interrupted your little story. Pray do continue."

"You speak excellent English."

The German looked taken aback. "Why thank you, it is very kind of you to say so. It should come in useful soon, don't you think?"

"How do you mean?"

"Why Frank, when we rule your little island as well as the rest of Europe."

"Do you rule Europe?"

"Why yes Frank, forgive me, you would not know. Marshal Petain has... how do you say... asked... no, begged for peace and will sign an armistice this very evening."

Frank's head fell forward. He felt the tears rise to his eyes, but he forced himself to look up again at his captor. "What day is it?"

"Saturday Frank. You have been our... our guest for over three days now, but you were asleep for most of the time. Saturday the twenty-second of June."

Frank stared at the man. Saturday? Had he lain unconscious for three days? His stomach lurched and he realised that if that was the case he had not eaten or drunk properly since he had left the chateau on the previous Monday. He licked his lips. "May I please have some water? Wasser."

"Wasser! Sprechen sie Deutsch?"

"Nein... no, it's just that my mother had a German friend, Gisela... she died at our house and is buried there in... oh, it's a long story."

"But an interesting one Frank, and one that I want to hear." The man pulled over the chair and sat in front of Frank, leaning forward. "Tell me Frank. Tell me of Gisela and your mother."

Frank swallowed hard. "Please Herr... I'm sorry I don't know your name."

"Weber."

"Please Herr Weber, may I have some water?" Weber looked up beyond Frank and gave a slight nod. Frank heard the soldier behind step back and go to the door. He concentrated hard. If he was to tell this man about himself he had to make it convincing, otherwise... otherwise he was sure that what had happened already was only a foretaste of what they could do to him. He cleared his throat. "I am Frank Balfour. I was born in Gloucestershire in 1915, nine months after my father was killed in the Great War. My mother was a nurse at the front... she was captured but freed again by the Americans. She met and fell in love with a French officer... he had been wounded... eventually they married and he brought her... and me to live with him at the chateau, the Chateau de Janvier outside Germigny."

The soldier entered and walked across to them. He handed a mug to Weber and stood once more behind the chair. Weber stood and bent down, offering the mug to Frank's lips. Frank drank deeply, savouring the musty-tasting water as if it were the sweetest wine, feeling it coursing through his body and flowing into his empty stomach. He choked and Weber withdrew the mug and handed it over Frank's head to the soldier. "Please continue," he said quietly.

Frank swallowed. He licked his swollen lips. "Armand, my father... sorry stepfather." He noted the raised corner of Weber's lip and the look of incredulity. "No honestly, I am telling you the truth."

"Of course you are Frank. Please continue."

"My stepfather Armand Taillefer adopted me as his heir and when he died... in a tragic accident, he left me his estate, including the chateau and the iron works in Chateauneuf which still bears his name."

"You own the iron works in Chateauneuf? Sorry you owned the iron works, for, of course, they are now the property of the Reich."

Frank nodded his head. "Yes. Yes you can ask the manager Monsieur Leclerc... he will vouch for me."

Weber looked intently at Frank. "Will he now? Well we'll see, but please continue... tell me of this woman Gisela."

"My mother... my mother when she was freed by the Americans... there was a German soldier. He was wounded... he died... but before he died he asked my mother to contact his wife... she did so after the war and they became friends and I..." He paused, uncertain whether to continue.

Weber leant forward, detecting Frank's reluctance to continue. "And you what Frank?" His eyes blazed, and he glanced briefly above Frank's head at the soldier.

Frank knew that he must continue talking if he was to avoid another beating. "I became friends... well he is my best friend really... with Gunther, her son."

A look of wonder came over the German's face. "Your best friend is German? We have a British spy in Germany through you?"

Alarmed, Frank sought to correct himself. "No! No! Gunther is not a spy. We have been friends since we were boys, before all this... before our countries went to war with each other."

Weber stood, the chair grating as he pushed it back on the stone floor. He half turned as if to walk away, but then suddenly and without warning whipped around and slapped Frank across the side of his face with the back of his hand. His eyes opened wide and a drip of spittle issued from the corner of his mouth. "You lie!" he screamed. "The whole thing is a lie, is it not?"

"No!" Frank pleaded through his broken lips. "No it is the truth and I can prove it if you'll let me."

Weber turned, a contemptuous sneer on his face. "Oh you can prove it, can you? Tell me Mr Balfour, how can you prove it?"

"Ask Leclerc to identify me. Ask in the village... they'll all tell you of the English boy who inherited the chateau and..." He paused. "The photograph you talked of. That will prove I'm telling the truth."

"I haven't shown you the photograph."

"Precisely, but I can tell you that the corner is torn from it."

"The corner is torn from it?" He sneered. "And how precisely can that prove anything? Of course you know that the corner was torn, it was in your pocket!"

"Yes, but you'll find the torn corner in the top drawer of my bedside cabinet at the chateau de Janvier... my home." Frank stopped and stared at the openly scathing look on the man's face.

"I don't believe you Mr Balfour, or whatever your name is. Shall I tell you what I think? I think that you are either a British spy, in which case you will be shot. Or else you are a French man fighting for the British, in which case," he smiled thinly, "you will be shot."

Frank swallowed hard. "I assure you Herr Weber, I am not a spy. I have dual citizenship and I was called up to fight for France, no more and no less. I am Frank Balfoure of the Chateau de Janvier, owner of the Taillefer iron works in Chateauneuf, and if you wish to do so you can ask Leclerc and whoever else you wish, to verify those facts."

"Why should we bother?"

"To assure yourself that you do not have a spy..." He stopped as he saw Weber's hand drawn back once more to strike.

"Don't you dare to tell me what I want to assure myself of..."

"I do not wish to tell you what to do Herr Weber, I merely wish you to believe me..."

Hatred and anger flared in the German's face. His eyes flashed and his lips drew into a cruel, thin line. Frank knew what was coming, but he determined to stare at the man, even as the hand was raised and the back of it smashed into his cheek. His head rolled to the side and again his senses swam, but he fought to retain them and once more looked at his attacker. "I am telling you the truth Herr Weber. Please believe me and please ask Leclerc."

"Leclerc! Leclerc is a Frenchman. Tell me why you think I should believe the word of any inferior?"

Frank swallowed hard. "I... I cannot... except that..." The blow fell, and this time blackness followed it.

He awoke alone in a dark cell and flexed his limbs, relieved to find that he was no longer tied to a chair and instead was lying, unfettered, on a hard straw palliasse. He shifted position and the dust that rose from the bed made him cough. The cough in turn brought on a blinding pain in his head and he grasped his temples in both hands, rocking from side to side as it seared through him.

He retched but nothing came. There was nothing to come from a body devoid of all food for God knows how many days, starved even of the water that it needed to sustain life itself. He slid his legs off the bed and forced himself to sit upright, still holding tight to his head for all the world as if it would fall off. Gradually his eyes adjusted to the gloom.

There was no window, and the only light there was seemed to filter through the small grill in the door off to his right. The room was about two metres by three and was completely unfurnished with the exception of the iron-framed bed upon which he sat. A movement in the corner by the foot of the door attracted his attention, and he gingerly leant forward to investigate.

A simple metal tray lay on the floor, upon which there was a metal mug and plate. He tried to focus on their contents. Again he detected movement on the plate. Frank tried to stand. Immediately, almost as he left the safety of the bed, his legs gave way and he crashed forward, reaching out to save himself as he hit the floor. His hands slid across the rough, damp stone and made contact with the tray edge just as the rat leapt from the plate with a squeal and ran over his hand and under the door. Waves of revulsion ran over him, followed by absolute despair as he saw that the precious mug of water had tipped over.

For a while he lay there, his fingers exploring the wet tray, his face pressed close to the floor, but then gradually he managed to force himself to sit upright and shuffle his back to the wall. He reached down and gently removed the plate from the tray, lifting it up close to his eyes to see in the dark what was on it. A single hunk of bread, of indeterminate age, and even that had been all but consumed by the rodent. He gagged as he brushed off the semi-dry droppings and lifted it to his mouth. He bit off a hard mouthful and sat desperately trying to chew. He managed to reduce it to a dry powder in his mouth, but nothing on earth would make it go down, however hard he swallowed.

Frank put the bread in his lap and reached out for the tray. Unsteadily, his hands shaking with the effort, he raised it to his lips, tipping it as gently as he could to take in the precious liquid. He drank through clenched teeth to filter out the droppings, which he knew would be there, but even as he was prepared for it, when one finally came into contact with his lips he could not resist jerking the tray away and spluttering out the precious water. He cursed himself for his weakness, feeling the wet in his lap, knowing that here was water that he needed in order to survive. Gently he put down the tray, and picking up the bread soaked it, holding it down and mopping up the spilt water. He broke off the wet crusts and put them one by one in his mouth, chewing slowly, swallowing carefully, as he kept his mind firmly fixed on his need.

The empty, yawning pit in his stomach craved more but there was none to be had. His mouth, still dry but now capable of summoning up some trace of saliva, felt sore and his lips felt as if they had increased in size threefold.

He pushed himself up the wall, his legs shaking with the effort, and stopped at about half height, resting and pushing back against the cold, damp stone. It was some sort of cellar. It certainly wasn't a purpose-built prison cell. He sniffed at his hands. Coal. He smelt coal. He was imprisoned in the coal cellar of a chateau! If he was in a coal cellar then there was presumably some sort of coal hole.

Frank placed his hands behind his back, palms against the wall. He pushed and stood unsteadily on his feet for a moment before turning slowly, keeping one hand on the wall whilst the other stretched out to balance. He stood looking away into the blackness from the direction of the door and then stumbled forward, searching for a chink of light, feeling along the wall with his hands to the corner and up along the wall at the far end of the small room. There, where the shadows had merely seemed deeper, he found the sloping shute which would lead up to the hatchway. Would that be bolted? Surely it must be? Would it come up outside the sight of the sentries or at their very feet?

He stood at the foot of the shute sniffing up, searching still for signs of daylight, but none were to be seen. Standing on tiptoe, his legs started to shake uncontrollably, the muscle spasms running up his thighs. His breath came in short gasps and his fingernails clawed at the shute, worn smooth by years of grinding, tumbling coal. He felt himself sliding down the wall and turned, as his knees buckled beneath him, to fall slumped sideways against the foot of the wall. His head swam and waves of giddiness rode over and through him. Gradually he pulled himself together and straightened his legs to sit back. He drew his knees up and rested his head on them and slept.

He was awakened by the sound of the door being flung open to reveal the figure of a German soldier in the dim light of the doorway. "Stehen sie auf! 'raus!" the figure cried.

Frank looked up, torn between relief at seeing another human being and fear at what was to follow. He turned over onto his knees and, holding on to the wall raised himself uncertainly to his feet.

"'raus!" came the impatient voice of the soldier as Frank stepped forward. Hands grabbed him and propelled him through the open door into the grey light of the passageway beyond. He concentrated on staying upright, despite the shaking of his weakened legs. Another soldier greeted him with a grunt, and as he half turned the first one came up behind him so that the two of them were able to push him along the passage.

Frank's legs buckled after a few steps and the two soldiers stepped forward to grab him under his arms. There was light ahead, streaming in visible bands through the dusty air. A staircase leading up to the right. Frank hesitated, breathing deeply, trying to summon up the energy to mount the steps. The soldiers behind grunted again and overtook him, grabbing each of his arms as they passed on either side. Frank fell forward, painfully wrenching his arms in their sockets. He tried to push with his legs to relieve the strain as he was hauled up the staircase and through an open door into a wide hallway. So like the chateau... so like home, even down to the door beneath the huge staircase leading down to cellars.

For a brief moment he took it all in, breathing in the clean, fresh summer air that flooded through the open double doors in front of him, but then the two soldiers prodded him forward and along the corridor. "Halt!" they cried in unison as they drew level with a door. Frank stopped and waited meekly as one reached past him and knocked on the door. A muffled reply came from within and the soldier turned the handle.

The door opened to reveal a large study or library. Frank's eyes wandered up and around the room as it presented to him through the open door. Row upon row of shelves greeted him, stuffed with books and manuscripts. A large window straight ahead looked out on to rolling lawns, again so reminiscent of those at home that a lump came into his throat. A sharp push in the middle of his back, this time a push rather than a blow, sent him reeling into the body of the room, where he stood drunkenly swaying, his eyes fixed on the open gardens beyond.

"Monsieur Frank! Oh Monsieur. Oh..."

Frank turned his head slowly to the sound of the familiar voice, his heart leaping. Leclerc. Was it Leclerc? "Leclerc," he mumbled, "is it you?"

The big man rose from a chair seated in front of a desk over to Frank's right and came towards him. "Stop there!" came the order and Leclerc stopped in his tracks, turning to the source of the command. Frank, too, looked up and beyond his friend into Weber's thin, cold face. He swayed as his captor smiled his cruel smile and extended his hand, pointing back to the chair Leclerc had vacated. "Please be seated Monsieur Leclerc," he commanded quietly.

Leclerc looked at him briefly, noting the menace in the voice. He glanced briefly, apologetically at Frank and resumed his seat.

"Thank you," said Weber.

Frank stood, his knees buckling. He extended his arms to maintain his balance, but looking up saw the ceiling spinning as he sank to the floor. Leclerc made as if to rise, but a snapped finger from Weber made him stay where he was. One of the soldiers who had escorted Frank into the room stepped forward, but stepped back as Weber barked "Lassen sie ihn!"

"Do you know this man?" Weber asked Leclerc.

"Why yes... yes of course, he is..."

"He is a British spy!" Weber screamed.

Leclerc looked taken aback. He shrank into his seat. "No... no... it is no..."

"Not true! Not true! Then what is true Monsieur?"

Leclerc tried to speak. Terror seemed to have taken his voice. Oh what a terrible week it had been. The factory had been spared apart from some peripheral damage to some outbuildings, but then he was told that the newest of their machines were to be made ready for transhipment to Germany... and now this. An early morning knock at the door and he had been carried off in a vehicle with no explanation at all, his wife left on their doorstep speechless with fright. He looked at Frank. Poor boy, what had he done to deserve this other than an accident of birth? He swallowed hard, tempted almost beyond endurance to forsake the boy for his own sake. 'How could you even think of that?' he remonstrated with himself. 'The adopted son of Monsieur Armand, God rest his soul, how would I live with myself?' He looked into the cold, grey eyes of Herr Weber and his blood froze.

"Do you know this man?" Weber asked quietly.

'If I say no then he'll be convinced that I too am a spy,' thought Leclerc, pleased now that clarity was beginning to come to his mind. 'If I say yes, then I need to convince him thoroughly.' He cleared his throat. "I..." His voice failed and he swallowed again and coughed lightly. "This is Monsieur Frank Balfoure. He was the adopted son of my beloved friend Monsieur Armand Taillefer... he left him his estate to include the Chateau de Janvier outside Germigny-des-Pres, together with the iron works, of which I am the manager." He stopped looking into the eyes of Weber, desperately trying to hold his gaze in the face of the German's penetrating stare.

"Do please continue Monsieur..."

"I told you so," Frank whispered from the floor.

"Silence!" Weber shouted. Leclerc jumped visibly in his seat and clutched his hat to his breast. "Tell me of the family of this prisoner," continued Weber.

"His... his family?"

"Yes. Tell me of his family. I want names and all of his background, and you...", he indicated Frank on the floor, "...I want no word from you or you will be very sorry. Very sorry indeed." He turned to Leclerc. "Please continue."

Leclerc cleared his throat yet again. "His mother was... is an English lady, Madame Violet... I never met his true father... he was killed in the Great War. They... that is Monsieur Armand and Madame Violet... they met as she was a nurse, and after the war they were married until his... until his accident." He looked up at Weber, who waved his hand in the air in a circular motion indicating that he was to continue. "He... when Monsieur Armand was killed they moved back to England when the boy would have been..." He turned to Frank, but Weber thumped the table top, forcing him to look away. "I don't know... twelve... maybe thirteen."

"Ha! So we are supposed to believe that he finds himself in France after all these years purely by accident, are we?"

Leclerc looked puzzled. "No... no Monsieur. He... he has lived in France by himself since 1936 and I have been teaching him the business."

Frank looked up from the floor into the eyes of Leclerc. "Thank you Monsieur Leclerc," he whispered.

"Take him away," Weber shouted to the soldiers. Frank looked up, surprised, as they grabbed him and hauled him to his feet. He had expected in his mind that the corroboration of his story would see him riding home with Leclerc, but he saw now that this was not to be. The soldiers spun him around and dragged him to the door, pausing only briefly to open it. In that brief moment, Frank looked across at Leclerc's shocked face. He smiled and Leclerc raised his hand momentarily before Frank was dragged from the room and the door slammed shut.

A heavy, brooding silence was left in the room. Leclerc nervously fingered his hat. "What... what will happen to him?"

Weber stood and walked around the desk. "He will probably be shot," he said matter-of- factly.

"Shot... oh no Monsieur... but why?"

"He is a Britisher in French uniform and therefore a spy, or he is a Frenchman fighting for the British against the Reich." He smiled his thin smile. "Either way he is guilty, do you not agree?"

Leclerc stood. "I beg of you Monsieur, he is a good man and he... he cannot be, his best friend is one of your countrymen..."

"Ah that would be... who would that be Monsieur Leclerc?"

"Gunther. Gunther was... is his best friend... he was here in August of last year just before... just before..."

"Before your country declared war."

"No. No... well..." He noticed the menace in Weber's eyes. "Well, yes... if that is how you see it, but the fact is that Monsieur Frank and Monsieur Gunther were the very best of friends."

Weber leant forward. "Good enough friends to transcend their duties to their country?"

Leclerc looked shocked. "No! No Monsieur... Gunther is fighting somewhere in the German army and Frank was fighting for France. Both of them are simply doing their duty, but that does not... has not stopped them worrying about each other."

Weber smiled. "How very touching." He stood. "Thank you very much for coming to see me Monsieur Leclerc. We shall not detain you further." He stood, picking up the telephone on the desk as he did so. Leclerc sat still, too shocked by all that had happened to really comprehend what was going on. He watched Weber's face as the German spoke into the telephone.

"Eh... what about Monsieur Frank?" he ventured as Weber replaced the receiver.

Hard, grey eyes transfixed him. "I suggest that you get on with running the factory previously owned by that gentleman and remove him from your thoughts. Is that clear?" Leclerc rose, fingering his hat rim, turning it around and around nervously. He went to say something, but before he could get the words out Weber came up to him and barked. "As far as you are concerned, Monsieur Frank Balfoure is dead. Is that perfectly understood?"

Leclerc jumped back, his nerve completely gone now. He nodded mutely and turned for the door.

Back down in the cellar, Frank hunched against the wall, sitting on the floor, his knees drawn up to his chest. Leclerc had identified him. Why then was he still incarcerated here in this filthy hole? Surely now they would let him go and re-join his fellow soldiers as prisoners of war? Surely now they would let his family know that he was alive? But how could they do that? How could Leclerc tell his family that he was alive? No post would go to England. No telephone connection could be made. Despair wracked him and he hugged his knees close as tears of frustration and fear filled his eyes.

Leclerc walked out of the double doors into the daylight. The soldier escorting him stepped forward and held open the door of the vehicle for him to enter. Leclerc breathed deeply and stepped forward. He stopped, as across in the far corner of the yard he saw soldiers marching, following two others dragging a man between them. Frank? So that was where they were keeping him. They disappeared around the corner of the building as Leclerc took his seat and the driver stepped around the car and got in. The heat of the day beat down on the roof and Leclerc reached forward for the window and slid it back as they started off and headed towards the gates.

A burst of gunfire jolted him in his seat, and as he turned around to the sound, the soldiers marched back around the corner slinging their rifles across their shoulders nonchalantly as they sauntered back across to the main building. Tears sprang into his eyes and he slumped forward in his seat, his head in his hands.

***

The sound of heavy iron-clad boots on the dusty stone of the passage made Frank sit up on his bed. Was it daytime? He stared hard at the thin shaft of light coming through the grille in the door. Was that electric light or was it the thinner grey of daylight as it found its tortuous way to his cell?

He steeled himself for what was to come. Would he be dragged out and beaten again? Would it now be his turn to face the gunfire that he so regularly heard from somewhere up above? Perhaps he was going to be freed? No, he was not going to be freed. He knew that. He waited silently, calculating the distance that the marching feet had to come. They stopped. That was not outside his door, they had not come close enough. What was happening?

A door opened. He heard the rattle of the key in the lock, the protesting screech of the rusty hinges, the crack as the wood was flung back against the stone wall. Voices. Voices speaking loudly in German. Another sound. Another voice. A thinner voice whimpering in the darkness. Was it French? It must be, but it sounded so frightened, so alone. 'Do I sound so desolate?' he thought.

The door slammed shut and the heavy boots tramped away up the passageway and on up the staircase. Silence. Frank felt a vague and irrational sense of disappointment and then chided himself. Fearful solitude was no reason to welcome the approach of even an enemy. He gripped the grille, his ear cocked as he listened for clues.

He put his mouth to the opening. "Is anybody there?" he called softly.

He switched his ear back to the grille and listened carefully. Nothing.

"Is anybody there?" he called again. He waited, searching through the darkness, seeking to penetrate it with his thoughts.

"Hallo," a woman's voice whispered.

Frank's heart leapt. Company. French. Female? He was not alone. "My name is Frank," he called. "What's yours?"

"Annette."

"Are you alright Annette?" Silence. He craned his neck trying to interpret the sounds. Crying! The woman was crying. "Can you hear me? he called urgently. "Why are you in here?"

"Frank."

"Yes."

"Speak to me Frank. Tell me of life. Tell me things to take me away from this."

Frank held on to the grille, his mouth pressed up against the opening. Slowly at first, hesitantly he began to talk about his life. He recounted the years at the chateau, the death of Armand and the years spent wasted at boarding school. He told of Slater and could sense her instinctive dislike. He told of Florrie, Joe and Lizzie, and to the question "Was she your lover?" could only mutter "No."

"She should have been Frank."

"How do you know that?"

"It is in your voice."

Frank rolled away from the grille. Lizzie. He concentrated on the memory of her. Her smiling face turning to him as she ran down to the river in her bathing suit, the raised hands, the curves of her lovely body. The body of a full-grown woman banishing the vision that had comforted him all his youth. "She is to marry another," he said quietly.

"I beg your pardon."

Frank put his face to the grille. "She is going to marry another man."

Then silence.

Frank thought that perhaps the woman had gone to sleep and he turned from the door and prepared to lie down.

"It makes no difference to how you feel," Annette said softly.

Frank started. It makes no difference. Does it make a difference? He turned back to the grille. "What makes a difference is that we are in two countries with a war separating us for... forever for all I know."

There was another long silence. Then she spoke again. "Thank you Frank."

"For what?"

"For helping me forget for a few moments."

Frank smiled to himself. "It helped me to escape for a while too."

"Goodnight Frank."

"Goodnight Annette."

Doors banging open, the clatter of metal and doors slamming shut again awoke Frank. He rolled off his bed as his cell door opened. A hand appeared and plonked down a bowl of what smelt like cabbage soup.

The hand withdrew into the shadows then returned and threw down a hunk of hard bread, which bounced off the tray and disappeared into the dark. The figure stood, keys jangled, and the door slammed shut.

Frank knelt in the dark, feeling for the bread. He found it, and picking up the bowl of tepid liquid returned to his bed. He sipped the almost tasteless liquid, dunking his bread to soften it. The rat would go hungry today.

"Frank?"

He looked up from his meal. "Annette?" He stood, taking care not to spill his precious food and crossed to the door. "I'm here," he called softly.

"I'm so frightened Frank." Frank put down the bowl on the floor and concentrated on the small grille.

"Have courage Annette. They'll probably let you go today."

"They won't."

"How can you be so sure?"

"I'm Jewish and a Bolshevik."

"A what?"

She laughed now. A light laugh that told of girlish joy, even within this grim setting. "We would have been enemies before all this."

"Perhaps in your mind. Never in mine."

The laugh again. "Enjoy your breakfast Frank."

Smiling, Frank bent down to retrieve his bowl. His smile faded as his hand touched something furry, which scampered off and under the gap under the door. He grabbed the bowl and lifted it up to the dim light. The bread was gone. "Damn," he hissed.

"What's wrong?"

"The bloody rat's taken my bread." Again, the laugh that brought the light back into the gloom. He smiled and then he too started to laugh as he sat down on the bed, holding his precious bowl out before him, trying desperately not to spill the contents as his shoulders shook.

They finished their soup, and for about an hour the two of them said nothing as they sat there in the gloom. Eventually Frank stood again and called out. "Your turn. Tell me about yourself."

"What do you want to know?"

The sound of boots on the stairs precluded any answer. Frank stood back from the door waiting and listening. The marching boots stopped outside his door. The lock turned and the door flung open, letting the sparse light into his cell, revealing him standing there, his hands gripped nervously in front. A hand jerked a signal at him and he stumbled out through the door into a grip on each arm.

Frank twisted his head, enquiring silently as to their destination, but his searching look was met with no answer. Cold fear gripped him. Was this it? Was he now to face what he had feared, what he had listened to and dreaded for all these days. They approached a door on the right. Why had he not noticed that door before? He turned his head as they drew level, and for a brief moment he thought he caught sight of pale flesh and dark eyes, but then he was swept on past.

"Good luck Frank," came a voice.

"Good luck Annette," he called back.

The soldier on his left released his grip momentarily and swiped at Frank's head before seizing his arm once more. "Stille!" he hissed.

They turned up the stairs and propelled Frank up them towards the light. Why did the light that he had so craved now seem so threatening? A strange, irrational wish for the dark solitude of the cell came over him. What had seemed to imprison him now beckoned him back with a promise of protection. They turned out of the doorway at the top of the stairs and proceeded straight across the hallway to the open doors. This was it then, no further interrogation. They had finished with him and now he was to be disposed of.

He blinked, blinded by the bright sunlight. He stumbled on the unseen steps and fell forward, out of the grip of his escorts, onto the rough, hard, packed sand. His palms scraped across and he registered the loss of skin, felt the grit tearing into his exposed flesh. Hands gripped him once more and he was hauled to his feet. Where now? Across the yard to some place of execution? He steeled himself for the last walk and set into a wearied rhythm to match the soldiers. Suddenly they stopped and pulled him to a halt in front of a small van-like vehicle. Frank stood, swaying slightly as they released their grips on him and pulled open the rear doors. One of them jerked his thumb in the direction of the van's interior. Frank looked at him for a moment, trying to decipher what was going on.

Why would they want to put him in the van just to take him across the yard and shoot him? "Schnell!" the soldier shouted. Frank stepped forward and climbed into the rear. A parting thump on the back and the doors were slammed shut on him, leaving him in total darkness. He waited for the engine to start, wondering where they were taking him and why.

Silence. No engine noise. No sense of movement. What was going on? He shifted position and lay on his back. The sun beating down on the roof of the van made it warm inside. At first he savoured the heat after the chill of the cellar, but as time wore on it became more and more oppressive. He reached up to touch the bare metal of the roof and pulled back quickly as it burnt his already injured hands. If he was left in this oven for too much longer he would surely die.

Just as despair was about to overcome him he heard the sound of approaching soldiers. The doors opened and the rush of heated air out of the vehicle was replaced by a welcome inrush of cool. Three figures stood in the light, two large with one smaller one between them. Annette? The soldiers propelled her into the body of the van and she crumpled up in Frank's lap as the doors were slammed shut. The van rocked slightly as the soldiers got in. Frank cradled the woman in his arms as the engine started and the vehicle moved off, slowing down as he guessed they were approaching the gates. It stopped and he heard voices before it started moving again, and they were thrown sideways as it swung out into the road.

"Sorry," he whispered.

"What for?"

He smiled in the dark, aware that he was still holding her. Aware also that she showed no inclination to be released from his embrace. He could feel the air quickly cooling the hot metal and breathed a sigh of relief. Where were they being taken? If they were going to kill them then surely they would not waste the petrol and time to transport them away from the execution ground at the chateau?

The van rumbled over some sort of strips in the road. He felt the front wheels cross them and then, almost immediately, the rear wheels. Smooth, then again, the same rumbling pattern. The van swung right and they were thrown against the side with a crash. He thought he detected the sound of laughter as the brakes squealed and the van came to a halt. He heard the doors opening and the footsteps coming around to the rear. He braced himself for what was to come as the doors opened, blinding him. For a second he sat blinking in the bright light, seeing nothing but the dark shapes of the soldiers standing by the doors.

"'raus! 'raus!" they shouted.

Frank released Annette. She crawled out on her hands and knees before being grabbed and bodily lifted out. Frank shuffled and slid his way to the rear of the van and dropped his feet to the ground. Once more he felt his arms gripped and he was pulled from the body of the vehicle and flung away. He reeled on his feet, struggling to maintain his balance as he looked around. He was in a rail yard. Not a station but some sort of freight loading platform. Other prisoners, men in French army uniforms, were being unloaded from lorries and herded up the ramps and into cattle trucks. A prod in his back from the muzzle of a rifle made him step forward. He turned, questioning his escort, and was greeted with another thrust of the rifle, forcing him to go away from the queue. Why did he have to go in the other direction? Annette joined him.

He looked into her face for the first time. She was about nineteen or twenty years old. Small, no more than to his chest, and slim. Her dark hair was bobbed at the shoulder and her pale face was turned up to his. Dark, almost black eyes set deep in her elfin face studied him intently. The mouth, surprisingly wide for such a face, opened, smiled and spoke. "Pleased to meet you Frank," she whispered.

He smiled down at her. "Pleased to meet you Annette," he replied.

Another jab in the back pushed them on in the opposite direction to the steady stream of prisoners shuffling along the ramp. They made eye contact with some, but for the most part the vacant, haunted expressions that were returned showed no emotion or greeting.

They halted at the foot of the tailgate of a truck, which was disgorging its last passengers. One of the two soldiers standing by it turned as they arrived. Frank raised his arm in a questioning gesture, but the young soldier misread his intention, loathing and fear written in equal measure on his astonished face. Frank held his hands, palm open in supplication. For a moment the young soldier seemed nonplussed, but then he reversed his rifle and swung it back to club at Frank.

"No!" Annette screamed as she pulled Frank back. The blow missed, but the two of them bumped into the soldiers standing behind them, who cursed and struck out. Frank felt the blow to his head and his senses swam once more. He crumpled up and would have fallen forward to the ground had it not been for Annette grabbing him and supporting him to the ground, as best she could. She knelt beside him, cradling his head.

"Auf!" screamed the young soldier, kicking Frank in the side. He struggled to rise, knowing that to do otherwise would lead to much worse. Annette assisted him to his feet and the two of them stood holding on to each other as the last of the lorry's occupants climbed down.

Why were they being made to get onto a lorry? Why weren't they going onto and into the rail trucks? The soldier jerked his thumb up into the body of the lorry, indicating that they should get in. Frank stood back briefly to allow Annette to climb up and in before painfully clambering up. It was empty, with four rows of bench seating, one at either side of the truck and two back-to-back down the centre. Frank pointed to the off-side front and the two of them shuffled over and sat down, expecting the soldiers to join them. None did, and, instead, the two that had escorted them in the van said their goodbyes to the other soldiers, returned to their vehicle and drove off.

"Are you alright?" she asked, extending a slim, white hand to touch his head. He nodded, smiling ruefully. She fingered the cut on his temple, pushing back the hair. "You'll have a scar there for life, but it'll be hidden by your hair to some extent."

He grinned painfully. "It's my brain that won't heal. That feels as if

it's been scrambled with all the blows my head has received of late."
He looked into her eyes, gently taking hold her hand, noticing the
dark blue and yellow bruising to her wrists. He studied her face. A
nice face, open and fresh, marred now by the dark rings beneath her
large eyes and the livid bruising to her cheekbones.

A shout right beside their lorry distracted both of their attentions
from each other. A head appeared over the rim of the lorry tailgate,
bald, rimmed with grey hair. Spectacled eyes peered over the top
as Frank moved forward to assist the older man into the truck. He
heaved him in and passed him back to Annette as another elderly
man climbed laboriously up and in. The two newcomers sat down
wearily on the nearest benching, nodding and muttering their
thanks. "Danke." Frank returned to sit at Annette's side, his brow
furrowed. Why had they thanked him in German?

The day wore on and gradually in ones, twos and threes more
and more prisoners were added to their lorry. For the most part
these were ordinary-looking folk who sat quietly in their seats like
so many passengers waiting for the bus to depart. The only hint of
abnormality being the way so many of them clung to each other, the
fear that hung in the air and the whispered conversations in other
languages.

Gradually the lorry filled up, and when there were about thirty of
them the tailgate was swung up and latched into place. Two soldiers
climbed in, pushing and gesticulating for the other occupants to
move forward. They sat, one in each rear corner of the lorry, their
rifles resting butt-first on the floor as the lorry engine roared into life
and they set off.

Frank stole a glance at Annette. He reached for her hand and
squeezed it reassuringly. She clasped hers over his and they sat
there looking out and back at the passing countryside. Gradually
the movement of the lorry induced drowsiness in the girl and she
rested her head against Frank. He put his arm around her and held
her close, his chin resting on her hair.

For two hours they travelled, with all of the prisoners remaining in complete silence whilst the two soldiers laughed and joked with each other in loud voices, shouting and slapping their thighs from time to time. Eventually they pulled off the main road onto a side road, which in turn gave way to an unmade road. The lorry started to bump and buck as they hit potholes, causing the occupants to cry out as they sought to keep a grip on their seats. The soldiers burst out laughing as one unfortunate old man lost his grip and slipped to the floor. Frank rose uncertainly to help, despite Annette's imploring look.

The soldier on the opposite side to them saw him rising and shouted something. The soldier on their side made as if to rise and Annette clawed frantically at Frank, pulling him down. Just then the lorry ran onto a smooth patch of road and the old man was able to regain his seat. The soldiers relaxed and went back to their private conversation.

"Frank you must be careful," Annette chided. "If you're to survive this you must not get beaten again... I warn you."

Frank turned to her. "Why? Do you have experience of this sort of thing before today?"

"I..." She looked up at him. "It's not only German soldiers who can be brutal to those that they perceive as enemies." She looked up at him, her face set seriously.

Frank nodded. "Perhaps you're right. I... well I..."

"You can't possibly know Frank. Why should you?"

The lorry slowed and pulled off the road to the left, bumping over what was obviously now rough grass. Trees appeared at either side of the track they were following and cold fear gripped Frank. If they had driven them all this way to some place way out of sight, then... he shivered. Annette sat closer to him and he looked down into her face, seeing the same fears echoed there.

The trees separated and the lorry slowed to a stop. Shouts from the front of the vehicle distracted their attention for a moment as the soldiers at the rear stood to lean out along the side, calling to their comrades. The lorry jerked forward and, as the soldiers swung back into its well, they framed the view the other occupants had of timber and wire gates set in a high- wire fence, as they closed.

The lorry halted and the two soldiers jumped down, turning and reaching up to unlatch the tailgate. "'raus!" they called, "'raus!" The occupants stood and shuffled single-file towards the back, down and off. Older prisoners struggled to dismount, uncertain as to how to negotiate the drop. Frank pushed forward in the lorry and bent down to take the hand of one old man as he clawed frantically at the bare metal. "Relax," he called down, "let me take you." The old man looked up at him, fear written large in his hollow eyes. Frank smiled and the man let go, trusting his meagre weight to Frank, who, despite his own weakness, was able to lower him gently to the ground.

A German soldier stood back watching them come off. His eyes made contact with Frank's and, much to Frank's surprise, held his gaze. Normal eyes, which in normal circumstances would elicit a smile of greeting, but here seemed incongruous. An officer stepped into view and said something in the soldier's ear. Immediately he was galvanised into affirmative action. He stepped forward, accompanied by two others, and they proceeded to assist the prisoners to dismount, pushing the men to one side and the women to the other as they did so.

"We're to be separated it seems," said Frank as the last of the occupants was handed down and he and Annette prepared to dismount.

"Take care Frank," she whispered as she jumped down. A soldier pushed her off to the right, where she joined the small group of women, and as Frank landed he was pushed to the left and the larger group of men.

"Marsch!" came the order, and the two files marched beside the lorry, on past it and towards another set of gates, which were swung open by guards as they approached. They passed through into an open area about twice the size of a football pitch, ringed by the two wired fences topped with coils of barbed wire. At each corner of the huge square, timber supports rose up to platforms, on which were mounted machine guns. The one on the right in front of them was further advanced than any of the others and its four-sided roof timbers were already in place, although not yet clad. Beyond the fence, in a clearing behind the compound itself, long wooden huts could be seen, three in all, set in an open horseshoe. These were obviously the huts that housed the guards, as from their open doors and windows men in uniform dangled, idly watching the activities within the wire.

Frank looked around. To the left of the open compound there were three huts, each about twenty metres long by about six metres wide set out in a line, each three metres apart. To the right and at the far end there were piles of lumber and stacked panels, which were obviously meant for erection to the same geometric pattern. A lot more people were expected here. No other shelter seemed available within the compound, and it certainly didn't look like some sort of elaborate killing ground. He glanced across at the group of women marching along on the same track as them about six metres away and caught Annette's enquiring look. He shrugged his shoulders.

In front of them, set out on the grass in the warm afternoon sunlight, were two tables, behind which sat two soldiers to each. It reminded Frank of the school room, but here in the beauty of a French forest evening, with the sun shining and the birds singing, the menace seemed bizarre.

They formed a single file in front of each desk, the men to one and the women to the other. Frank stood, moving forward slowly as each man in front of him was processed and ushered across to stand in a tight group in the centre of the compound, watched over by armed soldiers. He noticed that the smaller number of women had already been processed and looked across to see Annette. She was talking, a worried expression on her face, to an equally worried-looking older woman, who raised her hands palm up to the sky and lowered them repeatedly. So intent was he on watching them that he failed to realise that the line of men had moved forward, leaving a large gap between him and the man in front of him in the queue.

A tap on his shoulder and he turned to see, once again, the young soldier he had seen on their arrival. He indicated the space that had opened up in front of Frank. Frank apologised and stepped forward.

He reached the desk. "Name?"

"Frank Balfoure."

"Nationality?"

"Fren... French and English." The young soldier marking off the names and writing down the information beside each one looked up at this unexpected answer. Quite apart from his mental inability to contemplate anything different to that which was written down on his sheet, there was no room on it for anything out of the ordinary. "I am French and Eng... no British. Dual nationality."

The soldier looked up at him. He glanced at the other young man sitting beside him. He shrugged his shoulders and the first man stood and called out to the officer standing off at the side. He walked across, an enquiring look on his face. He bent down, looking over the young soldier's shoulder, listening intently to the man's explanation of the problem.

"You are British or French. Which one?"

"I was born in England but obtained French citizenship by adoption. I live in France and was serving in the French army when I was captured."

The officer stared at him. "Your father was British?"

"Yes."

"Your mother was British?"

"Yes. Still is. She lives in London."

"British," said the officer, stabbing his finger down at the space reserved for the answer to the question.

"Religion?" said the soldier.

"Church of England." The soldier looked up at the officer again.

"Christlich," the officer commanded.

"Next," called the soldier as Frank stepped aside to allow the man behind to come to the desk. The officer stepped back and silently indicated for Frank to join the group waiting in the open. Frank sauntered across to join Annette, and the little group waited whilst the remainder of their number were processed.

When all had been checked the officer stepped forward, flanked by two soldiers. He stood in front of them all as the quiet conversation died. For a moment he stood silently examining them, staring, it seemed, at each one individually. "Good afternoon," he said in perfect French. He repeated the greeting in equally perfect English, waiting whilst the silent questioning looks went from person to person. "My name is Major Mundt," he continued in French. "I am the temporary kommandant of this camp and you are the first..." He smiled. "...the first guests to arrive. There will be others, and it is your task to assist in the assembly of the rest of the huts and to complete the layout of the camp. Work will commence at first light tomorrow morning. For this evening you will accommodate yourselves in the three huts already assembled, women to the first hut and men to the other two. There will be no fraternisation between the sexes other than during work. Is that understood?"

He waited, and when there was no answer he repeated the question. This time there was a chorused reply of "Yes."

He nodded his head in satisfaction. "This is a holding camp. You will be processed here whilst the army consolidates its position in the country, and in all probability you will then be reassigned to other camps or prisons. Any attempt at escape will be punished by death. Is that understood?"

This time the group knew that a voluble answer was required and it was given. The Major stood back. Frank looked at him. He was a soldier, not a prison guard, and it was obviously irksome to him that he should be faced with his present task. Nevertheless Frank knew enough about men to know that, unwelcome as his post was, the man would see his duties through rigorously. He meant what he said.

The young soldier came around the group and stood just in front of Frank. He noticed Frank looking at him and turned to face him directly. "You are British?" he asked in English.

"Yes," replied Frank.

"I speak a little English," the young man volunteered.

"Good," said Frank encouragingly.

"Yes, I would be happy for you to teach me better."

"I would like that," said Frank.

"Yes," the young man enthused. "I would like to be posted to England when the British are defeated and it is good, ja, if I speak English very well."

"Very good," said Frank, not knowing whether to be amused or annoyed. He switched back to French. "What do we do about food and toilet arrangements?"

The soldier seemed disappointed that his first English lesson seemed to be over. He waved his hand over to an area straight in front of them. "Cook house not ready yet. Use that area. Food will be brought in for you to cook later. Toilets and showers there." He pointed to an area screened off with canvas about one-and-a-half metres high and a single standpipe with a hose leading from a bowser positioned between the inner and the outer fences. The group was drifting over to the huts and Annette and Frank joined them, Annette going to the first one, reserved for the women, and Frank going to the last one.

He stepped up and into the hut, surprised to find that even though he was the last across, he was alone within it. He turned in the door and made as if to leave. "Not to your satisfaction Mr Balfour?" said the officer as he started to step down.

"No. No Major, it's just... well, it's just that everyone else seems to have gone to the other hut."

"Is that a problem?"

"No. No, but I thought that maybe..."

"I think that this hut is where you will stay Mr Balfour. After all, most of those other men are Jews or Bolsheviks."

Frank looked at the man. There was no enmity in his voice and he seemed totally unaware of how offensive his remarks were. If he tried to point out the error then he would probably fail to understand, and in all probability would take offence. Self-preservation took control. "Thank you Major. This hut looks perfectly suitable." He turned and went back into the hut. It was completely bare of furniture with the exception of triple wooden-slatted bunks built back against the wall down each side and a single iron stove set on a concrete base in the centre. If he was to be here for a long time then a bunk close to the stove would be the best, and one of the top ones would probably be the most private. But for the moment, at the height of summer, and in the absence of any other occupants, he would take one close to the door.

Footsteps on the timber flooring warned him of the fact that the officer had entered behind him. He turned to look at the man. At any other time and in any other situation they could have been friends, but the fact was that this man was his jailer. He must not forget that and he must never let his guard down. "Will I be here long?" he asked.

"I don't know. My orders are to construct the camp and we will then hand it over to other authorities. We are soldiers, not prison guards."

Frank nodded his understanding. "I am a soldier too."

The officer looked at him. "The Gestapo obviously suspect that you are more than that."

"The Gestapo cannot understand that a man can love two countries."

Mundt smiled. "How then can you reconcile the fact that the British have just sunk the French fleet with the loss of huge numbers of French sailors?"

Frank looked astonished. "I... I can't... except that... well I cannot think that they did it lightly."

Mundt smiled. "I am a soldier. I must not concern myself with such things." He turned and walked slowly to the door.

"Would you shoot us if we attempted to escape?"

The officer stopped. He turned and looked directly at Frank. "Of course." Frank inclined his head in acknowledgement. Mundt returned the gesture, turned on his heel and left the hut.

***

From deep within the house the calls of "Coming" could be heard, and as they got nearer to the door they were joined by the sound of coughing. A heavy curtain was swished across and bolts were withdrawn. Ernest stepped back and down from the step, looking up expectantly as the key was turned and the door opened. "Good afternoon," he said cheerily.

Crowe peered down at him, his brow furrowed, his eyes squinting. "Good aft... do I know you sir?"

"You damned well should Crowe. It's me, Matthews."

"Matthews? Matthews? Matthews! Good heavens man, is it you?"

"It most certainly is old chap," said Ernest laughing. He mounted the steps and extended a hand, which Crowe took in both his, clasping it warmly.

"Well come on in dear fellow. Come on in." Crowe released Ernest's hand and ushered him through into the dark hall, piled high with stacks of old newspapers tied up in bundles.

"Not drawn the blackouts yet?" enquired Ernest.

"Can't be bothered old chap. Can't be bothered, leastways not at the front. Such a bloody fag trying to get them right again by the evening. Here, come through into the dining room, we can sit there. I usually use that room nowadays since..." The two men picked their way down the hall, with Crowe pointing out obstacles as they went.

"Yes, I was sorry to hear of your loss."

"Yes... eh thank you. Thank you. You too old chap... although I hear..."

"That I have taken up with my maid?"

Crowe grinned. He dug Ernest in the ribs. "You're among friends Matthews, old man. Among friends, don't you know." He winked.

Ernest thought about a riposte but decided the better of it. What was the point of trying to explain. Nothing would change. The man would say, "Oh certainly old chap. I understand old chap", but he wouldn't. None of them could understand the happiness, the fulfilment he had with Alice. And, given other circumstances, neither would he have done in a previous life. They went through into the dining room and Crowe bustled ahead to clear the table of stacks of books and papers. The French windows, their blackouts still taped to the glass, were open to the garden, allowing the light to highlight the dust that rose in clouds.

"Take a seat old chap," said Crowe, pointing down to a chair which he pulled out from under the table. "Well it has been a long time, hasn't it?"

"It certainly has," said Ernest as he sat.

Crowe came around the table and sat opposite him, leaning across observing him intently. "Lost all your money I hear."

"Yes. Yes I was in fact made bankrupt, but I'm pleased to say that I'm now discharged."

"Discharged eh? Good."

"Yes. The eventual realisation of all of my assets plus a little help from Frank... my grandson... you remember?" He leant forward. "Actually Crowe, that's the reason I'm here. I need your help."

Crowe leant back a little, the alarm showing on his face despite his best efforts to hide it. "Help? What sort of help... err. I'm not actually..."

"Nothing material old chap," said Ernest. Crowe visibly relaxed. "I just want to know if through your contacts in the Red Cross... well the truth is that we've not heard of my grandson Frank since just before the invasion of France and... well... we're getting a bit worried."

Crowe put his elbows on the table and cupped his hands together, breathing through them. He moved them away from his mouth. "Was he in France at the fall?"

"Yes. He had just been called up from reserve, so he would have been in uniform..."

"And you've received no notice of him being posted as a prisoner of war?"

"None whatsoever, but the point is, he would have been in French Army uniform."

Crowe leant back in his chair, his hands down by his sides, gripping the seat as he rocked back. "I see. I see, so... he didn't escape at Dunkirk with all the others?"

"No, unfortunately. If he had done so, of course he would not have gone back, only to surrender. He would have stayed here. No, it looks as if something has befallen him in France itself."

Crowe rocked forward on his chair. He rubbed his chin thoughtfully. "If he's not posted as a prisoner of war then... have you tried the French?"

"The French?"

"The free French. Do they know anything?"

"No, that's the point. Violet has already contacted them and they have no news of him at all."

"Well I really don't see what else can be done," said Crowe quietly.

Ernest fixed his old friend with his gaze and extended his hands across the table towards him, the index finger of his right hand pointing directly at Crowe. "You could get the Red Cross to write to his home or to his factory asking for news. I can't... well..."

There was silence, then Crowe stood. He delved around in the sideboard and came back to the table on Ernest's side bearing a pad of paper and a pen. "Write down the names and addresses of the people you feel might know and I'll see what can be done."

Ernest smiled up at his friend. "Thank you," he said as he took the pad. He wrote the name and address of Frank and gave the names of Philippe, Marie and Jean-Claude. Then he wrote down Leclerc's name, giving the factory address. "If you or your people can make contact with any of these people then I'm sure... I hope that we can know what's happened."

"I'll do my best old chap."

Ernest rose. "Thank you Crowe. It's just that... well it's just that I... well I became... am very fond of the boy... man and... you know."

Crowe clapped his hand around the shoulder of his old friend. "I do know," he said. "Cup of tea before you go?"

***

A soft flapping sound in the still of the night shot Frank back into wakefulness. He stirred on the hard boards of his bunk and lowered the blanket to peer over it into the darkness of the hut. A shadow moved against the faint light coming through from the high-level window and he held his breath. It came closer, feeling its way towards him. He sat up. "Who's there?" he whispered into the dark.

"Me," came the softly breathed reply.

"Annette?"

"Yes. Where are you?"

"Over here. What's the matter, what do you want?"

There was no reply, as such. She reached his bunk then released her grasp on the dark blanket she held about herself. For a moment he saw her naked whiteness, but then she slipped onto the bunk beside him and pulled his cover over herself, snuggling into the crook of his body. He sensed the earthy, smoky smell of their existence barely masking the warm, musky odour of her body. He propped himself up on one arm and breathed into her ear. "What are you doing here? If they catch you we'll both be... What's happened, is anything wrong?"

"Nothing." She turned over on her back. "Nothing now."

"Annette, are you trying to get us both shot?"

She touched her finger to his lips. "No, it's just... it's just that... the lights will be working tomorrow."

"So what?" he whispered.

"So this is the last chance for you to do something for me."

"What?"

She giggled lightly. "What do you think?" His serious expression was lost in the dark. He felt the heat rushing into his loins, and as she moved against him he gasped. She drew back. "You've done it before, haven't you Frank?"

"Yes. Yes of course, but..." Brief memories of past liaisons, most of them quick, fumbling, loveless affairs, rushed into his memory.

"Do it to me Frank. Please."

"Why?"

An edge of anger, of fear of a rejection, which she had not envisaged, crept into her voice. "Why?"

Frank stroked her face tenderly. "Why Annette?"

She sat up. "Because I have... I am a virgin, and before very much longer that will be taken from me, probably against my will." She threw her arms around him and pulled him back down on her. "I want to give myself freely Frank, to know love just one time before it all... before it all gets greedy and nasty." She lay back, her small body half under his. In the dark he could just see her face, the eyes staring up at him.

"Are you sure?"

In reply, she raised her head to his and kissed him full on the lips. He felt the urgency, her open lips searching his mouth like a blind puppy at its mother's breast. He ran his hands down her slim figure, over her small, hard breasts. She gasped as he rolled her nipples between his thumb and forefinger, pushing up against him. She raised her knees, pushing her heels against the hard boards as his hand travelled on down, over her stomach and on into her pubic hair. Frank pushed down with the heel of his hand and she writhed as his fingers spread and searched within her, feeling her wetness.

Gently he straddled her and positioned himself between her legs. He arched his back, raising himself from her, pushing himself against her opening. For a second she hesitated, but then she raised her knees and pulled him down and within herself. There was a moment of stillness, but then his hips started to move rhythmically. Annette transferred her hands to his bottom and pulled him again and again down and within her. She started to moan in time with his thrusts, and as they got louder he stopped. "Shhh," he whispered. "Try to be quiet."

She grinned back up at him in the darkness. He couldn't see it but he suspected. "What are you laughing at?"

"It's so wonderful," she sighed. "I never dreamt it would be this nice."

"Why thank you mademoiselle," he chided, starting to move within her once more. Annette turned her head, her eyes closed as she concentrated on the warmth that was spreading within her being. She began to pant and Frank, unable to hold himself back any more, came as she reached the height of her passion and slipped over the edge of reason. Frank was aware almost too late that her cries were rising into a yelp. He rolled aside and clapped his hand over her mouth, trying desperately to contain her ecstasy, giggling as he did so. For a moment she struggled, but then she too subsided into a fit of giggling and the two of them rolled around on the hard board delighting in their joy, she of discovery, he of the first truly wonderful sexual experience of his life.

Their giggles subsided and they lay entwined, kissing, pecking at each other and nuzzling close. "Thank you Frank," she whispered.

"Thank you Annette," he said. "That was wonderful. You're a bit of a natural at this."

She grinned up at him. "Well," she said coquettishly, "perhaps after a bit more practice." She reached down between them and took hold of him, gently rubbing and stroking him back into arousal.

"Have you no decorum girl?" he asked.

"None whatsoever kind sir," she replied, opening her legs wide and guiding him back within her.

He paused as he reached full entry. "Try to be quiet this time," he whispered.

"I'll try," she said, giggling as she squirmed against him pushing up into his groin, trying to start him off again. "I'll try, but first take me back to where you just took me and this time pretend I'm... what's her name... Lizzie."

"What?!" he recoiled, shocked.

She pulled him down again. "Pretend for me Frank, so that I can feel what it is to be loved."

Gently this time, without the urgency of the first time, they moved against and within each other, matching their movements and their breathing. As they both climbed once more to the thresholds of their joy Frank closed his eyes, and despite his misgivings thought of Lizzie. His eyes flickered open, catching a glimpse of the slim, white body beneath his, spinning him back in time and on and up into a crescendo of passion, which he released within her in a shuddering climax, which she matched perfectly.

Frank awoke from a dreamless sleep. He felt whole and more complete than he had felt in a long while. Darkness still reigned, but a faint streak of light crossed the night sky beyond the windows. She was leaning on one elbow, looking down at him. "I've got to go Frank," she said quietly. She stood naked before him and he sat holding out his hands to her, seeking once more to hold her. She danced sideways, picking up the blanket and wrapping it around herself as she ran to the door. She opened it and looked out, checking that the coast was clear. "Goodbye Frank," she whispered, and then she was gone.

It was light when he next opened his eyes. He stretched on his bunk feeling, luxuriating in, the dull ache in his groin and the faint yet discernible odours of his liaison. Had it really happened? Of course it had, and he now had to face the consequences. How would he react to her? How would she treat him? It wasn't as if they could avoid each other. Why should they want to? But they were prisoners, and as such he would now feel an added sense of responsibility towards her, which time and circumstance might make difficult.

Shouts from outside told him that once more the day was beginning and the work of construction of the camp would soon commence. Strange, they had spent the past few weeks as prisoners constructing their own prison but it had never felt quite like that. The soldiers who were their guards had almost become friends as they worked alongside each other, often stripped to the waist in the sun so that an outsider could not have told captive from captor. They had taken breaks together, lying on the dry grass, passing food and water, occasionally even wine amongst each other, for all the world like... well like members of the same club on a camping trip.

Muscles, which had been thin and wasted, filled out. Skin that had been ghostly white took on a healthy tan. Eyes that had been sunken and lost glowed with health and happiness in the clean forest air. Mundt kept himself aloof from most of the prisoners, but would often stop by and chat with Frank. He was a career officer in the Wehrmacht, and although he never actually said so, Frank felt that he was uneasy with the idea of being made a jailer and that he longed to get back to the business of pure soldiering.

That he had difficulty in reconciling his natural humanity with his acquired distrust of races considered inferior to his reflected in his attitude to the prisoners under his control. He confessed a liking for poetry to Frank and showed a profound knowledge of, and love for, the works of Shakespeare. Frank had never really taken to such things, but he introduced Mundt to an elderly Jewish woman, originally from Poland, who he had seen clutching a copy of *As You Like It*. After that, Frank would often watch as the two of them sat on a pile of logs chatting away peacefully. The old woman would laugh and raise her hands, gesticulating with pleasure as the two of them reminisced about their great passion... until the old woman touched him in her excitement and Frank would notice the visible stiffening, the doubt and the distrust reappearing in his demeanour. He often wondered if the old woman too noticed Mundt's withdrawal, but whether she did or not, she had the sense to ignore it and by carrying on, the moment would pass.

They had all worked wonders. A workforce of just under thirty prisoners, most of whom were of advanced years, together with an equal number of young soldiers, had, between them, succeeded in erecting a total of seventeen huts, which now stood empty and waiting for... for who knows what, thought Frank. Wash houses and showers too had been erected, as had a kitchen hut, although as yet no equipment was available.

After only a few short weeks, the prisoners took a perverse pride in their own prison and many of them, Frank included, relaxed and settled down to enjoy an existence which had all the promise of being a pleasant one.

All that promise changed one morning. Frank opened the door and stepped out into the early morning sunshine. He was bare-footed, and as he stepped onto the grass he curled his toes, feeling the dew squeezing between them. He raised his arms in the air, stretched, yawned and rubbed his eyes. "You there!" screamed a voice in French.

Frank looked up, amazed. Who amongst the prisoners was so excited at this time of the morning? He searched for the source of the voice and found it soon enough in the person of a gendarme striding across to him. French? The man was a French policeman! Did that mean that some event had turned the war around? Were they all free? He smiled as the man came up to him.

The blow caught him unawares and he spun off sideways, clutching his jaw. "What did you do that for?" he cried as he straightened up to look the man in the face.

Hatred greeted him. "Get into line you foreign bastard," the man screamed. "Get into line."

Into line? What was the man talking about? Frank looked around. In the centre of the open square between the lines of huts he could see his companions grouped together, cowering, their hands together. He searched for Annette, but then a cuff on the back of his bemused head sent him sprawling towards the other prisoners. "Where's Major Mundt?" he asked of the gendarme as he stumbled forward.

"Silence" was the only reply he got, together with a thump in the back. Gratefully, he saw Annette. She signalled him with her eyes and he slipped into the line beside her as the gendarme stood back.

Frank looked around. They were surrounded by armed gendarmes standing in lines, their guns pointing towards the prisoners. "What's going on?" he whispered.

"French are taking over the camp," she whispered back out of the corner of her mouth.

"French? Well that's good, isn't it?"

"I don't think so." She paused as Major Mundt, in company with a senior gendarme, walked through the outer and then the inner gates towards them. Frank, in company with many of the other prisoners, relaxed as the familiar figure came to stand in front of them. They waited for him to speak, but instead he merely nodded in their direction and then turned and shook the hand of the man who had accompanied him.

Briefly he glanced back at them all, then he turned on his heel and walked away and through the gates to a waiting vehicle. He got in and it set off, followed by three other lorries, filled with their erstwhile guards and companions.

The Capitaine waited silently as the prisoners watched the departing convoy. He observed the dismay in their faces and matched it with his own of complete disdain. These foreign swine were mourning the departure of the conquerors. That they were all in league, and that the fault for the defeat of France lay in their hands, there could be no doubt.

He waited until the vehicles were practically out of sight and the sound of their engines no longer dominated the quiet of the forest day. Then, in a thin, reedy voice, he began to address them.

"We are the patriots of the Etat Francais. You are our prisoners and you will obey all orders given by me and my men. You and your kind have engineered the defeat of France, but I promise you that we will build the new France free from the slovenly influences of foreigners like yourselves, free from the disease of Judaism and Bolshevism. Is that clear?"

Silence greeted him. "Is that clear?!" he screamed as his men moved forward, menacing the small group with their guns.

"Yes," came the muffled reply from downcast mouths.

"Yes sir!" the man screamed.

"Yes sir," came the frightened reply from as many lips as could muster sound.

The man stiffened. He breathed in deeply and puffed out his chest, revelling in the importance that circumstance, fate and his own belief had thrust upon him. He stood back as an underling came forward. The two conversed secretly together for a while as Frank and his companions watched, torn between despair and fascination.

Orders were barked and gendarmes strode in amongst them wielding their batons, forcing them into ordered lines. "You will respond to your names as they are called out and you will go to the places you are directed!" yelled a gendarme, stepping forward with a sheaf of papers in his hand. He proceeded to read out the names, and as each prisoner responded they were directed to various parts of the camp. Older men seemed to be separated from younger ones and similarly with the females. Annette's name was called out. Frank registered her full name for the first time. Annette Frieda Winklesdorf.

She squeezed Frank's hand briefly as she strode forward, and with barely a backward glance was directed, at a run, to one of the huts at the top end of the camp.

Frank stood, observing the weeding out of the inmates. Each time the gendarme opened his mouth to speak he anticipated his own calling, but each time it was not to be. Eventually he was left alone, standing in isolation as the last of his companions marched off to his designated position. Frank prepared to step forward to receive his orders but none came, and instead the gendarme dropped his sheaf and walked away. Something was wrong. What was it? Had they found out about last night? Was he about to be punished? Surely not? Annette had been taken away in company with some of the other younger women, so it couldn't possibly be that. Could it?

"Balfoure?"

Frank turned to his right. Three gendarmes approached, two of them armed. "Yes," he replied.

"You are to go with these gendarmes, who will accompany you to Paris."

Frank swallowed. "Paris? Why do I have to go to Paris?"

The man swiped him across the face. "You are a prisoner. You do not ask why, you do as you are told."

Frank's heart sank. Paris? What on earth would he find there? The senior gendarme turned to the other two, and oblivious to Frank's ability to hear, instructed them that the prisoner was to be escorted to Fresnes by train, after which the two of them were to return with all speed. Fresnes? Prison? Why must he go to prison rather than stay here in the camp? He wasn't Jewish, but he was foreign like the rest. Fear grabbed his very being. Annette. He would be unable to say goodbye.

The two gendarmes grabbed him, one by each arm, and before he could do anything about it he found himself handcuffed with his hands behind his back. They pushed him forward, out through the first gates, then the second, which were swung open as they approached. A car was waiting, the engine running. One gendarme got in the front passenger seat whilst the other forced Frank into the rear seat and got in beside him.

"You are lucky," the man beside him said.

"Lucky?"

The man laughed. "To be leaving this place."

"Why, what's to happen here?"

The man who had got into the front seat turned around and leant over. "This camp is going to fill up with filthy foreign Jews," he sneered. He turned back and spat out of the window, waving the driver to get going.

As the car pulled away, Frank looked out of the oval rear window at the camp disappearing into the forest behind him. He shivered as a troubled memory came back to him, a dim reminder of a forgotten episode which now seemed to be repeating itself.

September 1940

"Oh I feel so powerless," Violet wailed. "So helpless. Here am I down here all safe and sound while poor daddy..."

"While your daddy's pleased that you and the boys are safe."

Violet looked up from the bowl. She raised her hands, all covered in flour. "Oh Florrie, I didn't mean to sound so ungrateful. It's just that I'm so frightened for daddy and Alice... and for my... our... dear Frank."

A shadow crossed Florrie's face at the mention of Frank. No word had been received about him, and the longer things went on the more the gnawing fear grew deep within her. She glanced across the room at Violet, busy with the pastry-making. 'There she is making food for my daughter's wedding,' she thought, 'and she's no idea that it's her son Lizzie should be marrying by rights rather than that lummox George.' She sighed. She'd tried to talk to Lizzie, to tell her that she was making a mistake. She'd even plucked up the courage to mention Frank and say, lightly, so as not to give too interfering an impression, that she'd once thought that the two of them might... well, hit it off.

"Nonsense mum," Lizzie had replied. "Frank doesn't think of me that way. He thinks of me as his little sister, nothing more." Florrie had seen the slight flush in her daughter's face which gave away her true feelings. But she had continued. "Anyway, he's in his precious France and that's where he'll always stay."

Florrie hadn't pushed the issue. Sometimes you just had to let things go. Lizzie wasn't her possession any more than Frank had ever been and they had to make their own way in the world, even if it was a pity. She brushed the back of her hand over her forehead. "How long do you think it will take to get some news from France?"

"I don't really know," replied Violet. "Daddy says that Doctor Crowe promised to write immediately, but, if you think about it, the

British Red Cross have got to write to the International Red Cross... in Switzerland I think."

"Or the German Red Cross?"

"Do they have one? Anyway, they've got to write overseas and then they've got to write to the new authorities in France and to Frank's friends and... well it could take months I suppose."

"I don't know how you can bear it," said Florrie, wiping her hands and crossing to her friend.

Violet turned to her as she approached. "I have to Florrie, for the sake of the children and for all our sakes. Frank's a grown man now. I shall never stop loving him... none of us will, but we have to get on with our lives and right now..."

"...right now we've got a wedding to get through and an awful lot of food to prepare."

Violet laughed. "Oh Florrie, you're so marvellous. Nothing really gets you down, does it?" She turned back to her bowl and dug her hands back into the mixture, humming a tune as she kneaded the contents between her fingers.

Florrie stood for a moment observing her. 'No, nothing really bothers Florrie. That is... except everything. Frank most of all. Lizzie and this disastrous marriage... even your father, who I've never even met.' "That's right. Nothing gets me down," she whispered, trying yet failing to keep the edge out of her voice.

Violet picked it up immediately. She stopped what she was doing and shook her hands free of the cloying mixture, grabbing a cloth and wiping them. "Florrie. Oh Florrie, I'm so sorry, you're upset. What's wrong?" Florrie shook her head, waving her hands in front trying to deny her feelings, despite the tears that welled in her eyes. "It's nothing really."

"Nothing? Florrie you're crying."

Florrie's hands dropped. The tears flowed from her eyes. "I know... I know."

Violet held her. "What's wrong Florrie? Please tell me."

She tipped Florrie's chin up and looked earnestly into her eyes.

"I'm so worried about Frank," Florrie admitted.

The tears burst into Violet's eyes. All the fear, the emotion that she had been burying, hiding beneath a 'life must go on' attitude, crumbled then before her friend's frank admission. The two women flung themselves into each other's arms and sobbed freely. Eventually Florrie recovered sufficiently to be able to lead Violet to a chair at the table. She sat her down and pulled another around to sit beside her.

"I'm sorry," sobbed Violet. "I've tried to hide it all but I'm so frightened Florrie."

"Me too." Florrie sniffed and reached within her apron for a handkerchief. She blew her nose loudly, dabbed her eyes as dry as she could, and put it back in her apron. "Oh I'm sorry," she said, half retrieving it, "do you need a hanky?"

"I've got one," said Violet, gently leaning over and reaching within her skirt pocket, trying not to get the remains of the flour on her clothes. "I've always got one." She withdrew the handkerchief and held it up and open for Florrie to see. Florrie noticed the monogrammed 'V'. 'What a funny time to be boasting of posh hankies,' she thought. Violet noticed her quizzical look. "Frank's father gave these to me," she said quietly. "I've never been anywhere without them ever since."

Florrie extended her hand and gripped Violet's bare arm, squeezing it gently in a comforting, reassuring gesture. "I'm sorry Violet, sometimes... well sometimes I forget the pain you've had in your life." Violet raised her hand to stop her, but Florrie insisted on carrying on. "Frank's daddy... Frank... Ar... what was his name?"

"Armand."

"Armand. Yes Armand, and then that other fellow you married..." Violet started to giggle. Unsure what precisely was funny, yet infected with the giggling, Florrie smiled. "What's funny?"

"It's just that... that..." She giggled again, combining the mirth with the tears, which still flowed. "It makes me sound as if I've... well there's been a few, hasn't there?"

Florrie smiled. "More than some, less than others. Hardly in the trollop league."

Violet leant across and cuddled her friend. "Oh Florrie, you're a treasure. You cheer me up no end, you really do."

Florrie patted Violet's back. "And you cheer me up my dear. You and all your lovely boys that you've always let me share."

Violet looked serious. She looked away out of the window for a moment and then back into Florrie's face. "Not always." She held Florrie's gaze, noting the slight furrowing of the brow. "I was jealous of Frank loving you, you know." Florrie went to speak but Violet held her hand up. "Let me finish. When he contacted you again... when he was at school... I was so jealous. I think he knew it because he tried so hard to tell me not to worry... but I was Florrie. I was."

Florrie looked at Violet. "Course you was. Wouldn't be natural if you weren't. I was jealous too you know."

"You?"

"Yes me... well not jealous I suppose, but believe you me when you came and took Frank that first time I could have swung for you deep inside, I really could."

Violet looked serious. She stared ahead trying to recall that fateful day when she had reclaimed her son from his home, here with this lovely woman.

She turned and fixed Florrie with her eyes. "I don't blame you. I'd have been the same in your shoes.

"Thank you," said Florrie quietly.

"What for?"

"For understanding."

"Oh tosh. What are we doing raking over all this. It's now that's the problem. This bloody war. Frank missing, God knows where. Daddy and Alice in London with bombs dropping all around them now... poor Lizzie and George getting married the day before he has to go off to heaven knows where. Oh Florrie, I hate this damned war... all war." She buried her head in her hands. "Oh what are we to do?"

Florrie laid her hand on her arm again and shook it gently. "We have to be strong and we have to be there for them all when they need us, that's what we have to do."

Violet smiled. "As well as get these cakes ready."

Florrie smiled back. "As well as get these cakes ready... Miss Violet."

"Miss Violet!" Violet laughed. "Yes you used to call me that, didn't you... or Miss Matthews. Ever so formal."

"Well you was quality from London," laughed Florrie.

"Quality? I was a fallen woman."

"Ah yes, but you'd fallen from higher than we could ever go."

"Oh get away with you woman." The two of them giggled as they returned to their chores, smiling across at each other.

***

"Prisoner Balfour!"

"Yes sir," Frank replied, getting to his feet.

"Prisoners Picard, Bellanger, Baudron!"

"Sir," came the replies.

"Get your things together and come with me."

"Where to sir?" Frank ventured.

The prison guard turned. "You are going to work."

"Work?" Bellanger queried.

The guard laughed. A hollow, mirthless sound which echoed along the corridor, bringing men in other cells to the bars to see what was going on. "Work. You remember work, don't you?" He looked through at Frank. "You too, Englishman."

Frank grinned amiably. "Oh yes, I remember work. Building guns for the French army and then using them. Yes I remember work alright."

"Phaa, what would you know you bloody foreigner. Your lot ran away."

"I was a soldier for France and I never ran away. What regiment were you in?"

"Yes. What regiment were you in sir?" queried Picard.

The guard looked angry and uncomfortable. "I was here guarding criminals such as you," he said defensively. He drew himself up to his full height and banged his clipboard on the bars. "Get ready now!" he yelled.

"Yes sir. Coming sir," came the reply from four mouths, each one trying to stifle their laughter.

Frank laid his jacket open on the bed and filled it with his meagre possessions: a toothbrush and a twist of paper containing a mixture of ash and soot gleaned from the boiler in the dining hall, a tin mug and plate with the one bent spoon and his precious spare underclothing, seized in that last-minute dash from the chateau. He shut the jacket over them, tucking the bottom up and folding the collar section down before tying the sleeves around to make a bundle. Two German guards appeared, armed with rifles. They stood aside waiting for their French colleague to deal with things.

"Stand back," the guard commanded. They all stepped to the back of the cell and he took his keys from their ring and opened the door with a crash. He stepped back away from the door. "Out you come now. Stand in twos." Frank shouldered his bundle and stood beside Picard in the corridor whilst Baudron and Bellanger sauntered out to stand behind them. "Right, quick march," yelled the guard. The four of them marched off down the corridor. As they drew level with the waiting German soldiers they slipped their guns from their shoulders and held them at the ready. Frank inclined his head in mock politeness and the two soldiers fell in behind them, down the corridor towards the stairs. Choruses of goodwill greeted them as they passed each cell and followed them up the stairs to where they stopped in front of the locked gates. The guard bustled forward, nervously trying to keep clear of his dangerous charges. "Prisoners for transfer," he called through the bars to the German soldier sitting at a table to the side of the upper corridor.

"Papers!" the new man demanded. The guard detached a sheet from his clipboard and handed it through. The soldier took the paper, turned back to his desk and compared the names on it with those on his own list. He turned back and opened the door.

"Forward march!" the guard cried, standing aside as Frank and his companions stepped through the gates and marched off down the upper corridor, followed by the two armed German soldiers. Ahead Frank could smell fresh air. City air maybe, but after the weeks of confinement in the cells below it smelt good, and their pace quickened. They stepped out into the sunshine, and for a second or two the four of them stood stock still savouring the air, feeling the warmth on their upturned faces. But then the two soldiers behind them prodded them forward and across the open square towards a lorry waiting with its engine running.

Frank looked around as they crossed the yard. Long red, white and black banners hung down the building, and from each high tower the swastika flag flew. Beyond the building, humming in the air, he could hear the sounds of the city. Out there people were going about their normal daily lives, laughing, living and loving, whilst in here... in here all life existed in suspension. He shivered. What lay in store for them now?

At the rear of the lorry they waited for instructions. "Auf sein!" came the call, and he and his companions climbed up and inside. Frank seated himself quite near the back, hoping that by doing so he would be able to see out and observe the city as it passed, but as the two soldiers climbed in themselves they motioned him forward and out of their reach. The vehicle started off, stopped briefly at the gates and pulled out into the traffic beyond. Frank craned his neck to see out.

The smells and sounds of the city wafted through to him. Fresh bread as they passed a boulangerie, the acrid stink as they drew abreast of a pissoir. Life! The cries and shouts of men and women. God it would be wonderful just to wander slowly amongst all of this, to draw strength from its diversity. He turned to Christophe Picard. "Do you know where we are going?" he whispered.

Christophe shook his head. "I don't know at all," he said quietly. "If I could see the sun I could tell what direction we were heading, but as I don't know where we're coming from that won't be much help, will it?"

Thierry Bellanger hissed across at Frank. "I think we're heading north."

For about an hour the lorry chugged through the busy streets, with Frank and the other prisoners trying all the time to keep a note of their direction, looking out in vain through the narrow aperture of the open canvas at the back, for sight of any known landmark that would confirm their suspicions. Eventually, the signs which had served them no purpose as they read them from the back began to show that Paris was in the opposite direction to the one that they were travelling in and, as they entered open country, with the sun directly behind them, they were able to confidently predict that they were travelling north out of Paris. Jean Baudron leant across and tapped Frank on the knee. "Perhaps they're going to drop you off at the ferry on the way so you can go home." Frank burst out laughing in spite of himself.

"Stille!" yelled one of the soldiers. Frank stifled his laugh, confining it to a smile and a wink in acknowledgement of his friend's humour.

The afternoon wore on and the lorry continued to drive northwards. Frank felt his eyes grow heavy. He glanced at his companions. Each one looked tired and occasionally their heads would loll to one side before anticipation, combined with anxiety, jerked them once more into wakefulness.

Frank slipped into a reverie. He thought about the camp he had left behind, about Annette. Would he ever see her again? He recalled his last night in the camp and the motion of the lorry, combined with his memories, sent a hot thrill through his loins. He crossed his legs and looked up guiltily at his companions to see if his thoughts were guessed at, but each seemed lost in his own reverie. What a wonderful night that had been. He had no illusions about his feelings for Annette; they were not those of love, for all the fact that he felt a warm sense of friendship with her, but... had he just used her? Had she just used him? No, not in any mean way. They had drawn comfort from each other as friends. "Pretend I am Lizzie," she had said, and he had. He conjured up the image and closed his eyes the more to savour the memory.

Poor Annette. Was she safe? What was in store for her? Jews throughout Europe were open to increasing persecution as the last slim barriers to civilised behaviour were deliberately torn down by German directives. Latent anti-Semitism, combined with the French authorities' deliberate attempts to place all blame for their ignominious defeat at the hands of any foreigners, was the order of the day. 'Well Frank,' he thought, 'you yourself are at the receiving end of that train of thought. Even so, not being Jewish was a distinct advantage, as had been demonstrated by the attitude of even a reasonably fair man like Mundt.'

And where was Gunther? If only he could make some sort of contact with him, then surely Gunther could help him out of this predicament? Maybe, maybe not. After all, Gunther himself could be at risk through their very friendship. He smiled to himself as he recalled the first time Gunther had appeared amongst them, decked out in his Nazi regalia. How proud he had been, how haughty. And then when he, Marcel and Pierre-Luc had laughed at him he had got angry at first and then hurt, before he finally realised the stupidity of his posturing amongst friends who knew him so well.

What was Gunther's attitude to the ill-treatment of Jews and politically undesirable people? Frank tried to guess the mind of his friend. There was no way that he would openly, even dream of defying any direct order, but there was equally no way the friend he knew so well could commit the kind of acts he had heard of and witnessed since his incarceration... was there?

No. There was no doubt about it. Gunther would not shirk his legitimate duty, but as long as his friendships and the memory of them were there to remind him, he would try as far as was practicable to temper them with humanity. He must do. 'Please Gunther,' Frank prayed silently. 'Please remain a good man, one that I can call a friend when all this is over.'

The afternoon wore on, and by now the sun was low off to their right as they looked out of the rear of the lorry. The two German soldiers gripped their rifles in front of themselves, leaning down onto them, dozing quietly. Thierry shifted his position and moved quietly along the bench towards the back of the vehicle, merely trying to get a better look. One of the soldiers seemed to sense his proximity because he suddenly started up, shouted out and grabbed his rifle, pointing it at him. The other awoke and he too swung his rifle around to cover the others. Thierry raised his hands. He forced himself to grin inanely. "It's alright. It's alright," he cried. "Kamerad, it's alright!" He shuffled back along the bench, his hands still in the air until he reached his old position, where he lowered them slowly, still grinning at the two soldiers.

They relaxed at last and struck up a low conversation with each other. Thierry looked from each of his companions to the other, a wry apologetic smile on his face. Frank shook his head. That could have been nasty.

"What's that?" Jean pointed out of the rear of the lorry. "Have we been going south after all?"

The others looked at where he was pointing off to the left, behind them. Three massive pyramids threw themselves up on the skyline.

Frank laughed. "Pit heaps. Slag... waste from the mines," he explained.

"Mines, what mines?" Christophe asked. "Where are we?"

"We must be near Lille, just south of the Belgian border," replied Frank. "I used to see these when we came across to Calais."

"Well what on earth are we doing here? Unless we're being taken all the way to Germany," said Christophe fearfully.

"No don't be silly," said Thierry. "If they wanted to take us to Germany we'd have been put on a train."

"That's true," said Frank, just as the lorry slowed down and turned off to the right, onto a minor road. For another half an hour they continued in this general direction before coming into a small town laid out in the flat lands in a dismal grid formation, its uniform houses stretching away along its mean streets. The lorry slowed again and stopped. German voices, shouts of greeting. The two soldiers in the back leant out and called along the side of the vehicle at friends. Frank and his companions sat still, wondering just where they were and what was in store for them. The lorry jerked forward and the two soldiers swung back in, laughing and calling out as it slipped through and under the raised barrier and on into, what seemed to the group in the back, some sort of industrial yard. They swung to the left and bounced over several potholes. Behind them now they could clearly see the winding towers of the colliery and the massive grey buildings of the pithead. Everywhere smelt of the coal dust which permeated the air and coated everything in sight.

"I think we're to be miners," Frank ventured. Silence greeted him as his companions stared out at the scene laying itself out before them. The lorry bounced on past more grey buildings clad in corrugated iron. It stopped and the two soldiers jumped down. "'raus!" they called up into the lorry and stood back, rifles at the ready, as the four prisoners shuffled along to the rear and climbed down to huddle in a group, looking around themselves. To their right they could see a barbed-wire compound, double-fenced as usual, with a small wooden hut beside a single personnel gate no more than a metre wide, manned by an armed soldier. Dogs barking? Two enormous beasts ran around the corner between the fences and jumped up at the wire, growling horribly. The guard in the hut called out to them and they backed off and sat staring at the new arrivals, their lips drawn back over white fangs.

The drone of aircraft overhead caused all present to look up. Above them lines of aeroplanes, in loose 'V' formations, flew north-west, and as they watched more followed. Frank turned and looked back in the direction they had come from. Stretching as far as he could see to the horizons in the east and the south, wave after wave of bombers were flying north and west.

The German soldiers pointed up into the sky, laughing. One tapped Frank on the shoulder, pointing up. "Gute, ja?"

Frank ignored him and instead turned to Thierry. "Looks like London is in for a roasting tonight," he said sadly. Thierry nodded his agreement.

The gate opened and, escorted by the same guards who had accompanied them from Paris, they marched through, along the tunnel of wire separating them from the slavering dogs and through a second gate into the compound. Here there were four huts, of similar design to those Frank had already helped to construct in the forest, laid out in a precise line with, it seemed, a regulation three metres between each. The soldiers called back to the man on the gate, waving at the huts. "Drie," he called back, and the soldiers indicated to Frank and his companions that they were to enter the third hut.

Frank opened the door. The layout was exactly the same as he had known back at the camp. Triple-height bunks down each side, this time furnished with thin mattresses. No other furniture other than a small iron stove in the very centre of the hut and a few planks of wood nailed roughly together to form benches set around it. Lines were strung from side to side at all three levels, each holding clothing hanging up to dry and making movement up and down the hut next to impossible.

The other three crowded in behind Frank as the door was shut once more, throwing the hut back into semi-darkness. A figure rose from the benches and came towards them, ducking repeatedly out of sight as he negotiated the lines.

"Hallo. Welcome to our little home," he said dryly in a whisper. "My name is Pierre."

"Hallo, I'm Frank," said Frank, whispering back. "This is Christophe, Jean and Thierry."

"Pleased to meet you," said Thierry, holding out his hand and speaking in a normal voice.

"Shut up!" came a voice from within the hut.

Pierre put his finger to his lips. "You must be quiet they're sleeping, they've just finished their shift." Frank nodded his understanding. "Find yourselves a bunk at the other end of the hut and get some rest, you'll be working at two."

"Two?" whispered Jean.

"Two o'clock tomorrow morning."

Frank groaned. "What about food? We've not had anything since this morning in Paris."

Pierre laughed silently. "You'll get fed after your work shift at two o'clock the next morning."

"What about toilets and water?"

"Water we can help you with, but tomorrow when you come back from the pit you'll have to bring your own. We wash at the pit and you can pee in a bucket. There's one down there at the back."

Frank grimaced. "God I'm starving," he said to Thierry.

"Me too," his friend replied. Christophe and Jean looked miserable.

"Best get some rest lads," said Pierre, pointing down the hut. "You've got a bit of a shock coming tomorrow."

'I've had a bit of a shock today thanks,' thought Frank as he wove his way in and out of the laundry, his nose wrinkling at the smells of bodies, coal and cheesy damp material, 'and London's in for a bigger one tonight.'

He stopped and listened. The drone of aircraft could still be heard overhead. 'God, would anything stop the German war machine from overrunning the planet?'

***

Ernest hurried down the street. Ahead of him the whole sky seemed lit up, flames surging into the night sky, making a mockery of any blackout precautions. In the distance, searching shafts of light forced their way through the smoke, waving and dancing through the night. He heard the 'crump' of more bombs falling in the distance... then closer, much closer, he heard the howling whine of more. He crouched against the wall, feeling the shock through the air and the ground shaking beneath his feet. Bells now, from behind him. He clasped his tin hat to his head and turned to see a fire engine coming down the street towards him.

It passed him by and screeched to a halt, unable to proceed beyond the fallen-out front wall of a building still smouldering from the night before, standing there beside the road like some gigantic empty fire grate. He heard shouts and ran forward.

"How do we get to the High Street mate?"

"The High Street?"

"Yes old fella, High Street, Tower Crescent!"

"Tower Crescent?"

"Yeah Tower Crescent! Come on mate, quick as you can."

"Eh... yes... if you back up from here and go to the left there. No... no, the second left... because the first one's blocked... you'll get there."

"Thanks mate." The instructions were relayed back into the cab as the engine reversed.

The flats! 'Oh God, I'm too old for all of this,' Ernest thought as he scrambled over the rubble. He slipped and caught his knee on the protruding corner of a brick and winced in agony, rolling over to clutch it to himself as the pain waved over him. He drew his breath in short gasps, trying desperately to control his beating heart. 'Now

now, Ernest old chap,' he chided himself, 'pull yourself together, there's work to be done tonight.' His chest wheezed as he fought to exhale. 'Bloody chest! I do hope Alice is safe,' he thought, and a half smile came to his face at the thought of her snug in their little Anderson shelter, fitted out for all the world like one of those seaside chalets he remembered from... from when? From when he and Elsie had taken the young Violet to the seaside at... where was it? Frinton. Yes Frinton. All those years ago... all gone now. Elsie gone, Violet away safe in Devon, thank God... Violet! What would she do? How would she react when she got his letter telling her that there was no trace of Frank apart from Leclerc's story, which all but confirmed that the poor dear boy was dead?

Ernest felt the tears come into his eyes. He had grown to love that boy... the man that he had become. He shifted his position and stood unsteadily, testing the knee. It hurt but it bore his weight. 'Best get going Ernest,' he commanded himself. 'Best get going.' He climbed to the top of the heap and reversed himself to carefully make his way down the other side, crabbing down on his hands and knees until he found secure ground.

He turned and made his way limping down the road to the High Street, keeping as close to the edge as he could, stopping as he reached the junction. Billowing clouds of smoke and ash blew down the street, folding and unfolding in the garish light of the flames. Even at this distance he could hear shouting and see movement within and around the conflagration. He turned and ran up the High Street towards the commotion. As he reached the small green in front of the horseshoe of buildings, he stopped dead at the sight which confronted him. The left-hand angle of the horseshoe had received a direct hit and had literally folded in on itself, tearing a great gap in the building. A pudding of clay and mortar filled the broken void. Six floors compressed into a pile of debris less than two storeys high, lit by the ghastly flares of burning gas, exhaling vast clouds of choking dust and smoke. Could anybody possibly be left alive within this mess, Ernest wondered, as he stumbled forward to stand beside the fire engine.

Already, ladders were being thrown up against the heap and men were scrambling up, searching, calling out for survivors. At ground level more helpers were busy investigating any crevice or entrance, however small, which promised access to the interior, lying on their bellies and calling into the wreckage.

"Get that gas under control," yelled a senior fire officer, and two men ran to the arched entrance in the standing centre block to search for stopcocks.

The officer turned and saw Ernest standing there, his tin hat awry, his mouth wide open. "Don't just stand there," he cried. "Get in and help."

Ernest looked at him. Help? Help. Yes he must help, that was his job... but how? What? What could anyone do in this hell? He shook himself and started forward to the foot of a ladder. "Not up there old man," another fireman called. "You stay down on the ground and help when we pass things out." Ernest nodded. The other firemen must have found the main gas stopcock, for just then the flares, which had burnt so brightly, suddenly died down, leaving the scene illuminated only by the lights from the vehicles and the many torches which now wove amongst the ruins.

Ernest looked up and across at the other wings. Shattered windows trailed their curtains into the night. From some of them, frightened and shocked faces could be picked out surveying the horror. And beyond all this, happily in the distance for the moment, they could all still hear the sound of bombs falling, the crashing of anti-aircraft fire, the tinkling, almost feeble sound of bells ringing their alarm.

"Here's one," a voice shouted in front of Ernest.

"Where?" another called. Ernest stepped forward and knelt gingerly down beside a fireman lying prone on the ground with just his lower torso protruding from a small gap under a broken framework of joists.

"I'm here," Ernest volunteered, tugging the man's half-hidden jacket.

Another man joined them. "What've you got mate?" he called in to the first man.

"A woman," came the muffled reply. "She's alright... leastwise her head is free, but she's completely buried up to her neck... I can't free her like this."

"Can you see her?"

"Yes, my torch is in here. She's looking at me but not saying anything... see if you can raise that load of timber."

Ernest stood back with the other man. The web of timber seemed fairly secure in itself, even though it disappeared to within the main heap. Gently they raised it and it moved upwards, releasing a shower of dust and pulverised bricks. "Steady mates," came the gasping voice of the first man from beneath. "You'll choke us."

"Sorry!" Ernest shouted. He looked around and saw what he wanted in the form of an old curtain or tablecloth protruding from the rubble. Gently he tugged at it and it slid free. He knelt down and passed it through to the man. "Put this over your heads... it should stop most of it going on you."

"Thanks," came the reply, and a hand reached back to pull the cloth within the void.

The other man came forward with a length of stout timber. "You take this, old man," he instructed, "and when I lift, prop it under." Ernest took the wood and stood at the ready as the man put his shoulder underneath the main trimmer and pushed upwards. "Ready?" the man panted as he forced himself up as high as he could reach."Ready when you say," Ernest replied, moving forwards to crouch beneath.

"Now!" cried the man, and Ernest pushed the ragged end of the timber hard up underneath the structure. The other man let go and joined him in pulling the prop upright. For a second the two of them hung on to it, gasping.

"Down here mates," called the first man as he sat up out of the rubble and threw off the cloth. Cradled almost in his lap was a head, which in any other circumstances would have been mistaken for a clay model, the ghastly beheaded remnant of a lifelike statue. The head blinked and the mouth moved feebly. Large, fear-filled eyes stared at her rescuers, barely hiding the madness that lurked within. Her scarf, once brightly coloured and patterned no doubt, but now sharing the same featureless hue as its wearer, still clung to her head, knotted at the front. From beneath it, curler-bound hair dared to peek, breaking up the outline of her furrowed brow. A wicked phalanx of spear-like lathes pointed at her head, and across her shoulder lay the length of joist that both trapped and preserved her.

Ernest and the other two knelt down beside her and started to remove the soup of dissolved masonry that surrounded her below the neck. Above them a scrambling sound, footfalls and a cloud of dust raining down on them warned of others searching amongst the wreckage. "Careful up there," Ernest called, "we've a survivor here."

"Sorry mate," came the reply from above. "I'm trying to get this one down... a goner I'm afraid."

"Try not to stand on that section of timber there," the first man called up, shining his torch on it to illustrate his point.

"Right'o mate," came the reply. "I'll go around the other way."

"You hold her head and keep talking to her whilst we dig," the first man instructed Ernest. Ernest nodded and slipped in to lie cradling the woman's head, looking over her shoulder as the other two gently removed any objects they could actually grasp. Gradually they uncovered her shoulders, and then ever so slowly her upper chest came into view. "She's holding onto something," cried the first man. "What is it love?"

Silent eyes flickered open and the mute madness rushed from them. Ernest leant forward, dusting away the powdered debris. A round object like... like the top of a head, the hair matted down... stiff. "She's holding a child!" Ernest cried. "A little girl."

The others bent forward and felt around the head, shining their torches, feeling down within the dust for signs of life. The first man looked up at Ernest and shook his head. The eyes of the woman followed his glance and then slammed shut. "Let go my love and we'll get you both out of there a lot quicker," cajoled the second man.

"Yes, let go of the child my dear and we'll get you both free," begged Ernest. The woman tightened her grip on her cuddled burden. Ernest shook his head sadly. "We'll have to dig them out together or not at all I fear," he whispered.

"I guess you're right mate," said the first man. "Come on, let's get this lot clear."

Ernest looked up through the web of timber, beneath which he was crouched. Above and beyond the building he could still hear the sounds of London at war. Anti-aircraft fire tore great holes in the sky, which opened in a fiery starburst and shut with a thunderous clap. Occasionally high in the sky above, through the din on the ground below, he could hear the throbbing of unseen aeroplanes bringing with them their cargoes of death and despair. The timber lying across the woman's shoulder shifted and Ernest felt her wince, felt her upper arms relax. "Prop that timber or we'll all be crushed," he urged. The first man stopped his digging and backed away, searching for a suitable piece of timber. He returned and he and the other man forced it underneath the main timber, propping it down to a large boulder of shattered masonry.

They resumed their digging, aware now that all around them others too were engaged in similar tasks. Occasionally a cry would be heard that a live person had been found and excited men would scramble up into the wreckage to help. More often the call was that yet another body had been located and silent rescuers would pull and prise it loose to hand it down.

The child's body was now almost totally revealed, curled up as if asleep, nestling in the crook of its mother's body. "Let me take the child my love," Ernest whispered in her ear. "Let go now and I'll take her." The woman tightened her grip. "If you let me have her, I'll hold her for you... just there where you can see, and then when you're free you can have her back."

The eyes opened. The head turned, fixing Ernest with their silent stare. The chin lifted and the arms relaxed a little as the three men held their breath. Ernest leant forward to take the child from her arms. She released it slowly into his embrace as Ernest watched her face the whole time, expecting at any moment to feel her snatch the child back. The eyes remained open, fixed on his caring face. As he watched, tears flowed from the corners and coursed down her cheeks, carving furrows in the make-up of filth that coated her. The child was free. Ernest shuffled back and stood, as promised, in full view. The other two men seemed to breathe again and bent to their task as Ernest cradled the dead child in his arms.

The chief fire officer came across. "Live?" he enquired. Ernest turned to him and shook his head slowly.

"Put her over there," the man instructed in a loud voice, pointing to a line of grey shapes laid out in lines on the grassed area in front of the flats, before walking off into the night.

Ernest looked across at the woman, hoping against hope that she had not heard. The eyes were open, fixed on him in an unswerving stare, daring him to move. Ernest stayed put, even resorting to rocking the dead child in his arms. Finally the woman was free and the two men gently lifted her up and out into the open. Ernest followed them as they carried their charge across and sat her gently down on the ground. She reached up to him as he approached and he placed the child within her embrace. Slowly she stroked its tiny forehead, singing tunelessly as she did so whilst Ernest and his companions stood transfixed.

A cry went up. "Live one!" All three men turned away and looked up, to half way up the mound. Waving arms could be seen, topped by a pinprick light of a torch. "Up here," the voice called. The two other men glanced briefly back at the woman and then turned and rushed across and up ladders towards the calling. Ernest stood for a moment watching them go, then he too took one last look at the woman and headed back in. There was work still to be done.

As daylight beckoned, the all clear sounded and once more London faced the morning like a wounded beast, wreathed in the smoke of ten thousand cuts, howling its defiant anguish at the heavens. More helpers arrived, some neighbours or former occupants of the ruin who had taken shelter elsewhere, and climbed up into the jumbled mess calling out for friends, relatives and loved ones. The fire officer who had told Ernest where to put the child came by. "Have you been here all night?" he asked. Ernest nodded, too tired now to even speak. "Go home now old fellow," the man gently said. "There's many more here now to help and you need to rest. You look done in."

Ernest nodded once more and turned back towards the High Street. He saw then the lines of bodies and the men and women moving amongst them, gently lifting the shattered remains of humanity into long canvas bags, which they deftly tied up, sewing the string through the eye holes provided and pulling them tight. He looked around for the woman but she was nowhere in sight. Somewhere in the lightening day a mother wandered alone with her dead child, singing the tune that she would sing through the madness and despair of years to come. He sighed heavily. Best get home to Alice. Best get on.

***

Pierre-Luc and Marcel sauntered along the gravel road leading by the edge of the forest, a basket piled high with mixed cep and girolles on Marcel's arm. "Your turn," he gasped. "I reckon there may be five kilos here."

"I think you're right," said Pierre-Luc, hefting the basket and picking about amongst its contents. "Good ones too. When we get to your place we'll have to divide up what we've got."

Marcel laughed. "Pity about the deer."

"Never mind the deer, what about that boar?"

"I've no interest in the boar. You know that."

Pierre-Luc laughed. "Does boar count as pig?"

"Of course it does."

"Well it's a pity we didn't have a gun so we'd have the deer for you and the boar for us... do you realise... oh well we didn't and that's that." Marcel laughed aloud. "What's the matter now?"

"I was just thinking, there's me... lost my job, a social outcast. I don't think the authorities would be very happy if they found me wandering about amongst the woods with a gun."

Pierre-Luc smiled ruefully. "And I'd be arrested as part of a Zionist plot to overthrow the Reich."

Marcel looked at his friend. Since they had slipped back home after the fall of France, managing, thank goodness, to escape both the ignominy and the danger of formally surrendering, life had become increasingly hard. Oh, Pierre-Luc was alright... he had just gone back to work on his father's farm, for all the world as if he'd never left. But as far as he was concerned, being Jewish was not a very good idea at the best of times in Europe. Being Jewish under the Reich was a distinctly dangerous state of affairs. He'd slipped back into work after his return and for the first few weeks all had been normal, but then the works manager had called him in and told him quite bluntly that his services would no longer be required.

"No longer be required!" A charming euphemism for "Get out you Jewish bastard" and "I've been waiting to say this to you for years." He looked across at his friend, carrying the basket, still searching instinctively amongst the grass as they walked for yet another mushroom. If it wasn't for Pierre-Luc and his family, and of course dear Jean-Claude and Marie, then he and his family would have really been in trouble. Shops and cafes that he and his parents had frequented, neighbours that they had called 'friend', no longer wished to deal with them. He recalled, bitterly, the guilty stares as they explained that they had nothing personal against them but... but they would not, dared not trade openly with them.

What was going to happen? Would they just continue to be ostracised or would action be taken against them? Should they go into hiding and, if so, where should they go? The chateau? No, the Germans had shown more than a little interest in that recently. According to Jean-Claude, those worms, Armand's sister Nicole and her husband Henri, had arrived one day in the company of a German officer and shown him around the establishment, for all the world as if they owned it. Poor Frank, he would turn in his grave... if his friend even had a grave. His thoughts turned to his old friend. Leclerc had told them of his experiences and the terrible sights he had witnessed. No room had been left for doubt that Frank had been cruelly executed on that day... and for what? Frank hadn't done any more than he and Pierre-Luc had done... any more than Gunther had done.

They'd joined up like all young men of their age to fight a war that was none of their making. He sighed to himself and Pierre-Luc picked up on his mood.

"What are you thinking about?"

"Oh, I was just thinking of Frank and how... well you know, and then I was thinking of Gunther."

"Gunther is our enemy now." Marcel stopped and Pierre-Luc turned to him.

"You can't really believe that?"

"Of course I can. Frank killed. Your life in ruins..."

"My life's not in ruins."

Pierre-Luc shook his head. "I'm sorry Marcel. I'd love to think that Gunther was still our friend, but he wears the uniform... wears it with pride come to that... he wears the uniform of our enemy."

Marcel shrugged his shoulders. "If he was here he would help us."

"I'm sure he'd want to, but could he actually do so? Could he bring Frank back to life?"

For quite a while the two of them walked along in silence, each lost in his own thoughts, each trying to cover up his own emotions in the search for yet more mushrooms. A host of glorious fungi could have been laid out before them and they would not have seen them, so engrossed were they both in containing their feelings. They neared the crossroads where to get to Pierre-Luc's they would have to turn right, whereas Marcel's house was just along on the left. "Are you coming in?" Marcel asked.

"Yes. Yes I said so. We need to divide this lot up," replied Pierre-Luc.

They could hear voices from the house, less than two hundred metres down the road. "Looks like we've got company," said Marcel, moving inquisitively to the middle of the road. He stopped. Outside the house a grey-green lorry was parked, and as he watched he could see his parents being dragged from the front gate towards the vehicle by German soldiers! He started forward but Pierre-Luc grabbed his arm, putting the basket down and, in one almost simultaneous motion, used the momentum of Marcel's own forward movement to swing him around. He let go and his smaller friend fell backwards to sprawl in the ditch. Pierre-Luc picked up the basket and moved to the middle of the crossroads as if he had just arrived there and was about to turn right. "What are you doing?" Marcel yelled from the ditch.

"Saving your life and mine as well probably."

"What do you mean?" said Marcel, scrambling to his feet and crawling up the bank.

"Stay there, for God's sake!" Pierre-Luc hissed.

Marcel stopped. "They're taking my parents away. Do you expect me to just stay here and let them?"

"Can you stop them?" He turned and pretended to pick up yet another mushroom. "There are about ten of them, all armed."

"I can't just let them take my parents."

"Marcel!" Pierre-Luc commanded. "Would your parents want you to be taken as well, for that is what will happen... and me as well I shouldn't wonder."

Marcel subsided again into the ditch. "What should I do?"

"Creep back up the other side of that ditch and across to that stack of sheaves, keeping the hedge between you and the house."

"And what about you?"

"I'm alright... if I'm alone. I'll carry on walking slowly in the direction of my house, pretending to search for mushrooms. If I don't come back, make your way to my house after dark." Marcel looked up at his friend as Pierre-Luc nonchalantly bent down and pretended to pick up a mushroom from the verge opposite. "Go quickly!"

Marcel crawled up the bank and along by the hedge as Pierre-Luc wandered slowly down the road. He paused as he reached the end of the hedge and looked across at his friend. Three metres of open field separated him from the sheaves. Pierre-Luc half turned. "Go!" he hissed, and Marcel dashed forward and into and within the straw. Pierre-Luc hefted the basket and walked off alone down the road.

When he had gone about twenty metres past the junction in the direction of his house, the lorry passed him. Soldiers leant out of the rear, calling to the driver, and it screeched to halt just in front of him. Inwardly Pierre-Luc's blood froze, but he smiled as two of them dismounted and walked towards him unarmed.

"Papers," the man asked as he approached. Pierre-Luc put down the basket and reached inside his jacket, handing the papers over. The soldier flicked them open, glancing perfunctorily at the details and up into Pierre-Luc's face. He handed the documents back and Pierre-Luc pocketed them.

"Mushrooms?"

"Yes," Pierre-Luc replied, picking the basket up again and proffering it for inspection.

"You find these in forest, ja?"

"Yes, in the woods and some at the side of the road." He pointed along the verge. "You want some?"

The soldier looked pleased. "Ja. Ja... thank you very much." He took off his helmet and held it out. Pierre-Luc put down the basket and filled the helmet and then did the same for the other man.

"Jews?" Pierre-Luc asked, nodding towards the lorry.

"Ja Juden," the soldier replied, staring intently at him. Pierre-Luc spat into the grass and grimaced. The soldier's face relaxed back into a smile.

"Schnell Horst!" came the call from the lorry and the two soldiers picked up their helmets and returned. Pierre-Luc picked up his basket and walked on. As he levelled with the lorry the soldiers leant out and thanked him. Deep within the lorry he could just make out his friend's parents staring out at him without any show of recognition. He waved his free hand as the lorry drove off. The two soldiers returned his wave. Marcel's father blinked a signal.

Pierre-Luc walked on, pretending interest in the verge and his search for mushrooms whilst all the while keeping his eye on the departing lorry. He waited until it had gone out of sight and then walked back along the other side of the road, still keeping up the pretence of his search, even to the point of bending down and pretending to pick occasionally. He reached the point where he was level with the straw sheaves. "Are you there?" he called out.

"Of course I am," Marcel called back. His head poked out from between the sheaves.

"Stay there!" Pierre-Luc hissed urgently. Marcel stopped. "Let me go along the road towards the house and see if it's all clear."

"Why, they've gone haven't they?"

"The lorry's gone but they may have left a guard behind."

Marcel laughed deprecatingly. "To prevent burglary and damage I suppose."

"No you fool," said Pierre-Luc in an exasperated tone. "To wait for you. Do you imagine that they just came for your parents? No they came for you all."

Marcel's head disappeared back within the sheaves. Pierre-Luc walked on towards the house. "I'll whistle three times if it's safe," he called back.

He reached the gate in the low, neatly clipped privet hedge dividing the small house from the road. It lay drunkenly twisted, hanging from one hinge, kicked open in an action of brutal vandalism which would have required more energy than opening it properly. Beyond, down the straight path bordered with impatiens, now crushed beneath the weight of many boots, the front door lay open, jammed down to the floor of the narrow hall.

Pierre-Luc called within the building. "Is there anybody there?" No reply. He walked slowly down the path, wary that at any moment he might be challenged. Crude strokes of yellow paint formed a Star of David on the bright cream of the render. The lower edges of each defiling brush stroke running and dribbling as if to accentuate its savage intent.

He entered and stood aghast in the hall, looking into the lounge. Above the fireplace the mirror was broken, its empty frame still clinging to the wall encircling the scrawled words 'Jude'. On the hearth the broken remains of family pictures were piled and, on top of the pile, someone had defecated.

The furniture was strewn around the room, cushions torn and rent, their stuffing pulled out and scattered. What had they wanted? Did they think that the furniture that had so often comforted this poor family and all their friends contained wealth beyond imagination? He turned from the room and peeked across and into the bedroom, Marcel's parents' bedroom. Here too the bed had been thrown over and ripped by a hundred slashes from a bayonet. A prayer shawl lay crumpled on the floor. He bent to pick it up, but stopped as he realised that some bastard had pissed on it. Nausea swept him. These were his friends. What reason could prevail that would sanction this? He stumbled from the house, picking up the basket on the way down the path, and headed at a jog back towards the sheaves.

As he drew level he called out. "Marcel. It's all clear."

Marcel crawled out from the straw. "I thought you were going to whistle."

Pierre-Luc waited for his friend to join him. "I was but... I think it's best if we get going... get away from here."

Marcel looked up at him. "What about my house? I need to get some things... after all I don't know when I'll get back."

Pierre-Luc put the basket down on the ground and put his hands on his smaller friend's shoulders while looking seriously into his eyes. "You shouldn't go in there Marcel... you wouldn't..."

"Wouldn't like it? Well I don't like much at all at the moment Pierre-Luc, so what's going to change?"

Pierre-Luc noticed the edge of near hysteria in his friend's voice. He let go of him. "Go on then... but don't be long. I'll keep watch. If I whistle once hide, if I whistle twice then come quickly."

Marcel nodded and ran off down the road and into the house. Pierre-Luc picked up the basket and stood watching each way along the empty road. He waited for about ten minutes and was about to call when Marcel came out of the door carrying something at arm's length. Pierre-Luc watched as he disappeared around the side of the building. After a few minutes he returned and came hurrying down the road, wringing out the prayer shawl.

"I washed it in the butt," he gasped. "It was my father's... I will keep it for him."

Pierre-Luc nodded. He put the basket down and removed all of the mushrooms. "Put it in the bottom here," he instructed. Marcel laid the shawl reverently in the basket and the two of them piled the mushrooms over it. "Come on. We'd better get going," said Pierre-Luc. Marcel nodded. He glanced back at the house one last time and the two of them set off at a run towards Pierre-Luc's home.

April 1941

"You look tired Ernie," said Alice. "Do you have to go out tonight?"

"I should, but to tell you the truth, Alice, I don't think I can make it. My whole body aches and I feel as if the flu is coming on," Ernest replied, letting one hand flop off the arm of the chair whilst he rubbed his forehead with the other.

"Oh Ernie, don't go tonight. Stay here with me, you're not well enough. When Dave calls for you I'll tell him you're ill."

"He'll be here any minute, it's nearly dark already."

"Besides, we have to meet Violet and this young girl tomorrow don't we... what's her name?"

"Lizzie."

Ernest coughed and held his head in his hands. "Ooh, I feel all hot."

"I expect you do. I tell you you're sickening. I shouldn't wonder if I don't have to go alone to Paddington tomorrow. Is that short for Elizabeth?"

"Is what short for Elizabeth?"

"Lizzie," Alice repeated. "Oh really, Ernie, you're not with it are you?" The doorbell rang. "I'll get it. It's bound to be Dave and I'll tell him..."

"No really Alice... I'd better go."

"Nonsense Ernie Matthews, you're not well enough and that's that." She bustled out of the kitchen and through into the hall, bending back through the door at the last minute to wink at him. "Besides, I'm fed up with being all alone in our little shelter. It'll be nice to have some company."

"I'm not well enough for that," he protested in pretence. "Have pity on an old man."

"Old man my foot," she grinned. "You're only as old as you feel... and you can feel a young one... me."

"Phaa," he exclaimed lightly as the doorbell rang again and she pulled the door shut as she crossed to the front door. He smiled to himself, listening out for the hum of muffled conversation. He had overdone it lately. Who hadn't? Who could, hand on heart, claim to have had a proper night's sleep in weeks... no months? He was in his seventies now and perhaps he really did have something coming on. Seventy! Who'd have thought it? Alice, bless her... she was... how old would she be? Fifty-five? Yes she was... well nearly. 'Ten years older than Violet. Ten years older than my daughter, and she's my wife,' he pondered.

She'd stuck with him though, through thick and... no through thin really, because since they'd finally come out into the open with their relationship there hadn't been much thick. Still they'd been lucky with Violet, and before she'd left for Devon they'd all got along just fine. He missed her though... her and the boys. Slater's boys, Ian and George. Nice boys though... despite their father, who they happily didn't seem to take after. And Frank. Frank had been with them for quite a while before he finally decided to set up home in France.

He sighed. Poor Frank. Could he really be dead? Somehow it didn't feel that he was. 'I can't quite put my finger on it,' he thought, 'but I don't feel he's dead... I feel... I feel like he's out there somewhere. Oh, in trouble no doubt, but out there nonetheless.'

He heard the front door close and footsteps coming back across the hall.

"There," said Alice as she entered the kitchen. "He quite understood. I told him you were poorly and he agreed with me that you'd been overdoing it."

"For a man of my age, I suppose."

"He didn't say that."

"He might not have done but he meant it, I bet."

"Silly," she chuckled, busying herself with filling the flask.

The air raid sirens started, wailing into the evening air. Ernest got to his feet and went to the back door, looking over towards the east and the south. Already he could see the flashes as bombs fell, and in between the sirens' wail he could faintly detect the sound, almost the feel of bombs falling. "Looks like the docks are getting it again," he mused, shutting the door. "We'd best be thinking about going to the shelter."

"No, we've time yet. Time enough for you to go and get yourself cleaned up and ready for bed and time enough for me to finish this flask and make us a sandwich," said Alice. Ernest shivered. He really didn't feel that well and it would be good to be in the warmth of the shelter with Alice, even if the wicked woman had obvious designs on him. A smile played on the corner of his lips. "Go on get on with it," she chivvied, "or we'll both be blown to bits."

Ernest got to his feet. He crossed to behind Alice and put his hands around her waist. She squirmed her buttocks back into his crotch. "Don't do that love," he murmured, "or we'll never get anywhere." Undeterred, she continued to move against him whilst at the same time busying herself with the preparation of the sandwiches in front of her. A repetitive thumping announced the falling of more bombs, only this time they were much nearer and Ernest raised his head from her shoulder in alarm. "Best get going my love," he whispered, patting her waist and pulling back from her a little. She turned to face him, holding her arms out to him.

"Give me a kiss, then go and get ready," she breathed.

Ernest stepped forward into her embrace. 'God I'm a lucky man,' he thought, as their lips joined.

A howling whine rent the air and he broke off the kiss in alarm. The whine rose to a shriek, followed by a series of huge explosions, each moving closer. Ernest felt his own face go white, saw Alice's look of concern. The lights flickered, dimmed, and then rose again. He stared into her eyes as the air was torn apart, and for a split second the very essence of their being and of everything around them seemed alive with a strange prismatic beauty before the blackness of destruction and death tore them from this world.

***

Violet sat holding the letter from her father in front of her, trying to read it in spite of the train's movement. She stared down at the folded paper, going over the words yet again in spite of the fact that they were burned into her memory. '...Leclerc says that after he was taken out, he thinks he saw poor Frank being dragged away and executed'.

She felt once again the tears flood into her eyes and the paper in front of her blurred. Splashes dropped onto it as she rested it in her lap. "Here Violet. Oh Violet," soothed Lizzie as she crossed from the facing seat and sat cradling her. Violet turned and sobbed into her breast as Lizzie patted and stroked the back of her head. "There there, Violet," she crooned. "Nothing's sure. He 'thinks he saw' it said. It never says that he's sure."

Violet raised her head to look into the young woman's eyes. So like Florrie's. Calm and reassuring yet with a fire that she so envied: one that she herself once possessed. She would have made a good match for her Frank... no she would only think of him as a big brother, surely. "I'm sorry. It's just that..."

"I know. We all know and we all loved... love him... and I'm sure in my heart that he's out there. I feel it here." She clutched her clenched fist to her breast.

Violet sat up. "Do you? Do you really?"

"Yes. Yes I do." She turned to Violet and looked her straight in the eye. "They always say that you do know, you know."

Violet stared at her nodding her head, trying to fully comprehend what she was hearing. "Who knows, dear?"

"They say that you always know about... about someone you love."

Violet wiped her eyes with her hand. "Do you mean...?"

Lizzie nodded, her eyes fixed firmly on Violet's. "Oh my dear, I didn't know."

Lizzie smiled wanly. "Neither did he, it seems."

"But you married George."

"Yes," she sighed. "I married George. I thought I didn't... that Frank didn't and..." Her eyes filled with tears. "It was so difficult. He was going away to war. Frank didn't reply in the way that... I couldn't... I didn't seem to be able to get out of it and..."

"Shhh dear, don't upset yourself."

Lizzie waved her hand. "No. No I want to tell you. Oh Violet it was awful... that night, the night of our wedding... well, it was just terrible because I realised and somehow... somehow so did George."

Violet's mind flew back to the night she had married Slater. "Oh my dear, how awful for you."

"Yes," said Lizzie, taking out a handkerchief and wiping her eyes, "and the next day with him going away and all the family... well I had to sort of pretend."

"And you made a pretty good job of it, I can tell you. I never realised for one."

"Mummy did."

Violet smiled. "Florrie would. She's your mum... and she's practically Frank's mum as well."

Lizzie picked up on that straight away. "Doesn't that worry you?"

"Worry me? No. It would have done once, but not now."

"Give me a cuddle Violet," said Lizzie, opening her arms.

"No, you give me one," laughed Violet, falling into them. The two of them rocked in each other's embrace, their tears turning to a kind of joy at their shared love and concerns. At length Violet patted Lizzie on the back and said, "Come on now. We're nearly there and we don't want father to see us like this, do we?"

Lizzie laughed. "He'll think we're a right couple."

The train slowed, and through the window Violet could see the approaching station. She peered forward as they curved into it. How many times had she arrived by train to be greeted by her father? And in how many differing circumstances? Poor daddy. He'd had to greet a sullen daughter on her return from, what seemed to him, a shameful episode, the birth of her illegitimate son, Frank. She smiled a self-deprecating smile at the thought.

On a happier note, he'd met her here when she brought Frank back on the way to marry Armand.

The brakes squealed and the two of them stood to retrieve their luggage from the rack. "I wonder what it's like in London with all these bombs," said Lizzie.

"I don't know. I expect we'll find out though."

"It's alright for you, you're not staying long."

"Well you wanted the job up here, young lady," said Violet primly but in jest. "Fair worried your poor mum to death it has."

I know," said Lizzie. "But I expect that I'll be safer in this job than anywhere else really, you know. Apparently the bunker is completely bomb proof."

The platform rose up to greet the train and enveloped it in its sheath of concrete. Violet slid the window down to look forward and along the platform, holding her hat to her head. "I can't see him," she called back into the carriage.

"Maybe he's waiting beyond the barrier."

"Yes. Yes I expect you're right dear," said Violet as the train stopped. She put her case down briefly on the seat to open the door and then picked it back up again and dismounted. Lizzie joined her on the platform.

"Can you see him?"

"No, can you?"

"Silly," Lizzie laughed. "I've never met him."

Violet stopped. She turned to Lizzie, her mouth open. "No. No of course you haven't have you... oh, I am getting silly in my old age."

"Old age nonsense: you're a young woman."

Violet winced and resumed walking. "Nice of you to say so darling, but hardly true."

They passed through the barrier and stood just beyond, under the clock in front of the entrance to the underground. Violet glanced over to the car and taxi ranks across to the left, remembering the time when Ernest had met her in his new motor car. 'Poor daddy,' she thought, 'I did give him a bit of a hard time that day.' Where is he now? What could be keeping him? She'd told him twelve o'clock. Was he ill? "We'll give him a bit longer," she said, "then we'd better take the tube."

Lizzie nodded. "Alright by me."

She looked around. Above them the great canopy showed gaping holes, and around them broken and fallen masonry had been swept into neat piles. Their feet crunched on perfect squares of glass lying scattered like jewels on the concrete, driven from their wired embrace high up in the roof. She shivered. "It's a bit chilly here though. Why don't we go over there and get a cup of tea. We can see from there if he comes."

"Good idea," said Violet, picking up her bags.

The two of them picked out a table from which they could keep an eye on the main concourse and sat there drinking tea for the next hour, with Violet becoming increasingly worried as she constantly scanned the platform for her father. Lizzie sensed her friend's concern and shared it, but couldn't help being excited by the whole prospect of being in London at this time. The city had a frisson about it, which she felt she could almost touch. Everywhere people seemed imbued with a sense of meaning... of urgency. Men in all kinds of uniforms, obviously conscious of them as symbols of potency; women, some of them also uniformed, striding around, sure of themselves. A vibrancy seemed to emanate, a sense of purpose that touched everything and everyone.

Violet saw the sparkle in Lizzie's eyes, saw the sigh and guessed the reason. "Exciting, isn't it?"

Lizzie turned to her. "Yes. Yes it is... it's so..." She waved her hand to encompass the whole scene. "It's a war and yet I can never remember feeling so alive! Is that wrong?"

Violet smiled and put her hand out to the younger woman. "No dear, it's not wrong. I feel it myself to an extent, although in my case it is... well it's tinged with sadness that yet another generation of young men..."

"Oh Violet I'm so sorry. I didn't mean... oh you will forgive me, won't you? I wasn't thinking."

"Silly. Of course I forgive you. We're worried about Frank... and George of course. But that doesn't mean that one can't get caught up in the excitement. I'm just so worried about daddy. He should have been here by now. I wonder what's delayed him."

Lizzie looked at her watch. "Look, let's get the tube. If he turns up, he'll realise where we've gone."

Violet looked up and over the station concourse. No, he wasn't there. She chewed the corner of her lip, thinking. "Right. Come on," she said rising, "let's get moving."

They made their way across the concourse, through the sandbagged chicane and on down and into the underground. Violet marvelled at how little everything had changed considering its new nocturnal usage. The lights still burnt brightly, their glass shades still intact. The curved walls still bore the same signs, the same advertising slogans that she recalled, only now they sat alongside War Department posters whilst others were defaced with stickers proclaiming the incentive 'See it through'. In places, nails and hooks worked into the crevasses in the tiling bore testimony to their night-time use as clothes hangers, and slightly more and varied litter than average on the line indicated that at times each station was crowded with refugees from the war overhead.

Lizzie marvelled inwardly as the tube train arrived and its doors slid open to beckon them within. She gazed, fascinated at the tunnel walls as they whizzed by, the looping strands of cables waving in front of her less than a foot from the glass at times. At Kings Cross, she marvelled at the strangeness of it all as they changed lines, battling their way down the draughty tunnels, up and down long staircases.

Eventually they emerged into the daylight at Highgate station. "Is this where you come from?" Lizzie asked as they picked their way out into and down the street.

"No. No I come from Finchley."

"Is that far from here?"

"No, not far. Not far at all really." She paused as their way was impeded by a fallen pile of masonry spewing across the pavement. A path had been cleared about eighteen inches wide and the two of them carefully picked their way through to the other side. They turned left in front of a row of shops now open to the elements, their upper storeys reduced to a hollow facade. Neat stacks of salvaged items were piled up in front of each shop, and from within them more goods were constantly being passed to an army of willing helpers, supervised by groups of tin-helmeted policemen and uniformed men. Violet scanned the faces looking for Ernest. No wonder he hadn't come, he'd have been busy with all of this lot. She felt her spirits rise.

"What a mess," she remarked to a group of helmeted firemen standing, blocking the pavement as they looked across the street, pointing up to the unsupported brickwork.

They broke off their deliberations and stood aside to let them pass. "Sorry, ladies," one of them said.

"Yes and there's more to come down yet an' all," said another.

Lizzie felt a thrill of fear. "What, you mean more bombs?"

"More bombs? Oh I see what you mean. No miss, I mean that all that lot will have to be pulled down before it falls."

"Oh," said Lizzie, feeling foolish.

The man picked up her embarrassment, seeming to realise that she was from out of town. "Mind, there'll be more tonight. Gerry'll be making his rounds about six, I don't doubt."

"Well, we'd better get on then Lizzie," said Violet. "Come on my love, let's get home. Goodbye gentlemen."

"Goodbye ma'am... miss," said the man. "Take care now."

"We will," laughed Violet as the two of them walked off down the road. They turned right and trudged up the hill to the top, where they turned left yet again into what Violet thought was her street. She stopped, uncertain of her whereabouts. "That's funny, I must have missed a turning," she mused aloud. She put her bag down and looked around. Yes, there was the old chestnut tree at the corner. The white house on the corner opposite. This must be the road, but what was so different? No, it couldn't be. She must be in a similar street. She picked up her bag and retraced her steps a little way back down the hill. Lizzie followed, uncertain as to what exactly was going on.

After about twenty yards Violet stopped again beside a red pillar box. She turned and looked at Lizzie. "This is it... that must be it... oh Lizzie I'm lost."

"How can you be lost?"

"I don't know, that's the problem. It's just that everything looks so different..." She paused. "No, this is the hill and this is the post box... so that must be our road. Oh you must think me so silly." She rolled her eyes skywards. "Come on, let's get home."

They walked back up the hill and turned left, Violet walking ahead, staring from side to side. Where were the houses, that row of smaller houses that led into their street? They seemed to have gone, and in their place there was only empty ground littered with broken brickwork, opening on to rows of empty gardens. The street widened and here again something was different.

The trees! The trees had gone... well all but one, which still stood defiantly. Why had they cut the trees down? Did they need the firewood? No, surely not.

A strange horror gripped her and she ran down the road oblivious to all else but her search. She stopped dead staring at her gate, still neatly shut against the street between its framing hedge.

Nothing beyond! Nothing beside! An empty space where once a home had stood, cleared now, she could see as she got nearer, into a pile of rubble no more than ten feet high. Lizzie stopped, the truth dawning on her. Violet dropped her bags and stepped through the gate. She walked in a daze up the straight path, noting the familiar front door now lying on the grass as if placed there by someone who would be coming for it later. Nothing. Her home was gone. She felt a creeping numbness in her brain, a refusal to accept what her eyes were showing her. No it couldn't be. Daddy would be along in a minute to tell her how silly she was and take her to where her home really was.

A blackness, such as she had never felt since that dark day when Dieter was killed, folded in on her and she stood, head bowed, forcing her tightly clenched fists into the sockets of her eyes in an attempt to blot out this awful reality. She started as hands rested on her shoulder and then slipped down to embrace her from behind, and for the first time, as they held her tight, she realised that she was shaking, trembling like a leaf. She turned. "Daddy?" she cried in a strangled voice.

Lizzie held her tight. "Shhh, he's probably gone to stay with friends."

"Who's that?" called a voice from over the hedge, and both women turned to look.

"Hallo. We're in here," Lizzie called out. A head appeared, a young man's head with a mop of curly ginger hair atop a freckled open face with a ready smile.

"Hallo, my name's Dave," he said, opening the gate and stepping through. "What are you doing in here?"

"What happened here?" said Violet, stepping forward earnestly, causing the young man to stop and step back, a little intimidated.

"Bomb. A bomb last night, just after I called for him."

"After you called for him... you mean he wasn't here?"

"Oh no, he was here alright."

"But you said you called for him."

Dave hesitated. Who were these women? "Do you mind me asking who you are?" "This is Violet, Ernest's daughter," Lizzie confided, stepping forward and gripping the young man's arm. "Can you tell me where he is?"

The boy swallowed. "Oh dear... he's at the..." He lowered his voice and leant forward conspiratorially. Lizzie leant forward and he spoke quietly into her ear. "He's at the morgue... him and his missus."

Lizzie pulled back. "What for?"

Puzzlement was written all over his face. "What for?" he said loudly, "'cause they're dead. That's what for."

Lizzie spun round in time to see Violet slump to the ground in a dead faint.

May 1941

"Here we go again," whispered Pierre.

Frank smiled as he shuffled forward, keeping pace with Pierre, seeking the centre of the cage. They stood, surrounded by their fellow prisoners, their hands folded in front of them, bare feet curling against the cold of the metal floor, thin grey pyjama suits barely keeping the chill of the early morning air from their bones. Behind them, regular miners entered the cage and stood chatting to each other, like any normal workmates meeting up for the new day and travelling to work. Frank glanced up at them, standing there, seemingly oblivious to the presence and plight of their fellow countrymen... fellow miners now.

'Strange,' he thought, 'how they can accept the hierarchy of them being free men and us being slaves... of them being dressed in thick trousers and jackets with stout boots... helmets and lamps, whilst we stand here, half starved, shivering in thin, coarse cotton clothing, barefooted and bareheaded.' He could hear them talking now. The general talk one would expect of working men going about their daily lives. He listened as they spoke of meals, of wives and girlfriends. He closed his eyes and tried to imagine the warmth, the luxury of these simple comforts that they held so tantalisingly before him.

Never once had they spoken to him or the other prisoners in any normal manner, other than that which was necessary for the general communication required in the mine. Never once had they enquired as to why any of them was there, why they suffered so in their midst. They seemed to be able to shut out from their minds that these were human beings, Frenchmen like themselves, not beasts.

Frank looked up and caught the eye of one fellow. He spoke quickly before he could look away. "Do you have any food?" He held his hands out palm up, cupped, beseeching.

The man shook his head and looked away guiltily. "Please, anything," Frank begged.

"Tomorrow," the man whispered. Then he turned and continued his conversation.

A bell rang twice and the cage doors swung down and slammed shut with a loud metallic clang. The bell rang once more and the conversation ceased as the cage dropped like a stone into the inky blackness.

Frank felt his empty stomach lurch. Cold air drawn down by the rushing cage cut through him and he shivered, seeking comfort in the closeness of his fellows. His bare feet seemed almost to hover over the floor of the cage and the only sound was the rushing air, the only light, the flickering pin points from the miners' helmets dancing from face to face, glancing off the formless walls of the shaft.

A screaming sound from way up above them announced the application of the brakes in the winding tower and all braced themselves for the rapid deceleration they knew would follow. Frank bent his knees slightly, feeling his body rapidly increase threefold in weight. His thigh muscles quivered with the strain, and beside him Christophe sagged. He reached out for him instinctively, and as he did so linked hands with Pierre, similarly coming to their friend's support. The cage slowed now and the walls beyond it started to take on form. Gradually, as it slowed still further, the lights picked out the hewn rock no more than three-hundred millimetres from each bar of the cage.

The cage bottomed with a bump. Another bell rang and the doors swung up and open. The miners turned and stepped out into the dimly lit tunnel, striking up their interrupted conversation once more. They walked across to the open carts of the underground train and climbed in, sitting talking as they waited for it to depart.

"'raus! 'raus!" came the order. Frank looked up from within the cage. Two German soldiers, their rifles slung over their shoulders, stood in the tunnel, beckoning them out and pointing to the other side. They filed out and stood in a loose group across from the cage by the curve of the wall.

The train departed. The gates slammed shut. A bell rang twice and the cage rose and disappeared up the shaft. Frank and his companions spread out, turning their backs to the tunnel as the warm air drawn from within the depths of the mine played around their thin frames. All too soon, they knew, it would be replaced by the icy draught of the returning cage.

For the moment there was peace. The two soldiers relaxed against the wall of the tunnel, chatting quietly to each other, and the small group of prisoners stood or sat in silence awaiting their orders and the coming toil. The air stopped moving, announcing that the cage had reached the surface. Frank listened out for the sounds of the mine. Beyond the faint noises coming down the shaft and the barely discernible vibration far down into the loader tunnel, he could detect the sounds of the earth talking in creaks and whispers.

The tunnel was about six metres wide. The floor was flat bedrock, upon which were spiked the twin sets of narrow gauge railway lines that carried the carts and trains, loaded with men and equipment, through to the face. The ceiling was about three metres high, supported by great hoops of iron, set about a metre-and-a-half apart, jacked up into the roof and held in place by feet, bolted to the uprights.

In places, the almost unimaginable pressures of the earth above had twisted these great hoops, buckling them down and turning them over to reveal their channel formation. Down these conduits a stream of fine particles ran to form heaps at the floor, which passing traffic distributed to form a coating of dust and debris up to fifty millimetres deep in places. At times, Frank and his fellow prisoners had been set to work to clear this away from the tracks, but at other times, barefooted as they were, they welcomed its soft cushion.

From every other hoop, a bare light bulb hung from rubber-coated wiring, lit by the huge generators way up on the surface, powered in part by the gases that were drawn off from the mine which would otherwise kill by suffocation or explosion. Frank remembered how, when he had first arrived, a German soldier standing guard over them had nonchalantly gone to light a cigarette. A miner had rushed up to him and snatched it from his mouth, dashing the box of matches from his hand. For a second the soldier had seemed stunned, but then he had reacted, slinging his rifle off his shoulder and pointing it menacingly. The miner had tried to explain in French that a lighted cigarette could cause an explosion, but the German obviously understood no French. He continued to gesticulate with his rifle until, finally, another miner had gone across and mimed the act of lighting a cigarette and then an explosion.

Frank smiled to himself. He swore that even in the half light of the tunnel he had seen the German go white at the realisation of just how dangerous his unthinking action could have been.

Along the tunnel there was the sound of approaching carts. A pit pony, its hooves muffled by the thick blanket of dust, wearily pulled its way up the tunnel to where the group of prisoners stood. The air started to move again. Cold air, signalling the return of the cage. The two soldiers pushed themselves off the wall and stood ready.

The cage arrived, loaded with props, accompanied by just two miners. The doors swung up and open and they stepped out. "Right, get this lot loaded into the carts," they called. The Germans stepped forward, their rifles held horizontally before them, making pushing motions as they urged the prisoners towards the cage. The drover unhitched the pony and led the beast back and around to the other end of the line of carts.

Frank teamed up with Pierre, as he always tried to do, whilst Thierry and Christophe formed another pair. Pierre was no miner... leastwise he had never said that he was, but he did, nevertheless, show an uncanny understanding of the whole mining process and an instinctive feeling for the mine itself. Frank well remembered the time when the two of them had been working on extending the loader gate, to push the face forward. They had both been hacking away at the rock face from a ledge about two metres off the level of the floor. Frank had swung his pick one more time at a large lump that seemed to want to remain where it had been since the dawn of time and Pierre had stayed his hand. In the glimmer of the light from the small lantern they had placed on an outcrop, Frank had seen Pierre put his fingers to his lips, then cup his hand over his ear in a signal for Frank to listen.

Beyond and behind them, Frank could hear the sounds of the face being worked but nothing else. Pierre had pointed to the roof more urgently, then tugged at Frank's arm, pulling him back. They scrambled off the ledge and dropped back to beyond the newly installed hoop.

"Hey there. Get back to it," a voice had shouted in French. A guard had rushed forward to quell this mutiny but Pierre had simply turned to face him, one finger to his lips, the other pointing to the ceiling. The guard had stopped, unsure as to just what this dishevelled, blackened creature was trying to convey. Then the miner who had shouted out joined them.

"What's up?" he demanded.

Pierre had pointed again to the roof, just above where he and Frank had been working only minutes before. The miner had looked quizzically at him and then stepped forward, his ear cocked in the direction Pierre was pointing. Frank had followed, curious as to just what his friend was afraid of.

"Quiet!" the miner called, and all about them had stopped their work and backed away from the face. Frank listened as hard as he could. Faintly, he could hear a strange sound seeming to emanate from within the rock. He placed his hand against the wall and detected a tremor. The sound was clear now, a sound that was neither high nor low in pitch, a sound like no other he had heard, a sound that seemed almost to be speaking to them. "Back!" cried the miner, and all around had fled back up the tunnel, turning after about twenty metres to watch and wait. For a brief moment, friend and foe, freeman, soldier and prisoner had been equal in their fear as the almost undetectable sound had risen suddenly to a roar. Then the roof above where Frank and Pierre had been working fell in, blasting rubble and dust up the tunnel to where they waited.

Frank shuddered at the memory as he grabbed one end of a shaft of timber picked up by Pierre and backed out of the cage and over to the waiting train. They paused briefly to gather their strength before heaving it in and returning for the next. For an hour the prisoners worked silently, until the last cart was filled and the cage was empty. The miners walked to the front of the train and the drover hitched the beast to the tow. He urged it forward to take up the strain. Hooves dug into the soft dust of the floor and slipped as the pony swung to the left, seeking a firm foothold. "You men, push!" shouted the free miner.

Frank and Pierre started forward, followed by the rest of their group. The two guards, unable to comprehend what the miner had shouted, turned in alarm as their prisoners suddenly seemed to be converging towards them in a frighteningly purposeful manner. Frank stopped, extending his arm to prevent Pierre moving forward. The others formed up behind them as the two guards swung their rifles off their shoulders and crouched in a firing position.

'How easy it would be to take them,' thought Frank. 'Even if the rifles were loaded, and that was far from certain because surely even the Germans would know that a rifle shot down here could cause disaster... even if they were loaded, how could these two young men hope to succeed against ten, however tired and hungry they were.' He shook his head to clear the thought. 'Don't be silly Frank. Even if you did and you survived the attempt, where would you go? The exits would be sealed and they would all be hunted down in the darkness or die starving in the lonely depths.'

Frank held up his hands and pointed over the heads of the guards. He mimed the act of pushing. The guards looked puzzled. A miner came down the train and stopped as the frightened guard on his side swung his rifle towards him. He looked across at Frank. "What's the problem?"

"He's misunderstood things. We moved for..."

"Ah I see," interrupted the miner. He turned to the guards, his hands held in the air, palms out, towards them, smiling. He pointed to the group of prisoners and then to the last cart, dropping his arms and miming a pushing movement. The Germans looked at each other and visibly relaxed, two frightened young men in an unfamiliar environment in a strange land. They half smiled the sheepish smiles of men who knew they had nearly made fools of themselves and stood aside, gathering back their dignity in shouts and orders to the prisoners to heave to and push.

With the aid of the prisoners the train started off, and soon the momentum of the carts, gently assisted by the steady pull of the pony, left the group of prisoners to continue their march alone along the tunnel, spacing themselves out as far as the guards would allow so as to try and avoid stubbing their bare toes on any sharp or projecting object.

They reached the coalface. Ahead of them the tunnel continued, cutting its way through into the earth in tandem with the parallel tunnel, unseen at the other end of the seam. From deep within it they could hear the sound of drills and hammers and the crashing of metal as the supporting hoops were forced and fixed into position. The prisoners were divided up and seven of them were detailed to go forward with the two miners into the tunnel. Pierre, Frank and Thierry were held back and told to commence unloading the carts. Christophe, finding himself in the wrong group, tried to turn back to stay with his comrades but a guard saw him. He ran forward shouting and pushed him away. "See you later," called Pierre. Christophe relaxed. He waved half-heartedly and turned and followed the others.

The guard re-joined his companion as the three remaining

prisoners set to, unloading the train, stacking the timber in neat piles at the edge of the tunnel.

To the right, beyond the solid pillar of rock left as the wall of the tunnel, was the coalface. Barely one metre high, with a seam of sometimes less than four-hundred-and-fifty millimetres thick, it was a scene of intense and noisy activity.

Men, free miners and prisoners crouched or lay hacking and drilling at the face, pulling the coal and waste rock from it and pushing it back onto a conveyor running parallel with the face. Behind them there was clear space of no more than two metres supported by the props that were constantly being fed into the mine. Behind that were the splintered remains of the props that had been dislodged in order to let the ceiling down as the face progressed, lessening the pressure on the working area.

Sometimes the earth would close up silently as if reclaiming its density with dignity, but occasionally there would be an alarming crash as whole sections slammed shut and great puffs of dust and debris were forced forward.

An empty train arrived and the two ponies whinnied their greetings as they met head to head, nuzzling each other in affection. "Hurry up and get this lot off," yelled the drover as he unhitched the two ponies and led them off into a side tunnel. Another man bent down and coupled the two trains together, ready for their trip back up the gate to the cage.

Unloading the carts was easier than loading them as the props were now at the right height and they didn't have to bend to pick them up.

Within an hour the three of them had taken off all that ten of them had loaded in the same time. The ponies, fed now and watered in their subterranean stable, were brought back and hitched to the double train, which then set off back up the tunnel.

"What do we do now?" asked Pierre of the remaining miner.

"Jam!" came a call from the face off to their right.

The miner held his hand up at Frank and his crew and stepped through into the face. "What's up?" he yelled.

"The conveyor's bloody well jammed again," came the muffled reply. "Have you got anyone to clear it, or we'll have to take men off the face."

"Me and three men here."

"Well get to it then," came the order.

The miner ducked back through into the tunnel. "You three come with me. We've got to clear the belt."

Frank and the others moved to the opening in the tunnel wall and ducked through. The two guards, realising too late what was happening, shouted and ran across. The miner held his hand up, indicating that all was well, and ushered them through as well. The guards stopped, looking at each other. Being made to stand around all day in this tunnel far below the surface was one thing, but crawling into spaces nearly half one's height was quite another. They shook their heads and indicated that they would wait in the tunnel. The miner ducked back through. "Looks like your friends don't want to go with you," he laughed.

"We'll miss them terribly," said Thierry.

"Maybe so," said the miner, "but for now we've got to clear this belt. Follow me." He crawled through and, bent nearly double, proceeded to skirt the stopped conveyor. Frank and the others followed his light, trying to keep up with him, feeling their way through alongside the rollers, bumping every now and then into props and aware all the while of the awful no-man's-land off to their right.

They must have crawled for about a hundred metres before the miner in front stopped. Frank saw his light cease to move, but Pierre and Thierry following on behind and bumped into him in the darkness. "Here's the problem," the miner called back. "A rock's fallen off and jammed under these rollers."

He slid aside, backing under the slope of the dropped ceiling, pointing his lamp at the jam. Frank and Pierre moved forward and seized the rock, tugging at it. It wouldn't move. "Can't budge it like this," Frank gasped. "Can they reverse the belt?"

"Yes, but someone will have to go forward to tell them."

"Will they take notice of me?" asked Pierre.

"I don't see why not," replied the miner. "Tell them Jacques sent you." He waved Pierre away and turned to Thierry behind him. "Reach up there and get one of the picks." Thierry stood as far as he could and reached over the belt.

"Can we have a pick down here?" he called to the men lying across the other side on a ledge by the face.

"You can have mine with pleasure," came the reply. A hand reached over the gap presenting a pick, handle first. Thierry took it with a mumbled thanks and handed it to the miner they now knew was called Jacques.

"Right," he said, hefting it. "Let's see if we can free this thing." He swung the pick at the rock, seeking to wedge it between it and the rollers. "Pull on this," he called to Frank. The two of them tugged at the pick but nothing budged. Thierry, trapped behind Jacques, was unable to help in the confined space.

"Best leave it for a moment," said Frank. "If they reverse the belt whilst we've got this in there, we'll be in trouble."

Jacques looked at him. "Yes, you're right. Back off a little."

They waited in the dark, lit only by the light of Jacques' helmet pointing here and there as he idly looked about himself. The belt jerked into forward motion and then stopped. Jacques cursed and the belt reversed, crunching the large rock back, pushing the belt up and off the rollers to tip its contents back over onto them. "Bloody idiots," Jacques muttered. "Right, let's get this lot clear."

"You alright down there?" a voice called from above and over the other side of the belt.

"Yes. Just covered in the bloody stuff, that's all," Jacques called back. "We'll have this cleared in a little while."

"Take your time," the voice called back. "I'm enjoying the rest."

The three of them tugged and pulled at the rocks, pushing some back into the void behind them and placing others back on the belt, either side of the original jam. They worked in silence, more by feel than anything else, until they had finally cleared all the dropped spoil except for the large rock that still jammed the belt up and off the rollers.

"We need to lift the belt off the rock so that we can pull it clear," puffed Jacques.

"We'll never lift that weight unless we clear the whole belt," protested Frank.

Jacques thought, rubbing his chin as he did so. He turned and looked around and back into the void, his eye alighting on a length of steel rail discarded back against the settling earth. "That," he pointed. "Get that here." Frank looked where he was pointing, beyond the line of main props to the unsupported area. A shiver of apprehension ran through him. "Go on, it won't kill you," chided Jacques. "I'll light the way from here."

Frank and Thierry crawled forward together along the beam of light. They dropped to their bellies, wriggling through the fallen rocks, aware of the loose ceiling above them and the fact that at any moment the life could be crushed from them. Frank felt forward for the steel, gripping it tightly and pulling. It didn't move. "It's jammed in," he called back to Jacques.

"Pull harder. It'll come," he called back.

Thierry slithered in alongside Frank. For a moment the two of them lay gasping together, then Thierry reached forward, his hands clamping around and locking onto Frank's grip. "Pull on three," he whispered. "Ready?"

"Yes."

"One, two, three. Pull." The two of them tugged at the rail. It moved towards them with a metallic scraping. Above them the rock loosened and a shower of small particles rained down on them as they buried their heads in their arms, fearing the worst.

"Are you alright?" Jacques called, his lamp lighting up the cloud of dust billowing from the void.

"Yes, I think so," Frank called back.

"Did it move?"

"Yes."

"Come on then. Let's have it."

Frank and Thierry shuffled back, keeping their grip on the rail. They pulled once more and again buried their heads into the floor as another shower of rock fell from the ceiling. "I'm not happy about this," Thierry whispered to Frank.

"Me neither," he replied. "Come on, a couple more pulls and we'll be back under the support."

They moved back, holding on to the rail, which now slid more easily. Frank felt his feet touch the props and changed direction to avoid them. Jacques bent down and crawled in between them. "Well done lads," he said, reaching forward and gripping the steel. The three of them moved back, pulling the rail with them as far as the belt, its full length still extending past the props and into the void. For a moment they leant back against the hard rollers to get their breath back. A sudden creak and a whining sound alarmed them and the prop next to and between Frank and Jacques seemed to tremble. A wedge of rock tumbled down from the ceiling about a metre from them in the void, then all was still.

"Everything alright down there?" called the same voice from the ledge above.

"Yes. Just a little fall but it's alright now," Jacques shouted back. He rolled over from his sitting position and knelt down. "Right," he said, "you two pull that rock there over to here, and we can lever the belt up."

Frank and Thierry rolled the rock he'd indicated along to where he was. Then Frank went behind him so that he and Thierry flanked Jacques, who slid the rail forward, over the rock and under the belt, pushing down on it. Nothing moved. Again the three of them pushed down. Jacques transferred his whole weight to it, and the belt lifted. "Right, us two will hold it... you..." He indicated Frank. "... you reach forward and pull it free. Frank gingerly let go of the rail. The bar slipped down a little and Jacques redoubled his efforts, lying across it. "Quick!" he yelled through clenched teeth. Frank hesitated. He never knew from that day forward what made him do so, but in spite of knowing the urgency of the situation... knowing the strain his two companions were under, he hesitated nonetheless. "Come on," hissed Jacques.

Frank straightened up on his knees and prepared to reach forward. Without warning, the belt jerked into forward motion for about a metre, taking the end of the rail with it, sweeping its full length in an arc. It pivoted on the rock, carrying Jacques and Thierry with it, knocking aside the two nearest props, the first of which fell onto Jacques, crushing him and grinding him along the floor to lie with its length across his chest. Thierry felt himself swept back by the rail as the other prop crashed to the floor behind him.

Jacques lay unmoving, his helmet lamp pointing up to the ceiling. Thierry recovered and reached forward to him. "Are you alright?" he asked, shaking his shoulder.

Jacques cursed through his teeth. "Winded," he said wheezing. "Get this thing off me."

"Frank," Thierry called. "Are you alright?"

"I'm fine," said Frank. "I'm..." He stopped as a grinding noise came from above. "Back! Back Thierry!" he screamed. Thierry, on his knees, rolled backwards and jack-knifed over as the whole section of ceiling seemed to detach itself in almost slow motion, folding down into the void. Frank saw him scrambling on his hands and knees back up the direction they had come from. Jacques raised his hands in the air as the ceiling descended towards him and the rock pinioned the timber prop, crushing it down into his chest.

For a moment his arms remained outstretched, but then, lit only by the glimmer from his helmet light, they fell back onto his lifeless body. Frank cowered in terror as the whole roof seemed to continue to fold in on them, crushing the edge of the conveyor. He threw himself flat on the floor, his hands over his ears, convinced that at any moment his life would be crushed from him.

Then silence. Total silence. He was aware that he was holding his breath and he breathed out with a gasp. For a moment he could see nothing, but then as he opened his eyes and reached forward to rub them clear of the dust he was aware of the still shaft of light shining up from Jacques' helmet lantern. Gently he reached forward to touch Jacques' leg. He tugged at the trousers, feeling no response.

He rolled over on his back. The slab of rock that had detached itself had remained more or less whole. That was what had saved him. The void was no more and he was cut off from the face on the ledge above by the rock, which now leant upon it, leaving a triangular gap no more than six-hundred millimetres wide at the base by four-hundred-and-fifty millimetres in height. Frank bent his head down on his chin and looked along his own body. There, not more than ten metres away, he could see light. He had to get there! Above him the rock groaned and he felt the panic rising up as he threw himself back over onto his stomach and crawled backwards, feeling his way blindly with his bare feet.

He must have travelled like this for about five metres before he felt a touch on his foot which did not feel like that from a rock. A hand grabbed his ankle and squeezed. He rolled over and propped himself up on his elbows. Light. There was a bright light. "Who's there?" he called, aware that his voice was shaking with panic.

"Pierre. It's me. What happened?"

"The belt moved forward," Frank gasped. "We were trying to lever it up but it moved forward..." His voice rose and Pierre patted his foot.

"There Frank, calm down. You're alright now. What about the others?"

Frank gulped. "Sorry Pierre, it's just..."

"Ah, don't you be sorry," said Pierre softly.

"Jacques... the miner is dead, I think. Thierry went back the other way. I don't know if he made it or not."

"Are you sure Jacques is dead?"

"I'm pretty sure. Oh Pierre, can we get out of here please I've got a bad feeling."

"I know you have Frank but wait... look at me." Frank looked down the length of his own body at his friend. "It's bigger here Frank... see I can kneel. There's a sort of hole here and then the tunnel goes on until it's clear just back there. He held up the lantern for Frank to see. As he moved it back and aside Frank imagined that he could also see other lights at the far end and hear other voices calling out.

He shuffled towards Pierre on his bottom. Pierre backed away, allowing him to move into the wider space. Frank sat up, his head in his hands staring at Pierre. "Can we go?"

Pierre held his hand up. "Frank. Frank there's a chance for one of us to get out of here."

"One of us," said Frank alarmed. "What do you mean one of us?"

Pierre laughed gently. "I don't mean out of this hole, Frank, I mean out of this place."

Frank looked puzzled. "How do you mean Pierre?"

"One of us could swap clothes with Jacques."

"Swap clothes with Jacques?"

"Yes... and escape... Oh, they'd find out eventually, but by then it would be too late, you'd be well away."

"Me? Why not you?"

"Because... well I don't know, but one of us has got to try."

"I'll toss you for it."

"You can do what the hell you want as long as you hurry up about it." He searched about on the floor for a stone. Picking one up, he put the lantern down and put his hands behind his back. "You choose, left or right."

"Right."

Pierre brought his right hand forward and held it out, fist clenched. Frank gasped as the hand opened and the stone dropped from it. "You go. Now I'm going to leave the lantern here on the ground and then I'm going back down the tunnel to fetch a pick."

"What do we need a pick for?" Frank asked.

"We don't, but neither do we want that lot coming in here, and as long as I'm blocking the tunnel they can't get in, can they?"

Frank smiled at his friend. "No, I expect not... but what am I to do?"

"Crawl back there and pull our friend to here and swap clothes with him as quick as you can, then when I come back we'll bang about a bit and then drag him out dressed as you."

"What about his friends? They'll see I'm not him."

"Black your face as much as you can... after that we'll have to trust to the fact that they're Frenchmen after all." He turned and crawled off down the tunnel, leaving Frank alone.

Frank steeled himself for the task ahead. Every fibre of his being wanted to flee this trap, to follow Pierre to comparative safety and familiarity, but he knew in his heart that this was really a chance. 'If you don't do it Frank, you'll surely die down here sooner or later,' he thought to himself. 'Might just as well die trying to be free.' He turned over on his belly and crawled back up into the darkness, feeling forward all the while for Jacques' body. His hands made contact with the dead man's boots. Was he trapped? Would he be able to pull him free? After all, the prop that had crushed the life out of him must still be there.

He reached forward and grabbed the ankles. He pulled hard. At first nothing happened, but then, to his surprise, the body moved easily towards him. The head lolled to the right and the helmet fell off, its light pointing forward, momentarily blinding Frank. He shielded his eyes, looking along the body. The shattered prop lay beside the dead man's head, sheared off by the guillotine of rock that had forced it down and finally broken it through Jacques' caved-in chest.

'Leave the helmet,' thought Frank. He hesitated. 'No, it'll be useful disguise... and if I leave the light on it'll prevent people looking directly at me.' He shuffled himself forward, up and over the body. He felt the roof pressing down on their combined thickness and shuddered as his hands felt into the warm, sticky depression that was once Jacques' chest. His face was now centimetres from that of the dead man's. He stared down. How long had he known this man? An hour, maybe an hour and a half? To this man, Frank had been as nothing, an expendable source of work, there only to be used in the endless production of the mine... yet looking down at his face Frank could feel nothing but pity and a terrible sense of loss. He reached forward for the helmet and shuffled back down the body.

It took him about a quarter of an hour to finally get himself and Jacques back to the small cave and then another ten minutes to get the man's clothes off and to change into them himself. Pierre's head appeared in the small opening leading out to safety. "Alright?" he asked quietly.

"Yes I think so. I've just got to get my clothes on to him and that's not easy."

"Did you take his underclothes off?"

"No. Why? I didn't like to."

"Take them off and stuff them somewhere where they can't be seen or found."

"Why?" asked Frank.

"Because, silly, if they think it's you that's dead, they'll not waste the clothing and the minute they see posh underwear on the body they'll realise it's not you."

Frank sighed. He was right. "Pity it's not you that's going Pierre. This was your idea and you seem to be better at it than me."

"You drew the stone."

"Did I? Did I really, Pierre?"

Pierre smiled. "Get him ready whilst I bang away for a bit with this pick to make it sound as if something's happening down here."

In the confined space it wasn't at all easy to get his old clothing on the body, but by pushing and pulling, and with a few tears which worried Frank at first, until he realised that the more dishevelled the better, he finally got Jacques ready for his new role as a dead prisoner. Pierre raised his head up and looked at the dead man. "Push the smock into his chest and get it all bloody," he commanded.

"Pierre?" said Frank, horrified.

"Do it," hissed Pierre. "It's no good him looking as if he's just been dressed, is it?" Frank put his hand on the dead man's chest. He pushed down gently, feeling the sticky wetness rise up through the thin cloth, the broken bones grinding below his fingers. "Harder!" Pierre insisted. Frank looked away and pushed down as hard as he could with the flat of his palm. A long moaning sigh issued from the dead man's mouth and he snatched his hand away in terror. "Right," said Pierre. "I'll go out first and you follow, pulling our friend behind you, and Frank..."

"Yes?"

"Good luck, my friend. Once we're clear of this and back in the gate, you don't know me. Understood?"

"Understood," nodded Frank, a strange lump in his throat. "Thanks Pierre, and good luck yourself."

"Just you get back to England and give them hell Frank... for me, eh?"

"You can count on it."

It took them another twenty minutes to get through to the end of the fall. Pierre came out first and handed his pick to the waiting group of men crouched in the confined space. Frank wiped his bloody, wet hand in the dust and smeared it all over his face before donning the helmet. "Get clear back to the gate," he called. "I've a casualty here and we need to get him to the surface as quickly as possible."

Pierre indicated to the group that they needed to back off down the conveyor towards the gate and surprisingly they obeyed him, turning and making their way back. He turned and helped Frank with the body, half dragging, half carrying it to the end and into the gloomy tunnel.

A miner stepped forward. "Is he dead?"

"I think so," said Frank, bent over, supporting the body, trying to keep his face out of direct view. "I need to get him to the surface."

"Shall I help him?" Pierre volunteered.

"No," said the miner, "you'd better wait for the Germans or we'll all be in trouble." He pointed to a young man standing by the conveyor controls. "You, Guy, it's your fault this happened by all accounts, you help me and Jacques to get this man up top." The other man came over and Frank relinquished the body to him. The miner in charge took hold of the legs. "Right, let's get to the cage. You follow on Jacques, you've had enough for this shift. The rest of you get this bloody mess cleaned up."

The two miners set off down the tunnel carrying the body, and Frank followed on behind as quickly as he was able, his weakened body screaming out at the continued effort, his footsteps stumbling in the unaccustomed boots. They reached the cage and the leading miner, the younger man, swung the gate open and stepped in, followed by the other two. Frank found himself standing right beside the charge miner as the bell rang and the cage started up towards the surface.

"Locker number forty three," the miner whispered in his ear.

"I beg your pardon?"

"Locker forty three. That's Jacques'... your locker."

"Thank you... how did you know?"

"Should I not know the body of my oldest friend and school chum?"

"I'm sorry... there was nothing I could do. When the belt moved forward it... it took the bar with it and he was crushed by the roof as it... as it pressed down. I'm sorry. Are you going to give me away?"

"Would I have told you his locker number? When we get up top we'll dump the body in the infirmary, then you follow me. Alright?"

The cage reached the surface and Frank was dismayed to realise that it was still daylight on a beautiful May afternoon. Miners, German guards and two orderlies from the infirmary greeted the cage and, in a moment of panic, Frank held back until the firm grip of the miner steadied him. The dead body was the main focus of attention as it was placed on a stretcher. The two orderlies perfunctorily examined it before throwing a sheet over it and carrying it across in the direction of the infirmary.

"What happened?" came the question on many lips.

"You tell them Guy," the older miner instructed the younger one who had accompanied them up. "I'm going to get cleaned up." He flashed a look at Frank as he reached in his pocket for his tag, detached his lamp and handed it to the tallyman before striding off in the direction of the showers. Frank dug into his top pocket and was relieved to find the tag. He held it out for the tallyman, who took it.

"Lamp?"

"Lamp? Oh, the lamp." He reached up and detached it from his helmet and handed it over wordlessly. Then he held his head in his hands in feigned despair, but real fatigue, and walked off, shrugging off questions with a shake of his head. Guy started to explain what had occurred and Frank found himself alone and outside the group of men. He turned and followed the purposeful figure of the other miner striding across to the building containing the showers and lockers.

Twenty minutes later Frank stepped out into the afternoon sunshine dressed in the dead man's clothes, his cap pulled well down on his head.

The other miner stood momentarily beside him. "Right, listen," he said. "We've got to go out through that gate and I can't actually be with you because when they find out what's gone on I don't want to take the blame."

"I'm sorry I don't want to involve you."

"It's not just me. Jacques' wife will have to be told and she'll want his body."

"Won't they just bury it thinking it's me?"

"And if they do that they'll think that Jacques has just run off, and where would that leave her?"

Frank sighed. "What do you suggest then?"

"I'll go to the gate. The guard's name is Herman, my name's Pierre. I'll stop and talk to him and you walk straight through, calling out 'Hello' to him, by name."

"Right," said Frank. "Where do I walk to?"

"Go straight up the road and take the second on the right. When you're out of sight, stop and wait for me."

"Thanks."

"Don't mention it... but remember, if anything goes wrong you're on your own. I'll be as surprised and upset as everybody else." He smiled. "I'll even help recapture you."

"I understand," said Frank. He stepped back into the building as Pierre strode purposefully across towards the gate. He waited until he was over halfway there before setting off himself on what proved to be the longest, most difficult walk of his life. So concerned was he with not attracting attention that it became difficult even to place one foot in front of the other with any degree of normality. Even staying upright suddenly seemed to be a trial, which needed every last drop of concentration.

Ahead of him, Pierre had mounted the steps and was engaging the guard in conversation, without so much as a backward glance at Frank as he approached. His mouth felt dry, his tongue two sizes too large. He fought the impulse to flee, willing himself to walk steadily on to freedom.

"Good afternoon Herman," he called out cheerily as he passed.

Pierre waved his hand up in the air without turning or ceasing his conversation. From within the hut came a muffled greeting, and out of the corner of his eye Frank was aware of a figure rising behind the glass. He walked on, expecting a challenge at any moment but none came. Second on the right, Pierre had said. The urge to get clear, to get out of sight, was nearly overwhelming as he passed the first turning, but he held his course and continued on to the second road, turning right into it without a backward glance. The gatehouse disappeared from view, hidden by the first house, and Frank slowed down and stopped. His breath came in short gasps and his legs felt like jelly, but he was out. He was free!

***

'Why were they all looking at him,' thought Frank. He saw Pierre-Luc and rushed over to him, grabbing his arm. "Pierre-Luc, where are you going?" he cried. "Why did you just walk away from me?" The man looked down at this deranged creature clinging to his sleeve. He tried to shake him off, but Frank persisted. "Come on Pierre-Luc, let's find Marcel and go down to the river." He stared up into his friend's face.

"I am not Pierre-Luc. I do not know you," the man said. "Leave me alone or we'll both be in trouble." He wrinkled his nose at the smell of days without washing, nights on the bare earth under hedges and in ditches. Frank gripped the man's sleeve all the harder and dragged himself up, pulling his face close.

"What's the matter?" he gasped as all before him seemed to swim in and out of focus. The man recoiled from his breath, the breath of someone who had hardly eaten in days. Frank fell away still, gripping his sleeve. "Help me Pierre-Luc," he cried as his legs began to buckle. "Why won't you help me?"

"What seems to be the trouble here?" said another voice, unheard by Frank.

The man turned. "Father," he said, relieved. "This man... could you please call the gendarme."

The priest raised his hand. "I don't think that will be necessary.

Help me to get him to my house and I'll take care of him."

"But Father, you don't know who he is," the man protested.

"He is a young man who is obviously sick and in need of help."

"Father, I warn you," the man persisted. "He could be dangerous... an escaped criminal."

"In whose eyes? The eyes of French... or the eyes of Germans?"

The man shook his head as Frank subsided back against the wall and finally let go of his sleeve, sliding down to sit between them. "Pierre-Luc. Marcel," he mumbled, and then in English, "Violet, oh Violet, where are you?"

"Help me with him. Quickly now, my son," the priest instructed. "Just around the corner and we'll be safe." The man looked at him for a moment and then the two of them assisted Frank to his feet and started off down the road. As they reached the corner and prepared to turn down the side road, an open-topped motor car pulled up beside them.

"What is going on here, Father?" a German officer enquired, leaning out. The priest stopped, his arm still around and under Frank's armpit linking with the other man's, supporting his whole weight.

He turned his head, retaining his position so as to keep both Frank's face, and that of the other man's, facing away from the enquiring look of the German. "A little too much wine at lunch time I fear," he called over his shoulder. Frank slumped down and the two men hefted his weight back up.

"Gunther?" Frank mumbled quietly, and then in English, "Is that you Gunth..." He stopped as the priest dropped him purposefully and then hefted him back up again, cutting off his words.

"What did he say?" the German asked.

"Something about his girlfriend," the priest laughed. "I think that's the reason for him being in this condition."

"He has my sympathies then," replied the officer, smiling. "Get him home." He tapped his glove on the dashboard, the driver slipped the vehicle into gear and they drove off. With no further urging the priest and his companion turned off the road and down the side road. They moved quickly for about twenty metres before the man stopped, his breath coming in short bursts.

"My God, Father, that was a close one."

"It most certainly was," agreed the priest.

"I'm still shaking," the man said. "Can't we just put him down here out of harm's way... after all, we don't know who he is."

The priest looked across at the man. "Help me with him to my house and then get you gone," he said in a harsh voice.

The man picked up the tone of admonishment in the priest's voice. "Father, I've a wife and family to think of," he wailed.

"Help me to get him to my house... it's just fifty metres further and then you can go. The German didn't see your face... you're quite safe."

The man nodded. "Come on then, let's get it done." They lifted Frank's dead weight as best they could and half carried, half dragged him the rest of the way to a small middle terrace house. The man paused as they reached the front door.

"No, not there," the priest commanded. "Through the arch and by the back door." They carried Frank through and set him down on the step, leaning him back against the door. The man stood back and the priest reached in and under his robes and came out with a key. He inserted it in the lock and opened the door. Frank fell back with it as it opened and the priest allowed him to gently subside onto the tiled floor of the small kitchen beyond. "Go now," the priest ordered.

"But don't you want help with...?"

"No, I can manage now. You go... and thank you my son." The man mumbled something and then was off. The priest stepped over Frank's body and grabbed hold of his hands, pulling him into the centre of the room. He let them down again and stepped back over to shut the door.

"Father? Father, is that you?" A small woman in a grey dress with a clean white apron came through and into the room. She stopped at the sight of the prone man on the floor, putting her hands up to her mouth, her eyes wide and questioning.

The priest stepped back around Frank and stood beside her. "Madame Giry. Please help me get him into the front room... we'll put him on the couch for now."

"But Father... who is he?"

"I don't know madame, but I'd hazard a guess that he's in some sort of trouble with the authorities and that he's not eaten for some time."

"But Father... if he's a criminal..."

"I do not think this young man is a criminal. From his condition I would say that he has been in a long captivity but also..." He hesitated. "He was speaking in English."

"In English!" She gripped her hands together and held them to her mouth. "Oh Father, we will be shot if we harbour him."

"And we will be damned if we give him up."

"Does anybody else know he's here?"

"Bertrand Gaudet helped me carry him here and a German officer saw us but..." He held his hand up at the horrified expression of the woman. "But he thought he was a drunk, and to be honest when I first saw him, so did I."

"But Bertrand Gaudet will have heard him speak in English."

The priest thought for a moment. "Maybe, but maybe not... anyway, we'll have to trust to his sense of honour."

"Phaa, Bertrand Gaudet's sense of honour. How long will that last... until he gets drunk himself?"

"Maybe, but what else can we do? We'll get him cleaned up and then move him as soon as we can. I'll speak to someone tonight. Now let's get him through there and then I think if you could heat up a little soup, I'm sure that some food will do wonders to revive our new friend."

The two of them grabbed an arm each and dragged Frank across the floor, through the door and across into the tiny, dark sitting room. They let his arms fall for a moment as the woman bustled back to clear away the carpet, and then the two of them dragged him to the front edge of the couch and manhandled him up and onto it. "My God, he smells horrible," grimaced the woman.

"Yes, I think we'll get him out of these clothes and get rid of them," said the priest. "He can have some of mine in exchange."

"We need to clean him up a bit first," said the woman. She looked down into the face of the priest as he looked back up at her from where he was kneeling beside the couch. She smiled and shook her head. "Don't worry Father. I may be a widow now but there'll be nothing I've not seen before. I'll get some water ready and some towels, you go and find him some fresh clothing."

The priest smiled. "Thank you Madame Giry," he said, rising to his feet and rubbing the life back into his knees.

In the next hour they managed to strip the filthy clothing from Frank's body, in which he'd spent the best part of a month on the run. They cleaned him up as best they could and dressed him in fresh clothing from the priest's own wardrobe, although they had to retain his boots as those of the priest proved to be far too small. They sat him up, still barely conscious, and the woman gently and patiently spooned broth into his lips. Gradually, as the food entered his bloodstream, he began to take notice of his surroundings and address his companions, convinced, unfortunately, that they were Marie and Jean-Claude.

He rambled on to them about domestic matters that required attention around the chateau. He asked where Philippe was and if Violet was coming soon. To their confused replies he merely asked more questions, until at length the priest stood in front of him and, in a voice of authority, demanded that Frank look at him and pay attention. "Monsieur, what is your name? Think now!"

Frank looked up at him, his face troubled. "Father? Father René? Is that you?"

The priest leant closer. "No. Father René is not here. My name is Father Brault. This is my housekeeper, Madame Giry."

Frank concentrated hard. Not René... Father Brault he'd said. Had he? Where was everybody? They'd all been here a few moments ago. He looked around. Looked down at himself. What... whose clothes were these? He looked up into the concerned face of the priest. "Where am I?" he whispered.

The priest smiled. "You are in Barbizon." To Frank's enquiring look he continued. "South- east of Paris. How far have you travelled?" Frank looked from the priest to the woman, his senses suddenly alive and wary.

The priest correctly interpreted his reluctance. "Oh, it's alright my son, you are among friends here. You're quite safe."

Frank looked from one to the other, searching and finding the reassurance he now needed. "I came from Lille."

"Lille?!"

Frank nodded.

"On foot?" the priest asked.

"At night mainly, but... today... I thought I was home."

"In England?"

Frank shot a look up at the man. "England? Why do you say England?"

The priest smiled warmly and sat down on the couch next to Frank. "Because, young man, you have been speaking in English."

Frank grimaced. His eyes closed and his head dropped. "Oh no, I haven't, have I?"

"I'm afraid you have young man, and at one point it was in the presence of a German officer..." He saw Frank's horrified look and raised his hand to still the outburst. "No. No, you're alright, he didn't hear anything, but another did, and for that reason as soon as you are able, I want you to be ready to move."

"Where will you take me?"

"To God's house of course, my son. We shall make you comfortable in the tower until we can... until you are ready to go." He placed his hand on Frank's arm. "Where do you head for, my son?"

"Germigny-des-Pres, near Chateauneuf-sur-Loire."

"And what do you hope to find there?"

"My home. The Chateau de Janvier and... my name is Frank... Frank Balfoure," Frank said proudly, pleased at last to be able to announce the fact.

The priest's face looked serious. "Are you sure? Your papers are in the name of Jacques Menthe."

Frank looked at him. His senses swam and he tried hard to engage his thoughts. He did live there, didn't he? Why, then, should he not go there? Was this man, after all, not to be trusted? Why did he think his name was Jacques? He looked into the eyes of the priest, and from them across at the woman standing just inside the door to the kitchen. "I don't understand."

The priest leant forward and took Frank's hands, holding them in his lap. "If I am not very much mistaken, your arrival at home, wherever it is in France, would not be a good idea."

"What... what do you mean?"

"I mean, my son, that it is my guess that you have escaped from some sort of custody and that you will need to be very careful if you are not to find yourself back where you have just come from... or worse."

Frank stared at him. He was right of course. He knew he was right... but the loss of the dream was too hard to bear. He had thought he was home, had thought that even if not, he could go there soon and now... now he knew that would not be possible. His head dropped and he recovered his hands and leant away from the priest, looking over the edge of the couch to the floor. "My name is Frank Balfoure. I am English but of adopted French nationality. I live... lived at the Chateau de Janvier near Germigny-des-Pres, Chateauneuf-sur-Loire. I was captured by the Germans in June 1940... sent to prison camp, prison and then... then to work in the mines. I was a soldier in the army of France but they thought me a spy..." He stopped, staring down at the floor. There was silence in the room, broken only by the ticking of the clock on the mantle.

The wave of sanity Frank had ridden on for the past few minutes broke on the shingle of doubt, scattering his reason. "Where's Violet?" he demanded in English. "She'll tell you it's the truth." The woman moved into his field of vision, concern written all over her face. The priest held his hand up for her to stop. "There you are, Violet," Frank said. "Tell them who I really am... go on please."

The priest put his hand on Frank's arm and stood. He indicated the couch and waved for the woman to give him a cushion from the other chair, which he placed at the end. "Lie down my son. You are tired. Lie down for a while and we'll talk when you feel better."

Frank looked up at him, bewildered. "Armand?"

The priest nodded his head. "Yes, it's me, my son. Rest now. Lie down." Frank lay across, putting his head on the cushion, drawing his knees up. His eyes flickered and then closed and the priest and the woman stole from the room.

Later that evening the woman crept back into the room. She knelt down and shook the sleeping figure on the couch. "Monsieur. Monsieur. Wake up."

Frank's eyes opened. The concerned face of a strange woman observed him from her position, kneeling in front of where he lay. Who was she? He closed his eyes, thinking that perhaps if he did so she would go away but, as he opened them again, she was still there. He sat up and looked around the room. Where was he? A priest entered the room and he searched his face, looking for some clue as to why he was here.

"Ah you are awake," the man said.

The woman spoke. "Do you remember us at all? The Father brought you here earlier today, but you were very tired and..."

"...and a little confused," the priest interrupted. "You told us your name was Frank Balfoure from near to Chateauneuf, yet the papers you had on you say that you are one Jacques Menthe... although the photograph on those papers is certainly not you."

Frank thought hard. His conversations with them came back to him as if they were some half-remembered dream. The room he sat in seemed to be from the same dream. Was this now still a dream or was this real? He stared down at the face of the woman and held her gaze as she stood, and the priest joined her to stand just in front of him. He shook his head, seeking to clear his thoughts. "What is the date?" he asked.

"It is Friday the 20th June 1941," the priest replied.

"Just over a year."

"Just over a year what, my son?"

Frank smiled. "Since I was captured."

"As an Englishman or as a Frenchman?"

Frank smiled wanly. "Oh, I've told you have I... how many others have I told?"

"Just us two, but there is also a chance, I'm afraid, that another man, a man who helped me bring you here, also knows. That is why we have to move you now."

The woman left the room and the priest sat down on the couch next to Frank. Frank looked at him. "Thank you Father. It would seem that I may have put you in danger. Do you think this other man will betray me?"

The priest shrugged his shoulders. "Who knows. There are enemies amongst friends these days."

"And friends amongst enemies," Frank mused aloud, thinking of Gunther.

The priest turned to him and observed him carefully. He shook his head. "My calling would have me believe so, but... but it is very difficult to hope that at present."

The woman came back into the room carrying with her a tray, upon which there was a plate of bread and cheese, an opened bottle of red wine and two glasses. She waited whilst the priest pulled over a small table and then set the tray down on it. The priest indicated the food. "Eat now, my son, and then we must go and settle you down for the night. Wine?"

"Yes please, just a little," said Frank. He looked up at the woman. "Thank you so much. Could I ask for a little water with the wine." He laughed cynically. "They did not serve wine at my last place of residence, and I'm afraid it might go to my head."

Madame Giry smiled and went from the room, returning immediately with a jug of cold water and another glass. Frank took the jug and poured the water into his wine. The woman smiled and took the glass back into the kitchen. Frank ate quickly, feeling the strength coursing back into his body. He drank deeply of the watered wine, marvelling that far from dulling his senses it seemed, rather, to rejuvenate his spirits. The priest raised his glass to Frank and drank to his health.

At length the food was all gone. Frank felt an unfamiliar lump in his belly and a slight case of heartburn. Simple fare it may have been, but he had not taken the like for over a year now and it would take some time for his shrunken stomach to adjust once more to real food.

"Well," said the priest, "I think we'd better get along to the church. I have evening vespers to perform and we need to get you settled. Madame Giry will follow on with some things for your comfort, but I think it best if you slip on this habit and walk with me." He indicated a black robe lying over the chair back and stood.

Frank nodded his agreement. He put down his glass and rocked back, preparing to rise. He leant forward as far as he could and pushed down with his hands. His thigh muscles began to shake and he would have sunk back were it not for the woman and then the priest rushing forward to support him. "Phew," said Frank, "I'm a little weak. Thank you."

The priest held on to him and the woman hurried over to the chair and picked up the habit. She returned. "Hold your arms out straight in front of you," she ordered. Frank did so and she expertly reversed the gown and slipped it over his outstretched arms and over his head. The priest pulled the hood over.

"Right now," the priest said. "We have to walk to the church. It is about five-hundred metres away and you will have to walk beside me unaided. Do you think you can do that."

Frank nodded. "I'll certainly try."

The priest observed him sternly. "You must, my son. It is important."

The woman opened the door to the hall and then went forward to the front door. Frank and the priest followed her, his guiding hand on Frank's arm. "Ready?" the woman asked. Frank nodded and she opened the door and stood back out of sight. The priest stepped out and waited briefly as Frank joined him.

"Concentrate," he ordered. "This way." He turned and walked up the street, back towards the main street. Frank fell in beside him, his every thought tuned towards walking in as natural a fashion as possible.

The priest struck up a measured stride, which Frank copied, and, after what seemed ages but in reality was only a few minutes, they reached the church. They mounted the steps to the heavy oak doors. At the top step Frank stumbled and would have fallen were it not for the priest reaching out for him and drawing him close. He held Frank tight as he turned the handle and then guided him in, shutting the doors behind them.

Frank slumped in his arms. "Sorry Father," he whispered.

"It's alright my son, nobody saw." He helped Frank over to the centre aisle, turning briefly in the direction of the altar to cross himself, before leading Frank over to a small door. He stopped at this door and leant Frank against the wall whilst he opened it with another key from his belt. "We have to climb some steps now," he said.

Frank gasped. "To the top? Father, I don't think I can make it!"

Father Brault laughed. "No, not to the top. Just one floor and there's a room where we keep the spare bell ropes and things like that. Quite apart from anything else, if you went to the top you'd be deafened by the bells."

"Thank goodness for that," Frank laughed. "Come on then, let's get it over with."

It took fifteen minutes for the priest to help Frank up the stairs and into a small dusty room piled high with coils of bell rope. He propped Frank against the wall as he rearranged the various piles into the semblance of a bed, over which he threw a huge velvet curtain which had been folded up in the corner. Then he indicated Frank to lie down, which he did so gratefully.

There was a sound on the staircase, which alarmed Frank until the door opened and Madame Giry came through, carrying a bag. "Did anyone see you?" the priest asked.

"No Father, I came out the back way and along and through from behind." She stepped forward into the room and placed the bag beside Frank. "Food and a bottle of water and another bottle for... well you know."

"Thank you, madame," Frank mumbled.

"Take off the habit," the priest asked. Frank sat up and the woman helped him get it off. He watched as she slipped it over her own head and turned to the priest. Father Brault noticed his quizzical expression. "Two priests entered. Two will leave." He laughed lightly. "A fellow priest visited the church with me and has now gone home to his own. If anyone asks about the drunkard we picked up, we gave him some strong coffee and sent him on his way, hours ago."

***

"Ah, Mrs Slater, do come in. Take a seat."

"Thank you, Mr Maxwell," replied Violet, sitting in the chair indicated.

Maxwell sat as she did and then leant forward, his hands held before him on the desk, clasped as if in prayer. "So sorry, Mrs Slater.

So sorry to hear of your sad loss."

Violet looked up into the solicitor's eyes. "I presume you mean the house?"

Maxwell frowned. He sat back a little and placed his hands, palm down, on the desktop. "No. No, Mrs Slater. You misunderstand me. I meant your dear father and his... eh... wife."

Violet looked deeper into the man's eyes, seeking to establish just what he did feel. Her searching gaze was reflected back at her. The wall that he had long since erected around whatever feelings he possessed remained intact. "Thank you," she whispered.

He leant back in his chair, his hands clasped again, the two index fingers gently tapping his lip. "So... from my inspection the house is reduced to... well... nothing."

"It is all gone and we... the boys and I are homeless... on top of which Mr Hitler has taken away my income."

"Yes. Yes, I... I do feel that these are circumstances that the late Mr Slater could not have envisaged." Maxwell removed his fingers from his lips and drummed them on a sheaf of documents on the desk in front of him.

There was a long silence, which Violet finally broke. "Is the invested money safe... the money that produces the income for the boys?"

Maxwell frowned and looked serious. "Yes. Yes... well most of it, but..."

"But?"

He looked up as if caught out in his reverie. "Yes... well nothing... nothing is at all as it should be at the moment, is it? Some of the investments are secure, some... some have suffered... as all else has."

Violet sat forward. "Is the income secure?"

"No... no. There is a capital sum, but now that the house has gone I fear that it will not be sufficient.

Violet sat back in her chair. Her head dropped. "So we are consigned to poverty, are we?"

The silence came back, broken only by Maxwell's gently drumming fingers. He coughed. "No... well there is one thing that... no, I don't suppose... no, it's silly."

Violet looked up. What was he up to? "What's silly, Mr Maxwell?" she asked.

"No. No really... I shouldn't have said anything," he said, waving his hands in front of himself as if to clear the air of some imaginary fog.

Now Violet was sure he was up to something. "Well if you say so, Mr Maxwell," she said innocently. She gathered her skirts about herself, picked up her handbag from the floor and leant forward as if to rise from her chair.

"It's just..."

"Yes, Mr Maxwell? It's just what?" She sat back in the chair and clasped her bag in her lap, her face turned up to his in expectation.

Maxwell coughed. "Well it's just a thought." He leant back in his chair and swung around slightly, towards the window, so that his profile was visible to her but he would not have to look her directly in the eye. "The trust document." He indicated it with a sweeping motion of his hand. "The trust document has as trustees myself and Mr Enright, my... my partner... shortly to retire."

"Yes," said Violet. "Yes I understand that, but what..."

"What I had thought... what I had wondered is, if, in the light of all that has taken place... and bearing in mind my own future plans... well whether..." He coughed. "I had entertained the thought that perhaps Mr Enright and myself could appoint alternative trustees."

There was silence again, during which time Maxwell continued to stare out of the window whilst Violet studied his face, searching for any clues as to his real intentions. "Alternative trustees?"

"Yes, Mrs Slater." He swung back around to face her directly.

"But who?"

"You."

"Me?!" Violet pointed to herself.

"Yes you, Mrs Slater. You... and one other person could be nominated as trustees of the estate to administer it for the benefit of the children, until such time as they reach their Majority."

Violet sat still, stunned by this suggestion that had come out of the blue from, of all people, Maxwell, Slater's friend and accomplice in her humiliation... of all people... for him to suggest... "But what about you?"

"Me?"

"Yes, what about you? Surely you want to continue... your fees... what about your fees?"

"Ah well, that's the other part of my suggestion." 'Here it comes,' thought Violet. 'Now we get to hear just what's in it for Mister Maxwell.' "My fees were in fact settled long ago and any commissions I might receive are... well to be frank, with the passing of time and the diminution of the value of the assets..." 'And your own raiding of them,' Violet thought. Maxwell cleared his throat and leant forward, looking directly at Violet. "If, simultaneously with the transfer of the trusteeships, I was to receive... or purchase the interest in the Highgate land at... well let's say for a nominal sum, then I am certain that I and my fellow trustee would be able to agree to such a suggestion."

'You crooked old fox,' thought Violet, trying to resist the impulse to smile. She swallowed. "How... how much would be left... available in the... err."

"Enough to buy a modest house in the country, which I would, of course, arrange as soon as you had found one."

"And income? Would there be any income?"

His hands, clasped earnestly in front of his face, opened up and framed his pious expression. "Alas no, Mrs Slater, but you would at least have a roof over your heads."

'You swine,' thought Violet. 'You've bled it dry.' She smiled to herself, careful not to let it be seen on her face. 'Some friend to Slater you turned out to be, Mr Maxwell. Friend whilst there was profit to be made and fees to be paid, but now... oh what the hell. It was better to be free of all of this. How daddy would have laughed.' The chill came back into her heart, and with it the stark realisation that she and the boys were in fact homeless and dependant only on the continuing charity of Joe and Florrie.

"Who would be the other trustee?"

"Anybody you care to nominate, Mrs Slater... as long as..."

Violet smiled wryly. "As long as it's not my son Frank?"

Maxwell coughed once more. "Well yes err... only because... well as the document specifically excludes him from any benefit I hardly..."

"You needn't worry, Mr Maxwell, he's dead."

"Dead? Oh my dear Mrs Slater, I had no idea. How?"

"Shot by the Germans... tortured and then shot..." Her head dropped and she reached in her pocket for a handkerchief. She wiped her eyes and looked up into the face of Maxwell, expecting triumph to be reflected there, but instead, to her utter amazement, she saw what passed as genuine concern.

His eyes lowered. "I am so sorry, Mrs Slater. I expect that before it is ended this war will touch each and every one of us."

'Fine sentiments,' thought Violet. 'It will undoubtedly touch and enrich your wallet.' She smiled briefly and almost recoiled from the returning smile. It was too late to form or feel any friendship with this man, who had so cruelly connived with Slater, and since that time had forced her to go cap in hand for even the most meagre of incomes. 'But what's the point,' she mused. 'Let's get the whole thing settled with the minimum of fuss and I need never see the horrid man again.' She rose to her feet and extended her hand. "I shall seek out another who can join me as trustee and I shall start the search for a suitable property immediately," she said briskly. "I will see you in about a week's time and we shall discuss matters again."

Maxwell smiled thinly. "I shall look forward to that, Mrs Slater. I shall indeed look forward to that," he said shaking her hand.

Violet left the office and hurried to the tube and on up into town, to where she was to meet Lizzie as she finished work. She waited outside the government offices as the stream of secretaries filed out of the doors of the grey and solid building, their handbags and gas-mask boxes slung over each shoulder, their chatter the chatter of everyday young life.

She saw Lizzie coming down the steps and took in the detail of this handsome young woman she was growing increasingly fond of. Her smartly cut grey suit with its padded shoulders only served to accentuate her slim waist, and the single pleated skirt to just below the knee emphasised her long legs with the neatly turned ankles. She saw Violet and waved, her eyes lighting up her open, ready smile as she crossed to her. "Hallo, Violet," she breathed, adjusting her smart hat, set cocked to one elegant side on her head, as she leant forward to kiss her on the cheek.

"Hallo, darling," Violet replied. "My, you do look the bees knees. You look wonderful."

"Do you like it?" She twirled around, cocking her head as she did, so as to keep her eyes fixed on Violet's smiling face.

"If Florrie could see you now. She'd be so proud."

Lizzie stopped her pirouette and grabbed Violet's arm. "Where shall we go?"

"Well... well how about the Corner House? I need to talk to you darling."

"Sounds serious."

"It is," said Violet. "I've been to see Maxwell today and I need your help."

"Anything Violet. Anything."

"Come along then, let's get there and get a cup of tea and something to eat and I can tell you all about it," said Violet, steering her along the pavement and off down Whitehall in the direction of Trafalgar Square. They walked in contented silence for most of the way, happy in each other's company, but as they crossed into the square and passed Canada House, Violet pointed ahead to the National Gallery.

"That's where Frank and I first really met... well just up that road there."

Lizzie was silent for a moment, then she clapped her hand to her mouth and laughed. "Oh that Frank. I'm sorry, for a moment I wondered what you where talking about. Really? How was that?"

"I was at a demonstration just over there," said Violet, pointing to the corner of the square.

"A demonstration? My, what fun. What sort of demonstration?"

Violet smiled wryly and shook her head. "Suffragettes. We were demonstrating for that which you now take for granted."

"Really? Oh how exciting. I had no idea... and how did Frank's daddy come into that?"

"There was a fight... well the police started arresting us and a group of men started being horrid... we all ran in different directions." They crossed the road and started to walk up Whitcombe Street. Violet pointed ahead. "I ran up here pursued by some policemen." She stopped talking and they walked in silence as the memories flooded back to her.

"I had no idea," Lizzie enthused.

"Here. Here's where Frank grabbed me," said Violet, pointing to the indentation in the wall.

"He grabbed you? Was he a policeman?"

Violet looked into Lizzie's face, wondering for a moment, then she broke into a smile. "No. No, silly. Frank was in town delivering some documents for daddy and he'd stopped off to buy some shirts. He was just watching, and when I came running up the street he recognised me."

"And then what?"

He grabbed me and swung me into his arms and pretended that I'd been with him all along... oh he was so... oh well."

"And that's how it all started?"

"Yes. Well, I'd met him briefly at daddy's office beforehand, but that's... this is where we really met... and I was beastly to him." She laughed, shaking her head at the memory. "There he was trying to protect me and I was so angry, I shouted at him and ruined his new shirts."

They walked on, although Violet sneaked a look back before they turned the corner, heading for Leicester Square. They entered the Corner House and took a seat close to the window, looking out over and at the people hurrying by before the evening wore on and the inevitable raids threatened once more. Violet waited as the Nippy took their order, then she leant forward. "I want to ask you for a favour."

"Anything," said Lizzie earnestly.

Violet smiled. "Well, as I said, I went to see Maxwell today... the solicitor and trustee of the boys' estate."

"Good news?"

"Well... bad really... but good in another way I suppose..." She sighed. "There's not much left..." She caught Lizzie's shocked expression and waved her hand in the air in a gesture of resigned acceptance. "Oh I know, I know... he's probably been milking it for ages but there we are, there's little or nothing I can, or want to, do about it now."

"But what will you do?"

The Nippy arrived with a tray of tea and arranged it on the table. Violet and Lizzie leant back to enable her to place the various items, each one impatient to resume their conversation. "Thank you," said Violet as the girl swept the tray under her arm and departed.

Lizzie leant forward. "What will you do?" she repeated.

Violet arranged the cups and poured out the milk. She opened the teapot and peered inside, replacing the lid. "Needs to brew."

"Violet!" said Lizzie exasperated.

Violet looked her straight in the eye. "He's made me an offer. I allow him to buy the site of the Highgate house and he relinquishes the trusteeship of the estate to me and one other person."

"You would be the trustee... but surely that's what you want?"

"Yes... but..."

"But what Violet?"

Violet grimaced. "All there'd be would be a house. A house which I could occupy until the boys reach their Majority... that's all there is."

"No income?"

"No income."

Lizzie blew out. "But that's terrible, Violet. Terrible... oh you can't possibly let him get away with it."

Violet leant forward and poured the tea. She handed Lizzie her cup and then picked up her own.

She took a swallow of the warm liquid and then put the cup back down on the saucer. "I've had enough Lizzie. I just want to be free to make my own way."

Lizzie examined her for a while. Then she nodded her head. "Yes I suppose he's got you really, hasn't he? If you took it further you'd still be homeless in the meantime, and in the end you'd have no guarantee of getting anything out of him."

"None at all, and being a solicitor he's probably thought of all that and I'd end up with even less by the time the other lawyers had their slice."

Lizzie sighed. "So what do you want me to do?"

Violet laughed. "Well first of all, can I stay with you again tonight?"

"Of course you can, although we'll probably have old Mrs Jones asking more questions... is that all?"

"No. No I was going to ask... you are over twenty-one aren't you?"

"Yes."

"Of course you are. I was going to ask if you'd agree to being the other trustee."

"Of course. What does it involve?"

"Well nothing really, I suppose, once the house is bought... you'd really only have to come to Maxwell's office, when I've found somewhere, and presumably sign some documents."

"Well then the answer is most definitely yes."

Violet put her hand across the table and squeezed Lizzie's. "Thank you darling. Now I suppose I'd better start thinking of where to look."

"Do you want it in London or in the country?"

"Oh in the country, I think. The boys have got used to country life and really... well so have I."

"What about Devon?"

"I'd thought of that, but tempting as it is, I do feel such a long way away from all that I know there... I've decided to visit Jesse and to have a look around Tenterden."

"That sounds splendid. That would give me a chance to come and see you whenever I've got time off, and I've always wanted to meet her...Frank told me so much about her, although I'm bound to say much of it reminded me of mummy."

"I shouldn't wonder at it. That's decided then. I'll go in the morning. Now what shall we have to eat? I'm famished."

***

Once again, Violet found herself arriving unannounced and unexpected in Pudding Cake Lane, only this time as she walked past the other two adjoining cottages, something seemed different. Oh, they looked pretty much the same but... well the gardens of the first two seemed, quite frankly, unkempt, especially when compared to Jesse's little plot. All of which was thrown to the back of her mind as Jesse opened the door and Violet found herself, once more, in that welcome embrace she so treasured.

"Violet, darling! Oh how lovely... oh how are you? Come on in and tell me all that's bin happening." Violet was bundled through the front door and into the well-remembered sitting room. "Sit you down. Cup of tea? Of course you will." Jesse made her way out and into the kitchen and Violet could hear the kettle being filled and placed on the range. 'She looks the same,' Violet thought. 'Older. More stooped. The hair now completely white.' Violet's heart froze at the terrible news she had to give, the effect it would have on this dear, sweet old person.

"Leave the tea for a minute please, Jesse," she called. "I need to talk to you first."

There was silence from the kitchen and then Jesse appeared at the door, a questioning expression on her face. "Bad news?"

"Very bad... please sit by me Jesse."

Jesse crossed and sat beside Violet, who reached out and held her hands in hers. "Jesse darling." Violet felt the tears well up in her eyes. She blinked them back. She needed to remain strong for Jesse this time. "Jesse... they think... they think Frank's dead."

The colour drained from Jesse's face and Violet felt her hands contract within her grasp. "No... how?"

"Executed... there's no actual confirmation but... but a friend thinks he saw it."

"Thinks he saw it?"

"Yes. That's as much as daddy..." Her voice cracked at the mention of her father. "...as much as daddy could find out."

"But surely... can't your father find out anything more... how did he find this out? Frank's in France, isn't he?"

"He is... was. Daddy went to see an old friend, a doctor who wrote to someone in the Red Cross... and all I know is what he wrote to me before... before..." She could say no more, and despite her best intentions she broke into uncontrollable sobs. Jesse reached forward and pulled her into her embrace, holding her there as she cried.

"There there," she soothed. "Jesse's here." She patted the back of Violet's neck.

"I'm sorry Jesse," Violet wailed. "I meant to be strong but..."

"...but some things are too much for a body," whispered Jesse.

Violet sat up, reaching across and into her bag for a handkerchief. She blew her nose and wiped her eyes as best she could. "Sorry," she said again, looking into Jesse's strangely dry eyes.

"There's nothing to be sorry about," Jesse urged, "but..."

"But what?"

"I don't feel that he is dead."

"Don't you? That's funny, Lizzie, that's Florrie's daughter, she felt the same."

"Does she love him?"

Violet nodded her head. "But she's married to her cousin George... by all accounts a terrible mistake."

Jesse looked concerned. "Can your father find out any more?" She started as Violet's eyes grew wider and then filled again. She watched as Violet's face crumpled, speechless with grief, and she opened her arms again to receive her distraught friend. "What... what's happened my love?" she asked gently. She held Violet in her arms as the sobs gradually died down and then released her as she came upright again and dabbed her eyes.

Violet gathered herself together, looking into the concerned eyes of this lovely woman. "Daddy... daddy..."

"Yes dear?"

"Daddy and Alice were both... killed." She summoned up all her emotional strength to finish the sentence. "Daddy and Alice were killed when a bomb hit the house."

"Oh no! Oh you poor dear... oh I'm so sorry."

"I've lost everybody Jesse. Everybody and everything."

"There now my love," said Jesse, reaching forward once more and taking Violet's hands. "You've not lost Jesse and..." Her face grew serious. "The boys. The boys are alright, aren't they?"

Violet saw the fear in Jesse's eyes. "Oh yes. Yes, sorry they're fine. They're at Florrie's."

"Phew. Thank God for that. For a moment I... well you know."

"I know." Violet nodded. "Sorry, I didn't mean to frighten you."

"Never mind me," Jesse chided. "It's you that's the one who's got all the worries. Now a cup of tea and then you can tell old Jesse all that's gone on and we'll decide what's best."

She released Violet's hands, stood and went out to the kitchen.

Violet sat waiting for her to come back, looking around at the well-loved room. She felt at ease in some strange way, almost... almost as if it were some kind of homecoming. Funny, she felt the same way when she was at Florrie's house. No wonder Frank had so loved them both, and how lucky she was to be able to now share his love for these two women. Oh, if only she could share his love... if only they were right and he was still alive. If truth be known, she too could not feel that he was really dead, however much her reason tried to convince her. Somewhere deep down she felt that he was out there... alone and frightened, but out there nevertheless.

Jesse came back into the room with two cups of tea. She handed one to Violet and sat down. "Now tell me all about everything," she said quietly.

Violet told her of Crowe's investigations and of the letter she'd received from her father which had caused her to go up to London with Lizzie in the first place. She told her in halting terms of finding the house destroyed and the subsequent hurried funeral. Jesse sat and listened quietly, without interrupting, letting Violet purge herself of all that was bottled up. She listened as Violet explained all that had occurred and all that was planned following the visit to Maxwell, and as Violet finished that part of the story Jesse held her hand up to stop her.

"Did you notice anything different as you came in?" Jesse asked.

"Well yes... yes now that you mention it." Violet's expression grew puzzled. "Yes I did... it seemed..."

"It seemed as if the two other cottages were untended... unoccupied?"

"Yes. Yes that's it." She looked at Jesse, waiting for her to continue.

"They are empty. Old Mrs Price died, who lived in the end one, and Mrs Brookes, the lady that owned all three, has gone to live with her relatives in Suffolk."

"Does that mean...?"

"That they're up for sale? Yes it does... all three of them in one job lot... that agent in the town... what's his name... the one by the little tea shop on the left before you get to the cobblers. He's dealing with them."

Violet stared at Jesse, joy replacing the top level of her feelings, submerging the pain and horror of the past days. "Why... why don't you see Jesse, that would be perfect... if I could buy all three cottages, then one day the boys would be able to have one each and you would be secure."

"And so would you if you were clever."

"How do you mean?"

Jesse smiled. "I have a life tenancy on this cottage, but I won't live forever. You could arrange the purchase so that when I'm gone you could live here, or at least have this part as your rightful base."

Violet's face dropped. "Oh Jesse, please don't talk like that... please... I've had enough of people dying... enough talk of death for a lifetime."

Jesse reached forward to her. "I'm sorry, my darling. I didn't mean to upset you, but you must realise that much as I love you all, there's as many waiting for me on the other side now as there ever could be here and one day, God willing, I'll meet them all."

Violet stared at this loving woman, envying her, her simple faith. She smiled and patted her hand. "Well not yet please, not for a good long time if you don't mind."

"No fear of that," replied Jesse. "I've far too much to do and it looks as if I've got two lovely boys to help with and our Frank to look forward to again."

Violet looked at her. "Are you sure?"

"About Frank? As sure as I can be." She smiled. "Now when will we go and see the agent?"

***

The lorry slowed down and Frank tensed himself in expectation of yet another road block, yet another chance of being discovered. Since he'd left Father Brault, the journey had seemed interminable.

He lay still in the straw, as all around and above the open crates of hens that hid him from view showered their rain of droppings and chaff down on the canvas that he sheltered beneath. The lorry started off again and he breathed a sigh of relief, raising the canvas a little as the hens settled down on their haunches and huddled into the wind. Father Brault had warned him of the danger, but he had insisted that he must go home first of all. He needed to be on home territory for just a while before he set off once more and perhaps forever for England. Besides, he could not continue to endanger both the Father and the ever-faithful Madame Giry.

Bertrand Gaudet had indeed betrayed them... well not deliberately... more in boastful drunkenness than any malice. But betray them he had, and by all accounts the good Father was extremely lucky to have been able to convince the Germans that he was entirely ignorant... innocent of the nature of his supposed crime. Frank smiled to himself in his bed of straw as he recalled how Madame Giry had described to him, how the Father had flung his hands to his face with shock and horror on being told that he had assisted an English criminal spy to escape arrest.

"How could I have been so silly?" Father Brault had proclaimed. How could he have been unaware of the danger to which he was so unwittingly exposing dear Madame Giry and himself? "Oh, pray God you find this man," he had beseeched.

Frank shook his head ruefully and then regretted doing so as the straw found its way into his collar. He reached back and down, trying to dislodge the irritant. He would need new papers. The priest had confirmed the name of Jacques Menthe to verify his own innocence, and in consequence he was now sought for the murder of poor Jacques. That the priest had not wavered for one moment in his belief in Frank's innocence was a remarkable testament to human trust, but nevertheless they had felt it better to dispose of the papers altogether. That way, at least, Frank could claim another name and hope to throw any captors off the scent.

Where could he get papers? Pierre-Luc. Pierre-Luc would help... if he was there... if he'd got back home... and Marcel. Marcel! What would have happened to him? No, he'd be safe. No one would betray them, would they? They were so well known and liked. He needed papers and then he needed to get to the coast and to England. Would he get a boat? Would any be able to sail out far enough? The Germans must have thought of that... he needed to talk it through with someone who knew the lie of the land.

The lorry slowed down again, and this time, as it stopped and he huddled beneath the canvas, he could hear German voices. Where were they? They'd been travelling for hours now since leaving Montargis, where he'd been taken first of all. They must be close to home by now, surely. His blood froze as the voices came closer and the lorry rocked as somebody climbed up on the side and peered into the load. Frank held his breath. His heart seemed to beat like a drum in his chest. Surely the soldier, for soldier it most certainly was, could hear his heartbeat. "Alles huhn? All are chickens?" the soldier asked.

"Yes, all chickens for the market at Chateauneuf," replied the driver. "Would you like one?"

"Ja. Yes like one," the soldier agreed.

"Come down then and I'll get one out for you," the driver laughed. Frank felt the lorry rock as the soldier jumped off and the driver clambered up in his place. He reached into one of the top boxes and grabbed a chicken by the neck. Frank felt the shower of straw as the rest of the birds in the cage panicked, but took the opportunity to draw breath in the noise and commotion. The driver jumped down from the lorry and handed the fowl to the German, who evidently took it as Frank could hear his guttural thanks. He waited whilst the driver got into the cab and started the engine, tooting his goodbyes to the soldiers as he slipped the vehicle into gear and drove off. 'God that was a close one,' thought Frank. 'How could the driver have remained so cool and calm?'

They drove for about ten minutes before the lorry slowed down again, swung left and stopped. 'What now,' thought Frank. 'Not another check. They couldn't go on defying chance, surely?' The lorry rocked. "Right, we're at Saint-Martin-d'Abbat," said the voice of the driver. "I've just pulled off to the left turning to Germigny-des-Pres and I'm going across the road to get some bread. Whilst I'm gone, you slip out and get away to where you're headed."

"Thank you," Frank called out, above the rising cackling of the hens. "Thank you for everything, and please send a special thank you to Father Brault."

"Good luck," the man replied as he walked off up the road, whistling. Frank lay still for a while, waiting for any attention that there might have been on the lorry to die down. If he was right, there was only one house which could possibly see the lorry and they had gone far enough down the lane for that to be difficult if he got out on the left-hand side. He slid back the canvas and then waited whilst the panicked chickens' noise died down a little. Then he slid the boxes above him aside and carefully lifted the boxes beside him over and on to them, clearing a passage towards the side gate. He crept forward, keeping his head low, and then vaulted quickly over and down to the ground, pressing himself against the side of the lorry, listening out for any sign of his discovery.

None came, and Frank reached back into the lorry and grabbed his bag. He opened it and took out a crumpled straw hat and a rake that had been stored against the side of the vehicle. He pulled the hat down onto his head, slung the bag onto his left shoulder and then shouldered the rake on his right, before marching off down the road, for all the world as if he were a labourer returning from a morning's toil in the fields.

The last time he had walked, or more accurately run along this

road was with Pierre when they had still hoped to escape. He felt
exposed. By his reckoning it was just past the middle of the day and
the sun beat down on him as he walked between familiar fields,
lingering briefly at the bridge and on and into Germigny. He stopped
at the church, gazing at the open door, his thoughts tumbling about
him, veering between joy and fear of his homecoming. For some
reason he felt compelled to go into the church, and as he entered its
cool interior he lent the rake up against the wall. Why did he want to
go in? He was not really religious.

He searched down the rows of pews, seeking to see if there was
anybody present. At this time of day it was highly unlikely. The
priest, Father René, would be at his home in Chateauneuf or away
on some pastoral duty.

Surely he wouldn't be here? But he was, and when he showed
himself, Frank found that he was not surprised.

He walked forward and stood just in front of the front row of pews,
watching the Father at his silent devotions. The priest rose, crossed
himself and bowed to the altar before turning to see Frank standing
there. "Ah. I didn't see you there, my son," he said. "Welcome. Sit as
long as you like."

"Thank you Father René," said Frank quietly as he took a seat on
one of the front pews.

The priest started. "Do I know you my son?"

Frank laughed wryly. "You should do Father. You married my
mother and father right here in this church."

The priest stepped down from the altar steps and crossed to stand
in front of Frank.

He peered down at his face, studying it intently as he stroked his
chin. "No. No, I am afraid that I cannot... I..."

"It is me, Father. Frank."

The priest's hand flew to his mouth. "My God!" He lowered his
voice to a whisper and joined Frank on the pew. "My son, you are
in great danger here. They have been asking after you everywhere."

Frank shook his head. "I expected that Father, but I need papers. I have no papers, and without them I cannot get anywhere."

"But here my son? Why here? This is where they will expect you to come."

Frank smiled. "I will go to the chateau. There are places to hide there that they will never find."

The priest's face registered his horror. "No! No, you cannot go there... of all places, you cannot go there."

"Why not Father?" Frank asked. "Jean-Claude and Marie... they are still there, surely?"

"Yes. Yes, they are still there, but Henri and Nicole are also there and..."

"Well Henri and Nicole will have to leave my house. They have no right."

The priest raised his hands to silence Frank. "Frank, the Germans have commandeered the chateau as their... well as their recreation house... whorehouse more like... and Henri and Nicole are the ones who introduced them to the chateau. They are in effect the hosts."

Frank's mouth fell open. "Do you mean that my house is now a German brothel?"

The priest nodded. "Well not exactly a brothel... not as such... more a sort of club house I understand where... oh Monsieur Frank, you must stay away from there."

Frank stared down at the floor. "Yes. Yes, I can see you are right... but where can I go where I will not endanger my friends." He turned to the priest. "Pierre-Luc. Is he back?"

The priest nodded. "Yes, he came back shortly after the surrender and he is working at his father's farm, although... although there has been some trouble."

"What trouble?"

"Your other friend, Marcel."

"Marcel?"

The priest shook his head sadly. "We are a divided people now,

Frank. You must understand that it will not be possible to trust people that you once knew... fear makes people behave in strange ways."

Frank interrupted him, grabbing his arm and shaking it. "Marcel. What of Marcel?"

Father René cleared his throat. "His family were taken quite early, but he escaped." Frank breathed a sigh of relief, but the priest held his hand up. "No. He escaped with the help of your friend Pierre-Luc, and for a while he hid at their house, but then..." He shook his head and closed his eyes. "But then he was betrayed... somehow he heard the soldiers coming and he fled from the house... thank God, for if he had been found there your friend's family would have been in terrible trouble. He fled into the forest, but he was caught two days later and taken away."

"Where to?"

"Who knows? One of the camps that we hear about perhaps."

Frank looked up at the altar and the priest followed his gaze. "I was there."

"I beg your pardon, my son?"

"I was in one of the camps." He turned to face the priest. "I was taken for a time to a camp where Jews and foreigners were kept..." He tugged the priest's robe. "They are manned by gendarmes of the Etat Francais. Frenchmen betraying Frenchmen."

The priest nodded. "I know. I know my son. Some of those same men are of my parish. I know."

"What am I to do now Father?"

Father René rose. "You need to find somewhere safe to hide, whilst we arrange for new papers. Can you think of anywhere other than the chateau?"

Frank thought for a moment. "Le Mesnil. The empty farmhouse. I could hide there for a while."

"Would that be safe? There are neighbours."

Frank smiled. "The two sisters. They would not harm me. They would not harm anything that Armand had loved."

The priest nodded. "Yes, you are right. You are perfectly safe with them." He stood for a moment, his index finger stroking between his lips as he thought. Then he turned to Frank. "You stay here until dark... you can hide in there until then." He pointed to a door leading into a side room used for storage. "Then go across country to the house. I'll leave here and go by the sisters' house and give them word that you will be there and they can bring you food."

"Thank you Father."

"It is nothing my son."

"Father?"

"Yes my son?"

"Is Leclerc alright?"

"Alright?"

"I mean... he was brought to where I was being held prisoner. Did he get home alright?"

The priest nodded. His face took on a grave expression. "He reported that you had been killed. We all assumed you dead until the Germans started to ask questions about you a month ago."

"No harm done then," Frank laughed. "As you can see, he was wrong."

"The priest nodded. "Yes, but I am afraid that your relatives... your mother was informed of your death."

Frank stood, his mouth open. He shook his head. "My God poor Violet... you mean she has thought me dead for all this time?"

"I'm afraid so my son."

"Leclerc... how did he..."

"The Red Cross wrote to him... came to see him actually, and he told them that you had been executed."

A horrified Frank turned towards the door and would have walked out were it not for the restraining hand of Father René. "No. No, Frank, you must not go out and you must not go near Leclerc!"

"Leclerc?"

The priest dropped his hand and his eyes, then he raised his gaze once more and looked at Frank directly. "Leclerc is... has a lot of contact with the Germans, he..."

"He would never betray me," Frank interjected.

Father René shook his head sadly. "Maybe not. Maybe. I don't know my son. I don't know anymore."

Frank sat slowly down again, his head in his hands. "Thank you Father," he mumbled. "You'd best be on your way. Who can I trust Father?"

The priest placed his hand on Frank's shoulder. "God, my son. Marie and Jean-Claude and your friend Pierre-Luc."

"Can you get word to Pierre-Luc?"

The priest nodded. "Of course I can my son, but for now let us confine things to him and the two sisters... to involve Marie and Jean-Claude at this stage would be to endanger them. Now I must go my son... I will see you again before you go. Where will you go?"

"England... to fight."

The priest smiled. "Bless you, my son. Bless you." He gathered his cassock about himself and left Frank alone.

For a while Frank sat staring at the altar, trying to form his own thoughts, trying even to pray, but then he stood and went across to the storeroom. He opened the door and slipped in. Inside there were several low benches. He placed two together against the door and lay down upon them. Within a few minutes he was asleep.

He awoke after dark, at first unsure of exactly where he was, but then it all flooded back to him and he rose quickly, rearranged the benches and slipped out of the church. He skirted to the left of the square, taking care to keep out of sight, and crossed the road. Now he had to get past the open doors of the cafe. He held his breath and then walked quickly past, his hat pulled well down on his head, his eyes averted. He walked on, his every nerve waiting for the challenge, and when none came he broke into a run until he was clear of the village and could turn right on to the narrow road leading past the farm on the left and on, over the open country, to Le Mesnil.

Arriving at the hamlet he skirted right, past the two sisters' house and on and left to the empty farmhouse. The gates were shut and he left them so and worked his way around the back and alongside the end of the left-hand barn of the typical horseshoe. He pushed at the door and it gave in, creaking open. He felt his way forward in the darkness and across to the open ladder stairs leading up to the mezzanine hay store, mounting the first, second and third steps before stopping and feeling the wall. The square stone moved in his hands and he rocked it gently from side to side, easing it from its bed. It came free and he felt behind and in the hole for the key he knew would be there.

Taking it, he replaced the stone and retreated back down the steps and out into the open night air again. He felt his way around the back of the house to the kitchen door, inserted the key and slipped inside, locking the door. For a long while he just stood, letting his eyes adjust to the dark. To his immediate left was the stone sink, and across, near to the entrance to the animal barns, he could just make out the cooking range. 'No chance of lighting that,' he thought. 'Thank God it's high summer.' He walked towards the front door leading into the open courtyard and peered through the glass. No sign of movement there. He felt along the wall to his right, feeling for the door to the main room and, finding it, fumbled for the latch and opened it.

The room's shutters were closed and he was faced with pitch darkness. Nevertheless, he knew where the furniture should be and he stepped forward into the room, his hands stretched out before him to encounter the old sofa. When he did so, he slid gratefully down onto it and stretched himself along its length. A peace came over him. He wasn't quite home, but he was on home territory at last. He closed his eyes and lay there thinking.

How to get to England? His first thoughts had been to head west for La Rochelle, or anywhere on the Atlantic coast, but the more he saw of how things were in the country, the more he felt that the seaboard would be so tightly guarded as to make any chance of escape from there impossible. East? Could he go east? It was difficult country to cross. Country he did not know well, and he had no doubt the Swiss border would be heavily guarded against just such a venture as his. So south? Through Vichy France to Spain, itself a fascist country but neutral, nonetheless. There was a chance that the border there would not be rigorously policed.

'Yes, that's it,' he thought. 'I'll head for Spain and then ship out to England or Ireland.'

A tapping sound on the kitchen door broke into his thoughts and he got to his feet quickly and quietly, feeling his way back to the open door and across the kitchen. He tapped once on the door and put his ear to it. "Monsieur, it is us," came a rough female voice. He didn't know which one of the sisters it was... come to that he didn't even know their real names... they had always been referred to as the two sisters, ever since their old mother had finally expired. He reached into his pocket, took out the key and opened the door. "Oh Monsieur Frank, it is you," they whispered in unison as they stepped into the room. Baskets were placed on the side and rough hands took hold of him and clasped him in an embrace. Leathery skin grazed his cheeks as kisses were planted on each side, and he was handed over to the sibling for a repeat of the welcome.

"Thank you. Thank you," he whispered.

The baskets were retrieved and thrust forward at him. "Food," one sister croaked.

"Drink," another urged.

Frank took the two baskets, one in each hand, and retreated across to the door to the main room, where he placed them on the floor. He returned and stood before the two women. "Thank you very much for your help," he said with genuine emotion. "I will try not to trouble you... I won't be staying long and I do not want to place you in any danger, so you must not come here too often and... and when you do, make sure you are not seen."

"We understand, Monsieur Frank," said one.

"When you need more of anything leave the basket outside," said the other.

"I will," Frank promised. "I will, and thank you again."

"Goodbye for now monsieur," the first one whispered. She leant forward and clapped him on the upper arm, squeezing it one-handed with a power that many a man would have envied. The animal smell of her body floated up into Frank's nostrils. She turned and the two seemed to merge into one in the darkness as they went through the door and out into the night. Frank sighed as he locked the door behind them. What wonderful people they were. Their lives were lives of unremitting toil and yet... yet they freely gave to him. He shook his head and returned across the room, where he picked up the two baskets, holding each one up to the faint light through the glass of the door to examine the contents.

The first one certainly contained bread, the unmistakable smell of home-made goat's cheese and a rough earthenware pot with a fatty topping which was obviously some sort of terrine or pate. The second, by its weight and the chinking sound it made, contained three or four bottles of dark and strong red wine, a knife and a china cup. 'I've enough here for a good party,' he thought as he retreated back into the main room with his booty and sat down on the sofa to eat.

When he had eaten his fill and dusted the crumbs onto the stone-flagged floor, he curled up on the sofa and fell into a deep sleep, the like of which he had not had in ages.

He awoke when it was daylight outside, as he could see from the sunlight streaming through the cracks in the shutters. He crossed to the window and put his eye to one of the cracks, looking out and south across the fields towards the Loire. Workers were in the fields. It must be late morning, he guessed, judging by the position of the sun. He squinted. He could just make out the dark shapes of the two sisters, standing side by side, their hoes in their hands, swinging in perfect rhythm as they crabbed sideways along the rows. He sighed.

What he wouldn't give to be out there with them in the fresh air, free... free. What was free? He was free from the prison, free from the mine, but he was just as imprisoned. He needed the toilet and he made his way through to the kitchen, across and out of the door leading into the animal barn. He stepped down onto its dirt floor and, taking a long-handled spade from the corner, quickly dug a small hole. He squatted over the hole and relieved himself before carefully covering it over, smoothing out any trace. No point in advertising that he'd been here to all and sundry.

He returned to the kitchen and washed himself quickly but thoroughly at the sink before returning to the living room, where he tore off another hunk of the rough country bread and poured himself another glass of the wine.

There was a noise outside in the courtyard and he stood quickly and peered through the shutters, trying to see what it was. A man passed the gates and disappeared off to the right, behind the thick laurel hedge. Frank whirled around and rushed silently over to the south window, his eye jammed firmly to the crack. His heart leapt with joy as Pierre-Luc rounded the end of the barn, his face one of consternation as he scanned the lifeless building and the firmly closed shutters.

Frank tapped on the window and Pierre-Luc came across. "Is that you Frank?" he called softly.

"Yes, it's me," Frank called back. "Come to the kitchen door." He turned away and rushed through, fumbling in his pocket for the key as he ran, reaching, unlocking and flinging open the door in time for his friend's arrival.

Pierre-Luc stood in the doorway, framed by the light, his friend's face in front of him beaming out his joy. "Frank!" he cried, stepping through and picking him up in a huge bearhug. "Frank, you're really safe."

"Pierre-Luc!" Frank almost shouted. "Put me down you ox. Let me look at you." Pierre-Luc let him go and stood back. The two friends grinned at each other, each taking in the details of the other's appearance and registering the changes. Frank's hands flew to his face in horror as he realised that the door behind his friend was open. He brushed past him. "The door! Oh what fools we are." He slammed it shut and locked it quickly before turning once more to his friend. "Not yet safe I'm afraid, Pierre-Luc. Far from it I'm afraid... I'm a wanted man."

"A criminal spy," Pierre-Luc laughed, "a danger to all society."

Frank grimaced. "A danger to you if you're not careful, my old friend."

Pierre-Luc's face dropped. "Yes. Yes, I'm sorry Frank... it's just that since Father René called last night I couldn't sleep. I just couldn't wait to see you. We thought... we thought you were dead you know."

"I know," said Frank. "At times I've been close to it as well, but... oh come on in. Have you had something to eat? The two sisters brought me food and wine. I've got plenty."

"No thanks," said Pierre-Luc. "God, it's good to see you. I'll have a glass of wine with you though."

"Ah. Well a cup really, and there's only one of them I'm afraid."

"Well we'll share a cup then. We've done that before... between four... not two usually."

The reminder of their fellowship took the top off their joy. Frank sat down, poured some wine into the cup and handed it up to Pierre-Luc. "Have you heard about Marcel?"

"You know he was taken?"

"Yes, Father René told me. Do you know where he is?"

Pierre-Luc shook his head sorrowfully. "No. No I don't, and it's so difficult to find out what's happened to him... or to his family... especially for me."

"Why especially for you?"

"Because somebody betrayed him. They came looking for him at our house... damned near wrecked the place... beat up my father to within an inch of his life before they gave up." He sat down beside

Frank. "If I ask around about Marcel and they find out they'll have the proof they need and... well you know."

Frank nodded. "I know. What can we do?"

"I don't know. The fellowship is broken. You're on the run, I'm afraid of my own shadow, Marcel's God knows where, suffering God knows what..."

"And Gunther?"

"Gunther?"

"Yes Gunther. You mentioned the fellowship... well Gunther is part of that fellowship and he's out there... God knows where..."

"He's here."

The hairs stood up over Frank's whole body. He turned to Pierre-Luc, searching his friend's face for confirmation that what he'd just heard had been said. "Here? What, in Germigny?"

"In Chateauneuf."

"You've spoken to him?"

"No."

Frank wrinkled his brow. "Then how? How do you know he's here and why haven't you spoken with him?"

Pierre-Luc reached forward and held his friend's arm. "Frank, Gunther is a German officer, an adjutant to the kommandant in Chateauneuf... he wears the uniform of our enemies."

"I don't care if he's dressed in bear skins. He's my... our friend..."

"Frank, do you honestly believe that Gunther would betray his country for that friendship?"

Frank stood and walked over to the fireplace. He stood for a while, his back to his friend, before turning slowly to face him. "I'm not asking him to betray his country. I'm asking him to honour a friendship."

Pierre-Luc crossed to his friend. "But don't you see Frank, for him to do that... for him even to acknowledge that friendship would be to... it would be a traitorous act in German eyes."

Frank stared into his friend's eyes, seeing within them the truth, the logic of his words. He dropped his gaze and slowly nodded his head. Pierre-Luc embraced him and the two stood for some time by the empty fireplace before returning to the sofa and their wine.

"How did you get here?" Frank asked.

"By bicycle!" Pierre-Luc smote his forehead. "I left it outside!"

"Oh my God, you didn't. Did you?"

"I did," wailed Pierre-Luc. "I was so excited about seeing you that I left it propped up against the gate." He rushed to the door and tugged at it. It was locked. Frank came and opened it and Pierre-Luc ran out and around the corner as Frank hurriedly shut the door and ran across to peer through the window. He saw Pierre-Luc grab the bike and waited impatiently as he came back around the house and in with the offending machine.

"God Pierre-Luc, if we're all to survive this war we've got to be more careful."

"I know. I'm sorry," said Pierre-Luc.

"Did anybody see you? Was anyone out there?"

"No. No, I don't think so... well only some chap walking his dog."

"What?"

"He'd gone past. Honestly Frank. He was just a man out walking his dog... a Frenchman, not a German."

"Do you know who he was?"

"No."

"What sort of dog?"

"A Labrador. A golden one."

"Oh my God."

"What?" asked Pierre-Luc, horrified at this turn of events.

"Henri has a golden Labrador."

Pierre-Luc raised his hands to his head and rocked from side to side. "Oh hell, what do we do?"

"What can we do? We have to hope that nothing is suspected until at least dark and then perhaps I need to move on."

"Pierre Fabrice has a golden Labrador. It could have been him."

"So do Jacques and Martine at the end. But we can't be sure, can we?"

Pierre-Luc shook his head dejectedly. "No. Oh Frank, I'm sorry. I just didn't think that a bicycle could be such a problem."

Frank smiled. "Never mind. It's done now. Listen old friend, you slip out now and I'll get out tonight and meet you. Where shall we meet?"

Pierre-Luc thought for a bit. "At Marcel's house."

"Marcel's house, surely that's not a good idea."

"It's a perfect idea. The Germans wrecked the place and everybody knows it's abandoned, so nobody will think anyone's in there."

"Right, and it's close to the forest if I need to hide some more or get away quickly." Pierre-Luc turned the bicycle around to point it out of the door and stood back as Frank prepared to open it. "Ready?" said Frank.

"Ready. I'll see you tonight at Marcel's."

"Yes, and in the meantime see if you can ask around about papers."

"No. No, I can't do that," said Pierre-Luc. "If they know you're in the area and I start asking questions like that they'll latch on to it and..."

"Yes, you're right... but I do need papers."

"Father René mentioned it. I bet he's already making enquiries from... well from the Resistance."

"Is there one?" asked Frank.

"Yes... yes, a bit disorganised, but yes, there is... they meet in the forest apparently, but they've not done much yet."

"Good... well I'll see you tonight... and Pierre-Luc?"

"What?"

"Don't bring the bike."

Pierre-Luc smiled apologetically. "I most certainly won't."

Frank pulled open the door and peeped out. Across the fields he could see a horse and cart and two or three figures standing beside it. He poked his head out, looking either way, his hand held out.

Then, satisfied that the coast was clear, he waved Pierre-Luc quickly through and shut the door, locking it almost immediately. He rushed through the house to watch as he came around the side of the house with his bike and disappeared again around the back of the barn. 'Pray God nobody noticed,' Frank thought as he turned back to the sofa and lay down on it.

As the day wore on and nothing untoward happened, his fears subsided and he admonished himself for giving Pierre-Luc such a hard time over his mistake.

It wasn't Pierre-Luc's fault that he found himself flung into this situation; a war zone in his own playground, his friend in danger... and a danger to them both. Nobody had trained any of them to live within this environment. But there were lessons that would have to be learnt fast if they were to survive it.

He dozed through the afternoon, helped by the food and the strong wine, and woke again properly as evening approached. He stretched his limbs on the sofa, shaking the life back into his cramped legs, and swung around to sit with his head held in his hands, rubbing his temples. A noise! A heavy footfall. Instantly his senses were alert.

His head swung round to the window behind him as he detected a scuffling sound in the courtyard beyond. He held his breath, seeking anonymity in silence, and then stood suddenly as the kitchen door crashed open and a second later the front door to the courtyard did likewise. They were in the kitchen and after moments, that seemed like an eternity, the door to the living room crashed open to reveal three helmeted figures. Two of them stepped through and into the room, their rifles pointing at Frank's wildly beating heart.

He didn't hear their voices. All reasonable sequence of senses seemed to desert him in his terror. He watched their mouths move, saw the coldness in their eyes, recognised, just in time, the jerking motion of their weapons and raised his hands in the air in surrender. A strange calm seemed to return to the house and his brain as he watched the two soldiers fan out to either side and the third step into the breached door. Young men, men of his own age, yet in this circumstance alien in all respects.

The soldier in the doorway moved aside and back at a command from behind, and another figure took its place in the doorway, standing just back into the kitchen. He was uniformed, yet different. He wore high boots, into which the trousers were tucked. A smooth, tailored jacket and a high-peaked cap pulled down on the forehead, obscuring any vision of the face. The figure barked a rapid stream of commands at the soldiers and Frank watched, amazed, as the two within his room backed towards the door and out, all the while maintaining their guard. They stepped back through the door and the officer stepped forward, a wicked and heavy-looking pistol in his hand, pointed directly at Frank's chest. Frank heard the heavy sounds of booted feet running around the house and into the barns, heard the crashing of things being flung aside in their ordered search for others.

There was a long silence in the room and then the officer stepped forward and swept the cap off his head. Frank gasped as he stared into Gunther's face. "You're safe..." he blurted, and then his words were cut short by a heavy gloved blow to the side of his face which caused his nose to bleed instantly and profusely. He lowered his hands to stem the flow and was rewarded with another blow, lighter this time but hurtful nonetheless.

"Silence," Gunther barked. "Take off your belt... slowly."

Frank looked into his friend's face, his mind numb with the sense of betrayal. "Gunth..." he started to say, but again the blow fell and his head dropped as he fumbled with his belt, removed it and handed it meekly to Gunther.

"Turn around," Gunther ordered. "Face the fireplace and put your hands behind your back." Frank did so and stood there waiting. He heard Gunther place the gun on the table and then felt him step forward and grab his hands, looping the belt around his wrists and pulling it into a tight, yet strangely not too tight, knot.

Gunther leant close to Frank, pulling on the belt, his mouth close to Frank's ear. "When we get to the river, undo the belt, jump and run down the bank and into the water... understood?"

Frank's heart leapt with joy. He went to turn round and face his friend but Gunther jerked on the belt. "Stay!" he shouted. He lowered his voice to a whisper. "Swim out, and when you hear the gunfire pretend you are hit... do you understand?"

"Yes Gunther... oh I'm so glad you're safe..." The sound of the other soldiers returning empty-handed stifled his words, as did Gunther's cruel yanking of his arms, spinning him around to face him at last. Gunther sneered and raised the gun to Frank's chin. "To think that I once allowed you to call me friend," he screamed in French. He jerked the gun upwards, forcing Frank's head back, then he turned and barked an order to the soldiers. They grabbed hold of Frank and bundled him out of the room through the kitchen, out into the courtyard, through the broken gates and across to an open vehicle standing there, its engine still running, facing towards the river.

The first soldier to reach the vehicle opened the rear door. Gunther stepped forward and grabbed Frank, hurling him into the rear seat before getting in beside him. The soldier shut the door and ran around to the driver's side. Gunther ordered the other two to remain on guard at the house and keep a look-out for other criminals whilst he took the prisoner into Chateauneuf. Then he tapped the driver on the shoulder and motioned for him to move off.

The driver put the vehicle into gear and started to swing, as if to make a three-point turn, before Gunther stopped him, telling him that if he continued on to the river the track would loop around and re-join the main road. The driver nodded and they set off.

As they passed the fields before the levee, Frank looked across at the two black-clad figures hoeing the rows. They looked up briefly, showing no recognition, and then turned back to their work. Frank glanced at Gunther and his look was returned with the faintest nod of recognition before he leant forward and struck up a conversation with the driver. Frank tried to follow their conversation, struggling to recognise words and phrases in the stream of their speech. He gathered, from inferences, that Gunther was making towards him, that he was actually telling the soldier about his former relationship with him. An impression that was reinforced when, during a bout of raucous laughter, obviously at his expense, Frank himself tried to say something and Gunther cuffed him none too lightly on the side of the head with his pistol, drawing yet more blood.

"Stille!" Gunther screamed, before resuming his conversation with the driver. Frank sat there in the back seat, his head ringing, the blood running freely from his nose and temple. They topped the levee and the driver looked around at Gunther with a questioning look on his face. Gunther urged him on and they passed through the belt of trees and arrived at the river, where they turned right, skirting the bank. Frank fumbled discreetly with the belt around his wrists as Gunther leant forward, giving directions to the driver and making comments and references to features as they passed.

The road dipped down and to the left, to avoid a huge Scots pine tree growing on the bank, before rising up again. The driver slowed as the vehicle dipped into the drop and then swung down into the chicane, changing gear at the bottom in order to take the rise. Gunther's boot tapped urgently against Frank's ankle as he flung himself sideways to counteract the tilt of the vehicle. Frank leapt to his feet and jumped over the side of the vehicle, just as the driver pressed down on the accelerator and committed himself to the incline.

Frank rolled clear and stumbled to his feet, hearing as he did Gunther's shout above the roar of the engine. He ran hell for leather down the bank and into the water, forcing his way through the sticky mud and rushes to belly flop into deeper water. His legs kicked and the trousers slid down to his ankles, but still he flailed his arms, striving for yet deeper water and the far bank.

Faintly, he registered that the roar of the engine had died. He heard shouts as he finally got out of his depth and the swirling current took him and swept him from the bank. The crack of pistol fire rang out as, unseen by Frank, Gunther leapt from the vehicle and fired off generally in Frank's direction. The driver struggled to maintain the vehicle at the crest of the rise, reaching forward for the handbrake. Gunther holstered his pistol and ran across and round to the driver's door, screaming at him to pass him his rifle. The driver let go of the handbrake and reached across for his weapon, flinging it out at Gunther as the vehicle started to slide on the loose sand. Gunther grabbed the gun and ran off to one side, where he knelt, looking out at the desperately swimming Frank, now approaching mid-stream.

The driver stabilised the vehicle, pulling hard on the handbrake and leant out to watch as Gunther took careful aim. He fired. Frank heard the shot and waited a split second before he threw up his arms and stopped paddling for a moment. He felt the bullet tear through the water inches from his right side. Feebly he started to swim again, this time with little or no conviction or power. Another shot rang out. He jerked his body in a convulsive movement, taking a deep breath as he did so, before relaxing in a face-down position and letting the current take him.

On the bank, Gunther turned to the driver, a broad smile on his face. He blew on his knuckles, shook them and rubbed them on his lapel in a gesture of triumph. The driver doffed his helmet to him.

In the water, Frank floated face down as the current carried him away downstream towards Chateauneuf. His lungs felt as if they would burst and he began to panic at how he was going to draw breath, but just as it seemed that he could hold on no longer, he felt the current swirl him around as he struck a whirlpool and he allowed himself to roll over in its hold, grabbing a breath as he did so. He paddled beneath the surface with one arm and rolled once more to continue floating face down.

On the bank, Gunther stood and walked back to the vehicle, handing the rifle to the driver. He thought for a moment and then instructed the man to continue on their way, reasoning that they could collect the body as it came past Le Chastaing, where they could retrieve it from the river without having to get wet themselves. Then he leapt into the vehicle, the driver slipped it back into gear and they moved off.

Frank felt himself carried into deeper and more dangerous eddies. He rolled slightly in the water, breathing and listening out for any signs from the bank, and was rewarded by the sound of the vehicle obviously driving away, behind the group of willows that now divided the main stream from the road. It was getting considerably darker now, and within the hour it would be nightfall.

He jack-knifed in the water and removed his trousers from around his lower legs, struggling as he forced the wet cloth over his boots. The river slowed slightly, and with his legs free he struck out as quietly as he could for the bank and the group of trees, reaching them with such considerable effort that, by the time he finally grabbed one of the trailing fronds, he was quite exhausted.

Hauling himself clear of the current, he lay for a moment in the muddy shallows to regain his breath and gather his thoughts. Gunther had not betrayed their friendship! How could he ever have doubted him? Pierre-Luc had been wrong... was wrong. Pierre-Luc! He had to meet Pierre-Luc at Marcel's house. If he didn't show up, Pierre-Luc might go to Le Mesnil looking for him and that would be disastrous... but how to get there? If he cut back along the road, he would have to go past the two guards waiting at the farmhouse. On the other hand, if he cut across country, straight towards Saint Martin, he could avoid any habitation until the outskirts of the village and then cut around and behind the houses and on towards the forest and Marcel's house.

He struggled through the slimy mud of the river's edge and up the bank. He looked down at himself, naked from the waist down, and laughed. If he wasn't careful, indecent exposure would be added to the list of his crimes. Well at least the coating of mud served to cover up the whiteness of his skin. He carefully breasted the rise and struck out across country towards Saint-Martin-d'Abbat.

It was some two-and-a-half hours later when an exhausted, yet still wary Frank, finally approached his old friend's house. The broken gate registered on his mind and he held his breath as he approached the prone door and stepped in, feeling his way forward down the dark entrance passage, smelling the smell of open decay that now pervaded this once happy place. His hands found the open door to Marcel's parents' bedroom off to the right and he swapped walls and felt for the sitting room doorway that he knew would be there. He gained it and peered into the gloom, feeling with his foot for any obstruction.

"Is that you Frank?" Pierre-Luc whispered from the darkness.

"Yes, it's me," Frank breathed back. "Where are you?"

"Over here on the sofa by the fireplace. Mind... there's an upturned chair between here and you." Frank felt his way forward and into the room. His shin crashed against the upturned chair. "Told you," laughed Pierre-Luc. Then, as Frank got closer, "My God, what's that smell?"

Frank grinned in the darkness. "It's me."

"You? What have you been doing?" Frank joined him and sat down beside him on the sofa.

"I've been having swimming lessons."

"Swimming lessons... who from... what on earth are you talking about and... my God, you've got no trousers on!"

Frank laughed and reached out for his friend. He stayed his arm as they both heard a footfall in the passageway, and once more Frank's blood froze as the two of them turned to the open doorway to observe a figure standing there in the gloom.

"Good evening gentlemen," Gunther said.

"Gunther, how did you know I'd come here?" said a relieved Frank.

"I guessed," replied Gunther.

Pierre-Luc put a restraining hand on Frank's arm as he made as if to rise. Frank turned to him in the dark. "No, it's all right, Gunther's already saved me once." He quickly explained to Pierre-Luc all that had happened that eventful evening as Gunther crossed the room, felt for the chair, picked it up and set it upright before sitting on it.

Pierre-Luc listened with undisguised amazement as the story unfolded to its climax in the river. "I saw you in Chateauneuf," he said. "You gave me no hint of recognition."

Gunther laughed, the open laugh of one who was amongst friends and was, at last, at ease. "I can't go around greeting you all as old friends, can I? If I did that we'd all find ourselves in prison, or worse."

"How did you know I was at Le Mesnil?" Frank asked.

"Henri. He telephoned the kommandant's office to say that he'd seen signs of someone being there. I took the call and put two and two together."

"Chump," said Frank, digging Pierre-Luc in the ribs. "You and your bloody bicycle." He turned to Gunther in the dark. "He propped his bike up against the gate when he came to see me there."

Gunther shook his head in the dark. "You'll have to be more careful my friend... but perhaps this way is better."

"What do you mean?" Frank asked.

"I mean that now you are presumed dead. By the way, that was a brilliant performance in the river... for a moment I wondered if I'd actually hit you."

"Was pretty good, wasn't it? I thought I was going to burst at one point, but then the current swirled me around in time to grab a breath." He paused. "Hey, did you have to hit me so hard and so often?"

"Sorry. I had to make it real."

"Oh, you made it real alright... By the way, how did you cover up not finding my body?"

"It was dark and I explained that the current could take a body down or that you might be caught up on some trees. They'll search again in the morning."

Frank's hand flew to his face and he gasped. "I hope they don't find my trousers."

"Your trousers?"

"Yes, I had to take them off in mid-stream, they were preventing me from swimming."

Gunther thought for a moment. "Even if they do, and I think it's highly unlikely, I shouldn't think they'll connect them with you... they'll probably think a courting couple lost them."

"What are we to do Gunther?" Frank asked.

"Do?"

I can't stay here... I need to get to England." He waited in the ensuing silence. "Gunther?"

"Yes. Yes, I heard you," his friend replied. "I was thinking... Frank... Pierre-Luc, I can help you out to an extent but I cannot... I will not become a traitor..."

"We understand," Frank said quietly. "But me being here is a danger to all of us. I need to get away and you are best placed to help me."

"I know," Gunther said firmly. "I know." There was a silence as each man retreated for a moment into his own thoughts. Then Gunther spoke again. "You need to get across to Spain... you'll be interned there for a while, but eventually you'll get back to England, I'm sure."

"I'd figured that way myself, although I had reckoned on getting a boat rather than internment," said Frank. "Only there's one problem."

"What?"

"Weber took my British passport, and without that it would be difficult to prove that I was anything else except an escaping Frenchman with no papers."

"You could tell them who you were."

"Difficult... Leclerc has informed all in England that I am dead... executed by firing squad."

Gunther thought for a moment. "I could get the file. All of them are stored in the Marie... that's now the kommandant's office and I am his adjutant... yes I'll get it... what about other papers? Do you have papers?"

"No. I had the papers of a miner who died."

"A miner?"

"Yes, after prison I was sent to work in the mines near Lille..."

"Ah, that's where you were. I couldn't trace you after Fresnes."

"You looked for me?"

"Of course. You were saying about the miner's papers."

"There was an accident in the mine... we were trapped underground. A miner... I didn't know him... was killed and I took his clothes and papers to escape."

"My God, and here's me thinking my life had been turned upside down," Pierre-Luc interrupted. "Compared to what's befallen you I've had it easy... except for poor old Marcel."

"Marcel?" Gunther asked quickly. "What about Marcel?" He looked around at the broken home, now visible in part to them all as their eyes grew more and more accustomed to the darkness. "I mean, I assumed that he had fled... I know... I know that his parents were sent to Buchenwald, but I could not trace Marcel."

"He was taken and handed over to the Etat Francais. They came looking for him at our house but he escaped into the forest," explained Pierre-Luc. "They found him a couple of days later."

"Then he'll be at one of the camps," said Frank quickly. He turned to Gunther. "Can we get him out before I go? Please Gunther, we won't make any other demands on you but please... you owe..."

"I owe Marcel my life," said Gunther quietly. "But..." His voice became harder. "I will not do anything that might endanger a German life."

"Where are the camps?" Frank asked.

"Pithiviers... that's north of here."

"That's probably the one I was at," said Frank.

"Jargeau... no that's gypsies... and Beaune-la-Rolande. He'll be at Beaune or Pithiviers."

"Can we get him?"

Gunther thought hard. "Maybe... maybe, but it will be risky... you'll have to dress up in German uniforms and you... we could all be shot as spies if we're caught..."

"Well for my part, nothing's different then," Frank laughed.

Gunther stayed silent for a while thinking the thing through whilst the other two deliberately waited for him to take the lead. Eventually he broke the silence. "I will do this one thing and then you, Pierre-Luc, must go back to your farm and stay there. You, Frank, must leave for Spain. I'll get your passport and some French papers. And Marcel... well we'll have to see what we do with him if we find him."

"Thank you Gunther," Frank sighed. "Thank you."

"Yes. Thank you Gunther," repeated Pierre-Luc.

Gunther stood. "Right, you go home now Pierre-Luc and you, Frank, you hide out here. Stay hidden and do not go outside for any reason. I'll come here tomorrow lunchtime and we'll go first to Pithiviers and see if he's there. You'll have to drive, Pierre-Luc, and you'll both have to wear uniforms which I will bring... your rifles will not be loaded... I insist on that."

"Understood," said Frank.

"Me too," said Pierre-Luc.

Gunther held out his hand and the others, each in turn, shook his outstretched hand. "Until lunchtime tomorrow then," Gunther said as he left.

The other two waited as his footsteps receded down the pathway. Frank sat down and Pierre-Luc moved to stand in front of him. "Well, I'd better go then," he said quietly.

"Yes," Frank agreed.

"Who'd have thought it?"

"Pardon?"

"Who'd have thought that Gunther would risk so much for us."

Frank looked up at his friend, his face unseen in the dark. "I have never really thought... only in my darkest despair have I ever thought that he would be otherwise... but I warn you Pierre-Luc, after this we will not be able to rely on him further... without seriously compromising him."

Pierre-Luc nodded his silent agreement. "See you tomorrow then," he said and then, he too, was gone, leaving Frank alone with his thoughts.

He was hungry, hungry and thirsty, but there was nothing here for him. Pierre-Luc had unfortunately not thought to bring anything and neither had Gunther. Perhaps tomorrow. He stretched himself out on the sofa and slept.

Birds singing and a raging thirst, brought on in part by the fact that the only liquid he had drunk in two days had been wine, woke him. He stirred and winced as the sofa's broken springs dug into his aching back. He stood. What time was it? He crossed to the window and looked out of its broken panes. Ten... it must be ten at least. Good God, he'd slept here in total exposure, the doors open, the windows broken.

Thank goodness nobody had thought to look inside the shattered and defiled house. He looked around himself, shivering in disgust at the graffiti on the walls, the wreckage of what had once been a happy home in which he and all his friends had found comfort and love. What would Gunther think when he saw what his fellow countrymen had done? How would he rationalise his own feelings towards this kind of behaviour?

He wandered out into the passageway, idly looking into the rubbish-strewn bedroom. A pair of crumpled trousers lay on the floor beside the upturned bed, and he bent and picked them up. He held them against himself, checking for length. Too short by far, but better than nothing. He shook them inside out to remove unwanted beasts and then pulled them on before making his way out and into the kitchen area. Anything to eat or drink? He opened every cupboard but nothing remained within them and the tap, when he turned it, merely dribbled brown filthy liquid. 'Please Gunther or Pierre-Luc, think to bring me some food,' he thought.

He returned to the lounge and sat down to wait, daydreaming of home, of the chateau and of England. He must somehow get word to Violet that he was alive. How? Gunther could not risk trying to make contact with England. Keeping Gunther alive and beyond suspicion was in the best interests of them all now... and in the years to come. No, it would have to wait until he got to Spain.

Marcel. They were going to get Marcel. The fellowship should, with luck, be complete by the end of the day. He sat back and waited for his friends to arrive.

A whistle announced Pierre-Luc's arrival. "Did anyone see you?" Frank asked as his friend entered the house.

Pierre-Luc laughed. "No, not this time. I was very careful, and I walked here."

"Is that for me?" said Frank, indicating the basket.

"Yes. Yes, food and... well not wine... fresh milk and some trousers, although I see you've kitted yourself out already."

"Thank you my friend," said Frank, reaching out for the basket. "I'm famished... and thirsty too." He grabbed the small milk churn, flipped off the lid and drank deeply, luxuriating in its smooth coolness. He lowered the tin, breathing deeply as he wiped the white liquid from his stubble. "That's wonderful. You are clever to think of this."

"I didn't... well mother thought of it first... I told my parents." He looked into Frank's alarmed face. "It's alright... I didn't mention Gunther. They send their love. I thought of the trousers... and come to think of it, you won't really be needing them when Gunther arrives, will you?"

Frank nodded his acceptance and agreement. "Thanks anyway," he said, rummaging around in the basket and coming out with a large hunk of home-cured ham. He broke off a chunk and chewed on it, rolling his eyes heavenward in sheer pleasure.

"I also thought of this..." Pierre-Luc reached in his pocket and brought out a razor and a small bar of soap. "You'll need to shave if you're to impersonate a German soldier."

"Good thinking," said Frank, rising. "I'd better do that straight away." He stopped. "There's no water in the tap."

"Wait. I'll fill up a bowl from the butt outside."

"Be careful."

"I will." Pierre-Luc ran out into the kitchen and grabbed a battered pewter mixing bowl. Then he went to the door and peeked out carefully before running around and filling the bowl, returning just as Frank finished off the ham and took a last, grateful swig from the milk. He handed the bowl to Frank, who quickly made a lather and used the razor to scrape off his beard with the aid of a section of broken mirror.

The sound of an engine outside and a vehicle door slamming sent them into a momentary panic until Pierre-Luc verified that it was, in fact, Gunther. "Did anyone see you?" Frank asked as he walked in.

"No, but you'd better hurry. Ah, good you've shaved. Put this lot on quickly, both of you." He threw two bundles of clothing, two pairs of boots and two helmets onto the sofa. "Quick, the car's outside and I don't really want to attract attention. Frank and Pierre-Luc quickly stripped off and dragged on the unfamiliar uniforms. They forced on the unyielding boots and buckled them up over the trousers, then turned to Gunther for inspection. He looked them up and down. "Right, helmets on, let's go." Pierre-Luc reached down for his clothes, picked them up and placed them in a neat pile on the chair. Frank glanced up at Gunther and smiled. "Would you like to leave any other messages?" Gunther asked sweetly.

"What?"

"Your clothes, you clot." Gunther grabbed the clothing and handed it back to Pierre-Luc before tipping the chair back on its side. Pierre-Luc watched him, puzzled for a moment, and then realised his mistake. Frank shook his head, laughing.

The road was clear and there was no sign of life in any direction as they got into the vehicle, with Pierre-Luc driving, Frank in the front passenger seat and Gunther seated grandly in the rear.

"Do you know the way?" Gunther asked.

"Which one are we going to?"

"Pithiviers first and then, if he's not there, Beaune," said Gunther.

"Yes, if we skirt through and towards Bellegarde, we can turn off and head through the forest, through Nibelle and Chambon."

"Let's get going then." Gunther tapped the seat in front of him with his hand and Pierre-Luc, hesitantly at first, but then with increasing skill, drove off north.

They chatted as they drove, only ceasing their conversation as they approached checkpoints, through which they were waved through with the minimum of fuss. Gunther told them of where he had been in the early parts of the war, and it turned out that he had been within a few miles, if not closer, to where Pierre-Luc and Marcel must have been prior to the retreat.

"I'm lucky to be here," said Gunther.

"Not as lucky as we feel to have you here," laughed Frank.

"No really. I could have been sent... could still be I suppose, to Russia."

"Russia?" asked Frank incredulous.

Pierre-Luc looked across at his friend. "You don't know, do you?"

"Know what?"

"We invaded Russia last weekend," said Gunther.

"What?"

"You heard."

"But you must be mad," Frank laughed "We... the French that is, tried it once... it can't be done."

"By all accounts it is being done... they've reached Smolensk already."

"Good God!" Frank turned around to face his friend. "What do you think with all of this Gunther... how do you reconcile it all?"

"I... I can't reconcile it all Frank. I'm here and my knowledge of French and this area may keep me here, if I'm lucky, until it's all over."

"And how will it end, Gunther?" Frank asked quietly, fixing his friend in his gaze.

Gunther returned his look. His eyes, locked on to his friends, wavered momentarily. He shook his head. "I don't know Frank. I hope it ends with us all united as one people, but I fear not... I fear that it may divide us all even more."

"Even us?"

"Even us." There was a long silence, broken by Gunther. "But not yet... we have work to do."

They travelled in silence for a long while after that, until the forest started to break up and hint at the flat farmlands beyond. Before the main Paris road they turned off left, on to a bumpy minor road. Frank closed his eyes and tried to imagine his journey with Annette. "Left again here," Gunther ordered, and Pierre-Luc swung the vehicle left again on to an unmade track.

"This is where I was," Frank whispered.

"Here?"

"I'm almost sure."

"Will they recognise you?"

"No, I shouldn't think so. When I was here there were German guards under a Major Mundt... nice chap. I left as the French took over."

The forest opened out and the camp lay before them in the large clearing, almost exactly as Frank remembered it, although now the open area between the rows of huts was hidden from their view by a long guard hut with an open veranda, set just to the left of the main gates. Pierre-Luc slowed down and stopped beside the small flight of stairs leading up and into the hut.

"Now," said Gunther. "Frank and I will go in and demand that they deliver up the traitor, Marcel Fleisch, to us for questioning. Frank, you try to say nothing, and if you do have to say anything try and speak with a heavy German accent. You, Pierre-Luc, remain in the car with the engine off... pretend to sleep but keep alert. Open the door for me, Frank, and hand me that clipboard and pen."

Frank got out. He marched around and opened the door for Gunther, saluting him as he dismounted. A guard standing at the top of the steps drew himself to attention and saluted as Gunther, followed by Frank, mounted and stepped inside the open door to a small room with a counter dividing the space and a door leading off in either direction.

"I wish to see the officer in charge," Gunther demanded of a gendarme, sitting with his back to them, apparently studying a sheaf of papers.

The man turned around slowly, stood and walked across to the counter, looking across at Gunther with undisguised insolence. "Who wants to see him?"

Gunther stared at the man as he languidly removed his gloves. He slapped them and the clipboard on the counter top. "Leutnant Schmidt, adjutant to the kommandant at Chateauneuf-sur-Loire. Please inform your superior immediately that I wish to see him on a matter of urgent security."

The gendarme raised his eyebrows. "Wait here Leutnant, and I'll ask if he will see you." He buttoned up his open tunic, reached down to release the catch and stepped through the counter into the reception area. Gunther stepped aside as he came through and watched as the man adjusted himself and ran his hand over his hair before knocking on the door to the left of the counter.

There was a muffled "Enter" from behind the door and the gendarme opened it and stepped through, shutting it firmly. Gunther turned to Frank and smiled weakly. Frank returned the look. Gunther shrugged his shoulders, stepped forward to the door, and with one last glance back at Frank, nodding for him to remain. He turned the handle and went in.

The gendarme turned to face him. "Monsieur... Leutnant..." he spluttered.

Gunther held his hand up to silence him and looked beyond him at the officer sitting at his desk, a cigarette dangling from his lips. "Good day," said Gunther, side-stepping the gendarme.

"Capitaine Blondel," said the gendarme, "I..."

"That will be all, Lecoq," said the Capitaine as he removed the cigarette from his mouth, stubbed it into the nearly full ash tray on the desk and rose to his feet.

"Err... yes sir," said the gendarme. His look of annoyance was returned by a stony stare as Gunther stepped aside to allow him to leave, and then waited for the door to close.

"My name is Leutnant Schmidt, adjutant to the kommandant at Chateauneuf," he volunteered, saluting briefly.

The Frenchman returned the salute and sat back down again, reaching down and into the desk drawer for a packet of cigarettes. "Capitaine Serge Blondel," he said, indicating the chair in front of the desk. He offered the opened cigarette packet to Gunther.

"No thank you, I don't," said Gunther, sitting.

The Capitaine raised his eyebrows and cocked his head slightly to one side. "How can we help you, Leutnant Schmidt?" he asked, rocking back in his chair as he lit the cigarette, blowing a cloud of smoke into the air above both their heads.

Gunther's nose wrinkled. "We have received news of the possibility of certain individuals making contact with foreign agents, or having information which could lead to the discovery and capture of those agents."

The Frenchman leant forward and placed his hands on the desk, taking a proper interest in proceedings at last. "Really? How can we be of help?"

"One of the names we have is of a person that we believe might be held here and we wish to... to interview him as soon as possible."

"Here? But these are only Jews."

"This person is a Jew... he was a collaborator of the foreign agent."

"Name?"

"Fleisch... Marcel Fleisch."

The Capitaine rose in his chair and stood behind the desk. "Did you say Fleisch?"

"I did," said Gunther, slightly taken aback by this unexpected reaction to his mentioning of Marcel's name, but determined to retain the appearance of aloof authority.

The Capitaine came around the desk and clapped Gunther on the shoulder. "Well, I can certainly help you with the location of this scum, but I am not so certain that he will be much use to you."

"How do you mean?" said Gunther, rising.

The man smiled. He reached past Gunther and took his hat off the peg, clapping it to his head. "Come with me," he said, turning to the door and stepping out into the reception area. Gunther followed him.

As the office door opened, Frank, who had been standing quietly by the open door, moved aside and stood to attention. His blood froze as the Capitaine swept past him and through the open door, thankfully taking no particular notice of this humble German soldier. Gunther came out of the office hard on the man's heels. He paused briefly at the door and looked across at Frank's white face. Frank grimaced slightly and shook his head almost imperceptibly from side to side in a warning.

Gunther stepped to the door and down to the bottom step. Frank followed and stood on the step above him as Gunther carefully pulled his gloves on to his hands.

"It's Serge Blondel," Frank whispered.

"Who?" Gunther whispered back out of the corner of his mouth.

"Serge Blondel. We went to school with him. He was the school bully... we crossed swords several times. He'll know Pierre-Luc and me."

"This way Leutnant," called Blondel, motioning Gunther across the front of the guard hut towards the main gates.

"A moment please Capitaine," Gunther called back. "Follow me," he whispered to Frank. The two of them walked to the vehicle they had come in, where Pierre-Luc, feigning sleep as he had been ordered, made no response. Gunther cuffed him roughly over the head, screaming a string of invective at the startled man, all of which was, of course, totally unintelligible to him. Pierre-Luc sat up quickly, his face white and shocked, as Gunther stood back from the vehicle, placing himself so that his back faced directly back towards the figure of Blondel, standing not ten metres away. "That's Serge Blondel," Gunther whispered. "He doesn't know me, but he knows you and Frank. Keep your helmet on and avoid any direct eye contact with him." He turned and marched across to Blondel, followed by Frank, trying to look as military as possible yet remain unobtrusive.

In the car, Pierre-Luc scrambled to put his helmet back on his head before sitting bolt upright in the driver's seat and staring into distant space.

"Sorry to keep you Capitaine," said Gunther as they approached. "I cannot have my driver lolling about in such a fashion. It is demeaning."

"Quite. Quite," said Blondel, with barely disguised amusement. "Errr... this way." He indicated the main gates. A guard rushed forward from the inner gates and opened a small wicket gate in the outer gates, through which Blondel ushered Gunther before stepping through himself.

They marched across the fifteen-metre gap between the inner and the outer wire, with Frank and the French guard following on behind. A guard hut had been positioned inside the inner wire, just off to the right of the gates, obscuring Frank's vision of any of the inner compound off to the right of centre. But as he marched forward, Frank looked up and beyond the wire at the well-remembered lines of huts, many of which he had helped to erect.

Long lines of tables were set in front of the huts, and at these tables inmates sat or stood alternately, sewing the great mounds of serge-cut patterns heaped in the centre of each table. As the second wicket gate was flung open some broke off from their work to glance around, and for a fleeting second Frank gazed into their lines of vacant, anonymous eyes before a shout from several of the guards swung their heads back to their tasks.

"Uniforms for the German army," Blondel announced proudly. "About the only thing Jews are good for. Now Fleisch, you were asking after."

"Yes. Marcel Fleisch."

"Well he's here, but... well see for yourself Leutnant." He walked on past the hut and pointed off to the right, out of their field of vision. Gunther moved forward and looked in the direction he was pointing.

Two bodies swung from a crude scaffold, swaying gently in the warm summer breeze, naked from the waist up, their bare feet pointing to the ground. Gunther looked from them to the smiling face of the Frenchman, an enquiring look on his face. "Fleisch?"

The man laughed openly. "Yes, Fleisch... funny eh? Fleisch is flesh in German and that's all he is now."

Gunther stood looking at the man, trying to resist the urge to kill him there and then. Frank moved forward to stand beside him and look over at the bodies. He gagged and his stomach lurched, but he managed to retain his composure, looking away from the Capitaine back at the bodies. "Are you sure it's him?" Gunther asked quietly.

"Check for yourself. Would you recognise him?" said Blondel.

"Not personally," Gunther replied. "I've seen photographs."

"Check then," Blondel said, ushering Gunther over towards the bodies.

Gunther turned away and took a step forward. He paused and stepped back and over to Blondel, tucking his clipboard under his arm. "What caused this?"

"Insubordination. The other criminal was being punished, and your man Fleisch, a constant troublemaker, struck one of my officers..."

Frank noticed a warning twitch on the side of Gunther's face. "I had to make an example if discipline was not to be undermined."

Gunther stared at him, aware that his face muscle was twitching, yet powerless to prevent it. He drew himself erect. "Your actions may have jeopardised a very serious enquiry."

Blondel opened his arms and his face lost the triumphant look, taking on one of hurt pride. "I am sorry, Leutnant... how could we have known?"

Gunther continued to stare at him, aware now that the man was beginning to feel uncomfortable. Frank coughed behind him and he forced himself to avert his gaze. "Yes... yes, I think I should examine the body." He turned, gathered himself together and marched over to the scaffold, with Frank following close behind. Blondel watched them for a moment and then shook his head and retreated back to the guard hut.

Gunther walked slowly up to the bodies. The one on the left, to which Gunther concentrated his gaze, was an older man, his scrawny frame barely now even supporting the loose cotton trousers that hung almost down to his shrunken buttocks. Gunther stared long and hard at the poor wretch, unwilling... dreading his inspection of the second body. Finally, he tore his look away from the old man to the other body and, as it swung around, his hand involuntarily flew to his mouth as the tortured dead face of Marcel stared sightlessly down at them. He sensed that Frank was immediately beside and just behind him, but could not bring himself to turn to him or even speak. Marcel's head was cocked to one side, and from the bulging eyes, swollen tongue and the terrible rope burns to his neck, it was obvious that this was no breakneck hanging and that their friend had been hauled up and left to suffocate.

Frank stood beside his best friend, staring up at the body of the dear companion of their youth. "Thank God Pierre-Luc cannot see this," he whispered. "He would go berserk."

"I would like to myself," Gunther whispered back. The body swung again in the breeze, revealing its back, stripped raw, cut to the bone from the scourging he had received before death.

"Please," urged Frank. "Please don't do anything stupid."

"I'm not going to. Don't worry. Not now at least."

Frank glanced back into the camp. Along to their left the lines of huts marched towards the back of the compound, and just behind what he assumed was the cooking hut he could just see the horseshoe of huts occupied now by the French guards. "Could you do one more thing for me Gunther?" he asked.

"What?"

"Could you add another name to your list?"

Gunther turned and looked into Frank's eyes. "Are you serious?"

"Yes I am. There is someone... someone who was here. The thought of her being at the mercy of these animals is more than I can bear."

"Her?"

"Annette Winklesdorf."

Gunther retrieved the clipboard that was tucked under his arm. He took out his pen and wrote her name quickly, below that of Marcel. "Will she recognise you?"

"Yes... yes, I'm sure she will."

"Dressed like that?"

"Yes... probably... maybe... I don't know."

"Will she give us away?"

Frank thought for a moment. "No, I think she'll probably be less risk than Marcel... than Marcel would have been. She taught me how to hold my tongue."

Gunther smiled briefly. "Come on then." He glanced up at Marcel, looked down at the ground for a moment and then back up at their dead friend. "Shalom Marcel," he whispered, and Frank echoed his parting.

They marched back around the hut to where Blondel awaited them. "Was it him?"

"Yes. A pity. His information could have been very useful."

"I'm sorry," said Blondel. "How could I have known?"

"No matter," said Gunther. "Perhaps though, there is some other way that you may be able to assist?"

"Of course. How?"

Gunther consulted his clipboard. He appeared to study it carefully for a while, then he turned and looked directly at the enquiring Blondel. "The dead man had an accomplice, an associate, one..." He studied the clipboard again. "Annette Winklesdorf. Do you know of this woman's whereabouts? Our information is that she was here, but that she may have been destined for onward transportation."

Blondel looked uncomfortable. 'He knows her,' thought Frank. "Annette Winklesdorf. Annette Winklesdorf," Blondel mused. He turned to the guard standing by the open door of the hut. "Do we have such a person?"

The guard smiled. "Yes, of course we do Cap..." His words and smile faded in the face of his superior's obvious fury.

Blondel recovered his composure. He turned to Gunther. "Well, it would appear that we do have a woman by that name."

"Good," said Gunther. "Would you please arrange for her to accompany us..."

"Accompany you?"

"Yes. Is there a problem with that? We will wish to question her and we may need to use her to identify some others." Blondel's face fell. "Is there a problem with this?" Gunther said seriously. "I do, of course, have the kommandant's authority for this." Blondel stared at Gunther, the workings of his mind showing clearly on his face. Gunther held his gaze, unwavering. Blondel's eyes flickered from his to Frank's face, standing just behind Gunther. A puzzled frown crossed his brow for a moment. Frank quailed, and Gunther, sensing rather than seeing the direction of Blondel's gaze, brought his attention back to the matter in hand. "Capitaine Blondel," he urged. "The woman?"

"Yes... yes of course, Leutnant Schmidt." He turned to the guard.

"Where is the woman Winklesdorf?"

The guard smiled at him. "Well you should..."

"Fetch her here immediately," Blondel almost shouted.

"Yes sir," said the guard, clearly shaken. He came down from within the hut and, to the astonishment of Frank and Gunther, turned left and went out of the main gates and left again, outside the inner perimeter wire and out of sight.

"Shall we wait out by the motor car?" Gunther asked.

Blondel turned to him. "Yes. Yes, that would probably be better... or you could wait in my office."

"Yes... in your office... I think that would be better," said Gunther.

"Right then, this way," said Blondel, leading the way through the wicket gates and across to his office. Gunther followed at a respectable distance.

"Stand by the car," he whispered to Frank as he prepared to mount the steps. Frank nodded his understanding and marched straight across and around to the other side of the motor car where he stood, roughly to attention.

Pierre-Luc sat still in the driver's seat, his hands on the steering wheel, staring almost directly ahead.

"What's going on?" he whispered out of the corner of his mouth. "Where's Marcel?"

"He's... he's not here... don't look at me."

"Not here... then why are we waiting? Why can't we get out of here? If Serge Blondel recognises either of us we're done for."

"I know. I know," Frank whispered urgently, "but there is someone else."

"Who?"

"A girl I met when I was here." Pierre-Luc turned towards Frank, a look of astonishment on his face. "Don't look at me," Frank hissed.

"Sorry," said Pierre-Luc. "It's just that... well it must have been a pretty momentous meeting for us all to be risking our lives for it."

Frank smiled in spite of himself. "It was. By the way she may recognise me... I hope not, but if she does and she says the wrong thing it could get a bit sticky."

"What do you suggest?" Pierre-Luc asked.

"When Gunther brings her towards the car, start the engine and be prepared to drive like hell."

Pierre-Luc shook his head. "Drive like hell, he says. Drive to hell more like... how far do you think we'd get?"

"Shhh. Here she comes," Frank hissed. He kept his face looking forward, but his eyes followed the progress of the guard coming out through the wicket gate, leading a woman. It was Annette. The same eyes. Wisps of the same hair trailing from her headscarf. A loose cotton smock dress and rope sandals distinguishing her from the other prisoners.

Pierre-Luc started the engine and the sound of it roaring into life caused her to look over. She spoke to the guard. He laughed and pushed her towards the hut. She stumbled but picked herself up, her dark eyes flashing defiance at the two German soldiers waiting to carry her away. She reached the bottom of the steps and put her foot on the first rung. The guard put his hand in the small of her back and prepared to push her on and up but stopped as Gunther, with Blondel behind him, appeared at the top of the steps.

"Are you Annette Winklesdorf?" Gunther demanded in a menacing voice.

"Who wants to know?" Annette called up, before the guard behind cuffed her sideways to fall on the ground. She spun around on her knees and knelt there in the mud, looking up as Gunther descended the steps, casually taking off his gloves. He walked across to her and swiped her across the face, causing her to reel back.

"Yes that's her," Blondel shouted from the top step.

Gunther glanced back at him and then down at the woman at his feet. "Get up Jewess," he sneered. "We have some matters to discuss with you." Annette painfully got to her feet, the look of defiance now tempered with fear.

Her eyes flew beyond Gunther to the figure of Blondel, standing in the open doorway at the top step. "What now Blondel?" she screamed.

"Don't look at me bitch," he yelled back, "you're theirs now."

Gunther raised his hand for silence. "I am Leutnant Schmidt, adjutant to the kommandant at Chateauneuf. You will come with me." Annette, misinterpreting his requirements, made as if to mount the steps into the offices. "No... no, you will get into the motor car... we are taking you for questioning." Annette threw a stricken glance up at the cruelly smiling face of Blondel. She looked across at the equally unsympathetic grin of the other guard and then up into Gunther's determined face. "In the car if you please... now!" he shouted.

She retreated from the steps, looked across at the vehicle and, as Frank held open the door, started to walk slowly, as if in a dream, all the while looking back and beyond the wire to the compound which had been her prison and home for so long.

"Thank you Capitaine Blondel," Gunther said, saluting. "We will return the woman to you when we have extracted all the information we require from her."

Blondel sloppily returned the salute. He laughed loudly. "I expect when you have finished with her, she'll not be fit for much. Chuck the Jewess in the Loire for all I care."

Gunther smiled. "Maybe so. Maybe so." He turned and walked towards the motor car, grabbing Annette's arm as he did so, steering her none too gently around to the open door before forcing her in and getting in himself. Frank saluted him briefly and then jumped in the front passenger seat.

Pierre-Luc put the vehicle in gear and they moved off, the three men staring forward impassively whilst Annette looked around, panic showing clearly on her face.

Suddenly she leapt to her feet and vaulted over the open side before Gunther could stop her. Pierre-Luc jammed on the brakes as

Gunther rose to his feet, drawing his pistol from its holster. "Halt or I shoot," he cried to the fleeing girl.

Annette stopped in her tracks. Across to her right, the French guard had raised his rifle and was aiming it at her as Blondel cursed and pushed him aside, rushing down the steps towards her. She looked back at the determined figure of Gunther, his gun pointing directly at her. Wildly she searched for shelter, but none was to be found. The belt of trees seemed so far away. She relaxed. The resigned relaxation of someone who knows that they are beaten and that all hope is lost.

"Get her," hissed Gunther, and Frank, who had been kneeling in his seat looking back, dismounted and ran back towards her. He arrived at the same time as Blondel, who ignored him and swiped his clenched fist in a long arc, connecting with Annette's jaw, sending her reeling back, senseless, into Frank's arms. Frank grabbed her as she fell backwards, pinioning her.

He went to turn around with his catch but Blondel seized the opportunity to swing one more vicious punch at her. Frank saw it coming and swung her away from the blow, which sailed past in thin air. "Leave her," he growled at the furious Frenchman. "Leave her alone."

Blondel looked up into his face, startled both by the ferocity of his tone and the fact that he had spoken in French. Their eyes made contact briefly before Frank swung Annette aside, turned his back and dragged her back across to the car. He lifted her bodily up and into the rear seat compartment, where Gunther grabbed her and held her down whilst he ran around and got back in the passenger seat. "Go!" he yelled, his voice all but lost in the roar of the engine as Pierre-Luc put his foot down.

Behind them, a red-faced Blondel scratched his head, standing deep in thought as the car sped off.

"Did he recognise you?" Gunther asked.

"I don't know," Frank shouted back. "What's he doing now?"

Gunther glanced back. "He's just standing there. How long since he last saw you?"

"Properly... about five years I suppose, but I've seen him around from time to time."

"Not in a German uniform though," interrupted Pierre-Luc.

"No, not in a German uniform... I reckon he hasn't made the connection yet, but he's troubled... damn!"

"Yes," agreed Gunther. "Damn. But if I'd have gone after her, they would have thought that even stranger."

"How is she?" Frank asked.

Gunther looked at Annette slumped in the seat beside him. "I think she caught a hell of a blow on her chin. She seems unconscious... she's stirring... look, when you get to the end of the track, turn left instead of right. We'll go back by another route."

"Which way?" Pierre-Luc asked.

"Go up towards Pithiviers and then right through Boynes and Beaune-la-Rolande."

"Are we going to look for Marcel at Beaune?" Pierre-Luc asked.

Frank shot a look back at Gunther, who shook his head sadly. "No Pierre-Luc... there's no point," Frank said quietly to his friend, resting his hand on his arm.

"What do you mean there's no point?" asked Pierre-Luc, staring across at Frank's concerned face and swerving the vehicle across the road as he did so.

"Watch out," Gunther yelled from the rear and Pierre-Luc wrenched the car back into a line, narrowly avoiding driving into the ditch.

"Look, pull up over there and pull down that track to the trees," he said softly, his hand resting on Pierre-Luc's shoulder.

"Where?"

"There. Just there... see?" He pointed ahead.

"Yes, just here," said Frank. "Pull right into the trees and out of sight."

Pierre-Luc swung the car into the track. "What's up with you two?" he asked, looking from face to face whilst trying to control the car on the bumpy surface.

"Just up here... right that'll do," said Gunther. "Cut the engine for a moment."

Pierre-Luc turned off the engine and sat around in his seat, looking at each one of his friends in turn. "Tell me," he whispered.

Frank swallowed. He cleared his throat. "Marcel is dead."

"Dead? Where... how?"

"Back there," said Gunther.

Pierre-Luc's face swivelled from Frank's to his. He shook his head. "Is that what they told you... how can you believe them?"

"We don't believe them... we saw it," Frank said quietly.

"You saw it... well why didn't... I never heard anything."

"He was dead when we got there. We saw his body... hanging from a rope."

"Are you sure? It could have been someone else..."

Frank looked into his friend's eyes and held his bewildered look. He shook his head slowly, feeling, at last, the tears coming into his own eyes. "It was Marcel," he whispered.

Pierre-Luc swung around to Gunther, seeking confirmation and finding it in his sorrowful expression. "Well... why... why did you leave him there? We should still have fetched him home... we shouldn't..."

"We couldn't Pierre-Luc... we couldn't. Alive, we had a reason to take him, but dead... there's no story we could invent which would make it..."

"We couldn't... we just couldn't... don't you understand?" said Frank.

Pierre-Luc shook his head. "You got that woman, whoever she is."

"Yes, we got that woman... Annette," said Frank. "We got her to save her from what... we had to get her out of there when we saw..."

Pierre-Luc's eyes opened wide and the tears started. "They hurt him... tortured him, didn't they? Blondel... Blondel always hated him... I'll kill him..."

"No, Pierre-Luc, I will," said Gunther from the back seat, with an edge in his voice that quite shocked his two friends.

A movement from Annette distracted their attention. She moaned and held her head in her hands. Frank looked at Gunther and then got out of the car and walked to the door and opened it. Annette looked up blearily at this German soldier standing beside the motor car. She flashed a look back to the officer sitting beside her, the same officer who had been the first to strike her. She rubbed her eyes. "So you've brought me here to shoot me, have you?" she said, looking around and out to the trees beyond. She reached forward and put her foot out on the running board to dismount.

Frank took his helmet off. "We haven't come to shoot you Annette," he said softly.

Annette looked up into his face. Her brow furrowed. She looked down at his uniform and then back up and into his eyes as he discarded his helmet, throwing it onto the car seat. "F... Frank?"

"Yes... it's me," he said laughing, holding out his hands.

She turned back into the car, looking at Pierre-Luc, who was smiling too, despite the tears in his eyes. 'Why was the driver crying,' she thought. She turned back to Frank. He too had tears in his eyes. "Why have you all been crying?" she asked.

Frank nodded his head. "Annette... Annette, we didn't really come for you... I didn't even know until we got to the camp that it was the one I'd been at."

Annette looked at Frank, incomprehension showing on her face. "Well, why did you come?" She turned to Gunther, remembering... "You are Germans... aren't you?" She turned back to Frank. "Are you... is this all...?"

Frank reached forward and took her hand gently, leading her out of the vehicle. "Annette," he said in a soothing voice, "you remember I told you I came from England but that I lived in France?" She nodded and he continued. "Well remember, I told you of my friends at the chateau?" She nodded again. "We were four friends... me... Pierre-Luc there, driving... Gunther, in the back seat... and Marcel."

"Gunther?"

"Yes Annette, Gunther... he's a German officer... he's my friend and..."

"...and he's just risked his life... all our lives... to rescue you from Blondel," said Pierre-Luc.

Gunther stood and got out of the car. He held out his hand to Annette and she took it automatically, her face a questioning blank. "Leutnant Gunther Schmidt. Pleased to meet you Annette," he said seriously. "And I'm sorry for hitting you... I had to make it look convincing in front of that bastard Blondel."

Annette studied his face. For a while her face remained impassive, but then she smiled, marvelling at his blue eyes, his blonde good looks... his manners. "You... you make it sound as if you all know Blondel," she said. "Do you?"

"I have never met him until today, leastwise not as I remember," said Gunther.

"We know him alright," Frank interjected. "He was at the same school as us. He was the school bully and he hated Marcel..."

"He hated us all," Pierre-Luc interrupted.

Frank smiled weakly. "He hated us all, but he never did get the better of us until... until Marcel..."

"Marcel? Who is Marcel and where is he?" Annette asked.

Frank pointed back in the general direction they had just come from. "That was Marcel... the younger man, hanging... hanging on the scaffold... that's who we came for... too late."

Annette's hands flew to her mouth and she gasped. "Oh no... oh no... Blondel... no, I cannot say... I..."

"It's alright Annette," Gunther said. "We know... we saw what he did and he will pay for it. I swear he will pay for it."

"I hope I'm there to see it," Pierre-Luc said vehemently.

"And if I'm gone by then... well I'll just have to imagine it, won't I?" said Frank.

"Gone?" said Annette, turning back to him. "Where are you going?"

"I'm going to England, Annette. I have to get out of France. Oh, don't look so worried. I'm sure..."

"He's sure that you will be well looked after and you will be," piped up Gunther. The others all turned to look at him. He smiled and shrugged his shoulders.

Annette turned back to Frank. "You'll see... what's her name... eh... Lizzie. You'll see Lizzie. Oh Frank how..."

"See Lizzie!" laughed Pierre-Luc. "What's he been telling you?"

Frank blushed and Annette reached over and stroked his cheek. "Never you mind," she crooned. Frank smiled at her and then looked over her shoulder at Gunther.

Gunther returned his look. "I think we can guess at that one," he said, smiling broadly. "Maybe, now, he can do something about it..."

"Here, what's this," Frank laughed. "I thought that you..."

"Me? Me? She was always yours... only you, you dolt... you didn't do anything about it." He cuffed Frank playfully on the cheek and then turned and looked down the track, his face becoming serious again. "Right, introductions over, I think we'd better get a move on before Capitaine Blondel comes looking..."

"For his toy," said Annette tersely.

"What?" said Frank, appalled. "You mean..."

"I warned you Frank, didn't I? I told you that last night... you remember that last night, don't you?"

Gunther laughed out loud, pointing at Frank. "You're blushing again Frank."

"I am not."

"No, you're not really, but I think that perhaps you should be," Gunther laughed. "Come on, let's talk in the car as we go."

They all got back in and Pierre-Luc backed down the track to the main road, swung out into the empty carriageway and drove off.

Frank turned around in his seat. "What's the plan now, Gunther?"

Gunther thought for a moment. "I think... I think that we should drop Pierre-Luc off at Marcel's house so that he can change and then go home and lie low. You, Frank, should stay tonight at Marcel's house and Annette can come to my house."

Annette looked from Gunther to Frank. "I don't..."

"It's alright Annette," said Frank. "I promise... but he's right... it's just best that we aren't all in the same place tonight and Gunther can do all of the other things he needs to do."

"Will we see each other again before you go?" asked Pierre-Luc.

"Yes," said Gunther. "We will." He turned to Annette. "Annette, Blondel knows that I have taken you... he may suspect that I was accompanied by Frank... he didn't see Pierre-Luc as far as I know."

"No he didn't, thank God," said Pierre-Luc.

"Good, he didn't see Pierre-Luc, so he's got no proof because Frank's supposed to be dead... and we've got witnesses for that." He sighed. "So... so, if they find me with Annette, the most they can think is that I'm behaving like... like..."

"Like any other German officer taking whichever woman he wants," Annette interrupted.

Gunther smiled. "Like *any* other? Well in any event, nothing much will be done about it at any rate, even supposing Blondel does say anything. I'll say I questioned you about things, discovered that you had little or no relevant information and then..."

"Took me for your own plaything," said Annette lightly. "Are you sure you want to be associated with Blondel's soiled goods.

Gunther smiled again. "I would be delighted to have such a charming young lady as my house guest," he said, and this time Annette blushed. Frank smiled to himself and turned back around in his seat, catching Pierre-Luc's amused grin as he did so.

The rest of the journey back was uneventful. Occasionally they spoke, and Annette in particular was interested in being brought up to date with world events, all of which Gunther was only too happy to help with. Frank and, in particular Pierre-Luc, in the front seats, remained more or less silent, lost in their own thoughts of Marcel.

It was middle to late afternoon when the car slowed down at the crossroads and approached Marcel's house. Annette raised herself in her seat to look at the house as they drew level and stopped outside. She gasped as she saw the broken door, the shattered windows and the crudely scrawled Star of David. "You can't... you can't possibly stay here," she wailed, "it's... it's disgusting."

Frank turned in his seat. "It's Marcel's house. It's out of sight from any other and I'll be alright here... as long as someone drops me off some food."

"I'll bring you some later tonight," Pierre-Luc volunteered.

"Right!" said Gunther. "You two, get those uniforms off. Annette, what do we do with you?"

"Tie my hands in case we're stopped," she suggested.

He looked at her. "Yes, you're right. I've dropped off the guards and you would be... do you mind?" Annette shook her head and held out her hands, the wrists together. "Give me your belt, Pierre-Luc," Gunther said urgently. Pierre-Luc got out and, lifting his tunic, slid the belt through the loops and handed it to Gunther. Frank slid across and out and the two of them quickly removed all of the outer uniform garments to stand there naked except for their underwear.

"Some sort of outing this is turning out to be, boys," laughed Annette as she held her bound hands up in the air and lolled back in the seat.

"Stuff that lot in the boot compartment," Gunther ordered, "and then get out of sight." He climbed over to the driver's seat. "I'll see you both here in two days... that'll give me time to sort out some things for you Frank... and for you Pierre-Luc."

"Yes."

"Make sure you're not spotted coming and going from here. Wait 'til after dark."

Pierre-Luc grinned a wry grin, clapped Frank on the shoulder and the two of them turned and ran in. "And take care yourselves," he called back to the departing car as he and Frank turned at the door for one brief wave.

***

The gentle drone of the cicadas, overlaid with the higher trilling of the crickets, lured Frank into closing his eyes for a moment and he shifted his weight against the outcrop of sharp grey rock.

'Michel Dubrais. I am Michel Dubrais,' Frank thought. 'Last week I was Alain Legrand, an agricultural salesman from Lyon, and this week I am Michel Dubrais, a humble goatherd from the Roussillon.' As if to reinforce this assertion, a large glossy, brown and black goat appeared in his line of vision, outlined against the blue of the August sky. Long, shining, black, ribbed horns swept in two graceful arcs from its forehead, and yellow eyes, with their strange vertical pupils, stared down at him. The dull metallic clunking of the leader's bell sounded further up the hill and the goat lifted its head, in response, called and leapt effortlessly from its perch, up and out of Frank's sight.

"Tired already," grumbled Bertrand as he crested the rock and jumped down to where Frank lay.

"Tired? No, not really, just... well at peace I suppose. You know Bertrand, for all the world up here there might as well not be a war going on."

The old man shrugged his shoulders. "Makes no difference to me. There can be Frenchmen in Paris or Germans... my life is the same."

Frank rolled over and drew his knees up. "That's exactly what I mean... for two pins, I'd just as soon stay here and let the world get on with it."

"Well, that's as may be," the goatherd growled. "But we've a herd to watch and you to get to the border." He grinned down at Frank as he got to his feet. "We'll be there by nightfall."

Spain by nightfall. The end of freedom for a while, if Gunther was right. They'd intern him for up to nine months but then... then he would be back in England. Violet... Florrie and Joe... Jesse... grandad, Alice and the boys... they would all be there in England... and Lizzie. Lizzie would be there in England... but not for him... she was George's wife. Frank sighed as he reached up to grab a branch and haul himself up between two slabs of rock.

"You alright?" Bertrand called down from above.

"Yes. Fine thank you."

"Hurry up then."

Frank smiled to himself. 'Hurry up then. It's alright for him, he's used to climbing around like a mountain goat, living off, and as part of, the land.' He looked down at himself. What did he look like? A peasant, that's what he looked like, and any patrol that might, by chance, find its way through this impossible terrain would take him as such. Rough homespun smock jacket, baggy trousers tied up to his waist with string, leather chaps around his shins to ward off the thorns and spines of the maquis... all topped with a battered straw hat with a wide brim. How his friends back in Chateauneuf would laugh if they could see him now.

His thoughts rolled back to the days before he had left. Pierre-Luc had brought him food and drink for the two days after their excursion to Pithiviers but, apart from his visits, the time had been spent in unremitting boredom... tempered all the while by the fear of discovery or betrayal.

Nobody but the fellowship, Pierre-Luc's parents and Annette had known where he was... known anything other than the facts, as reported sorrowfully by the two sisters, that he had been taken by the Germans and carried off. News would have seeped back to Henri, no doubt, that his betrayal had resulted in Frank's death and Frank rued the hurt that would bring to Jean-Claude, Marie and Father René.

He stood for a moment to catch his breath, marvelling at the magnificent views down and over the hazy valley. Sharp limestone rock, its jagged forms carved by wind, sun and ice, stood out from the dark grey-green hues of the low maquis scrub. Here and there, brighter green stunted Mediterranean pines eked a precarious living from the baked soil, their roots tunnelling deep beneath the surface. Low prostrate oaks, their leaves like those of holly, lay across the stones, their spines scratching at his leather-clad leggings as he forced past. He shaded his eyes and looked up ahead for Bertrand, catching sight of him striding purposefully from rock to rock, using the hidden paths and trails that he had known since boyhood. What a man. Strength emanated from every pore of his being. Strength of character, strength of will and purpose, strength of body and spirit. Frank laughed out loud to himself. Even strength of odour... you could smell Bertrand from twenty metres, even if he wasn't with his beloved goats. Not a bad smell, more... well more like the goats themselves really, and the strong cheeses that they produced, which formed a large part of this simple man's diet. Bertrand waved down to him. Frank waved back and set to.

'The sun was overhead now and it must be close to the middle of the day,' Frank thought. 'Would they stop for a rest and something to eat, or would Bertrand want to keep going? There was no real rush to get to the border. If they made it by nightfall then fine. If not, well tomorrow would probably do as well. Bertrand would see him across and would then just carry on with his goats, looping up and around and back down the mountains in the timeless cycle of his life.' Frank crested another rock and leapt across to another before jumping down and following the almost invisible path winding through and ever upwards.

He felt good. He felt fit. His muscles, though aching, felt strong and bore the climb with relative ease. How different from the pale and weakened creature that had first stumbled into Father Brault's life in early June. Come to that, his friends back in Chateauneuf would hardly recognise him now, his sun-browned face, the hair on his head and in his full beard, bleached yellow blonde, the eyes creased against the constant glare.

When they had last seen him he had, on Gunther's instructions, dyed his hair black and grown a thick moustache, also dyed black, to fit with the first of his recent incarnations, Alain Legrand. How Annette had laughed when he had gone to Gunther's house on that last evening. "Look at you," she had cried, "you look like a Spaniard already."

"And you... you look like a fraulein already," he had joked, pointing at her newly blonde hair.

She'd blushed and knew that he had seen her blush, even though he made no mention of it. It wouldn't have been fair to burst her bubble of happiness in a life that by all accounts had held little for her up until then.

Gunther had come up behind her and put his hand proprietarily on her shoulder, calling them both back into the dining room of the little house on the Rue de Mouton, and she had turned to him smiling and then turned back to Frank and guided him into that last supper, for all the world like the mistress of the house.

The curtains drawn and the world outside banished, they had chatted and laughed, talking of old times, telling and recounting tales of past exploits and deeds... teaching Annette their history, their fellowship, helping her learn, for the first time in her life, that friendship need not rely on race or even class.

There had been sombre moments too, and Pierre-Luc had wept openly when she had described the treatment and persecution poor Marcel had suffered at the hands of Blondel right up to, and even beyond, his foul death. Gunther had sat there, his face a mask, only the slightest twitch in the corner of his mouth betraying the thoughts within, before Frank had called an end to any more misery and demanded that they all spend their last evening together in good cheer.

Pierre-Luc could not, in any event, go home that late at night without defying the curfew, and Frank's train was early in the morning, so they sat talking and drinking for most of the night.

Pierre-Luc had gone to bed first, followed, shortly after, by Annette, who kissed Frank on each cheek and hugged him tight, murmuring her thanks. Frank had looked over her shoulder at Gunther. "What do you think of our Annette?" he had asked when she had left the room.

"I think she is wonderful," said Gunther seriously. "A breath of fresh air... despite all she has been through."

Frank laughed. "She did that for me too. In a cellar with nothing but rats for company and regular beatings from Herr Weber... she brought me back to life..."

"Talking of Weber," Gunther had said reaching down and into his attaché case, "you'll be wanting these."

"What?"

"Papers... two sets, one in the name of Alain Rodot... real actually, apart from the photograph. Poor bugger got caught up in the fighting on a business trip and was killed. His papers were stored at the Marie. The other set are in the name of Michel Dubrais from the Carcassonne area, a soldier shot by Weber."

"I don't know what to say... thank you, I suppose."

"It's nothing, they were in our files at the Marie. These, you will be happier about." He handed Frank his British passport, French carte d'identite and the torn picture of Armand and Violet.

Frank had gasped as he reached out for them. "How in hell did you get them?" he had almost shouted.

"Shhh," Gunther had said. "You'll wake the others. Herr Weber has been called away, with many of his chums, to Poland or Russia, I think. He'll be back, but in the meantime his files are stored at the Orangerie at the Marie." He smiled secretively. "There was a break-in... by vandals or criminals, and some of the files were destroyed... burnt..."

"You crafty monkey..."

"Me?" Gunther had said with feigned innocence. "It was me that discovered the fire and shot at the criminals as they escaped over the walls and off towards the river."

"And which files were burnt beyond recognition?" Frank had asked, knowing all the while what the answer would be.

"Why, oddly enough, funny you should ask that... pass that bottle would you. As I recall, it was those files with surnames beginning with 'B' and those beginning with 'W'.

"How very odd... thank you Gunther."

"Don't mention it," his best friend had said. Well that was all very well. But Gunther had risked his life for him... and for Annette... and every day that passed with him still in France, even here in Vichy France, was a day when his discovery or capture could bring ruin down upon his friends.

Frank reached up for a hand-hold on a protruding rock and hauled himself up. The rock took his weight until just before he found his footing and then slid silently out of its seating, sending Frank tumbling down into the middle of a rosemary bush, which happily broke his fall. He lay there, slightly winded, until Bertrand's grinning face appeared over the top of the rock, looking down at him. "Feeling like a rest, are you?" he called.

Frank looked up at him, torn between anger and laughter, hurt pride and the recognised sense of the ridiculous. "Is it time for something to eat yet, Bertrand?" he asked. "I'm famished and more than a little tired."

"I'm already eating," said the man, holding out a hunk of bread to prove the point. "I thought you was about to join me when you decided to lie down for a bit instead."

"Very funny," said Frank ruefully, turning over in the bush and finding his feet again. "Very funny."

He joined Bertrand at the flat top of the rock under the shade of a pine tree, with what seemed like the whole of southern France spread out before them. It was obvious that Bertrand knew this spot and that this was where he often took his midday meals. Frank gazed out at the parched and tranquil beauty. This had to be as close to heaven as you could get to on Earth. 'In the next life he would be a goatherd,' he thought. He took the hunk of rough country bread from Bertrand, averting his eyes from the blackened and broken fingernails of this rough and ready man. No time to be fastidious up here. He accepted the hunk of very dry saucisson and the wedge of creamy, strong goat's cheese and sat back to eat.

"Wine?" said Bertrand, offering him the leather bottle.

Frank took it and, tipping his head back, directed the stream of strong red liquid into the back of his mouth. He swallowed, took another swig, and then handed it back to his companion. It was good wine and, surprisingly in this heat, thirst-quenching. He attacked the bread and gazed out at the view. Thinking of wine he smiled to himself. "What about all my wine at the chateau," he'd said to Gunther and Pierre-Luc. "It's one thing to have my house turned into a brothel, but another that they drink all my wine."

There had been a short silence before Gunther had tapped him on the shoulder. "Our Lady could help."

Frank had looked puzzled for a moment, and then it dawned on him and he broke out laughing. "What are you two talking about?" Pierre-Luc had demanded. "What on earth is so funny?"

Frank had had to tell him. He'd told him the secret that, up to then, only he and Gunther had shared, about the tunnels and the secret passageways in the chateau, which led to a statue of the Madonna in the garden. "But how can that help with the wine?" Pierre-Luc had asked.

"Because, my dear chap, there is access from the tunnel to the cellars," Gunther had explained, "and you and I..."

"And me," Annette had piped up.

"You and I can move the wine... and a lot more besides... down into the tunnel and away."

Frank grinned to himself and gnawed at the saucisson. What he wouldn't give to see Henri and Nicole's faces when they had to try and explain where and why so much wine was missing. They would have a very sticky time trying to get out of that one. He laughed out loud.

"Something funny?" Bertrand asked.

"Just thinking of back home," Frank said. "Any more of that wine?"

Bertrand handed over the flagon and Frank took another deep gulp.

"Not too much in this heat," Bertrand warned. "There's water in the bottle in your sack." Frank nodded his agreement and reached within his own sack, taking out the flagon. He took a long drink and then handed it across to Bertrand, who waved it away. "No, not me. I meant you," he growled.

Frank went to protest but thought the better of it. "How much further?" he asked.

"Not far. We're at the top now... it's level for a bit and then it goes down and that's the border... you'll be in Spain."

"And you?"

"Me? I go with the goats... they don't see no borders, they just see the maquis."

All too soon for Frank's aching limbs, the meal was over and the remains stashed in their sacks. The afternoon's walk proved easier, in some respects, as they no longer had to go uphill. Nevertheless, care had to be taken on the fissured rock and it was late in the day that Bertrand finally announced to Frank that they had, in fact, been in Spain for some time.

"Really?" gasped Frank. "You mean I'm free?"

"Until we meet the Guardia Civil," Bertrand said in a matter-of-fact voice. "Then you'll be back in prison."

"When do we meet them?"

"In about three minutes."

"What?"

Bertrand pointed ahead and down the hill. A narrow mud road

ran across the hill below them and then doubled back on itself and wound its way down into the wooded valley. At the crook of the first bend, there was a low mud-coloured hut with a deeply profiled red-tiled roof, set into the side of the hill in the shade of an acacia tree. "That's the Guardia post."

Frank gulped. He didn't feel quite ready to give up his newly found and oh-so-cherished freedom just yet, but Bertrand seemed intent on continuing on down and sealing his fate. He followed him with a heavy heart, wishing all the while that he could simply turn back and wander the hills with the goats again. Bertrand called out as they approached the hut, and his call was returned by a man in a strange three-cornered hat, carrying what appeared to be a submachine gun, with numerous other weaponry stowed about his belt.

"Ola, Bertrand," the man called.

"Ola, Xavier," Bertrand replied, jumping down the last section and extending his hand.

"Inglese?" the officer asked tersely.

"Si," Bertrand grunted as he crossed to the table set out in front of the hut and sat down, nodding a curt greeting to the other officer seated there, nursing a drink.

Frank climbed down the last section and stood nervously in front of the Guardia. He extended his hand in greeting. "Buenas dias" he said as brightly as he could muster. The Spaniard inclined his head slightly, but made no other move to return the greeting. Instead, he jerked the submachine gun he was holding with two hands in the direction of the hut.

Frank took one last, almost despairing look back up the hill towards France, sighed and then obeyed the man's directions.

***

The sun sank low on the western horizon, a great red-orange ball melting slowly, throwing its pink light through the scattered clouds and reflecting them across the limpid waters of the Loire. Across on the southern side of the river, a flock of whiskered terns rose from the sand as a grey heron languidly flapped over them, squawking his greeting to his mate.

A lone fisherman sat still on his stool, his eyes fixed on the distant float, gently bobbing in the current. He reeled in the line and reached down into his bag, taking out a small tin with a screw lid, into which nail holes had been punched at regular intervals. He rested the rod across his knee and reached forward for the empty hook. For a moment he gazed out over the tranquil waters. Then he opened the tin's lid, poked within it with his index finger and selected a wriggling worm, which he carefully impaled on the hook. He stood and prepared to cast.

"Fish not biting today?" a voice said from just beside and behind him.

He turned into the sun, screwing up his eyes and holding his hand up to shade them. "No, not good today," he said, still squinting. "Do I know you?"

"I think so Serge," said the voice as the fisherman leant forward into the figure's shadow, seeking to make sense out of dark shape and form. A high-peaked cap... an officer... a German officer. What on earth did he want with him on a Sunday afternoon at the river?

"I'm afraid I don't..." The figure moved to stand in front of him and he gasped as he recognised the speaker at last. "Schmidt?"

"Ja, Schmidt. Good afternoon Capitaine Blondel," said Gunther.

The Frenchman laid aside his rod and stood slowly, staring hard at the man standing between him and the river. He smiled thinly. "In some trouble, Leutnant Schmidt?" he asked, with a sneer in his voice.

"Me?" replied Gunther. "Now why should I be in trouble?"

"Because I remembered when you'd gone..." He laughed out loud and pointed at Gunther. "You thought you could fool me, didn't you? But I remembered that swine Balfoure's face, just as I remembered that little Jewish bastard Fleisch... and do you know what? I remembered you as well... you with your arrogant, leader of the gang rubbish... all rich foreign boys pretending they were better than any of us when all they were... were a Jew, a Boche and a spineless Englishman."

"And a Frenchman."

Blondel whirled around at the sound of Pierre-Luc's voice. For a moment his demeanour fell, but then it was quickly replaced by his usual bullish look and he turned back to Gunther, undisguised disdain on his face. "And a renegade Frenchman. So what? I've put paid to you all." He drew himself to his full height. "I've spoken to the kommandant's office... I telephoned them and told them all about you lot."

Gunther stood his ground. He glanced sideways at the last toppings of the sun as it slipped into yet another day's end, and then back at the man before him. "I know."

A slight quiver showed on Blondel's lips and he licked them nervously. "What do you mean 'you know'?"

"I took the call."

"You... you took the call?"

"I took the call. You will remember that I thanked you profusely for the information and promised to do something about it?"

"W... w... what do you mean?" stuttered Blondel, clearly becoming frightened.

Gunther slowly and deliberately removed the pistol from his holster. He stroked his fingers along its barrel as it lay in his open palm, all the while keeping his eyes fixed on the wide, bulging eyes of the man in front of him. Slowly he moved around in a circle to his left and Blondel followed his progress until Gunther joined Pierre-Luc and the two of them stood, side by side, with their victim between them and the water.

Blondel looked from one pair of pitiless eyes to the other, He took a stumbling step backwards and nearly fell over his own stool. "You can't! You can't!" he cried, his hands outstretched, his eyes pleading. "It's not right... it's not right."

"Was torturing Marcel right?" Pierre-Luc asked in a low, calm voice.

"No! No! It wasn't... I'm sorry... look, these things happen... they just happen... I didn't... it wasn't..."

A figure appeared on the bank: the figure of a well-dressed woman. Blondel stretched out his hand to the figure as it walked serenely down the grass and across towards the small group of men standing there on the sandy shoreline. A trim, elegant figure in a smartly cut suit, a fashionable hat perched atop her blonde hair. The woman stopped and Blondel visibly relaxed.

"Madame, madame... these men are threatening me... please fetch a gendarme or a soldier... they are renegades, traitors..."

Annette cocked her head to one side. She smiled sweetly. "Why, Capitaine Blondel, surely you recognise your old playmate?" Blondel took a sharp intake of breath and turned his body as if to flee, although his feet remained rooted to the spot as she continued. "Perhaps if I was naked and tied to your filthy bed? Goodbye Capitaine, I hope you rot in hell forever." She turned on her heel and walked a short way off. Blondel speechlessly held out his hand to her departing figure, lowering it as she turned and paused briefly. "Don't be long Gunther," she said, "I've a cassoulet in the oven." She turned and strolled elegantly across the shore and up the bank.

"Now look... look," gasped Blondel. He backed away from the determined couple in front of him, looking down with distaste as his feet encountered the mud and then the water. Gunther stepped forward, the gun now held before him, the dark eye of its muzzle pointing directly at Blondel's torso.

Blondel kept on backing through the water, getting ever deeper in the now rapidly fading light. It reached his knees and he stumbled and turned, abandoning all dignity as he struck wildly through and up to his waist. "Stop!" Gunther called, and the Frenchman turned, hope lighting in his eyes. The first bullet tore into his chest and he flung his arms into the sky. The second bullet took his brains out and scattered them in a pattering pink rain across the surface of the river as his body slipped beneath the waters.

Gunther holstered his gun. He turned to Pierre-Luc's white and shocked face. "I said I would kill him," he said quietly.

Pierre-Luc nodded, unable to speak. Gunther put his arm around his friend's shoulder and guided him across the sand.

July 1942

Frank turned the pages of his newspaper and changed the crossing of his legs. He glanced momentarily at the young man in the seat opposite, staring out of the window with obvious excitement at all that he saw. 'Undoubtedly on his way to the same destination as me,' he thought... 'probably his first time away from home.'

He turned the page and concentrated on the news. Little or nothing about France but, as he'd predicted to Gunther, the Germans were in trouble in Russia. Equally, the Allies seemed to be having a bit of a sticky time in Africa. George was in Africa. 'I hope he's alright,' Frank thought. 'Wouldn't wish him any harm... after all, Lizzie... oh Lizzie.'

What were they going to do? The other night at The Holt, in Enfield, when they'd checked in as Mr and Mrs Balfour, had been... he felt his cheeks go red and a familiar surge in his loins. How could they just pretend that this was how it would all end, that their lives would go on as if nothing had ever happened. Yet, effectively, that was what they had agreed. He closed his eyes, the newspaper shielding him from the prying gaze of others. Her smell, the warmth of her body, her hair on his face... it all came flooding back to him.

Three months of visiting, of cosseting... almost a continuous party since his arrival in Plymouth from Gibraltar had culminated in that night's stolen love. Frank glanced sideways at the passenger next to him, wondering if the old man sitting with his bag on his lap had any idea of his thoughts. He had done this before. In a lorry heading north out of Paris, he had daydreamed about the passion he had found with Annette and now here he was... he smiled to himself... here he was daydreaming about the real thing... all that Annette had provided the dress rehearsal for.

From a recently shattered Exeter, after a few blissful days with Joe and Florrie, he had caught the train up to London to be greeted at the station by an ecstatic Violet, accompanied by his stepbrothers, Ian and George, the former smiling and polite, the latter keen to pump Frank for information about his daring deeds and exploits and his terrible tortures at the hands of the Nazis. And standing there, just behind them all, had been Lizzie, smiling her own warm greetings over the heads of the others, flashing her secret special message of love, even as he had knelt down to hug the two boys.

He had gone on down to Kent after that, to be feted by Jesse and... well at times it seemed like half the county. And it had been about ten days later, when he'd gone back up to London, that he and Lizzie were finally able to meet and be alone, even if it was for just a lunchtime.

"What are you going to do now?" she'd asked, holding his hand over the table just as any lover would.

"I'm trying to get into the RAF," he'd replied.

"What? I thought they'd want you to join one of their secret services."

Lizzie was exactly right. They had. They'd asked him to come up and see them and they'd pumped him for all that he could tell them about troop deployment in and around Chateauneuf, about names of personnel and their duties... and he'd told them. He'd told them all that he could, but all the time he felt somehow as if he was betraying someone, although quite why he'd never really fathomed. He didn't want any more of that cloak and dagger stuff, not now, not for a long while. And besides, how could he just go back into France when Gunther and so many had made such heroic efforts to get him out. Gunther... how could he endanger his friend... even take up direct arms against him, by returning in such a way?

No, he'd made up his mind... in a funny sort of way, he'd made it up when he'd seen the German bombers going over northern France. He'd made up his mind that if he got out, that's what he'd do... and here he was, on his way to the RAF reception centre at Padgate. He'd wanted to be a pilot, even passed a selection board at Oxford, but when he was told that there was an eighteen-month delay for pilot training, he'd agreed to accept and report for training as a flight engineer.

The brakes squealed and the train slowed markedly. Frank lowered his newspaper. He caught the enquiring glance of the young man opposite and replied to the unspoken question. "Padgate... you?"

"Yes," the young boy confirmed.

Frank extended his hand across. "Frank. Frank Balfour."

"Eric Wood... from Palmers Green."

"Palmers Green? My famil... well some of them... my mother actually... come from Finchley and I lived at Highgate for a while."

The boy nodded, his slightly blank expression giving notice that, much as he knew these were towns in his general home area they were, nevertheless, foreign to him. The train stopped and Frank leant back and pulled in his feet to allow the elderly gentleman to pass between them. He fumbled at the door handle whilst trying at the same time to hold on to his bag. "Here, let me," said Frank. He stood as the man backed off, opened the door and sat back down.

"Thank you," the man mumbled as he dismounted.

Frank let the door remain open, grateful for the fresh air. Across, towards the back edge of the platform, some girls stood, surrounded by an admiring group of American airmen. Frank watched as the eternal mating game was played out. The males circling in display whilst the females responded with coy, submissive glances, interspersed with flashing looks of admiration and acceptance. If ever these young people had the time to watch a group of pheasants in the field they would recognise themselves. Lizzie would be prey to the attentions of every red-blooded male in London. How would she..."

His daydreaming was cut short.

"You got a girl back home?"

Frank looked back across at Eric. "Yes... no, not really... No. You?"

Eric grinned his boyish grin. "Yep. She came to see the train off in

London... you must've seen her, the one with the blonde hair in the pinkish... sort of flowered dress."

A vague recollection of the hard-faced girl on the platform at Kings Cross came into Frank's mind and he nodded. Lizzie had been there too, dressed in her suit, looking... well, fantastic... sophisticated, sure of herself, her bright smile illuminating the sadness of the occasion.

The guard's whistle sounded just as a large woman carrying a great array of bags hauled herself up and into the compartment. Eric grabbed her arm and helped her in, whilst Frank took her luggage and put it up in the rack. "Ta, boys," she trilled, plumping herself down beside Eric. Frank leant out and hauled the door around and shut as the train jerked into motion. He smiled a brief greeting at the new arrival as he sat back in his seat and then stared out of the window, seeking to concentrate on the memory of the night before.

"Names?" the sour-faced landlord had growled.

Frank had shot an unguarded look at Lizzie, fortunately unseen by the man. "Mr & Mrs Balfour," Lizzie had answered, pertly.

"Address?"

"Lilac Cottage, Pudding Cake Lane, Rolvenden Hill, Kent," Lizzie announced authoritatively. Frank smiled at the memory. Good old Lizzie. However suspicious the old man had been, when she'd rattled that address off with such conviction, she'd scotched any further enquiry. They'd followed him up the narrow, creaking stairs and along down the sloping corridor to their room, where he'd opened the door and cast his arm around in a half circle as if to indicate the facilities. "Bathroom and toilet's over there." He pointed further down and across the corridor. "There's no hot water." And then he was off, mumbling to himself as he went, leaving them there, standing awkwardly by the open door.

"After you," Frank had said, his tongue suddenly feeling three sizes too big in his mouth, his lips strangely failing to articulate the words properly.

Silently they had entered the room, glancing guiltily at the double bed. Frank had put his small brown suitcase on the floor just inside the door, whilst Lizzie had breezed over to the window and drawn the heavy curtains. He reached for the light switch just as the room was cast into darkness. "Eh... I'll just go... I need the loo," he said, backing out of the door. "You can unpack or... see you in minute. I'll knock twice."

And when he had got back to the room, having relieved himself and douched quickly, she had met him at the door and swept past him, brushing a kiss on his neck as she went. "Me too," she breathed. "Won't be a sec."

And then when she had...

"You boys going back to camp, then?" Frank jerked his thoughts back into the train compartment and looked across at the fat lady, beaming at him, nodding agreement to her own statement. 'You boys going back to camp, then?' he mimed inwardly, knowing that he must answer the question, yet unwilling to abandon the train of thought he had been on. "Yes. Yes... joining up."

"Me too," said Eric, his brow furrowing briefly as a podgy hand gripped his knee and squeezed it tight.

"Lovely boys. You take care now. Lovely boys." She grinned at them both in turn, shrugged her shoulders, folded her hands over her ample bosom and wriggled her bum back on the seat before settling down to a nap. Frank looked across at Eric, a half smile playing on his lips, and Eric returned his look with a slight raise of his eyebrows.

Frank closed his eyes and returned to his reverie. Lizzie had come back into the room to find him lying nervously on the bed. He sat up as she entered, shutting the door behind and turning the key. "Well, Frank Balfour," she'd said wickedly, adopting her native accent. "Where's them secret places of yours then?"

"Lizzie," he'd stammered like a virgin schoolboy. "Are you sure...?"

"Sure Frank Balfour? Sure? I've never been so sure of anything in my life and I've waited a long time for this..." She flung something across the room and his eyes involuntarily followed her panties as they landed on the floor by the window. Slowly, she unbuttoned her jacket and draped it over the chair by the meagre dressing table. He watched fascinated, aware of his own arousal as she slipped off her blouse, her skirt and her slip and stood before him totally naked, a wicked smile playing on her lips. She raised her hands in the air and then cupped her breasts towards him. "Guess who's a big girl now," she crooned as she slipped onto the bed and into his embrace...

Frank sighed heavily, feeling the effects of his thoughts, and the movement of the train, in his loins. He crossed his legs and glanced across at Eric, but he had nodded off, his head resting on that of the fat lady beside him. 'I mustn't think about it now,' he thought, folding his newspaper and placing it on his lap. But he did. He had to remember it all... insisted on remembering every last detail...

Gently, they had kissed at first, holding each other tight as they lay, she naked, he fully clothed, on the coarse top blanket. Then she had sat up, pulling him up into a sitting position as she removed his tie, unbuttoned his shirt and slipped it back off his shoulders. She sat back momentarily and then leant forward, tracing her tongue around his chest, circling his nipples as she reached down and undid his belt, fumbling with the buttons of his fly.

Frank had squirmed under her touch and her urgency, feeling his own desire reaching the same fever pitch. He swung his legs off the bed and stood, stepping out of his trousers, pulling off his socks. She jack-knifed on the bed up to the pillow end and pushed down the covers to reveal the white sheets, into which she slipped, her arms open wide, to receive him. He pushed his underpants down his thighs, revealing himself to her, and her eyes widened and she sucked her breath in.

His skin against hers, as he joined her between the sheets, had been the culmination of every dream he had ever had... how she would feel... how she would respond... and that response, when it came, had taken his breath away. She had pulled him over on top, opening herself to him in one simultaneous movement. For a fleeting moment he had felt himself at her entrance and then he had slipped into its welcoming wetness, only to be stopped momentarily before she reached up and pulled him all the way in, letting out a gasp which turned into a sigh as she did. He detached his lips from hers, his voice low. "You were..."

"I was," she whispered, as her hands held his head. "I'm not now."

Afterwards they had talked, as they lay there together, entwined in each other's arms. It appeared that George had been too drunk and too silly to do anything on their wedding night. Besides which, he had, with that courage brought on by drink, taunted her, dared her to deny that she would have preferred Frank, and, when she had refused to answer, thrown himself onto the bed and fallen asleep almost immediately.

The train lurched into a bend and the fat woman fell over onto Eric's lap. He snorted and she half woke up, sat more or less upright, smacking her lips and then leant heavily against him once more. Frank looked at the two of them sleeping there together, total strangers, like mother and son. He smiled and turned once more to the window and his own thoughts.

She had been a virgin, just as Annette had been. His brow furrowed. How could he ever explain to Lizzie what he and Annette had done, what they had pretended and how wonderful yet how inferior the pretence had been. Did he ever need to? Hopefully one day the two of them would meet and be friends and Annette... Annette would never do or say anything to hurt him... or Lizzie. She had wanted to be Lizzie for one night... to know love before the likes of Blondel used her body for their own insane fantasies, but she had never sought to supplant Lizzie.

War would make many things happen that peacetime could never forgive. Lizzie was alone in London, professing her love for him, yet holding him to no pact other than that, one day, if they were both free. 'Oh, how could she be free,' he thought sadly. 'George would come home one day and what then?'

No strings, she had said. Love me when you can and I'll be there for you. What sort of relationship was that? The only one he could hope for, that's what. George was not only her husband but he was family and there was no way either of them could countenance any sort of 'Dear John' letter, especially whilst he was away in a foreign land fighting for his life.

The train slowed as it entered the outskirts of a town. The fat lady, obviously sensing the journey's end, sat up, smiling apologetically at Eric. "We're here my loves," she announced as she shuffled herself forward on the seat, getting ready to disembark. She patted Eric on the knee one last time. Frank stood and assisted her to her feet. He opened the carriage door, handed her bags to her and stood back as she dismounted, and with one last cheery wave went upon her way. He smiled weakly at the still-seated Eric. "Well, here we go then. Let's get there."

Eric nodded and stood. Frank retrieved his suitcase from the rack and stood back as Eric got out. He followed him onto the platform, and for a moment the two of them stood, looking around as if expecting something to happen. Along the platform other men were standing in similar, self-conscious groupings, their suitcases or bags in hand.

Like them, Frank felt this strange sense of reluctance now that it had come to it, almost a desire to stretch out the moment before they would finally commit themselves.

"Where do you reckon we go?" said Eric.

Frank looked along the platform. An NCO was visible at the end, a clipboard in his hand. Frank pointed to him. "We'll start there, shall we?"

They set off down the platform, followed now by the gathering band of young men. Frank was the first to arrive at the barrier. He stopped in front of the Sergeant, Eric beside him and the others arriving behind him.

"Good morning, Sergeant," he said politely.

Cold, hard eyes stared at him from beneath the peak of his cap. The jaw jutted, and from a sharp intake of breath a rough, humourless voice barked out. "Bus's outside, look sharp now. Bus's outside."

They filed through the narrow entrance, across and out of the station and on to a double-decker bus parked there, its engine running. "Up or down?" Frank asked Eric, accepting that by circumstance they were together, and that in any event it was good to have another soul to share the experience with.

"Let's go up," said Eric. "Then we can see things."

They found a seat and it wasn't very long before the bus was filled almost to capacity. "That's enough!" the Sergeant shouted. "There'll be another one along in a while... you lot from there." He pointed his baton at the line. "You lot wait here for the next bus!" He mounted the tailboard and rang the bell for the bus to start.

As the journey progressed, the strange smell that they had been vaguely aware of on arrival increased. It was a cloying, sickly sweet smell that seemed to pervade the air and all about it, almost to coat the surface of everything around them. "What on earth is that?" Eric grimaced, holding his nose.

"I'm not quite sure," Frank replied. He looked across the aisle at another fellow. "What do you reckon that smell is?"

The other man shook his head. "No idea," he replied.

His companion in the seat next to him leant forward. "Soap factories I think. Horrible, isn't it?"

"It certainly is," Frank agreed, wrinkling his nose in disgust.

The bus stopped outside the gates of the camp and Frank waited as the others in the seats to the front got up and filed past before rising, followed by Eric.

They waited patiently as the queue shuffled down the winding stairs and, in consequence, were the last to disembark, stepping down onto the ground to stand, momentarily, looking about. Frank grinned at Eric. "Well here we go then," he whispered.

"Here we go then," Eric agreed.

The men who had just arrived seemed to be forming up into a loose grouping on the far side of the barrack square and Frank and Eric walked across and joined them. For a while they stood, uncertain quite what to do, or where to go next. A Sergeant marched across the square towards them.

"Attention!" he called as he arrived in front of them, stamping his boots hard down on the tarmac as he stopped. He took his baton from beneath his arm and pointed it at them. "Stand in line!" he almost screamed at them. "You are in the RAF now... stand in line!"

Frank picked up his suitcase, positioned himself more or less in the front row of the ragged line that was forming, and placed his suitcase back down on the ground. Eric stood beside him, his hands clasped behind his back, his glance shifting nervously from the Sergeant to his companions and back again, seeking confirmation that what he was doing was right.

The Sergeant waited impatiently, tapping his baton on his open palm. He waited until the group of men and boys were quiet and still, their gaze set upon him expectantly. "Right gentlemen, this is Padgate, this is your 'ome for the next few days. You will not be leaving 'ome, you will remain in camp. Is that clear?"

"Yes sarge," Frank replied, amidst a host of other mumbled answers.

The Sergeant's ears picked up Frank's reply from all of the others and he stepped forward to stand inches in front of him, his eyes blazing. "Sarge?! Sarge?!" he yelled into Frank's face. "This is not the bleedin' army! I am not 'sarge'! I am Sergeant to you. Is that understood?"

"Yes sir," Frank replied. "Sorry sir."

"Sir?!" the man roared. "I said Sergeant! Sergeant... I am not an officer, I am a Sergeant. Is that clear?!"

"Yes Sergeant," Frank replied, his eyes fixed, beyond the manic stare, on infinity.

The Sergeant stood back a pace and stared at Frank, looking him up and down as if he was something horrible that had just been deposited in front of him. "Name?" he barked.

"Frank Balfour, Sergeant."

"Balfour? Well Balfour, you seem to be a little older than most of these other chaps here, don't you?"

"Yes Sergeant, twenty-seven Sergeant," Frank agreed, his eyes fixed forward, looking over the head of the excited man in front of him.

"Twenty-seven. Twenty-seven, is it? Had a bit of trouble making our mind up about getting involved in this war, have we?"

"No Sergeant," Frank replied, aware of a slight titter of unease amongst his fellow recruits. The Sergeant also picked up the nervous humour. His eyes blazed and he swung around, searching the lines of men for the culprits. Silence fell before his gaze, like corn before the scythe.

"Behind you is your accommodation. You will fill them 'uts from left to right and assemble out here, in good order at fourteen-hundred hours sharp. Is that clear?"

"Yes Sergeant," came the reply.

The Sergeant took one last look at them, then turned on his heel and marched away. Frank exhaled and glanced at Eric. "Phew, I don't think he took to me."

Eric grinned his reply and the two of them picked up their cases and turned towards the huts. Hut 'A' seemed to be filling quite quickly, and Frank pointed to hut 'B'. "Go for that one," he said, walking across to it. Eric followed.

They entered the hut and stood by the open door. A corporal materialised from within his small room beside the entrance and pointed to a pile of small squares of old blanket. "You will place those under each foot and proceed around the 'ut at all times with them," he said. Frank looked down to where he was pointing. He looked beyond and into the hut, noticing for the first time the highly polished linoleum, the perfectly ordered lines of folded beds, and the neatly stacked biscuit mattresses. He smiled to himself. "Sumink funny?" the corporal asked.

"No corporal. Nothing corporal," Frank replied, bending down to take two squares. He placed them under his feet and stepped out onto the glassy surface of the linoleum, sliding his feet in a skating fashion to propel himself across to the first bed on the left-hand side of the hut. He stopped and observed Eric as he too skated across and took the bed next to his. The hut contained about twenty folded beds, ten each side. There were two coke stoves spaced evenly down the centre of the hut, their shining black stovepipes disappearing up through the apex. At the entrance, two smaller rooms were partitioned off, one for storage, the other for the hut corporal.

Frank put his suitcase down. He wondered quite where to sit. The folded bed was piled with the perfectly aligned mattresses, and to disturb it would almost certainly bring some sort of wrath down upon him, so he opted to sit on his case and watch the other occupants of the hut gradually skate their way in.

Just before two o'clock they skated across to the door, stacked their blanket squares and filed out of the hut to assemble, as ordered, in the square. Here they stood, ill at ease, as more and more uniformed men filed onto the parade ground and stood in blocks, partially obscuring their view. "What's up, do you think?" Eric whispered to Frank.

"I don't know, but something funny's going on," he replied.

Just then a drum beat started, and from a corner of the parade ground three men marched out to stand to attention in the centre, the middle man standing just forward of the other two. The drums stopped and orders were screamed out to bring the whole assembly to attention as two officers marched out to stand in front of the three men. Frank craned his neck forward, trying to glimpse what was going on. One of the officers stepped forward and read out something from a paper he was holding. He dropped his arm, holding the paper to his side, and stepped back.

"What did he say?" Eric whispered.

"I don't know," Frank replied. "Maybe it's some sort of award ceremony."

The second officer now stepped forward to stand directly in front of the middle man. He reached forward to the man's upper arm, and with a swift tearing motion removed the rank insignia, repeating the process with the other arm. Then he turned on his heel, returned to the other officer, and the two marched away.

For a moment the three lone figures stood there in the silence, then an order was barked and they came about and marched back across the square towards the entrance gate, passing between a block of uniformed men and the casually dressed new recruits.

As they drew level, Frank stared at the man's sleeves, still bearing the traces of cotton, the almost imperceptible fading, marking the stripes that had been removed. His gaze lifted from the arms to the face of the man. The eyes stared straight ahead as he marched, seeing nothing to either left or right, his rigid expression refusing to acknowledge the stares fixed upon him. They swept past and out through the gate to a waiting vehicle, which departed to the accompaniment of shouted orders and marching feet as the assembled audience was dispersed.

Gradually the square emptied, leaving the group of new arrivals standing self-consciously around wondering quite what to do next. A corporal appeared at the far side of the square and marched across, arriving in front of them with a great display of stamping hob-nailed boots.

"You is to form up in twos and proceed to the barbers!" he yelled at them, his face barely feet away from Frank. He pushed and prodded them into some semblance of order before ordering them to "Quick march!" across to a hut marked 'Barber', where he called them to a halt and ordered them to line up and enter as they were called. Frank and Eric waited patiently, moving ever closer to their turn as their fellow recruits came out two by two, their once styled locks now shorn into a uniform short back and sides. Eventually it was Frank's turn. He sat in the chair and a sheet was thrown around his shoulders, which had barely settled before the clippers were running up his neck.

"Nasty scars you've got there," the barber remarked.

"Yes," Frank replied, unwilling to elaborate further. He stared, horrified and amused as great clumps of hair tumbled down into his lap from the flashing shears and scissors. From the corner of his eye he could see Eric receiving similar treatment, and beyond his chair an airman swept the great piles of hair into a corner. 'What becomes of that,' Frank wondered. 'Am I going to be part of somebody's mattress?'

"That's it," the barber announced with a flourish. "Next!"

For a while they hung around outside the barber's hut in self-conscious groupings, acutely aware of their newly shorn looks, feeling the unfamiliar draft about their ears and necks, until the corporal returned and formed them up again to march them back across the square to another hut for a medical.

Once more Frank stood in line, watching the brief, almost perfunctory examinations, and as a space became free he was ordered forward and told to strip to his underpants.

"Name?" said the doctor, without looking up.

"Frank Balfour, sir."

"Age?"

"Twenty-seven." The doctor looked up at him, suddenly interested.

"Twenty-seven?"

"Yes sir."

"Any previous service?"

"Yes sir," Frank replied.

"Which one?" asked the doctor, standing and leaning forward to look more closely at Frank.

"The army sir... the French army."

The doctor reached up and touched the scars on Frank's forehead.

Instinctively, Frank flinched and pulled away. "It's alright son," the doctor soothed. "Bit tender still?"

"Yes sir... well no, not really sir, it's just..."

"How did you come by them?" He moved around to behind Frank and sucked in his breath at the sight of the scars on his torso, tracing their line with his finger tip.

"Gestapo."

"Gestapo sir!" the corporal standing away to the rear shouted. The doctor grinned and shook his head.

"Gestapo sir," Frank repeated.

The doctor nodded and smiled openly at Frank. "Carry on," he said. Frank turned on his heel and retrieved his clothing.

"Where now corporal?" he asked of the corporal.

"Get your clothes on and line up outside!" the man yelled, almost in Frank's ear. "Issue of uniforms and equipment from the stores."

The clothing stores proved to be the last exciting experience of that first day. They stood shoulder to shoulder in front of a counter, behind which a couple of older men in battle dress paraded up and down, peering over at them all, sizing them up and shouting back instructions to a scurrying band of airmen. Gradually a pile of clothing, boots and equipment built up in front of each man and they were instructed to try them on. In most cases that first look from the outfitters would produce an almost perfect fit. In the few where it failed, it would be rectified by a hastily produced replacement. In just a couple of instances the counter top would be thrown back, and by a series of pinchings of fabric and deft chalk lines, the garment would be marked up for the tailor and retrieved.

Luckily for Frank, everything fitted almost perfectly and he proudly carried his pile away and back across to his hut. Here there were lists of instructions and charts lining the walls, showing them all how to arrange and store the various items and how, where and when they were to be worn or utilised.

Over the next few days, all traces of their civilian existence and identities were, as far as possible, erased. And as Frank finally sealed up and addressed the suitcase containing his civilian clothing and effects and prepared to hand it in for dispatch home, he felt that he was, in truth, parcelling up his former life. Induction in the French army had been an almost casual affair, owing little or no relationship to the attention to detail and order accompanying his entry into the RAF. Here, all equipment had to be kept spotless and everything capable of being polished had to be until it shone and gleamed in the reflection of the linoleum. It then had to be laid out for constant and repeated inspection, in an established order, the slightest deviation from which would produce, at best, a stream of invective and, at worst, several hours of additional physical jerks.

For those boys away from home for the first time, the whole atmosphere of the camp, with its emphasis on reduction of personality in favour of a uniformity of character and purpose, proved to be terrible. For Frank, unappealing as the camp was, when compared to Pithiviers or Figueras and the regimes he had undergone there, he had very little to complain about, with the exception of the weather and the ghastly odour from the soap factories.

News of his past, and the almost incredible fact that he had had direct contact with the enemy, spread throughout his peer group and there was no doubt that the corporal who had been present at the doctor's examination had passed the word amongst the other NCO's. Frank's age, of course, meant that he was, in any event, looked up to by his fellow recruits. But as far as the NCO's were concerned, in a place dedicated to conformity, any singling out of an individual, other than for necessary disciplinary purposes, would have been seen as counter-productive.

On the last night that they were to be at the camp, however, when Frank was standing just outside the hut, looking up into the sky, the Sergeant who had ridiculed him on the first day marched by. Frank drew himself to attention as he passed. The Sergeant walked on by before suddenly stopping and retracing his steps to stand in front of

Frank, who remained at attention, his eyes fixed firmly into infinity.

"Evening Balfour," the man said.

"Sergeant," Frank replied, remaining at attention.

There was a long silence. "Carry on Balfour... well done Balfour," the Sergeant finally said. He looked into Frank's eyes as they momentarily flickered down and met his gaze.

No further words were spoken, but all that needed to be said was conveyed.

The next day, Frank and his fellow intake left Padgate under escort and travelled by train to Blackpool, leaving behind them the camp that, despite the fact that they had only been there a matter of days, would prove to be an enduring memory for all who would survive the war.

***

Gunther and Annette sat on the bench under the shade of the huge plane trees of Le Chastaing, looking out to the river beyond.

"It's so peaceful here," she murmured, cradling her swollen belly in both hands.

"Mmm," he replied, reaching out and placing his open palm on her stomach.

"Poor Pierre-Luc... having to go to work in Germany. Is there nothing you can do to get him out of it?"

"No, nothing... and in truth, with Weber back in town, he's best off away from here."

A shiver ran through Annette at the mention of Weber's name, despite the warmth of the evening. "Weber... he's bound to recognise me... I should go."

"I don't want you to go."

"But Gunther, this is silly, you're risking everything for..."

"For you? No, not just for you, for me. I want you with me... and him."

He touched her belly and cupped her chin in his hand, pulling her face towards his as he bent down to kiss her lips. "My fiery redhead," he murmured.

She laughed as she returned his kiss. "Better than that awful blonde... especially with my dark eyes and eyebrows. I looked like a tart."

He smiled and drew back to observe her. "How did you look when Weber last saw you... the same as at the camp?"

She pursed her lips. "Pretty much the same, I think. My hair was bobbed and very dark, and I was pretty scruffy of course... covered in bruises."

"Well then... whereas now... you are a sophisticated, well-dressed redhead..."

"And very pregnant," she giggled.

He smiled broadly. "And very... beautifully pregnant." His face became serious. "Seriously Annette, you've nothing to worry about. You are Annie Bertheau from the village of La Francais near Montauban and you have all of the necessary papers to prove that... on top of which you once went there and can describe the place. Stop worrying."

She grimaced and nodded her head. "Alright, if you say so, it's just..."

"It's just nothing... Please, when we meet Weber, just remain calm and it'll all be alright, I promise."

She shook her head. "I know, I know, but it's not just him. I'm French and I live with you... a German officer. You should see the looks I get from everybody... I can tell that they think that I'm some sort of collaborator... and after all I've been through..."

"After all you've been through it's hard to bear... but we know the truth, don't we? We know, Pierre-Luc knows, and so does Father René."

"Father René... what time is it?"

Gunther looked at his watch. "Five thirty."

"We must go. I said I would meet the Father at six for some more instruction on how to act in church."

Gunther smiled. "Is he making a Christian out of you?"

Her face turned up to his, indignant. "No he's not, he's just helping me give the appearance..." The answer trailed off as she caught his smile. "Well, I expect he lives in hope, but he's wasting his time." She laughed lightly. "Even a Rabbi would be wasting his time with me."

He bent down and kissed her on the lips, a tender kiss that turned, as she threw her arms around him, into a more passionate embrace. "Really, Leutnant Schmidt... and me in my condition. I think you'd better come and see the priest too," she said, laughing as she pushed him gently away.

"Not my type," he joked, standing and offering his arm to her. She stood awkwardly, taking his arm as she adjusted her dress. They walked back along the promenade, past the now reassembled bridge and on through the Place du Port, where they paused momentarily to observe the boules players going about their timeless game before proceeding up the Grande Rue du Port and turning into the Rue du Mouton.

Outside their own house they stopped briefly, and Gunther stepped up and opened the front door. "Are you coming in first or are you going straight over there?"

"No... I'd better go. I did say six o'clock. I'll only be half an hour."

He pulled a look of disappointment. "Oh well..."

"Guten abend," a voice said, and both of them swivelled around to observe the speaker. Weber smiled thinly and doffed his hat. "Good evening mademoiselle... Leutnant Schmidt.

Annette's blood froze and she felt the colour drain from her face. She reached out a hand towards Gunther, who stepped back and down towards her.

"Herr Weber. Good evening," he said lightly, remaining in French as he put his arm around Annette's shoulder. "May I introduce my house guest, Mademoiselle Bertheau." He patted Annette on the bottom. "She can't stop alas, she's got an appointment with the priest. Off you go dear, and I'll see you later."

Annette raised her face to his, catching the infectious smile, gaining strength from his courage. She took a deep breath. "Yes... yes I mustn't keep the Father waiting." She turned to Weber and smiled at him. "Monsieur," she said, inclining her head.

"Mademoiselle," he replied as she crossed the street to the priest's door. She knocked, and the two men stood silently watching as the door was opened and Annette was ushered in. As it closed, Weber turned back to Gunther. "Diese frau kenne ich!"

Gunther's heart skipped a beat. If Weber really did know Annette's true identity it would be disastrous. Maintaining as calm a demeanour and as normal a voice as he could muster, he replied, "Das glaub' ich nicht, sie ist vom Süden."

"Das ist komisch. Vielleicht täusche ich mich. Das ist komisch. Vielleicht ich mich daran," said Weber, scratching his chin.

Relief flooded through Gunther. "Ich bin mir sicher," he said reassuringly. "Ich bin mir sicher."

Weber adjusted his hat and pulled the belt of his coat tight around his waist. He nodded his head towards Gunther. "Ich muss jetzt gehen. Heil Hitler."

"Ja. Heil Hitler."

"Auf wiedersehen, Leutnant Schmidt."

"Auf wiedersehen, Herr Weber." Gunther affected a mild salute and then turned back to his door and went in. He closed the door and rushed through into the front room, standing back in the shadow looking out into the street. For a moment he could see Weber standing there, but then the man turned and walked out of sight. Gunther breathed out and relaxed. "Mein Gott," he whispered to himself. Had he got away with it? Would Weber really believe his assertion that Annette was from the south?

In the house across the street, a shaking Annette collapsed into the arms of the priest. "Hush my child," Father René soothed. "Courage."

Annette raised her face from his shoulder. "I'm so frightened Father," she said, her eyes pleading with him.

He stroked her hair. "I know you are my child, but you must be brave... I know what you have suffered..."

"No Father... not for me... for the baby... for Gunther. What would happen to him if..."

The priest smiled down at her. He wiped away the tears from her cheeks. "Bless you my child," he said quietly. "Bless you."

"He's a good man, Father... if only they all..."

The priest smiled. "If only they all knew that he had not shot his friend... that Frank was alive and well in England? And how long do you think it would be before that news got back to the Germans and Gunther was arrested?

Annette looked up. She nodded her mute agreement, her lips pursed. She glanced towards the window. "Has he gone?"

The priest let go of her and crossed to the window, pulling back the curtains to observe the street. "Yes... yes, I think he's gone... no sign of him anyway."

Annette crossed the room to stand with him. "I think I'd better go to Gunther, Father. I couldn't... I wouldn't be able to take in anything you said to me this evening anyway and..."

"Wait here for a while... he may come back. It's an old trick of theirs, and if he finds you over there when you said you had to be over here then... well it will add to his suspicions."

"What if he recognised me?"

"If he recognised you then he will need proof and you have all of your papers... and a pretty powerful protector... really Annette... no Annie! We really must all call you that, otherwise... If you keep your head and we all are strong and trust in God..." He saw her slight frown of disagreement and laughed. "If I trust in God for us all then... then we'll come through." She nodded her agreement and then held her breath as the priest suddenly raised his hand.

He put his index finger to his lips and pointed out of the window.

"There, what did I tell you... he's back and knocking on your door."

Oh my God, what do we do?" Annette wailed.

The priest turned to her. "We behave as if we've nothing to hide Annie... for Gunther's sake."

She looked at him, her wide eyes displaying her fear. She clenched her teeth and swallowed hard, closing her eyes, summoning up all her inner reserves. Her eyes opened and he could see from the set of her jaw that she had found what she sought. "See me to the door," she instructed. "Thank me for coming and talk about tomorrow night... about the flowers for the church."

He nodded and led her through to the door as Gunther opened his door across the street. "Herr Weber, guten abend nochmal."

"Guten abend." He stopped as the door to the priest's house opposite opened and Annette came out. She turned, as if she had not noticed them, speaking to the smiling priest standing within. "Thank you so much, Father René," she said in a bright and breezy voice.

"Thank you my child, and don't forget tomorrow evening will you?"

She laughed lightly. "No, of course not Father, I'll be round at six all ready and armed with my secateurs." She turned and seemingly noticed Weber for the first time. "Herr Weber... I thought you'd gone."

"Mademoiselle," he said, inclining his head briefly towards her. He turned back to Gunther. "Ich habe ein paar fragen."

Gunther looked from Weber's hard, intense face to Annette's as she crossed to them, a broad welcoming smile on hers. "Ich denke, es ist besser wir sprechen Französisch. Die dame spricht kein Deutsch." He looked at Annette as she paused beside Weber and then mounted the step to stand beside him. He put out his hand to support her. "Herr Weber has a few questions..." He looked at Weber. "Of us both?" Weber nodded. "I've suggested he speak in French, otherwise you won't know what on earth we're talking about." He slipped his hand around her waist and the two of them stood looking down at Weber, their faces open and enquiring.

Weber noticed the familiarity, and his aquiline nose wrinkled slightly in distaste. A thin smile played on his lips. "I was telling Leutnant Schmidt that I felt I had seen you before, mademoiselle."

Annette laughed. "Oh no, I don't think so monsieur, unless it's been around town. I come from the south of France and only got here by accident. I met Gunther in Orleans and we got talking and... well you know how it is, surely?" She looked down at Weber, an expectant expression on her smiling face.

He shifted his gaze and wrinkled his nose once more. "Yes I'm sure," he said, without enthusiasm.

"Would you like to see my papers, monsieur?"

"No... no, I don't think that would be necessary, madam..."

"Oh go on, you've obviously got me confused with someone else..." She reached into her handbag and drew out the documents, handing them to him with a smile. "There we are... and there's this other one which..." She looked up at Gunther, noting his concerned look of admiration. "Yes, it's in here... won't be a second." She disappeared into the house, leaving Weber leafing through her papers, a puzzled expression on his face.

He looked up at Gunther. "You took the Jew, Winklesdorf, from the camp," he said, continuing to speak in French.

"Yes," Gunther replied.

"What did you do with her?"

"I questioned her about any association she may have had with the Englishman... my previous friend... the one I shot in the river. She knew nothing of importance and I handed her back to a... to Capitaine Blondel."

He laughed out loud. "I think he thought of her as his property. Have you asked him where she is?"

Weber wrinkled his nose again. "Blondel seems to have gone missing."

Gunther laughed again. "Well perhaps he took a shine to the Jewess and they've run off together."

"Very funny Leutnant Schmidt. Very funny... I see you favour the Semitic look for your choice in women."

Gunther's eyes narrowed. "I favour many things in people, Herr Weber, and I do not..."

"Here we are... I knew I had it somewhere," said Annette, coming up behind Gunther. She handed through another paper to Weber, taking back the ones he had finished with. "My 'Certificat de Non-Appartenance à la Race Juive'. I got it when I first came north, just in case my southern looks were confused." She laughed heartily. "And me a good Catholic girl... what must the good Father think? It's bad enough me living in mortal sin with a Protestant and..." She touched her swollen belly with an apologetic smile. "But... well the poor man... I think that would be too much for him."

Gunther looked at her, as if examining her face for the first time. "You know you could be mistaken for..." He turned to Weber, taking the papers from the man's hands, holding them up, examining the photograph. He turned back to Weber. "Maybe it's the thrill of forbidden fruit, eh?" he asked salaciously. "Nearly, but not quite. Will that be all, Herr Weber?"

Weber stood looking up at the lovebirds on the doorstep. He grimaced in obvious distaste. "Wenn sie wünschen, wenn sie wünschen." He raised his hand. "Guten abend, Leutnant... fräulein."

"Guten abend," Gunther replied.

"Bye bye," trilled Annette, "see you again some time."

"Ich bin... I'm sure we will, mademoiselle," Weber said coldly. He stood for a moment observing the two of them. Then he turned on his heel and stalked off down the road.

Gunther and Annette watched him go and then, with a last quick glance to make sure that he was really going this time, they retreated into their house and shut the door. Gunther leant heavily against it, his eyes closed, breathing heavily. Annette slipped into his embrace and the two of them held each other tight for several minutes. At length Annette raised her head from his chest and looked up at him.

"Phew, that was hard, wasn't it?"

"It certainly was. I didn't tell you because I didn't want to worry you, but I did have a bit of a run in with him before."

"What about?"

"Frank. I had to put in a report about Frank."

"What did you say?"

Gunther sighed. "I told them that I had received information about the spy's whereabouts, that I had taken a detachment of men to capture him and that he had tried to escape... obviously presuming upon our previous friendship."

"Did they believe you?"

"They did. Weber didn't, but he has no proof... the driver verified that I had shot Frank and that he had quite obviously been hit and presumably drowned."

"Annette looked up into his face. "How could they believe that you shot your childhood friend?"

Gunther smiled ironically and shook his head. "Because that is what the likes of Weber and the rest of them would do."

Annette took his hand and led him away from the door and into the front room. "What more can he do?"

Gunther thought for a moment. He sat down on the couch and patted the seat beside for her to sit with him. "Nothing much. He can write to the Vichy authorities for information about Annie Bertheau and they will tell him that she was last known of in the Paris area... unless he can organise some sort of identity parade in what is, after all, a separate country, then..."

"Hold me."

Gunther turned to her and took her in his arms, rocking her gently. "We'll be alright, I promise," he whispered. She nuzzled up to him.

**

Frank stepped out from the giant hangar into the cold December air.

He paused and half turned as Eric joined him. "Phew, thank goodness that's over for another day."

"Yes," Eric replied. "My head's ringing with it all."

Frank smiled. "Did you understand it all?"

"I think so. Cor, it's bloody cold tonight, isn't it?"

"Sure is, and it's a Friday night in wonderful Blackpool. What do you suggest we do?"

"I don't know, there's so much to consider," Eric sniggered. "What do you suggest?"

"Well," said Frank, pulling up his greatcoat collar in an attempt to keep out the icy wind. "I was thinking, a slap-up meal at our new lodgings..."

"Served to us by the ever demure Mrs Bathgate..."

"A definite improvement on the late and unlamented Mrs Porter..."

"Not to mention dear, sweet Mrs Green..."

Frank mimed shock and horror. "Mrs Green... oh how my heart aches for her sweet charms." He chuckled, pointing across to the line of buses. "Here, we'd better hurry or we'll be spending the evening walking along the bloody shore." They picked up their heels and scooted across to join the line of their fellows queuing to get on the last bus. Frank arrived at the tailgate first and grabbed the upright, hauling himself up, apologising to the man in front of him as he bumped into him. He turned and held out his hand to Eric and heaved him onto the platform as the bus lurched forward, heading north towards the centre of Blackpool. Frank gazed out to sea. Five months. He had been here five months, but not all at the same billets.

They'd arrived in July, on what passed for a warm day in these latitudes, escorted for all the world as if they were prisoners rather than free men volunteering to uphold their country. Shouted commands had bullied them into line at the station before the column had set off down Talbot Road and turned right into Dickson Road, all names which would be burned into their memories over the next weeks and months.

He and Eric had ended up near the back of the line, so that they were amongst the last to be billeted as the column continually stopped off at houses in Dickson Road and others on Springfield Road. Eventually, when there were just eight of them left, they had stopped outside a seedy-looking terraced boarding house on the corner of Walker Street, close to the sea, which was, however, entirely obscured by the Metropole Hotel.

As they stamped to a halt outside, the door opened to reveal Mrs Green: thin-faced, in felt slippers, one of which still retained the original cuff of fake fur. A dirty white apron covering a shapeless print frock, her cold eyes scanned her unwelcome guests from beneath a fringe of curlers, scarcely hidden by the knotted scarf. "Do I have to?" she weedled.

"Eight for you Mrs," the corporal called down the path.

"Eight! And where do you think I'm goin' to put all me regulars."

"Now then Mrs Green," chided the corporal. "There's a war on you know." He pointed through the gate, hanging loosely on one hinge. "In there you lot."

They filed down the path and up to the front door, where for a moment it had seemed that Mrs Green was going to deny them entry, until at the last she seemed to relent, standing aside to wave them in with a sour, resigned expression on her face. "Straight up the stairs, the two back bedrooms... four to a room and, mind you, keep it tidy!"

Tidy! The place was filthy. Dust lay everywhere, seemingly stuck to all that it fell upon, glued by the grease that pervaded the air. Air? More like the reek of cabbage... the abiding smell that permeated practically every house in the area, almost as if a pot of the damned stuff was kept constantly on the boil as some sort of incense to ward off evil spirits. If ever he had his way, he would never eat the stuff again, leastwise not in England.

They'd spent the next month drilling and square bashing in the streets and squares at the northern end of the town, at times feeling more of a tourist attraction than a force being moulded to strike terror into the heart of the Nazi empire. Up and down they'd march, in Queens Square and along the shore by the Cenotaph, hour after hour in the failing British summer. Discipline was stiff. A corporal was God, and for minor offences, such as less than spotless buttons and boots, the punishment would mean having to clean either the whole billet or be put on a charge.

Illegal though it was, the former was often the preferred choice, as the official punishment could be seven nights marching in full kit for the full length of Blackpool promenade and back to the taunts of 'Jankers boys' from locals and holidaymakers alike. Happily, Frank and Eric avoided that dubious pleasure... though they came close a few times. Frank smiled to himself as the bus trundled across the tramlines. Cleaning out Mrs Green's house... no, seven nights marching would have seemed the better choice, even if only to deny her the pleasure.

When they'd left those billets for ones further to the south of the town and closer to the pick-up point for Squires Gate, they'd gone first to a very similar establishment run by a woman who could have been Mrs Green's twin sister. Mrs Porter had been her name. Frank smiled to himself at the memory and Eric caught his expression. "What's funny?"

Frank laughed out loud and shook his head. "I was thinking about Mrs Porter."

Eric grinned. "The potatoes?"

"The potatoes. What chumps we were."

"Chumps?" scoffed Eric. "At least we were the ones who put paid to her little scheme."

Frank snorted a laugh and shook his head. "Not before we'd peeled bloody mounds of the things." The bus pulled around behind the police station and drew to a stop on the open ground to the rear. Eric and Frank were the first off and they huddled into their coats and trudged off across Central Drive and on down Vance Road. The little scheme that Eric had referred to was the fact that at their second billets they had been set a task each evening -especially on the Thursday evening - to peel great piles of potatoes, ostensibly for their own consumption. Frank had thought it strange, and on that first Thursday he'd puzzled over the fact that of the eight of them in the billet, their entire week's ration of two yellow boiled potatoes a day would have hardly dented the quantity they had prepared. The mystery was partially solved for him on the following morning, when rising early after a particularly sleepless night he had pulled back the grimy curtains and seen a large man with a handlebar moustache manhandling great bins of peeled potatoes through the rear gate and into a handcart.

'Bloody hell,' he'd thought. 'Trust us to get the billet that's responsible for peeling potatoes for all the other billets.' And that was that... or it would have been if they hadn't walked past the Clifton Hotel later that evening and stopped outside a fish and chip shop. Frank had casually glanced in, and who should be serving behind the steaming counter but the same man he had seen that morning at Mrs Porter's. Of course they'd reported it immediately, and God what a fuss there'd been. It turned out that the man in the chip shop was Mrs Porter's brother and that all of the potatoes they'd been peeling had been destined for his establishment. They'd been removed from the billet of course, the last man scampering down the path with his belongings to a hail of abuse from afar from humiliated Mrs Porter, and found new accommodation at short notice in establishments not usually used by the services.

Eric and Frank had ended up in a pleasant little house in Charnley Road, owned by a Mrs Bathgate, a voluptuous redhead of about thirty-five years of age whose husband was serving in the army, somewhere abroad. To their absolute delight, they were the only two in the billet as the house had just two bedrooms, one of which Frank and Eric occupied, the other of which was used by their landlady.

But the greatest joy of the house was almost entirely unique. It possessed an inside bathroom and toilet, plumbed in by the eminently resourceful and absent Mr Bathgate; something that was practically unheard of for most other establishments in the town. Indeed, in the first billets they had been at, the toilet had been out at the back beside the coal shed and washing had been carried out in tin basins filled with a kettle.

The fact that their enlightened landlady had no objection to them using the bath, for a small payment, freed them from the dreaded bath parades which took up so much of many an airman's precious evening. Not that they were officially freed. Twice a week they had to parade in a pre-arranged street at seven o'clock in the evening, where the roll would be called and they would then be marched off to the municipal swimming baths to take a shower. The parade would form up as a long caterpillar, with two white hurricane lamps at the front and two red ones at the rear. As the column passed an alley or side turning in the dark, those who wished to skip the shower would nip out of the line, with the result that the parade got smaller and smaller as it progressed through the streets. Needless to say, if missing the showers was what one had in mind, it was necessary to avoid being a lamp carrier.

"Why don't we just tell them that Mrs Bathgate lets us bathe at her place?" Eric had asked one evening.

Frank had looked at him in astonishment before replying. "And how soon do you think it would be before we were moved out and a couple of NCO's moved in instead?" Eric had stared at him for several seconds and then nodded his understanding.

They reached the front gate and Eric opened it and stood aside to let Frank through before following him up to the front door, where Frank knocked and waited.

They could hear Mrs Bathgate bustling down the small hallway and the door opened to reveal the cheerful light framing the beaming face of their hostess.

"There you are, my loves," she trilled. "Cold and tired I've no doubt. I've a hotpot in the oven just as soon as you're ready." She grinned conspiratorially as they entered the hallway. "I expect you're off out on the town tonight, eh?"

Eric grinned. "Yes Mrs Bathgate. Thank you Mrs Bathgate." He turned and made his way up the stairs.

Mrs Bathgate reached across and dusted an imaginary mark from the collar of Frank's coat. "You going with him my love," she pouted, "or do you fancy an evening in?"

Frank smiled at her, flattered by the attention yet uncertain how to respond. "Well, I'm not sure yet Mrs Bathgate..."

"Joan dear. You can call me Joan."

"I'm not sure... Joan." He caught her enquiring expression. "I've promised Eric I'll go with him so... well."

She sighed. "Oh well... still you'll be hungry. You go and get that coat off and then come down for your tea. Oh, I nearly forgot there's a letter for you."

"Me?"

"Yes... it came this morning... a lady I think, by the writing." She reached past Frank, making quite sure that in doing so he got a clear view of her ample bosom as she bent down and retrieved the letter from the small table just beside and behind him. She straightened up, brushing against him, and presented the letter to him. "Girlfriend?"

Frank smiled thinly, recognising Lizzie's handwriting as he took the letter. "Sister."

"No girlfriend?"

"No. No, I'm afraid not." He turned and made for the stairs. As his foot made the first step he turned briefly. "Thank you. I'll be down in a moment."

In the hall, Mrs Bathgate shook her head. "No girlfriend... such a shame."

Frank made a self-deprecating grimace and then turned up the stairs. At the top he paused and, instead of going to his room, made for the bathroom and toilet. Once in, he sat down on the shut toilet seat and opened the letter to read.

My darling Frank,

Sorry for this hurried note. How lovely to get your letter and yes, yes, yes, I can meet you in Enfield on Thursday night but I can't stay longer than the one night because I'm expected back home for Christmas by Friday night, so have to catch the two o'clock train from Paddington.

Where are you going for Christmas? Kent? You can tell me when we see each other. Maybe you could come on down to Devon if you've got time.

I must finish now my darling, so that I can make the post with this letter. See you on Thursday, the 24th December, in Enfield.

Love and kisses,

Lizzie

xxx

Frank folded the letter and put it carefully in his top pocket. Just one night. After all these months they could have just one night. Oh shit... Still, one night with Lizzie was... he felt the heat rush into his body and consciously forced the thought from his mind. Mustn't get all excited now, there was a week to go yet... a week of avoiding the obvious advances of Mrs Bathgate.

By the time he met Lizzie, he should be promoted to leading aircraftman. That is if he passed the final tests. And when he returned... his heart sank at the thought of having to come back... when he got back they would be moving on to the fitter airframes course, although the venue wouldn't be changing.

Vickers had built a very large factory at Squires Gate under a huge span of roof. The building was divided by a concrete wall about fifteen feet high, and on one side they were building Wellington Bombers whilst on the other side was the school which Frank attended. There were no classrooms. Trestle tables, chairs, blackboards and screens were set out in blocks and used to display charts and circuits. From above, it looked like a giant draughtboard. Although to view it from that angle, you had to go up to the balcony, where the administration and trade test rooms were situated, making sure all the time that you didn't commit the cardinal sin of looking over into the factory section.

Frank pulled the chain on the toilet, to give the impression that he had been using it. He sighed. How petty some of the rules were. Mustn't look over into the factory, yet they were being taught everything there was to know about the aeroplanes they would shortly be flying. Mustn't be out after ten thirty at night, when within months they would be engaged in the twenty-four-hour-a-day struggle.

It really was incredible how strict everything was. Some landladies would secretly give a key to at least one man in the billet... Mrs Bathgate was getting one cut for him, she'd said... whilst others... others like Mrs Green would telephone the RAF police on the stroke of ten thirty to report those who were late.

Frank picked up his coat and reached for the door. One week to go. One more week.

**

"Has Mrs Balfour arrived yet?" Frank asked breathlessly as he juggled with his kitbag whilst trying to sign the register.

The old man behind the desk grunted and reached forward for the book. He stabbed his finger at a signature four lines above that of Frank. "Didn't you see that?" he asked suspiciously. "I'd 'ave thought you'd recognise your own wife's signature."

Frank smiled and bent over to peer more closely at the book. "Oh yes, silly me, I wasn't thinking... which room number are we?"

"Twelve, on the second floor, straight up the stairs, along the corridor, through the double doors and it's on the left," he growled.

Frank thanked him and made his way up to the room. He stood for a moment outside the door as a strange feeling of reluctance swept over him. He had waited so long for this moment and now that it was here, he was loathe to start the process that would lead to it being over. He put the kitbag on the floor, adjusted his tie and knocked three times.

"Who is it?" came Lizzie's voice.

He put his mouth close to the door. "Frank."

He heard sounds from within the room and stood back slightly as the door opened to frame Lizzie, standing there, stark naked with an impish grin on her face. "Good evening young sir," she said as she raised her arms above her head, palms up, and posed for him. "Can I help you?"

He grinned, casting a guilty look each way down the corridor before picking up his kitbag and entering. He dropped it on the floor as she draped herself about him, pushing the door shut. "Umm, you seem pleased to see me," he murmured as she nuzzled his neck, "and I see you've dressed for the occasion."

"I most certainly have sir, would you care to join me?"

He held her away, smiling down into her eager face, noting that despite her smile, her eyes showed a hint of blackness underneath, as if hiding some trouble within. "After I've been to the little boys room," he said, looking back at the door. "It's been a long journey."

"Well step this way young sir," she announced, sweeping her arm around in a circle to indicate a door off in the corner by the window. She let go of his hand and walked across the room as he stood marvelling at her figure, her complete confidence and lack of concern at her nakedness. She pushed open the door and wiggled her index finger at him to come to her. "We got the bridal suite," she breathed.

"The what?" he said as he walked across to her.

She reached up and undid his tie, flinging it back behind him onto a chair, before slipping his jacket off his shoulders. "The bridal suite... I told the old man that we were to be parted... perhaps forever." She smiled wickedly, but her eyes betrayed a flicker of some other emotion. He followed her into the bathroom. "I do so like a man in uniform," she whispered, "but I also like you..." She turned and looked him directly in the eye. "...naked. Your bath, sir." She indicated the already full bath. "Get in and I'll scrub your back."

Self-consciously, acutely aware of his erection, Frank stripped his clothes off to her murmured appreciation as she took each item from him. He stepped into the bath and lay down in the warm water as Lizzie carried his clothing out and deposited it on the chair, carefully folding his trousers and draping the jacket over the back. She returned to the bathroom, picked up the soap and lathered it before reaching in and down to smooth it over his torso. Frank closed his eyes and lay back with a contented sigh. His eyes flew open again as she reached between his legs and soaped him and he sat up quickly, splashing water over her and down onto the floor.

"What's wrong?" she squealed, giggling and reaching back into the water for him.

"Nothing," said Frank, squirming under her touch. "It's just that..."

"You're shy, Frank Balfour," she teased.

"Not at all you strumpet," said Frank. "It's just that... well if you don't stop soon... well I won't be able to."

Her eyebrows raised and she licked her lips salaciously. "Well," she said, deliberately adopting her native Devon accent. "You'm best get out of that bath and follow me, young sir." She held out a towel. Frank ducked down under the water to swill off the soap and stood, taking the towel from her and hurriedly pulling it about his body in an attempt to dry. She backed out of the door and he impatiently flung the towel down on the wet floor and, still dripping, followed her into the bedroom.

Lizzie pulled back the bedclothes and slipped onto the white sheets, reaching up for him as he slid in beside her. "You're still wet," she giggled.

"So are you," he murmured as he reached between her legs.

"Let's be wet together then my love," she sighed, arching her back. They made love slowly at first, but then with increasing passion until Frank became aware that their cries of delight and the banging and creaking of the large bed might betray them to all other occupants of the hotel. He stopped moving within her and held her close, nuzzling in her ear as her hands searched and clung to his buttocks. "Don't pay them no mind my love," she teased. "Them's only jealous."

Frank picked up one of the pillows and forced it down behind the headboard against the wall. He turned her around so that she lay across the bed and slipped above and within her, supporting himself on his hands. She smiled up at him. "Love me Frank," she pleaded. "Love me as you have never loved anyone before."

"I do," he whispered as he began to move slowly within her.

Lizzie raised her knees and clasped her feet behind his bottom, dictating his rhythm. "Love me enough for forever," she cried as tears flowed from her eyes.

He gazed down at her, his mind finding clarity, even as he felt the release building up within him. "Lizzie?" he almost shouted as they both came together in a crescendo which left her lying practically senseless, whilst he gently subsided down onto her before rolling off to lie beside her, breathing heavily. At length he raised his head and reached across to trace his finger across her mouth and up to her eyes, still wet with tears. He gave a short laugh. "I know I'm not the world's greatest lover, but I don't usually make girls cry," he said softly.

Lizzie turned to him, her eyes wide and glistening. "Hold me Frank," she begged. "Hold me."

Frank put his arm behind her head and cradled her on his chest as she lay on her side. With his free hand he gently stroked her damp hair, aware that with their initial passion out of the way, something which had been troubling her had come to the fore. "What is it Lizzie? Tell me," he asked softly. She murmured something which he didn't catch and nuzzled closer to him. "Sorry my love, I didn't catch that," he said.

Lizzie raised her head and looked directly into his eyes. "It's George."

"What of George?" he asked, aware that his voice sounded thick and unnatural.

Lizzie raised herself on one elbow and toyed with his chest. "He's coming home... injured."

Frank felt a constriction in his chest and his mouth went suddenly dry. There was a long silence, during which he stared into the middle distance whilst she continued to trace imaginary patterns on his chest with her finger. Eventually he broke the silence. "What are we going to do?"

Lizzie looked down at him on the bed. He returned her look, noticing that the face that only a few minutes ago had been so alive with love and passion was now drawn and tense. She pulled her lips into a half smile. "I have to go to him... I have to go home... I was going anyway, but now I have to go," she sighed, and stared up and beyond Frank's vision. "I have to go Frank, I can't let them all down... they're my family... all of them."

"Mine too," he remarked quietly.

Lizzie sat up, cross-legged on the bed beside him. "Yours too... that's the problem, if we..."

Frank too sat up, and shifted himself so that he sat back against the headboard, looking down the bed at Lizzie. "Oh I wish we could just run off to France... and be together."

"Frank... I'm not sure I could live in France."

"With me you could."

"I belong here in England with my family."

He swallowed. "Anywhere... as long as we could be together." He leant forward and placed his hand on her shoulder. "You don't love him, do you?"

Her head flew up and she returned his questioning expression directly. "No! No... well a little of course... but not like you."

"Then why can't we be together?"

A sorrowful expression crossed her face and she knelt on all fours, her hands on either side of him, her eyes looking straight into his. "Because of family Frank, you know that, don't you?" There was a silence before he nodded, almost imperceptibly, and she continued. "I love you Frank... I probably always did... ever since you first came to our door... but..." He went to speak, but she silenced him with a finger to his lips. "No, let me finish... we neither of us had the courage to risk letting the other know how we felt and we... I made the decision... it was difficult Frank... you were my brother in all but name and you gave me no hope that it would ever be any different..."

"I had the same problem," he said gently. "I wanted to tell you but felt unable to... I felt somehow that it was wrong of me to want you... my sister... in such a way... and then there was the war and..."

"You should have replied to my letter telling me how you felt."

He shook his head. "I should, you should have... we should have, what's done is done and now we have to put it right..."

"By breaking the hearts of our whole family? By shaming them all and dividing Florrie and Kate... is that how we have to put it right, Frank?"

Frank looked glum. He shook his head slowly. "What are we to do?"

"I don't know," she said. "I don't know... I'm going down to Devon on the two o'clock train tomorrow and you're going to Kent... how long are you staying there?"

"I have to be back in Blackpool on Saturday the 2nd. You?"

Lizzie sighed. "I don't know Frank, I'll have to see how he is... what's wrong with him exactly... before I decide."

They both lay silent for a while, each acutely aware of the other's presence yet deep within their own thoughts. 'If only the blighter had died,' Frank thought, then quickly corrected himself... no, he mustn't think that, he was Kate's son, their cousin... well Lizzie's in reality, as well as being her husband... and those facts had to be faced, however inconvenient. Would he be able to be a husband...

what would become of their love? A deep chill seemed to creep across him and he reached down and drew the sheets up and over them both. Lizzie snuggled into his body.

For a while longer they lay there quietly before Lizzie sighed loudly. "This won't do... I'm not going to be unhappy tonight of all nights." She flung her arm around him and held him tight. "Happy Christmas, darling Frank," she whispered as she kissed him on the lips.

"You too," he responded. "Listen, you're right, let's not spoil tonight, let's get dressed and go out and have a meal and then..."

"Then will you make love to me again?"

"And again, if I've got the strength."

She sat up in the bed, her eyes dancing. "I don't suppose..." She reached under the sheets and stroked him.

A small smile played at the corner of his mouth. "As it happens you do," he replied.

March 1943

"**I**s that you Frank?" Mrs Bathgate called out as he opened the front door of the little house in Charnley Road.

"Only me Mrs Bathgate," Frank called as he entered.

She bustled out of the kitchen, her face wreathed in smiles as she wiped her hands on a teacloth. "Now I've told you Frank, you must call me Joan. Where's Eric?"

"He's gone up to town to meet the trains."

Mrs Bathgate laughed. "To meet the girls more like. Will he be back for his tea?"

"No, he told me to tell you that he would get some fish and chips... he said to say sorry."

Mrs Bathgate grinned. "Oh it's alright, I haven't done anything special for tonight, just Spam I'm afraid, I couldn't get much else. Still, if he's not coming in there's more for you and me isn't there... that is unless you're going out as well... are you?"

"No... no I don't think so," said Frank. "I might slip over to the pub later, but I don't really fancy dancing tonight."

Mrs Bathgate smiled and turned back into the kitchen as Frank mounted the stairs. She stopped half way through the door, turned and called back. "Here, silly me, there's a letter for you, from that sister of yours I think... it's on the side there." She pointed to the hall table. "Go on in the front room and I'll bring you in a cuppa."

Frank's heart skipped a beat. He watched as she disappeared into the kitchen and then turned quickly and grabbed the letter, holding it up to the light. It was from Lizzie. He could tell from the writing. His mouth felt dry and his heart pounded in his breast. What would she say this time? Last time she had written to say that George was back home, blinded, and that she had decided that she must stay down in Devon to help with his recovery. At least she had expressed her love for him, told him that she would and could never love another as she did him, but that she could not and would not do anything to hurt their family. But that letter had left him feeling so desperate, so inadequate.

What would this one tell him? He crossed the narrow hall and went into the front room, closing the door behind.

He took a seat on the small sofa close to the bay window and laid the letter in his lap, looking down at it wondering at its contents, keen to know yet afraid of the message it contained. He sighed and opened it, holding it up high to catch the light from the window behind.

My darling Frank,

I hope that you are well. Everybody here sends you their love, especially mum of course, who misses you terribly and begs that you come down and see us whenever you can.

My darling - this is the hardest letter I have ever had to write in my life. You know I love you and I know you love me, but I must ask that you respect my wish that in future you think of me only as your sister and as George's wife.

George was terribly injured and the doctors say that he will never recover his sight. I have had to make some hard decisions and I have decided that my place is here with him and that I cannot bring the shame and humiliation on our family that would result from our continuing our affair. Please try to understand that this has caused me a great deal of pain but that my decision is final.

My darling Frank, I will never forget our love, but in future when we meet it must be as brother and sister, for all our sakes. Please Frank, help me in this.

George and I are reconciled as man and wife and we are expecting a baby in the autumn. I wanted you to hear this from me rather than from some other source.

I cannot say more, even though I wish with all my heart I could. I will always treasure the memories of our love and of our happy times

in Enfield. Keep safe my darling Frank, and please, please, please don't
allow this letter to divide you from us all, we love you so much.

All my love forever,

Lizzie

xxx

Frank let the letter slip from his grasp as he stared into space.
Brother and sister. George's wife. How could they ever just go back
to being that? They had been lovers... in his heart they were still
lovers, and had been even before he had ever laid a finger on her.
He felt the tears forming at the back of his eyes and swallowed hard
to stop them.

"Cuppa tea!" chirruped Mrs Bathgate as she pushed open the door.
She stopped at the sight of Frank sitting there, his face stricken. "Oh
my Lord, what's up love?" she exclaimed, putting the tray down on
the small table beside his chair. Her eyes followed on down to the
letter lying on the floor and she bent and picked it up, handing it
back to him. "Has something happened love, is somebody dead...
your mother?"

He took the letter soundlessly from her and then handed it back
up. "Read it," he instructed, his voice thick with emotion.

She held the letter in front of her. "No. No I couldn't. No Frank..."

"Read it," he repeated.

She cocked her head slightly and then sat on the sofa beside him
to read the letter. As she did, her brow furrowed. She looked away
and then sideways at him before reading it again, her head shaking.
"Well I don't know," she said sternly as she finished. "I've heard of
some pretty queer things in my time... and I'm no prude... but..." She
stood and faced him, her face flushed and angry. "But I must ask that
you leave this house immediately Mr Balfour."

Frank looked up at her, his expression turning to one of disbelief.
"Leave? Why?"

"Why? You ask why. This letter's from your sister and from the contents it would appear... no I can't say it, it's too horrible... what do you think I am... I can hardly believe what I've just read."

Slowly it dawned on Frank, just what she was reading into the letter. A half smile played on his lips. "She's not my sister... not my real sister... I was fostered by her mother, Florrie, until I was four, I never really met her until I was twelve... she's not my sister apart from the link with Florrie!"

Mrs Bathgate's face relaxed a little. "But you always said..."

"I know I did... I... we fell in love but... I was away in France and she married George, her cousin."

She sat back down beside him. "Well I must say she keeps it in the family."

Frank looked at her, his expression half way between annoyance and non-comprehension. "We were... we were in love."

Joan smiled. "I know love, but she's right isn't she? You can't blow a whole family apart... she knows that." She handed the letter back to Frank, putting her hand on his knee. "Here, do you fancy a drink? You look as if you need one." Frank nodded silently. "Good 'cause I could do with one myself and it just so happens that Mr Bathgate, God bless his little cotton socks, keeps his whisky in that cabinet." She got up from the sofa, walked across to the cabinet and opened it. "Yes here we are, finest malt whisky... now glasses... yes in the bottom here." She knelt down on one knee, the bottle in one hand, and took out two glasses, swivelling around to face Frank. His eyes took in the view directly up her skirt, noting the plump whiteness of her thighs. She smiled up at him and rose to her feet, bottle and glasses in hand. "There we are my love," she said as she handed him both glasses. "Let me be mother."

Frank held up the glasses as she poured out two very generous measures. She put the bottle down on the table and sat beside him on the couch, raising her glass to him.

"Does this mean I don't have to go?" he said quietly.

Joan smiled. "Course it does love. Course it does."

"Then cheers Joan," he said, chinking his glass into hers.

"Cheers my love," she replied, downing her glass in one gulp. He followed suit. "Another?" she said smiling. "Fair warms you up, don't it?"

Frank smiled. He reached forward for the bottle and poured another good measure into first her glass and then his own. He sat back into the couch aware that she had shifted her position to be closer to him and that her thigh was rubbing against his. "Feeling better love?" she whispered.

Frank did indeed feel better. The whisky coursed through his veins, driving out the cold, empty pit in his stomach, and he was acutely aware of the closeness of her soft body. "Yes thank you Joan," he said. "Much better... I knew that it was possible of course... no I knew that it was going to happen in a funny sort of way. She'd said as much when we were... when we were last together at Christmas... I realise that now. But... but to read it there..."

"She had no option love. You can see that, can't you? Her husband is sick... how did he lose his sight?"

"In North Africa... he was blown up..."

"Well there we are then... he's a war hero. She knows where her duty lies and so do you."

For a while they sat there content in each other's company, but then Frank turned to her. "Where's your husband Joan?"

"A long way away Frank... and when he comes home I'll be here for him, same as I've always been... but for now..."

"For now?"

"For now... well it seems to me that you and me is two ships on a stormy sea Frank, and you know what they say don't you?"

He grinned openly at her. "Any port in a storm?"

"Exactly." She put her glass down and reached down to her blouse buttons, undoing them slowly as she watched his face. His eyes flicked from her smiling face, back down to her bosom, to her face and back down again as she released her breasts. He drained his glass, put it down on the floor and fell forward into her arms as she cradled him, gently stroking the back of his neck. "Come to mother," she crooned. "Come to mother."

When Eric got back later that night, the house was in darkness and it wasn't until the following morning that he discovered the new sleeping arrangements; arrangements which pertained for the rest of that spring and summer.

There was, of course, a lot of good-humoured banter between the two of them about the situation, but by and large very little changed apart from the fact that life for the two of them became even easier. At one stage Eric bemoaned the fact that he couldn't have a girl in his room. "Honestly Frank, we may be fighting soon... you wouldn't want me to die a virgin would you?"

"Silly bugger," Frank had laughed.

"Oh but truly Frank, do you think she'd mind?"

"Of course she'd mind," roared Frank. "She's not running a knocking shop."

"Well you could have fooled me, listening to you two at night... fair puts me off me sleep it does," Eric had protested.

Frank had lashed out at him, laughing, and chased him into the hangar. Truth was though, that his relationship with Joan was, at that stage in his life, the perfect foil for all that had gone before. At times he caught himself looking at her critically, noticing the plumpness, the redder than quite natural hair, the dress sense that bordered on the tarty. At other times, however, he revelled in her joyous simple pleasure in sex and the plain fact that there was no commitment on either side. They both knew full well that come July he would be off and that their farewells would, in all probability, be forever... both accepted that with no regret or recrimination.

During that spring and summer, and with Joan's help, Frank was able to come to terms with the situation with Lizzie, to the point that he was able to write quite normally to her, congratulating her on the forthcoming baby and wishing her and George every happiness. He showed the letter to Joan before he sent it and she turned to him smiling. "There's my brave boy."

Frank grinned and shrugged his shoulders. "Thank you Joan," he said.

"Me? What for?"

"For helping me get over things... see things in perspective."

Joan laughed. "Well don't thank me... whatever a perspective is." They both laughed, and as usual their laughter turned to hugs and the hugs turned into kisses, which in turn meant that they ended up in bed.

On the last weekend that he was to spend in Blackpool, Frank took Joan to the Winter Gardens for the evening. She cleaned and pressed his uniform to perfection and then disappeared up into their room to change. Frank waited downstairs in the front room, looking about the small room where he had spent so many happy times. He heard her feet on the stairs, opened the door and went to the foot to await her. Down she came, a smile playing on her red lips, dressed in a fabulous frock of shining green hugging her ample figure to hour-glass perfection and contrasting beautifully with her red hair. About her shoulders she wore a black mink stole, which sent shivers of somehow forgotten memories through him.

"Good God Joan, but you look fabulous," he exclaimed.

"Why thank you kind sir," she replied, holding out her hand to take his. "Shall we go?"

They strolled up Coronation Street arm in arm to the Winter Gardens, pausing briefly as they arrived at the entrance. Frank cast his eyes up, for perhaps the last time, at the arched facade with the name 'Winter Gardens' picked out in blue tiles on the cream background. "Ready Mrs Bathgate," he said smiling.

"Ready Mr Balfour," she answered with a coquettish tilt of her head.

They walked up the steps and on through the doors into the foyer, crowded now with uniformed men and boys each vying for the attentions of the girls standing in giggling groups. Frank winked at Joan and she returned his wink as he escorted her on and up the sweeping marble steps to the concourse. To their left was the Victoria bar, its doors open, spilling noise and smoke out onto the passers-by. Frank spotted Eric earnestly chatting to a couple of blondes and waved cheerily. Eric saw him and waved them in for a drink, which resulted in him losing contact with the two girls, and after a while Frank and Joan wandered off to the Palm Court for a dance.

They spent the whole evening in each other's company, knowing full well that this was in reality their last night out together, wishing to take as much joy from each other as they could, knowing that without regret the following day would see them both move on in their lives. At nine o'clock Joan whispered in Frank's ear that she wanted to go home and he draped her stole around her shoulders and escorted her out onto the concourse. "I'll miss this place," he said thoughtfully, looking around at its seedy decadence, its patched-up tawdry decay.

"Just the place?" Joan asked.

"I'll miss you too Joan," he said seriously. "We've had a lot of fun these last few months, haven't we?"

"We certainly have my love, we certainly have."

"Will you be alright?" he asked.

"Me? Course I will." She winked at him and clutched his arm tight. "By next weekend there'll be another couple of lovely boys to choose from."

Frank laughed out loud. "Oh Joan, I'll never forget you."

"I should think not," she chided, "and when we get home I'm going to give you a few reminders to take with you."

Frank smiled at her and hugged her tight as they walked. "You're a wicked woman Mrs Bathgate."

"And don't you just love it."

They walked slowly down the road content, delighting in the warmth of the July evening, eager for the passion they knew was to come. They turned into Charnley Road and on to their house, where Frank stepped forward to open the front door, stepping aside to let her pass before he entered and shut it.

"A nightcap my love?" Joan purred.

"That'd be nice," said Frank, returning her smile, his tongue beginning to feel as thick as the bulge in his trousers.

He followed her into the lounge and watched as she turned, throwing off her stole and slipping the dress straps off her shoulders. He stood transfixed as she slipped, naked, from the falling dress and stepped from it holding her arms out to him. "Come and say goodbye to mother," she crooned.

***

In 1943 St. Athan, to the west of Barry in South Wales, was the largest RAF station, home to over 16,000 airmen and WAAFs. Being so large, the base station was divided up into a number of more or less self-sufficient living units, consisting of row upon row of wooden huts of a similar layout to those at Padgate. Heating, which wasn't necessary when they first arrived, but by the time they left in October was very welcome, was provided by three coke stoves, one in the Corporal's room and the other two spaced evenly in the main section of the hut.

"Is that all?" Eric complained as they arrived. "We'll freeze in the winter."

Frank laughed. "We only had one in France and precious little fuel at that."

"Ah, but it's warmer in France, isn't it?"

"Don't you believe it. Northern France can be a lot colder than here."

One thing that was familiar was the highly polished linoleum flooring and the consequent squares of blanket piled up at the front door. "Thank God I've still got my skating muscles from Padgate," Frank joked as he donned them on arrival.

Just as at Padgate, beds and kit had to be laid out correctly for inspection if disciplinary action was to be avoided. During the day, beds had to be closed up to half their length with the blankets folded to a uniform size and stacked on the piled-up mattress sections, with their kit laid out on top in a rigidly prescribed order. Everybody's various piles had then to be lined up from end to end of the hut. They all grumbled about the pettiness of it all, but nevertheless it taught them that each one was interdependent on the other, a fact that before too long would be vital to their survival.

For most of the airmen, but not for Frank and Eric, the facilities, even the huts, but especially the Mess Halls, were wonderful compared to those they had endured in Blackpool. Frank smiled to himself as he listened to his companions. If he had had to stay at Mrs Porter's then, he too, would probably have felt the same. As it was, he sorely missed the comforts of Joan's house, not to mention all of the other pleasures she provided.

When he'd first arrived he'd sent her a short note telling her that he had got there and wishing her good luck. He toyed with the idea of writing to her again, of keeping in some sort of contact, but then took heed of her instructions not to. 'Dear Joan,' he thought, 'she was a wonderful lady, and when Mr Bathgate got home she would happily and faithfully slip back into making him a wonderful wife, but until then... well some lucky young airman was probably, even now, availing himself of her charms.'

On a site as large as St. Athan, there was of course quite a lot of entertainment, and that entertainment obviously included a great deal of fraternisation between the sexes, limited by the rules which prevented the whole place from degenerating into a holiday camp. Eric threw himself wholeheartedly into a fruitless pursuit of every WAAF he came across, but Frank really didn't bother, feeling no particular need for female company.

Training school arrangements were much along the lines of Squires Gate, except that for the first time they were able to get close to and touch and feel the great beasts of war that they would soon be flying.

In September, Frank received a note to tell him that Lizzie had given birth to a baby boy on the 15th of the month. He immediately sent off a card with his heartiest congratulations, and just before the traditional Wings Presentation Ceremony he received a letter back, with a separate letter from Florrie. Both letters asked him if he would please be godfather to the boy, James, at a ceremony to be held in Chagford church on Sunday the 10th of October.

It quite puzzled Frank as to why the christening was to take place with the baby so young and why and how the date had been so conveniently arranged so as to coincide with his expected seven-day leave at the end of his St. Athan course... that is until he opened the letter from Florrie begging him to accept the undertaking and informing him that Violet, the boys and Jesse would be travelling down for the ceremony. Quite obviously all of the women had planned the whole thing around his availability and he had no alternative but to accept with good grace.

Before he left St. Athan though, he and Eric returned to their billet hut, took out their housewives and sat proudly sewing on their Sergeant's stripes and brevets.

"I wonder how long before I have to take these off again," mused Frank.

"Yeah, recommended for a commission eh? Perhaps it's your age."

"Cheeky bugger," Frank laughed, taking a mock swipe at him.

They finished up and packed their kit bags before collecting their leave passes and travel warrants covering them for their journey home and on to their next training unit at RAF Winthorpe in Nottinghamshire.

***

The organ swelled as the congregation filed slowly out of the church to stand in the clear cool of the autumn morning. Frank walked on a bit and then turned to watch quietly as Lizzie, the baby in the crook of one arm, led George into the weak sunshine. She smiled at the crowd of surrounding friends and family, her eyes darting from each beaming face in a successful search for approval.

Frank stood back watching all of the people he loved so much as they milled about the church steps, their faces wreathed in smiles, their very bearing a salutation to the joy of family life... his family life. He watched Lizzie's face as she returned the love that flowed about her. Her face, the face he loved so much, was animated, radiant with pride and joy... and beside her, clinging tightly to her arm, George's ravaged face pulled itself into semblances of the same expressions. Poor George! More like lucky George. No! However much he envied him and was jealous of him, the man had suffered and was suffering still, despite the obvious support and affection he was receiving from his family... from Lizzie.

She had greeted him on his arrival the night before, her face open with genuine affection... was it love? As she kissed him on each cheek, he imagined that her lips brushed his ear and her hands had squeezed his upper arms a little tighter than they needed to. No... he hadn't imagined it, but that was all that there had been to betray anything other than the sisterly love she professed. How gorgeous she looked now in her lovely cream suit: how female... how bloody sexy. For the first time since he had left Blackpool he felt the stirrings of desire, but strangely no inclination to further them.

He could see... anybody could see... that any outcome other than the one laid out before him would be so disastrous as to be beyond comprehension. No, if Lizzie was content with her lot and if she had the strength to carry it off then the least he owed her was to support her. He moved forward and within the body of people, seeking a passage through to the centre of attention. "Congratulations to you both!" he called as he approached.

George's face swivelled in his direction. "Frank? Is that you Frank?" His hand stretched out, feeling through the air, and Frank took it and was pulled in close. "Thank you for coming Frank," said George. "Thanks so much for today... it's good to see you... well you know?"

"I know," said Frank quietly, looking beyond George at Lizzie's upturned and smiling face.

"Jerry's had a go at you as well I hear," said George.

"I had a few scrapes," said Frank, fingering his temple.

"A few scrapes. From what I hear you're bloody lucky to be out of it alive."

Frank laughed. "Well it was a bit sticky at times, but you've obviously had a worse time of it."

George grimaced. "Yeah, well to tell you the truth I don't remember that much of it. One moment I was moving forward trying to keep a tank between me and them and the next... boooom! I was lying in the dark in a hospital bed."

"Is there any hope for your sight?" Frank asked.

Lizzie's face fell and she shook her head. George seemed to sense her gesture rather than feel it. His head flicked momentarily towards her and then back in Frank's direction. "No, there's no hope of that," he said softly.

Frank clapped his hand on the man's shoulder. "Guess if we go sledging again I'll always have to fetch your sledge back for you then."

For a moment there was a silence as George tumbled Frank's words in his mind, seeking the memory that he felt was there. Suddenly he laughed out loud. "Yes. Yes I remember, but how..." His unseeing face searched for Frank's. "You were only a baby..."

"Just one of the little things that stick in your mind... helped on a bit by other things." He lowered his tone. "Apart from the sight... is... is everything else all right... no other injuries?"

"No," George said, shaking his head. "Just my eyes... and chest." He coughed, a wracking cough that seemed to come from deep within his frame. "Aside from them, everything else is in perfect working order." He reached across to Lizzie and felt down her arm to the baby sleeping in its crook. "As you can see!"

Frank smiled and squeezed his old chum's arm. If anything, the man's injuries seemed to have brought back that spark that had seemed to die in the adolescent George. It was as if the struggle for normality had lifted his mind and allowed it to expand. He glanced up from his face and caught Lizzie's glimmer of thanks, the tiny nod of approval that she flashed at him.

"There you are darling!" came Violet's voice. "And how's my lovely, handsome pilot son?"

Frank turned to greet his mother. "Violet, I keep telling you I'm not a pilot, I'm a flight engineer."

"Same thing I'm sure. Anyway, you're still the most handsome man in the place, isn't he Lizzie?"

Frank's blood froze and he turned to Lizzie, a fixed, stony smile on his face. Lizzie laughed lightly, the brittle tone thankfully lost to all but Frank.

She gripped George's arm tightly. "Well one of them, yes, but there are others." Frank visibly relaxed and George turned his face to Lizzie's and puckered his lips as she swept a kiss on them.

"Have you seen Jesse?" Violet asked. "And come to that the boys?"

"The boys are over there playing around the tombstones," said Frank, "but Jesse... no I haven't seen her..."

"She's with mummy," said Lizzie. "They went back into the church together."

Violet laughed and shook her head. "I might have known. They met each other for the first time ever last night and they've been practically inseparable ever since."

"She's so happy to have been asked to be godmother to little James here, so proud she could burst," said Frank. "It was lovely of you to ask her especially as... well two of us from our family..."

"Mum and dad would have liked dad's sister... but she died last year and Lizzie and auntie Florrie thought of her," said George.

"She seems a lovely old lady... almost like an older version of auntie Florrie herself."

For a second Frank observed George, amazed at his perception. "Yes... yes I've always felt the same myself." He turned to Violet. "I'll go and find them."

"Would you darling?" said Violet. "Only I think we'd better all get going back to the house before it gets too chilly. Anyway, I expect this little mite needs something, doesn't he?" She tickled the baby under the chin. Lizzie nodded her agreement and smiled down at the baby, rocking him gently. Violet murmured softly, gazing down at the sleepy infant. She straightened up. "I'll see if I can round up those boys," she said.

Frank smiled. He watched Violet's departing figure and then nodded to Lizzie and went back into the church. He entered its cool, calm splendour and paused for a moment, looking about for the two women. They sat facing each other, their hands clasped, on one of the back pews, and at his polite cough they looked up from each other and turned to him. Frank detected a momentary flicker of something like pity in their eyes before each rose and smiled a welcome at him. "Are they ready to go yet, my darling?" Florrie asked.

"Yes, we're sorry... we were just having a little chat," said Jesse. Her gaze turned back to Florrie. "One we've been waiting nearly a quarter of a century for really."

Frank smiled. He stepped forward and embraced them both. "I can't tell you how happy it makes me feel to finally see you two together."

Jesse smiled up at him and put an arm around him. "We've always been together really... through you, even though we've never met before... and now..." A flicker of something flashed across her smile, but then it was gone.

"And now we have everybody we love in the one place and they're all waiting for us I expect," said Florrie cheerfully.

Frank stood aside as the two women shuffled out of the pews. He let them pass, arm in arm, and followed them out. 'How old is Jesse now?' he thought, noting her frailty... 'she must be in her early to mid-seventies.' A cold chill ran through him as the fact dawned on him that she wouldn't always be there. Dear Jesse, she had been so much to him ever since that first embrace on the path of her little cottage... one of the rocks upon which his life was founded. A beautiful, spiritual woman able to transcend generations with her love and now, as she approached old age, revered by two families united, as one, around the strange circumstance of his own birth and upbringing.

She had spoken to him once of life and death. Told him of how, when she left this life, she would go on to renew old friendships and loves.

He envied her the certainty that she felt, the comfort that she derived from her simple beliefs. When he'd told her once of his visit to his father's grave, she had sat there silent as he recounted his feelings and described the scene. As he'd finished, his voice choking with emotion, she had turned her peaceful eyes upon him and told him how proud his father would be of him and how she would tell him one day what a fine son he had.

How wonderful, he thought, to be able to imagine and believe in a far-off land where the sun always shone and where people like his father, Armand, Philippe and poor dear Marcel walked and laughed in peace and harmony.

They left the church and made their way across to the cars parked ready and waiting to take them back to the farmhouse. Florrie found Joe and the two of them, accompanied by Jesse, got in one car along with George, Lizzie and the baby, whilst Frank made his way to another car and got in with Violet, the two boys, Kate and George senior.

"How long are you staying down, Frank darling?" Kate asked.

"I have to go back tomorrow," Frank replied. "I'm catching the morning train."

"Oh darling, do you have to go so soon?" wailed Violet. "Can't you stay a few more days? When do you have to be back in the air force?"

Frank smiled to himself. "I'm always in the air force Violet, I've just got leave at the moment... I have to be in Nottinghamshire on Thursday, but I have some business in London before that."

"Is it secret?" Ian asked quietly.

"Yes, are you going to be a spy again?" his brother piped up.

"No, no it's not secret it's just business," Frank said to his two brothers.

"Oh but Frank, surely it can wait. Surely you can stay a little longer," said Violet, imploring. She turned to Kate and George. "Tell him to stay longer," she asked.

Lizzie's parents smiled and Kate went to speak, but Frank interrupted. "I have to go, honestly Violet... I need to see about... well I need to make some more arrangements for you." He stared meaningfully at her and her gaze wavered as she understood.

"Oh... oh yes. Yes I understand." She turned to face Kate and George's enquiring looks. "Frank... well Frank helps me and the boys with money since... well since Mr Hitler took away our income."

Kate and George looked across the car at Frank and smiled. He returned their look and then stared out of the window. It was a lie. He didn't have to go to London, but he could not contemplate staying for too much longer... not this time anyway. Perhaps next time things would be different, perhaps next time he would be more able to bear it all? There was nothing to arrange in London, it was already arranged. His deposits, which he had made before the war, would continue to support Violet and the boys as long as it wasn't too long before their assets in France were recovered.

Most, if not all, of the people who had been at the church went back to Florrie and Joe's house for the large buffet lunch that had been laid out in the second parlour. It was well into the afternoon before they gradually began to filter away and the immediate family members, Frank included, were able to take a breather from serving and entertaining them. By mid- afternoon, George said he was feeling tired and Lizzie escorted him up to one of the spare bedrooms and left him there to sleep. The twins went out with Joe to help with the milking whilst Violet, Kate and George senior sat quietly in the parlour talking about life in general and the war in particular.

Frank, at a loose end, went in search of Florrie and found her in the kitchen with Jesse. They looked up at him as he entered. "Oh there you are darling," said Florrie. "We were just going to come and look for you."

Frank pulled a face. "Why, have I done something wrong?"

"No my darling," soothed Jesse. "It's just that someone needs to have a word with you before they go and..."

"Who? Everybody's gone now except immediate family," said Frank, bemused.

Florrie's face became serious and she crossed the room and embraced Frank, guiding him back to stand immediately beside Jesse. "Lizzie wants to see you before she goes back home." Frank's heart leapt. "She said she'll be..." Florrie gave a short laugh. "She says she'll be with the river people by the secret pool and could you meet her there?"

Frank looked at Jesse's upturned face and then at Florrie. Each one, in turn, gave him a nod of encouragement. He disengaged himself and headed for the back door. As he reached it, Florrie called out gently. "Be strong Frank darling... like you were once before." He turned to her, his face open and enquiring, but she said nothing further and indicated for him to go.

Frank shut the door and walked across the gravel, across the small bridge over and between the two ponds and on down the hill, past the sentinel rock and on down to the gnarled willows at the river's edge. He paused momentarily and glanced back up at the house before turning left beside the river. The path dived into the woods and he followed it as it approached the clearing with the secret pool, where they had swum naked all those years ago. His heart beat faster and leapt into his mouth as he stepped into the open and saw Lizzie standing, her back to him, staring into the water. She turned at his approach and he noticed with a twinge, half way between disappointment and joy, that she was carrying the baby.

She smiled lovingly at him as he walked slowly across to stand in front of her. "You wanted to see me?" he said.

"We wanted to see you," she said softly. "Little James and me... James and I? Anyway, we wanted to see you."

Frank looked down from her smiling face to the sleeping infant. He reached out and ran his finger over the child's cheek. The eyes flickered but stayed shut. "Thank you for asking me to be his godfather," he said. "I'll do my best to be a good one but..." "Can't you see Frank? George can't see because he's blind, but surely you can see?"

His eyes shot back up to her face. "See what?"

"Frank, look at him. Look at him and think about how old he is and when... when we last made love!" Frank stared into her eyes, holding them, refusing to understand, to allow himself to understand what she was saying. It couldn't be... could it... no it couldn't. Was it? He looked down to the sleeping child and his hands reached out for it as she lifted the bundle and handed it to him. "He's your son Frank... yours and mine."

The tears flowed from his eyes as he bent down and kissed the child. Lizzie stepped forward and embraced the two of them, her head resting over the child's onto Frank's chest. "What are we going to do?" he asked, his voice choked with emotion. "What on earth do we do?"

"We've done it Frank. This is what we do. George is my husband and he needs me... and we all need our family."

"But what about us... what about me?

Lizzie turned away slightly, looking back at the river. "There can be no more us Frank... except our memories and this little secret... our son."

Frank's hunted look swept around, seeking, but not finding, solace in anything it alighted on. "But... but our child... my child... George will know... he will find out and he will hate you and destroy our son."

"No Frank he won't. George is blind... really blind. You can see and you didn't know until I told you. George loves the child. It's his whole life now... we're all he has..."

"Oh and I suppose I don't count... I suppose I can just be left with nothing?"

Lizzie faced up to him, the anger blazing from her eyes. "You have your precious France, you have your beloved chateau... and I... Frank I'm a married woman and we both knew that and I..."

"That's not fair Lizzie," he protested. "I love France because it's mine and because it has given me so much... because I loved Armand and he gave me... made me all that I am today, but I would give it all up to be with you... and little James here... all of it."

Lizzie's face softened. "Frank, you could never give up France and I wouldn't want you to. Oh, don't you see that even if you gave it all up it would be for nothing if we lost that which is most dear to us... our family?"

"Florrie would never desert us... she would understand..."

"She knows."

Frank stopped talking. His eyes swivelled around the clearing and then back to Lizzie. "She knows? You told her?"

Lizzie shook her head. "No. No I didn't tell her... I didn't have to, she saw immediately. She raised you from a baby after all."

"What does she say?"

"She says that we have done the right thing but that... she insisted that you know in case..."

"In case what?"

"Frank, there's a war on and you are going to be in great danger... pray God you're all right but... but Florrie insisted... and, in truth, I wanted you to know."

Frank stood silently looking down at the baby in his arms. He looked up at the sky through the treetops and drew a deep breath. "And if George... we're talking about my possible death so... if George dies... what then?"

She looked up to the sky and then back down into his eyes. "He may... he may live a normal life... he may become ill..." She swallowed and shook her head, momentarily closing her eyes. She opened them again and looked straight at him. "Then you'd be free to court me," she said softly.

"Free to court you! Damn it Lizzie, I love you. You love me... I know you do. I don't need to court you, do I?!" he exploded. "Nor should I be asked to wait... no, to hope, for the death of... God it's horrible!"

Lizzie stood firm in the face of his anger, her hands on her hips. "Frank I don't deserve this... do you think that I want you to be unhappy? Do you think that I don't wish that things were different?"

"Then make them different."

"I can't. No Frank, I won't... not while George lives." She reached forward to clasp his arm. "Frank, I need to know that you will do nothing to spoil things."

"Spoil things? Is that how you see it? Do you think that to be with me... for us all to be together is to spoil things?" He handed the baby back to her and she took it and cradled it in her arms, soothing him gently as he stirred at the raising of their voices. "How ill is George really? Presumably well enough to believe that he was capable of fathering the child... I mean he... the two of you... if he thinks that the child is his, then..."

"Then yes, we made love. Then and since. What of it? He's my husband and I'll not refuse him." Her eyes blazed again and she faced up to him. "Tell me that you haven't been with another woman since me."

Frank felt his face flush. "Well..." he stammered.

Lizzie's face relaxed. "Look Frank, I'm not angry, I don't expect you to go off and be a monk, you're a free man... free to make love...

to love who you want... do you understand? We said before... before all this, we agreed that we would not hold each other to anything we couldn't keep..." She held the baby in one arm and reached forward to touch him. "Frank, help me in this please. It's all I ask... that you help me in the knowledge that I... and George, will love and care for our baby. Please Frank, I'm begging."

He stood looking around the clearing trying to come to terms with all that he had just learnt. Was she just doing this to stop a family rift? Did she really... had she... was she now in love with George? How could she just throw away all that they had. Thoughts tumbled about in his head and he shook it to clear them. She was right of course. She and George were married. The child would have a stable background and would one day inherit the farm. What could he offer? France was lost to him. Anyway, she said she could never live there. Disgrace and shame... oh God she was right! Joan had said as much and he had accepted it until... until the baby... but even then, what right had he to pluck this child from the warmth of its whole family, to divide that family forever... the family his own birth had created. He stared down at the waters.

"Frank?" Her quiet voice forced its way into his thoughts.

He turned to her beseeching gaze and his look softened. He stepped forward and held the two of them close. After what seemed an eternity he released her from his embrace and cupped her chin in his hand. "Alright," he said quietly. "But on one condition."

"What?"

"That if ever life becomes intolerable with... if ever he finds out, then you contact me straight away."

"Frank I'm happy... George is happy. Nothing is going to go wrong."

"Promise me?"

"Alright, on one condition."

He smiled. "What?"

"That you keep yourself safe and always let us know where you are."

"I promise. If I can I will, but..."

"I know. I know... just as soon as you can."

"I promise."

"Kiss us goodbye Frank," she said, "then wait here while I go up to the house and get George ready to go home."

"Can't I come and wave goodbye... surely George would think it strange if I'm not there?"

"Frank," she said firmly. "George is blind. If he asks if you were there, I'll tell him I think so."

"Will I not see you again?"

"What time are you leaving in the morning?"

"I'm getting the ten o'clock train from Exeter. I needn't go if you want me to stay. I was only going..."

"...'cause you couldn't stand the strain. Go anyway Frank, this time... next time, stay longer... when we've both got used to the situation. When we're both stronger and can go back to being just brother and sister."

He smiled and nodded "You'll be alright?"

"Of course I'll be alright," she replied. "It's you that's going off to war, flying goodness knows what, goodness knows where. Take care Frank. Please take care. Now kiss me... and little James here. If I don't get back soon they'll think I've eloped."

"We could you know."

"Frank," she chided. "You know..."

"I know," he said. "I know, but don't be angry with me. I've had a bit of a shock you know... it's all a little hard to take in."

Lizzie laughed. "Kiss me goodbye will you Frank Balfour." Frank bent and kissed her long and hard on the lips. She moved against him, almost crushing the baby before she swung him on to her hip. For an eternity they kissed, searching within each other's mouths. Eventually she pulled back, took a deep breath and stepped away from him. "Stay here please Frank... wait 'till we've gone... let this be our goodbye. I don't think I could... I might give us away if you're there." Her eyes filled and he stepped forward and took out his handkerchief, wiping away the tears.

"Au 'voir, ma chérie... ma soeur," he whispered.

She turned and left the clearing. For a long while he stood staring after her, then he turned and sat on a large rock... the same rock he had changed his clothes on all those years ago. He gazed into the dark, swirling waters as they sang to the silent stones. 'Would that he could summon her naked form from beneath their surface now,' he thought. He shook his head slowly from side to side. 'I have a son... I am godfather to my own son.' He cast his eyes skywards, blinking the tears away. Frank, his father, had never known of him, he had gone to his grave never even knowing of his existence. Whatever happened he would know and he was glad.

What was going to happen? How could he just leave? He must... he had agreed to and he knew that there was no real alternative. He was going to war. How long would it take? Germany was gradually being hedged in. In Africa, in Russia and now in Italy, the tide was turning. Soon perhaps allied troops would be on the soil of France... Giraud and de Gaulle were reconciled... France. Did Lizzie really feel that she would have had to compete with a mistress called France? Surely not. He loved the place, loved the country, just as he loved England. They were both his home and he had homes in both. What good was a country without those you loved?

No, there was more to it than that. He had seen the affection, witnessed the closeness between her and George. It wasn't love in the sense that they had shared it, but something had happened between them and he had no right... no right at all, to question it. What was it he felt? Jealousy? Certainly. Guilt? No, not that. He smiled to himself... blankness, emotional blankness... so many feelings pureed together into an unrecognisable whole. For a moment he longed for Joan. How wonderful it would be to bury his senses and his body within her undemanding softness.

He rose and walked slowly through the woods to the edge of the fields, stopping as the path left the shelter of the trees. Faintly he caught the sound of car doors slamming, human voices and the tooting of a horn. They were going. She was going. A lump came to his throat and he swallowed hard. 'Steady now Frank. Pull yourself together.' He stepped from the shadows and trudged along the path and up the hill towards the house, past the sentinel stone and up, across the gravel and around to the back door. He pushed it open and entered. Florrie and Jesse were sitting there almost as if they'd not moved since he had left the room, although they patently must have done so in order to wave goodbye to the Brownfields.

Florrie rose to her feet immediately and hurried across to him. "Ah, there you are my love. Alright?"

Frank flashed a look across at Jesse, concern written all over her face. She knew! She knew. He could tell she knew. He looked into Florrie's eyes and found confirmation there. "You both knew, didn't you?"

Florrie embraced him, holding him tightly and rocking him in her arms as Jesse struggled to her feet and joined them. The three of them stood, holding on to each other until Jesse broke the silence. "I guessed today and..."

"And I couldn't hide the truth from her any more than I could hide it from myself," Florrie interrupted. She led the two of them back to the kitchen table and waited whilst Jesse resumed her seat and Frank sat in the chair beside her.

"How many people know... does Violet?" Frank asked.

"Just the three of us... and Lizzie of course. And that's how it must stay Frank, believe me, if Kate knew it'd kill her... let alone George."

"Has Kate gone?"

"No love, Joe said he'd take her and George home later. A cup of tea?"

"Not me thanks," said Jesse.

"Mmm, yes please Florrie." Frank looked at her as she rose. She smiled down at him and rested her hand on his shoulder. He cocked his head over and nuzzled it with his cheek. "What am I going to do?"

Jesse's hand stole across and took his. "You're going to be strong and you're going to think what's best for all of us... for all of the family," said Florrie.

"And you're going to know how much we love you and just how happy we both are and how much more important young James is to us," said Jesse quietly. "If Frank had known of you..."

"I thought of that, down at the river when she told me."

"Well there we are then. You know that baby James is here and I know who he really is... that's important to me."

Frank looked at the old woman he loved so much. He looked from her to Florrie and found the same love, the same comfort and understanding there in her face. "Alright... alright, we leave things as they are... until at least the outcome of this war."

"No Frank, we leave things as they are... for as long as George lives," said Florrie sternly. "That's what Lizzie wants and that's what's best for the family. I'll not judge either of you for what's happened, but by God I'll not let it break up my family."

Frank shot her a look and then caught Jesse's similar admonishment. He shrugged his shoulders and grinned sheepishly. "We leave things as they are... for the good of the family," he intoned.

Florrie bent down and kissed him on the cheek. "There's my good boy," she said. "Now who's for a cup of tea?"

"Did anyone mention tea?" said Kate as she entered the room. "Oh there you are Frank. You missed Lizzie, she had to take young James home and George was a bit tired. She'll be sorry to have missed you."

"It's alright auntie Kate, I met her outside and said goodbye to her. Anyway, I promised her I'd be back down before long and perhaps then I'll be able to spend more time here." He laughed lightly. "Perhaps the war will be over by then, eh?"

"Oh let's hope so. Let's hope so," Kate agreed. "Yes I'd love a cup Florrie dear, and so would George and Violet. Can I help?"

She bustled over to the range. Jesse shot Frank a look of approval and reached over to squeeze his hand. "That's my boy," she whispered. Kate didn't hear, but Florrie cast a glance back at Frank and nodded her agreement.

***

Frank and Eric walked into the crowded Operations Room. They paused for a moment, daunted at the milling throng of men standing around in loose groupings, which they took to be the crews who had arrived earlier from Operational Training Units.

"Well here goes then," Frank said to Eric.

Eric grinned at him. "I feel like I'm up for auction."

"Yes it's a bit like that, isn't it?" Frank agreed. He stopped and pointed across the room to a group of men standing close to the NAAFI tea trolley. "I think I'll try them... that's that chap... what's his name... Jim. Jim Baxter, from our hut." He turned briefly to Eric. "See you later and good luck."

"Good luck yourself," urged Eric, as Frank turned and walked across the room.

Jim Baxter turned as Frank approached, as if he had been expecting him to join his group. He smiled and held his hand out to shake Frank's. "Hallo again Frank," he said cheerily. "I'd like you to meet the rest of our crew."

He took Frank's elbow and guided him around until he stood within the open horseshoe of the rest of the men. "Chaps, this is Frank Balfour. Frank this is, from left to right, Tom Meredith, our navigator, Alec Coles, bomb aimer, Giles Fisher, our skipper, Roy Smith, who you've already met, our mid upper, and Dickie Holmes, tail-end charlie."

Frank shook each hand in turn as it was offered, returning the smiles of welcome. With the exception of Giles, who he guessed was a couple of years older than he was, the whole crew were in their late teens, early twenties. He turned to Jim. "So you're the wireless operator?"

"That's me," said Jim smiling.

"Have you had a cup of tea Frank?" Giles asked.

"No... no well... yes, I'd like one."

"I'll get it," offered Roy.

"Thanks," said Frank. He turned back to face Giles. "Err, I'm looking for a crew. Are you...?"

"Looking for a Flight Engineer? Yes. Yes we are. So Frank, tell us a bit about yourself."

"Well," said Frank, "I'm twenty-eight years old and I got my wings a couple of weeks ago."

"Where d'you come from Frank?" asked Tom.

"Well... that's not as easy as all that to answer. I..."

Giles interrupted. "What were you in before this?"

"You mean in the war?"

"Yes."

Roy returned and handed Frank a cup of tea. Frank thanked him and took a swallow. He'd known of course that he would have to tell his story before long, but was fully aware that its impact, its very incredibility, would cause a stir. 'Oh well, here goes,' he thought. "I was in the army, the French army until I was captured at the fall of my home town, near Orleans. I was imprisoned, sent for slave labour and finally escaped through Spain."

There was a silence, during which Frank was aware of the six men staring straight at him, their faces a mixture of emotions. Even the general hubbub of all the other voices in the room seemed to die down for a moment, although Frank realised it was only an impression as around them excited young men continued in their quest to form cohesive units of seven.

Giles coughed. "So you're French?"

"No... well both really, English by birth, my mother lives in Kent, my father... my real father died in the Great War, but my adopted father..." He shook his head, smiling, aware of how strange his story must have sounded to six Englishmen who had been expecting to meet a seventh.".. ..he's also dead. He was French and I now live... lived in his house in France."

"Did they do that to you?" said Giles, looking and pointing at the scars on Frank's temple.

Frank fingered his wounds. "The Germans? Yes. Yes, a certain gentleman by the name of Herr Weber and his friends."

"Bloody krauts!" exploded Roy. "I've said it before and I'll say it again, the only good German's a dead one. I can't wait to have a crack at the bastards."

Frank turned to face him. Roy looked into his face, expecting to see approval, but was surprised by the look of obvious distaste written there. Frank became aware of his unconscious expression and deliberately altered it, but not before it had been noticed by an observant Tom. "You seem to have a problem with that idea old chap," he said quietly.

Frank turned to him, feeling, it must be admitted, a little at bay. "No... well yes, to an extent. My best friend is a serving officer in the Wehrmacht and he helped me escape as a matter of fact... at considerable risk to his own life."

There was a short silence before Giles put his hand on Frank's arm. "War's a bloody business." He smiled openly at Frank. "I thought I was the one with the interesting history here. I was in the army as well, only it was the British army. I came off at Dunkirk and got into this lot via the African desert. Welcome aboard Frank." He extended his hand and then gripped Frank's with both hands.

"Does this mean that...?"

"...that you're our flight engineer from now on? Well yes, if you'll have us."

The rest of the crew crowded closer, each of them eager to shake his hand again. Across Roy's shoulder, Frank could see Eric receiving a similar welcome from a similar horseshoe of smiling young men.

The next two days were taken up with familiarising themselves with the Lancaster, the first aircraft that Frank had seen in an operational condition and the first time the rest of the crew had come across the four-engine aircraft after their initial training on Wimpeys. They were assigned to Pilot Officer Williams, who was to be their instructional pilot, and at 08.25 hours on the 23rd of October 1943, Frank was airborne for the very first time.

The aircraft was a fairly tired old Mk.1, which had seen operational service with 207 and 9 Squadrons before being converted to dual controls.

As he stood just behind Giles and Williams, the engine noise roaring in his head, despite the helmet and headphones, Frank felt a surge of exhilaration almost as great as that produced by the four Merlin engines as they hauled the great beast of war into the morning sky.

After four flights, Giles was cleared to fly further exercises without an instructor, although at specific points in their programme, Pilot Officer Williams would fly with them to check their progress or to demonstrate the next part of the flying training, which included 'fighter affiliation' or 'corkscrew evasion' and 'banking searches', all of which were designed to avoid or throw off fighter attack.

When Frank had amassed the grand total of sixteen-and-a-half hours of day flying and a further fourteen-and-a-half hours of night flying he was considered qualified, and they were on their way, now as an established crew, to a squadron and operational airfield that nobody had ever heard of: 630 Squadron at East Kirkby, in Lincolnshire. By chance, Eric Wood and his crew were also on their way to East Kirkby, but they were posted to the long-standing 57 Squadron.

Giles travelled from Winthorpe to East Kirkby on his Norton motorcycle whilst the rest of them took the train from Newark to the station at Stickney, the nearest to the airfield. They were met by a Bedford truck, and with their, by now, greatly increased amount of kit, taken for their first sight of what was to be their home for the next months.

Once they were officially signed in at station headquarters, they were shown to their accommodation, small Nissen huts, set out in well-dispersed groups quite some distance from the main airfield, and allowed to settle in. Then they made their way back to the main airfield entrance, where they produced their identity cards and, having been cleared through the barrier, continued on to the Squadron offices, large wooden huts situated between the hangars and the perimeter taxi track.

Here, they were allocated lockers in the crew room and issued with a Mae West lifejacket, parachute harness and Observer-type parachute, which they were told would be changed every month. As a flight engineer, Frank was also issued with a set of tools and a canvas tool bag, to which he later added a coil of electric wire, a few lengths of tubing and some other bits and pieces which he felt might be useful.

The airfield had only been handed over to the RAF on the 20th of August and 57 Squadron had moved in from Scampton seven days later. When Frank and his companions arrived some three months after that, some of the building work and the laying of paths had still not been completed, and with the coming of the wet weather, mud became an almost constant companion. Later in the year the frosts brought some relief, but in turn made it difficult to find any running water.

On the night of 26th/27th November, Giles had his first experience of operational flying when he did a 'dickie trip' to Berlin with an experienced crew. Frank was detailed to fly on an afternoon air test and night cross-country exercise with another crew; a horrible experience, as it turned out, as the crew had obviously not gelled and the navigator, bomb aimer and wireless operator managed to have quite a fight over a lost pencil.

Frank was hardly surprised when, in later weeks, he heard that

that particular crew had not returned from their fifth operational flight.

Eric Wood seemed to have settled in with his chosen crew. He and Frank still saw quite a bit of each other as they were in the same billet hut and they both still used the Sergeants' mess as Frank's commission had still not come through.

At 11:00 hours on the 2nd of December, a bright and frosty day, the names of Frank's crew appeared on the 'Battle Order' on the Squadron's notice board, with briefing scheduled for 13:00 hours in the operations room. They spent the intervening period checking their kit and going out to the allocated aircraft to check the systems and ensure that everything was in place. The engines were run up and they then left the ground crew to their tasks of topping up the fuel and oil tanks, arming and loading their cargo of a 4,000-lb 'Cookie', two 500-lb high explosive bombs and eight canisters, each of which contained 150 incendiary bombs of 4 lb each.

With feelings much the same as when they had been summoned before the headmaster at school, they assembled in the operations room at the appointed time. On a large blackboard, the names of all the crews and their aircraft details were shown, and at the top of the board was the code name for the target, 'Whitebait'. Berlin was also displayed on a huge map of Europe, showing the route to the target by means of coloured cords fixed on by pins.

After a general briefing they split up to be briefed by their section leaders, and at the end of it all the station commander gave them a few words of encouragement and wished them luck.

They filtered out and across to the crew room, where tea and sandwiches were provided and they could collect their next meal, consisting of an apple, an orange, two bars of chocolate and a Thermos flask of coffee, with a supply of 'Wakey Wakey' pills if they wished.

"Cor, I wish I could ring me mum and tell 'er I'm off," Roy moaned.

Giles looked at him seriously. "You know that all the telephone boxes on the base and even in the village are sealed as soon as battle orders are posted," he said in an admonishing tone.

Roy grinned up at him. "Just kidding skipper. Just kidding."

Frank caught Giles' look and silently acknowledged the older man's concern with a raising of his eyebrows. They filed across to the locker room to put on their flying kit, and on the way he bumped into Eric, his face flushed with excitement.

"Are you on this one Frank?" he asked.

"Yes, you too?"

"Rather... here we go then... see you when we get back and we'll have a jar and swap stories."

"Great idea," said Frank. He clapped his friend on the shoulder and lowered his voice. "Alright?"

The latent fear within the younger boy's face flashed through for a moment, before it was quickly submerged by the veneer of enthusiasm. "Fine Frank... honestly I'm fine... you take care."

"You too," said Frank, giving him a playful cuff about the ear. "See you later." Eric grinned and ran off ahead to re-join his crew.

At about 15:00 hours they were all ready and, carrying their individual flying bags and parachutes, they climbed aboard the crew bus to be taken out to the waiting aircraft. It was an ex 57 Squadron Mk.111, now with the code letters LE-M (Mother) painted on. Frank looked up at its dark shape as they approached. He felt much as he had done when, as a small boy, he had first stood on the high diving board of the lido, torn between a wish to turn away and the knowledge that he must go on.

They stowed their gear and parachutes and then stood at the side of the dispersal for a last chat with the ground crew, each man both eager to be off and, at the same time, nervous about what was to come. At about 15:50 hours they climbed aboard, started the engines and tested the systems. Giles called through to each crew member in turn to check their intercom was working, and also checked the crew call lights. As the engines warmed up they were run up, in turn, against the brakes to test the power, the propellers were exercised through the pitch control and the magnetos were tested. Frank then called out the pre-taxi check list, with Giles ticking each item off.

Giles signalled 'chocks away' to the ground crew, and when they signalled that it was clear, they moved out of the dispersal and taxied to the runway-in-use. It was 16:15 hours on a bright winter's evening.

As they continued around the perimeter track, other Lancasters were leaving their dispersals, some moving ahead of them and others following on behind. When they reached the entrance to the runway, there were two ahead of them waiting their turn so they stopped and carried out the pre-flight checks. Frank called the list and both Giles and he checked the items and verbally confirmed that they had made the check.

With radio silence in force, the movement of the aircraft was controlled by signal lamps from the black and white checked caravan at the side of the runway. A large number of officers and other ranks had congregated beside it to wave enthusiastically at each aircraft as it commenced its take-off run and Giles pointed them out to the crew.

Their turn came to line up on the runway, signalled from the caravan, and Giles slowly moved the aircraft into position and applied the brakes. He opened the throttles to zero boost to check engine response and then throttled back. A green light was flashed from the caravan and Giles released the brakes and gently opened up the throttles, keeping the port throttles slightly ahead to counteract the centrifugal force of the propellers. Frank kept his hand on the throttle levers until Giles called for him to move the levers to full power. Frank then continued to hold the throttles as Giles concentrated on raising the tail by gently pulling back on the control column whilst, at the same time, keeping the aircraft straight by use of the rudders.

The end of the runway seemed to be approaching terribly fast as Frank continued to call the air speed in order that Giles could confine all his efforts to controlling the aircraft and keeping it on the centre line of the runway. After what felt like an eternity, the speed reached the magic 105 mph and, as Frank called it, Giles eased the aircraft off the ground.

"Undercarriage up," Giles announced as they climbed on their way, having experienced and survived their first fully laden take-off.

Frank gave a large sigh of relief and looked across at Giles. The older man inclined his head to him and winked. Frank winked back and got on with his next jobs of entering all the times and occurrences in the engineer's log, computed fuel consumption against boost and RPM, oil pressures and temperatures, radiator temperatures, altitude and outside air temperatures.

As they climbed, due to the reducing air pressure it was necessary for Frank to advance the throttle levers to maintain the boost pressure. With continued increase in altitude, the throttle levers had to be advanced further, back to the gate, and as the height continued to increase the boost pressure started to drop.

Their navigation lights and IFF (Identity - Friend or Foe) were turned off shortly after leaving the English coast, and they continued climbing to 20,000 feet, by which time they were about halfway to the Dutch coast. The night was extremely dark, and it was a rather worrying thought that, hidden in the surrounding blackness, were 439 other four-engine bombers. As they crossed into Holland they were greeted by anti-aircraft fire and searchlights and Giles commenced the banking search routine whenever there was a lull in the fire, which could indicate the presence of fighters.

About 100 miles after crossing into occupied Europe, jamming by the enemy made it impossible for Tom to get any further navigational fixes. However, before that, he had been able to positively establish their position, giving him a good starting point for 'Dead Reckoning Navigation' to the target.

Nearly ten percent of the force turned back that night due to heavy icing. In Frank's aircraft, the cabin windows and windscreen were thickly coated with frost and, with an outside temperature of minus forty degrees centigrade, great care had to be taken not to touch any exposed surfaces.

They were in the third wave of aircraft, and as they approached the target they began to see that they were not alone. All around them other aeroplanes were silhouetted against the fires caused by the preceding waves of bombers, night-fighter flares and the 'Wanganui' marker flares. Fighters began their attack, the streams of tracer shells curling towards the bombers before they exploded in balls of flame.

Frank couldn't prevent a shiver of fear and anticipation as he watched the scene below and around him. Anti-aircraft fire seen from above was new to him. He had seen it from ground level during his short time in London, but was surprised at how the tracer shells initially appeared to rise so slowly to their height. When they burst, unless it was very close, there was no sound from the explosion over that of their four Merlins, just the flash and the large puff of black smoke.

Alec, the bomb aimer, was in his position in the nose and had the bombsight set up as he identified the marker flares. He armed the bombs, set the selector switch and called for the bomb doors to be opened. Giles set the bomb-door lever to the open position, calling out "Bomb doors open."

For the next five minutes, Giles flew the aircraft to Alec's instructions. "Left... steady... steady... right... steady... steady," he called, until, when he was satisfied, he pressed the bomb-release button. The aircraft lurched as it was freed of some five tons of bombs, but Giles kept the course and height steady for the photo flash to drop and illuminate whilst the synchronised aircraft camera took pictures of the area where their bombs would fall.

Frank craned his neck to try and see their own load fall, but it was impossible. He did, however, have many clear views of other aircraft dropping theirs and could see that the 'Cookie' fell in a wavering fashion, the 500-pounders tipped down at a neat 45 degrees and began a clean drop, whilst the incendiaries gave the appearance of a box of matches being emptied.

Alec called for the bomb doors to be closed. Giles set the lever to 'closed' and called for Tom to set the course to leave the target area. By the time they were clear of the target they had been over Berlin for some twenty minutes and Frank was able to evaluate his feelings. He couldn't say he was frightened, maybe because he had been too busy and had taken such a keen interest in all that had gone on. What he could admit to was a firm belief, probably shared to some extent by nearly every man there, that it would always be the other chap that got it.

Even after they slipped back into relative darkness, the fighter attacks continued and it was not until they crossed the Dutch coast and reached the North Sea that they were able to relax a little, drink their coffee and, in Roy's case, smoke a carefully shielded cigarette. Thankfully, all the crew except Giles were also able to visit the Elsan lavatory in the rear of the fuselage.

"God, I'm dying for a pee," Giles moaned to Frank as he got back.

Frank thought for a bit and then dived into his small bag. He came up with a funnel and a length of tubing, which he attached together, holding the tubing up to the hot-air discharge close to Jim's position to soften the rubber. He passed the funnel to a very grateful Giles and then fed the tubing out through the small chute in the fuselage, through which they pushed the shredded tin foil, called 'Windows', used to confuse enemy radar.

"Thank you," Giles sighed as he finished peeing. On later trips, Frank took the tube and funnel already made up. But Giles had to heed Frank's caution: "Don't let your willy get too close to the funnel hole," for if he did, the suction from the tube, flying free through the chute, would threaten to empty the pilot of more than just his urine.

As they approached the English coast the navigation lights and IFF were switched on, and when they could see the East Kirkby beacon flashing 'EK' it was time for Giles to make his VHF call. "Silksheen... Silksheen, this is Gauntly Mother, over."

They received the reply. "Gauntly Mother, this is Silksheen. You are no.3 to land, call entering funnel."

"Gauntly Mother, wilco," Giles replied.

They landed at midnight and the ground crew, who had been waiting, marshalled them into their dispersal hut and took down any preliminary reports of damage or equipment that was in need of attention. A little while later the bus arrived to take them to debriefing.

Frank and the rest of the crew entered the briefing room to be greeted by the station commander, the squadron commander and the station padre. The padre issued cigarettes and tots of rum for anyone who wished or needed them, and then each crew member was interviewed by an intelligence officer, who made copious notes of all that they had to tell. They also passed their logs to their section leaders before removing their flying clothing and stowing it in their lockers.

A crew bus took them to their respective messes, where they received their flying meal of steak, bacon, eggs, fried bread, tomatoes and chips, which they ate with great gusto. For Frank, however, hungry and tired as he was, the edge was taken off the euphoria of having survived by the knowledge that of the three aircraft from East Kirkby that had failed to return, one was that containing his friend Eric Wood. As he automatically chewed his food, a meal that many a civilian would have given his eye teeth for, Frank could not shake the vision of his young friend's eager face when they had last spoken. They had walked into Padgate together, gone on to Blackpool, St. Athan and Winthorpe together, and they had arrived at East Kirkby together.

And now... now that boyish charm was extinguished forever...

drowned in fire and space. He shook his head and put his knife and fork down.

"I'm bushed," he said quietly. "I think I'll turn in."

Jim Baxter nodded and stood. "I think I'll join you... it's been a long night."

At about noon they were awoken from a deep sleep to the news that they were on the 'battle order' again. Arrangements had been made for a brunch in the mess and they were to be at the briefing room at 19:00 hours. They had been allocated a Mk.111 aircraft, LE-Y (Yolk), and after their meal they went out to the dispersal and spent some time checking the aircraft, after which they returned to their messes for an evening meal and then made their way to the briefing room.

The target was Leipzig, the form of the briefing the same as for the previous night, and the departure was set for midnight. The outward route was to be a direct one towards Berlin, before turning south to the target, whilst the return was planned as a long southerly route passing to the north of Frankfurt. They were to take a full bomb load consisting of a 4,000-lb 'Cookie', with the balance made up with 4-lb incendiaries.

At about 22:30 hours they were once again at dispersal, with all their kit and equipment, where they checked the engines and systems. The ground crew chief made a few adjustments to the starboard outer engine and they re-tested it. It was then just a matter of waiting for the time to board the aeroplane and settle themselves in their respective posts.

They were airborne twenty minutes after midnight, the routine being the same as for the previous night, the same one as it would be for all their future operations together. At 20,000 feet they once again crossed the Dutch coast and headed for Berlin.

About halfway between Bremen and Berlin they ran into fighter flares floating in a direct line heading for Berlin, continuing well beyond the point where they turned towards Leipzig. "Looks like the Mosquito attack on Berlin has had the right effect," Frank said to Giles.

"Yes. Let's hope they've sent their night fighters there," Giles replied as he turned the aircraft to the new heading called out by Tom.

Although they kept their eyes peeled for any fighter activity, none was seen on that whole leg of the journey, but they did run into heavy flak near Magdeburg on their run into the target.

Suddenly a heavy shell exploded, at their exact height, dead ahead, and a few moments later it was followed by one bursting dead astern. Frank looked across at Giles as time froze for them both. It was known that the German anti-aircraft batteries had 'Predictor Gun Laying Systems', and they braced themselves for the certainty of the third shell, which would almost certainly burst between the first two.

There was little or nothing that Giles could do. No evasive action, no skill or effort would thwart the incoming missile. Frank's hand reached out in slow motion, he knew not what for, as his mind slowed down. The intercom crackled as Dick, alone in his rear turret, muttered an expletive and the aircraft gave a lurch. Frank's eyes opened wide as his brain waited for the extinction he knew must follow. He registered Giles' tight grip on the column, the jerk to the right and then back to the left as the aircraft miraculously continued in level flight.

A screaming in his earphones brought his thoughts back to reality. "Bale out... we're hit... got to get out...!"

He looked across at Giles. Giles shook his head. "Who was that?"

"I'm not sure," Frank replied, "sounded like Roy."

"Jim," Giles called. "See what the bloody hell's going on back there."

Jim disconnected himself from his station by the radio. He opened the rear cabin doors and peered down the fuselage. Plugging his intercom back in, he called forward. "Looks like Roy may have some trouble... he seems to be trying to get out of his turret. I think we may have been hit though... I can't see... I'm going to need some help."

"Frank," Giles ordered. "You go back and help Jim... and report any damage."

Frank signalled his understanding. He disconnected his oxygen supply from the main supply and reconnected it to his portable supply bottle, which he clipped to his flying suit. He turned and made his way behind Tom, who gave him a thumbs-up sign as he passed, through the doors and over the main spar as Jim made his way ahead of him. In the darkness they could make out the struggling shape of Roy as he tumbled from his turret, flailing his arms around. He landed on the fuselage floor ahead of them and made as if to rise, banging his fists on the side of the aircraft in a frustrated gesture as he subsided back to the floor.

Beside them, just forward of the mid-upper turret, they were aware of a jagged hole in the fuselage, and above them, at an angle, just aft of the turret, another hole where the shell had obviously torn its way out, without exploding. Frank's blood curdled at the thought of what might have been. If that shell had exploded, the whole tail section would have disintegrated and none of them would ever have got out. Inches further forward, and whether it exploded or not, it would have detonated the bomb load. He pointed to the two holes and shook his head at Jim in disbelief. Jim returned his look and then crawled over Roy and turned back to examine him.

In his panic to get out of the turret, Roy had obviously failed to realise that at 20,000 feet and with his oxygen supply disconnected, his efforts were doomed to failure. He lay on his back in a heap, his arms moving feebly, his mouth trying desperately to articulate the terror shining from his eyes.

Frank plugged in his intercom. "Minimal damage," he reported to Giles. "It went through without exploding... nothing seems affected apart from a few shell racks."

"What about Roy?"

"He's pretty much out of it... I don't think he was hit, but he does seem to be having some sort of a panic attack and he's only semi-conscious... oxygen starvation, I reckon."

"Get him to the rest bed and plug him in again," Giles ordered.

"What about the mid-upper gun?" asked Frank.

"Get Roy to the bed and then one of you will have to man the bloody thing until he comes around."

Frank looked across at Jim and signalled that they were to take Roy forward. Jim signed his understanding and the two of them dragged Roy forward, manhandling him onto the rest bed, where they reconnected him to the main oxygen supply and plugged themselves in to the intercom.

"Got him there... he's coming round," Frank reported.

"I need that mid-upper manned," yelled Giles.

As the oxygen reached into Roy's lungs he began to breathe deeply and he reached up for Frank, his eyes swivelling around in renewed terror. Frank fished about for his intercom and plugged it in. "It's alright Roy. It didn't explode... we're alright."

Roy's expression didn't alter and he swung his legs off the bed, shouting. "Bale out... got to get out!"

Frank flung himself down on him and pinioned him down on the rest bed. "Pull his oxygen out!" he yelled to Jim, "...and his intercom."

Jim reached over and disconnected Roy. As his struggles died down, Frank held on to him and Jim stood up. "I'd better take care of that turret," he said. "Can we get his suit off, it's pretty chilly up there." They tried to turn Roy over and get the heated suit off him but were unsuccessful. "Never mind, I'd better get up there," said Jim resignedly. Frank grinned at him and made a thumbs-up sign as Jim unplugged, turned and made his way back to the turret.

By then the renewed lack of oxygen, though unlikely to kill him, had rendered Roy practically helpless, and with considerable anti-aircraft fire and fighter activity building up, Giles called for Frank to resume his station and concentrate on fuel management. Frank got

Roy to his knees and dragged the semi-conscious man along to the cabin doors. He pushed them open and Tom, seeing him, rose from his table and helped him through with Roy. They parked him on the floor just behind Tom's seat and Frank resumed his station, standing to the right of Giles.

"Alright?" asked Giles, as Frank plugged himself back in to his position.

"I think so skipper," Frank replied. "He's on the floor behind Tom for the moment."

"We'll leave him there while we get on with this," Giles said tersely.

They ran on into the target, dropped their bombs on the marker flares and turned for home, each man more than relieved at their survival. Along the return route they flew into considerable air-defence activity off to the port bow, which Tom identified as the Frankfurt area defences. As a result, Giles turned the aircraft several points to starboard in order to give them a clearer track, and the remainder of the journey passed off without incident.

As they reached the Dutch coast, Frank leant across and reconnected Roy's oxygen supply and, when it appeared that he was prepared to remain calm, turned from him in order to carry out his own tasks. However, he left Roy's intercom unplugged. None of them had the time or the inclination to listen to his moans, or even his excuses, whilst they were still airborne.

They landed at East Kirkby at 07:15 hours as dawn was breaking in the east. Giles cut the engines as they parked on dispersal, pulled his helmet off and turned to Roy. "What the bloody hell was that all about!" he yelled.

Roy stood sheepishly. "I'm sorry skipper... I just... it nearly..." He swallowed hard. "I lost my nerve for a moment, skipper... it won't happen again, I promise."

For a moment Giles looked as if he were about to explode, then his face relaxed a little. "Make bloody certain it doesn't," he growled. "This time I take no action but next time..."

"There won't be a next time, skipper," said Roy.

"Right then, let's get to de-briefing and then get some sleep," said Giles. Roy turned and made his way back to the exit and the others followed.

The Moon period was now with them and the weather was particularly unsuitable, so it was not until the middle of December that the next 'battle order' appeared. In the meantime they had to make a few daytime training flights, and in the evenings they got to know the two local pubs, both called the Red Lion, one in the village of East Kirkby itself and the other out at Revesby.

The nearer one, in the village, shared its accommodation and doubled up as the local butcher's shop. An unprepossessing building by daytime, its small bar was, by night, a heaving throng of RAF boys and men clamouring for their next drink, waving their jam jars over each other's heads in an attempt to get served. Whole crews would often prefer to drink in this small, crowded pub rather than in the messes, as by doing so it meant that they could drink together rather than be split up according to rank. In an attempt, perhaps, at immortality, many a young man carved his initials on the tables, and before long those of 'F.B.' were added to the distinguished list.

On the afternoon of the 16th of December, they went through the now familiar briefing and once again the target was Berlin, with another midnight take-off. Frank couldn't help noticing that Roy's face seemed to have lost all its colour, but he put any doubts to the back of his mind as he attended to his section leader and the necessary fuel calculations.

Having donned their flying kit they jumped aboard the next available crew bus, which took them out to dispersal, where they proceeded with their individual tasks of checking the aircraft. By the time they had finished, Roy had still not arrived and Giles stopped a passing vehicle and asked the driver to report to the squadron office that he was missing. Just before zero hour they received a message to say that he could not be found on the base and that, as they didn't have a mid-upper gunner, they were to be taken off the detail.

Wherever he was, Roy was now in serious trouble. He had absconded from the camp after the briefing and both the RAF special investigation branch and the civil police were informed and brought into the hunt.

For the next four operational flights, they had to make do with whichever mid-upper gunner was available. Most of these chaps were competent and the runs were completed with little or no incident, but on a raid on Berlin on New Year's Day 1944, they were saddled with a young Canadian with no previous operational experience who kept on seeing imaginary German fighters that neither Dick Holmes, the rear gunner, or any other member of crew, come to that, could see. He blasted off at these shadows with cries of "Fockewulf Condor!", wasting a lot of ammunition in the process, and on one occasion even shot up a Lancaster within their group, although happily he was as bad a shot as he was a judge.

On the 2nd of January 1944, Frank's crew was again posted on the 'battle order' on the squadron notice board, and this time they had been allocated an aircraft - with the designation LE-W - which they had not flown in before. Once again the target was the by now almost routine one of Berlin, and they were given another relief mid-upper gunner by the name of Paul, a decent chap who had flown on several previous raids and displayed a great deal of confidence.

They left on schedule at midnight and headed for the Dutch coast, climbing 'on track' towards their normal 20,000-feet altitude. At about 10,000 feet, Frank started the procedure for changing the supercharger gear from 'M' to 'S'. There was no response and so he tried again, and again it failed. As the system on the Lancaster Mk.111 was electro-pneumatic, he checked the electrical fuses but they were all serviceable.

"I can't get the superchargers to switch to 'S'," he called to Giles.

"Have you checked the fuses?"

"Yes."

"Try one more time."

Frank reached forward to the switch above the starboard master engine cocks. He turned it but nothing happened. "It's no good skipper, it simply won't change."

"Can we go on?" Giles asked.

"Not a chance skipper. It'd be suicide," replied Frank.

"We'll have to turn back then," said Giles. "Tom!"

"Yes skipper," Tom answered.

"Tom, we're going to have to abort... set us a course to get us back home, will you?"

"Righto," said Tom. "But we can't just turn around you know... there's four-hundred others like us out there somewhere. Ease off to starboard and I'll let you know when we've left the stream."

When Tom was able to confirm that they were well clear of the track, he called forward to Giles with a heading which would take them back towards the Dutch coast and the designated North Sea jettisoning area. They reached it and Giles opened the bomb doors. Alec dropped the incendiaries in their canisters and then, when they were well clear, he let go the 'Cookie'.

At just after 02:00 hours they reported to the operations room, where Giles and Frank made a detailed report of the supercharger malfunction. Their report was received at first with a stony silence and then with obvious disbelief. Frank felt his temper rising at the implications, but a swift sideways glance and a meaningful cough from Giles warned him to keep calm. The section leader informed them that the matter would be fully investigated and they were dismissed.

Outside the room they were met by the rest of their glum-looking crew. "What did they say?" Tom asked. Giles shrugged his shoulders and made a deprecating gesture, shaking his head.

"They think we... I think they think we're turning LMF," said Frank bitterly.

"What? Surely... what can we do?" said Alec.

Giles spoke then. "Well, I for one have never lacked moral fibre and neither have you chaps. We'll just have to wait for the report. Come on lads, I need a drink and it just so happens I have a bottle of Scotch in my locker."

"For medicinal purposes?" Frank enquired.

"I bloody well hope so," replied Giles.

The following morning another crew were detailed to take the aeroplane up on an air test, and to the horror and disbelief of Frank and his crew they reported that not only had they been able to select the 'S' gear on the supercharger without any trouble, but that they had even attained an altitude of 23,000 feet. Giles and Frank were summoned immediately to the squadron commander's office and given a very stern dressing down, despite their continued denials of any wrongdoing.

It was, of course, fair to say that there were cases of early returns for dubious reasons, but what particularly incensed them was the sheer unfairness of being labelled as cowards when they had done all they could to avoid having to abort. Giles bemoaned the fact, to Frank, that if proof was needed of their dedication to the task then there was none greater than the time before, when despite being hit, despite the trouble they had had with Roy, they had carried on and dropped their bombs on target. "If only I could tell them about that," he agonised. "But I suppose that if I did now then I'd be in trouble for not reporting Roy at the time."

Vindication was to come, however, on the 5th of January, when, on returning from a fairly uneventful operation to Szczecin in an aircraft with the designation LE-R, they entered the briefing room to see that their bogey craft, LE-W, was marked on the board as an early return due to supercharger failure.

It didn't clear their names that night, but it did allow them to go to their beds feeling a little less down than they had all felt for a while. In the following days, the ground engineers were able to pinpoint the trouble. It appeared that there was a bad pneumatic pipe joint in the floor zone under the cabin, and when the 'Cookie' was loaded the distortion caused this joint to move, releasing the air pressure that operated the pneumatic jacks that changed the gears on each engine.

Their release from suspicion allowed them to settle back into the routine of operations with a clearer heart, and at the end of January John Soames joined them as their permanent mid-upper gunner. He was a lively lad of about nineteen years of age who integrated well with them all, both on and off duty, and allowed them to put the incidents with Roy and the supercharger behind them.

At about the same time, Frank received a letter from Florrie, which both delighted and saddened him in equal measure. Avidly he scanned for news of James and proudly lapped up the report of the baby's progress. Several times in the aircraft, often in the thick of battle, he had thought about him. Whatever happened, he knew that his seed would remain on Earth and the comfort he gleaned from that was immeasurable.

Florrie chatted on about the family and, as he read, Frank felt himself drawn back into the world of the Devon countryside. Lizzie was there, and she came alive in Florrie's words. If he closed his eyes he could picture her by the pool with their baby in her arms. The thought of her, the nearness of her in the letter, brought his feelings for her back to the surface... feelings he had deliberately subsumed in the safe, all-encompassing memories of the family as a whole. They were feelings which veered between lost love and... well... almost anger.

At times he had chided himself over his acceptance of the status quo... aware of a nagging suspicion that perhaps in his heart of hearts this was what he really wanted... but at other times... at other times he felt with a mind-numbing certainty that given the free choice he would run to her like a shot. But freedom of choice was not what he had. Lizzie was right, Florrie was right, they could not, and he should not, place his own feelings... his own lust, above the good of all those he loved. He cursed himself for the relief that this reasoning brought him, chastising himself for the shallowness and guilt it brought. Was this how Violet had felt all those years ago?

"Girlfriend?" asked Jim, passing by the end of his bed.

Frank looked up, his eyes questioning, his face displaying his incomprehension. "Pardon?"

"Girlfriend... Is that from a girlfriend? Only you seem pretty wrapped up in it. I reckon you've read it three times already."

Frank smiled. "No. No, it's from my... well from my foster mother... it just reminds me of a world... well one that seems a long way away just now."

"I know what you mean," said Jim sagely.

'I wonder if you really do,' Frank thought.

On Thursday the 10th of February, Frank and Alec Coles were surprised to be called into the squadron adjutant's office to hear the news that Roy had been apprehended and was being held in Nottingham prison. They were detailed to travel to Nottingham to fetch him and, feeling like schoolboys who had been given time off classes, they collected their travel warrants and set off by train. This was no easy journey in view of the number of changes of train that had to be made, and it was fairly late in the day when they finally arrived at the prison.

Once there, there was an awful lot of paperwork to be completed before they finally signed for 'one body' and took charge of a cheerfully smiling, and far from abashed, Roy. They walked out of the prison, for all the world like three old friends who had been reunited, and walked to the railway station with Roy chatting away, asking for news of all his old chums, seeming almost pleased to be returning home. At the station, however, they were informed that there was no possibility of them catching a train that night which would get them back to East Kirkby, and Frank made the decision that they would all go back into town and get a room at the YMCA.

They settled in, and after a, by their standards, fairly meagre meal, and faced with the prospect of a long evening with little or nothing to do, they decided to go out on the town for a bit.

"My last night of freedom," Roy moaned in mock anguish.

"What would sir like for his last request?" Frank asked.

"A gorgeous blonde, dinner at the Ritz and an ocean liner to the Caribbean," Roy replied.

"Would a night at Nottingham Palais suffice?"

"That would be very acceptable, thank you."

They entered the dance hall and made straight for the bar, where Roy immediately struck up a conversation with a big blonde girl from Heywood in Lancashire who was apparently down on a visit to another friend. "Oh, is she here?" Roy said, "only my two friends here wouldn't mind some company."

"She is," the girl laughed, "but she's with her fella... over there." She pointed, and the three men followed her directions.

"Never mind," said Roy, sweeping his arm around her shoulder. "Let's you and me have a little fun, aye, starting off with a bit of a dance."

They swept onto the dance floor and joined in the circling throng of dancers as Frank and Alec separated to each end of the bar in order to keep an eye on him. All night they sat, their eyes glued to the laughing figure of Roy and the big Lancashire lass, only coming back together as and when the couple got back to the bar.

"Why don't you lads have a dance then?" the girl asked.

Roy laughed. "Oh, they like watching me."

Frank smiled. "I know," said Roy. "Why don't you dance with Dora for a bit whilst I have a pee?"

Frank looked at the girl, seeing the doubt in her eyes at being fobbed off. "I, err..."

"Go on... I won't be long. You two have a dance and..." Roy turned to Alec. "D'you need one?"

Alec nodded and they left. For a moment Frank stood, uncertain of what to do. Then he looked at the girl. 'Oh what the hell,' he thought. "Come on then," he said cheerily, "just for a moment until he gets back."

The girl flashed her acceptance and they entered the circle of dancers, Frank putting his arms around her waist and holding her hand. He caught the scent of her, the faint musky odour of her hot body mingling with the cheap toilet water. Her softness flattened itself onto his body and his thoughts whirled back to memories of Joan. Round and round they danced, until a tap on his shoulder warned him that Roy had returned and he reluctantly handed the girl back to him.

He walked back to the bar. "Alright?" Alec asked.

"Fine. Fine, thank you," Frank replied. "I could do with a drink though... keep your eyes on chummy there."

"Oh I don't think he'll go anywhere without her," Alec responded.

"Don't you be so sure," laughed Frank, "our Roy's never been one to miss a chance."

The band leader called out the last waltz and the dance floor filled up. Frank cast a nervous glance into the melee and signalled for Alec to take up station around the other side. He lost sight of Roy and walked around to Alec. "Can you see him?"

"No. Not at the moment. He's... is that him?"

"I don't know... no. I can't see them anymore... go around!" shouted a frustrated Frank. He waited for the vast circle of dancers to come around as Alec ran around the outside of the dance floor, looking inwards. There was no sign of Roy or the girl, and as Frank stood there craning his neck Alec joined him and the dance finished. "Nothing?" asked Frank, more in hope than expectation.

"Nothing," Alec said resignedly. "He's done a bloody bunk."

"Oh shit," muttered Frank, "that's all we need. Now it's us that's for the high jump."

They stood and watched as the dance floor emptied, hoping against hope that Roy would materialise from its midst and their troubles would be over. Eventually, as the floor cleared and it was apparent that he had scarpered, they left the Palais and waited outside in the cold night air, wondering if perhaps he would still turn up.

"He's gone, hasn't he?" said a dejected Alec.

"I'm afraid so," Frank replied.

For about half an hour they stood shivering in the night air before deciding that nothing further was to be served and they returned to the hostel and bedded down for a fitful night's sleep.

The following morning they got up and left for the station. Dejectedly they showed their warrant cards at the gate and strolled along the platform to the waiting room. Frank opened the door first and stopped dead in his tracks. Roy stood there in the centre of the room, his face wreathed in smiles, his arms wide open in an expansive greeting. "Morning lads!"

"Bloody hell Roy, we thought you'd legged it," said Frank, bursting out laughing as much with genuine relief as humour. He turned as Alec came in. "Look who's here," he cried.

Alec's face broke out into a wide smile. "Roy!" he said as he stepped forward. "Where the hell did you get to?"

"I got to heaven dear boy. I got to heaven on a blonde."

"You didn't... what, that one you were with last night?"

"The very same," said Roy proudly. "Sneaked me up to her room, had her wicked way with me and sneaked me out again this morning at the crack of bloody dawn."

"You dirty lucky bugger," grinned Frank. "You dirty lucky bugger..." His face dropped. "But why...?"

"Why am I here? Come on lads, I might be lacking in moral fibre but I ain't going to let my mates down, am I?"

"You did when you didn't turn up that time," said Alec quietly. Frank shot him a admonishing glance, but Roy laughed it off.

"I said to Giles that it wouldn't happen again and I kept my word, didn't I... eh?" He raised his eyebrows and waited for an answer.

"You did that," Frank agreed.

"That I did... and if I'd've gone with you then I would have probably broken my word to a mate, and whatever Roy Smith is... whatever I do, I don't do that."

Frank smiled at Roy and put his arm around his shoulder. "Thanks Roy."

Roy returned his embrace and reached out to take Alec's proffered hand. "Now what time's the train home?"

The journey back to East Kirkby, though arduous, was uneventful, and later that day they handed Roy to the RAF police Sergeant and 'the body' was taken off their charge. Before the ink was dry on the paper, Roy launched himself at the door and made a dash for freedom, but the Sergeant, who had obviously anticipated such a move, made a superb rugby tackle and brought him to ground on the threshold. Frank and Alec stood there dumbfounded, caught halfway between astonishment and amusement.

Eight days later they were once again flying operationally, and this time the target was Leipzig. Once the green flare had gone up, the usual stream of aircraft moved from their dispersals and proceeded by their shortest routes around the perimeter track to the runway. Unfortunately, one of the Lancasters manned by a new crew and piloted by a young Australian, ran one of its main wheels off the perimeter track and sank deeply into the mud.

Every one of the following aircraft, including Frank and his companions, had to be turned around and were forced to take a different and longer route to the runway.

All the way to the target that night, they were harassed by night fighters and, despite the initial take-off delay, they, and the main force, arrived before the pathfinders. On a night as black as pitch, and constantly in and out of cloud, they had to orbit and wait, with aircraft coming in from all directions. Before the target flares were eventually laid Frank saw two collisions, and they were all extremely relieved when they could finally complete their mission and turn for home.

The following morning when they awoke, the sound of Merlin engines could be heard moving around the perimeter track. The Australian and his crew had been detailed for concentrated taxiing practice.

In the late afternoon they again attended a briefing, and this time the target was Stuttgart, with another midnight departure. On time, they left their dispersal and followed several other aircraft to the runway in use. The Lancaster in front of them was given the green light to turn on to the runway, followed by another green to signal take-off clearance.

As soon as the aircraft in front of them started its take-off run, they were given the green light to clear them for line-up. Giles and Frank watched the tail light of the preceding aeroplane moving down the runway ahead of them as they waited their turn for take-off. It appeared to be moving off to the left of the centre line and Frank shot a concerned glance at Giles, who shook his head in disbelief.

Suddenly there was an almighty flash where the tail light had been, followed by a tremendous explosion, which rocked their aircraft back on its wheels. Moments later they received their own green for take-off and headed off down the runway, with everybody on board holding their breath against the very real possibility of a sympathetic detonation of the 'Cookie'. This was coupled with the fear that there might be debris on the runway.

Luckily they lifted off without incident, leaving a blazing inferno on the ground off to their port. One of their problems had been resolved satisfactorily, but the other, the 'Cookie', would remain with them until they finally released their bomb load.

In the event, the trip was relatively trouble free apart from the fact that one-and-a-half hours into the flight the starboard inner engine suddenly throttled back and it proved impossible to restore it to any useful level. As the engine was causing severe drag, Frank feathered the propeller and shut it down and they continued on three.

When they finally got back to base, they discovered that the aircraft that had exploded had been piloted by the same young Australian who had come to grief the night before. This time, attempting his first fully laden take off, he had swung to the left, as they had seen, and as the aircraft had crossed the road, the undercarriage had collapsed and the entire bomb load had detonated, killing everybody on board with the exception of the rear gunner, who was blown clear and rescued with very little injury.

The blast broke windows up to 15 miles from East Kirkby and caused damage and confusion all over the camp. The one beneficiary was Roy, who calmly and quietly left his cell in the guard room through the hole that one of the main undercarriage wheels had made in the wall. He was never seen again.

Life went on with a constant routine of operations. Berlin, Augsburg, Berlin and Berlin again, until on the 10th of March they took part in their first raid outside Germany, against the Michelin Tyre Works at Clermont-Ferrand.

Frank was never quite sure, afterwards, just why he had such a bad feeling about the raid from the off. He supposed it was because he knew that this time he would be bombing French men and women rather than an identifiable enemy. He tried to put the thought from his mind, but the more he tried the more it came home to him that what he was about to do was in no way very different to bombing his own factory in Chateauneuf.

Down there, men and women were doing their jobs, not in any determined or deliberate effort to bolster the German war effort but merely to put food on the table. What they were doing was just the same as that which they had done before the war.

Giles must have read his thoughts because, as they left the briefing room and made their way to the aircraft, he had turned to Frank and asked him specifically if he was alright. Frank had smiled at him and nodded his head, and nothing more was said.

As they approached the foothills of the Massif Central and ran on south to the valley where Clermont-Ferrand nestled, they all knew that things were very wrong. The sky above them was clear and the bright moonlight was shining down onto solid low cloud. They could see Lancasters and Halifaxes in every direction and, before long, intense fighter activity started with them all silhouetted from above and below. Time after time they saw bombers holding a steady course, with a fighter flying on the same heading below it. Suddenly there would be a steam of cannon-shell tracers going upwards at about 45 degrees into the belly of the bomber, followed almost immediately by flames and then its disintegration in a massive fireball.

By the time they arrived on the target, the flames from below and the almost constant rain of bombs from above had all but obliterated the marker flares. Nevertheless, Alec was able to identify them and he called for the bomb doors to be opened. As he set up his sights, he guided Giles in with a steady and calm stream of instructions and called "bombs away" as he pressed the release button. Giles held their course steady for the photo flash and then peeled off to starboard in a long arc, which would take them out and away from the target.

Tom called out a course for home and they turned on it, heading roughly north, with Frank acutely but privately aware that each mile they travelled brought him not only closer to England and safety, but in addition took them ever closer to Orleans. As they approached Vierzon and Tom called out the fact to them all, he found his thoughts ever more on the ground below, and his friends and enemies who would shortly lie beneath him.

A strange dread that had bothered him all through the flight persisted and dragged at his thoughts, until suddenly it clarified in John's scream over the intercom. An ME 109 was closing in on them from their starboard quarter.

Frank stared out of the cockpit as the Messerschmitt tore out of the clear night sky, its cannon blazing, sending streams of tracer shells in their direction.

Giles banked to the starboard and dipped the nose as John opened up from the mid-upper and the enemy fighter swept over the top of them. "Where's it gone?" Dick yelled.

"Off to port about ten o'clock!" John shouted. He opened fire again as the fighter swung up into the Moon, rolled and swept back down, pouring fire at them. Alec now opened up for the short time that it was in his field of fire, but John continued firing as the plane rapidly closed on them, sweeping under their port wing. In a flash it was past and Dick, his turret at full turn to port, was able, at last, to shoot at it as it raced by and out of useful range.

For a brief moment there was relative peace, but then the port inner engine started to splutter and almost simultaneously the port outer closed down. Frank looked at his dials for a split second, registering the loss of oil pressure in both engines, the sudden reduction in the registered fuel and the corresponding increase in engine temperature.

"Feather both port engines!" Giles called across.

Frank reached across, pulled back the throttles and closed the master fuel cocks for the two engines. He moved quickly right and pushed both feathering buttons in and held them there. "Fire in the port wing!" John yelled over the intercom. Giles looked back and confirmed it to Frank, who, after an agonising wait for the propellers to stop turning, took his fingers from the feathering buttons, flicked up the covers and pushed hard on the extinguisher buttons. He craned his neck to see over and behind Giles and his heart dropped as, after a moment's hesitation, the flames once more rushed from the cowlings, streaking back across the wing.

"Time to go!" Giles cried. "Bale out! Bale out!"

Alec let go his triggers and dived to the floor of the nose compartment. He grabbed the handle in the centre of the hatch, lifted it slightly inwards and then turned and jettisoned it. The inward rush of air tore at them as Frank reached across and grabbed his parachute and began strapping it to his chest. "Alright skipper?" he shouted. Giles returned his enquiry with a thumbs-up, gesturing for him to go, and Frank slipped down and under the main console as Alec went out through the hatch. For a split second Frank hesitated at the brink. He was aware that behind him the others were preparing to follow, aware that they had, at the most, two minutes to get out. Yet he was also aware of his own strange reluctance to swap allegiance from the aeroplane to the empty space below.

He launched himself through the hatch. The icy blast grabbed at him, seeking entry into every crevice as he tumbled through the air, fumbling for his 'D' ring, praying that in his haste he had remembered to correctly attach the parachute to his harness. He pulled, and suddenly it was all gone... the tearing wind, the noise, all of it suddenly stopped and he felt himself swept to a halt, dangling from his harness whilst above him the blessed white canopy mushroomed.

To his left and slightly below him he could see another parachute, and instinctively he glanced upwards to the right seeking others. None were there, but in the far distance he could see the flaming trail of the bomber. He stared after it, searching in its path for the tell-tale white blossoms that would indicate his friend's safety, but none came. Instead, as he watched, horrified, the streak of flame expanded to a huge ball that disintegrated into a host of blazing sections spiralling down to Earth.

***

"Bless me Father, for I have sinned," Frank whispered against the grille. He waited until the priest's dark form leant forward, and he knew that his ear was close before continuing. "Father René?"

A discreet cough and then, "Yes, my son. Do you wish to confess your sins?"

Frank smiled to himself in the cool gloom of the confessional. It was Father René alright, no doubt about that. "No, not really Father, but I would like to meet you later in a safe place."

There was a short silence before the priest spoke again in a whisper. "Do I know you monsieur?"

"Yes Father, you know me... although I don't think you'll be very pleased to see me. It's Frank... Frank Balfour."

There was a sharp intake of breath from the other side of the grille. "You... you should not be here Frank. There's great danger for you... and for your friends."

"I know Father. I did not mean to come here. I have crashed. I was... am in the Royal Air Force and we were shot down."

"Are you injured?"

"No, but I am not alone. I have a friend with me... he's out there in the pews... over there near the door." A glimmer of light showed that the priest had pulled the curtain aside briefly, and then darkness reigned again.

"I see him. Does he speak French?"

"Not a word."

"Just the two of you?"

"I'm afraid so Father. All of my... the others didn't make it. It blew up with all of my friends in it. We parachuted down into the Sologne and made our way here. We need to be put in touch with anyone who can help us get back to England. I don't want to trouble Gunther again. How is he, by the way?"

"He's fine, and... look, we must finish now or it will look suspicious. Meet me later this evening. Now where...?"

"Do you know Marcel's old house?"

"Yes."

"Is it still empty?"

"Of course... yes, yes. I'll meet you there this evening. Now go my son, and take care. France is a very dangerous place for you."

"For everyone," Frank agreed. "Thank you Father. Until this evening then."

"Go with God my son," the priest whispered as Frank left the confession and walked purposely across the aisle.

He bowed briefly to the altar, crossed himself and then re-joined Alec.

"Was he there?" Alec asked as he sat down beside him.

"Yes. When we stand up, do as I do and then walk out of the church and down the road... try not to look as if you're worried or frightened. Alright?"

"Alright."

"Good, then let's go. Frank stood, and the two of them made their obeisance and left the church, turning left into the main street, across the Rue Migneron and down towards the river. As they passed the narrow side street leading through to the Rue de Mouton, Frank could not help glancing down, wishing with all his heart that he could simply walk up to and knock on the door of his friend's house. He knew he couldn't. Gunther would be pleased to see him, but that joy would soon give way to fear that his presence would be dangerous to them all, and that fear would then give way to anger. He hadn't meant to come here and now... now he must get away as soon as possible before he brought ruin on all that he loved.

They had landed in the Sologne, as he had told the Father, and spent the night huddled up in a hayrick on the edge of a small farm complex just outside Tigy. In the morning, as day had broken with that pale, peculiar light so typical of the Sologne, they had crouched back into the hay as a man and a woman had left the house, their hoes over their shoulders ready for another day's toil in the fields. For a long while they had watched carefully as the couple trudged across the open land and set to work hoeing together, in that timeless rhythm that was so familiar to Frank.

The house had seemed empty, but there was really no way of telling, so eventually they had crept across the yard and pushed gently at the unlocked door.

A dog had struggled to its feet by the open range, giving a low bark as it peered at them through eyes blue-glazed with age before laying its head back on the bundle of dirty sacking that formed its bedding.

Frank called out a greeting and they waited with thumping hearts for a reply. None came.

On the table the remains of a loaf of bread and a bowl, half full of tepid cabbage soup, remained as evidence of the occupant's breakfast. Guiltily they had divided it between themselves, dipping the hardened loaf into the thin liquid. Frank had smiled at Alec. "Cabbage soup for breakfast. What do you think of that?"

Alec gave him a wan smile. "Yes, and some other lucky bastard is tucking into my bacon and eggs back home."

Frank had laughed quietly. "Ah, but look what they're missing."

When they'd finished eating, it had taken them barely five minutes to find the rough clothes that they now wore. Pantaloons tied up with string, coarse woven jackets and, in Alec's case, a battered straw hat. They'd carried them over to the hayrick to change, carefully hiding their flying suits deep in the hay, hoping as they did that perhaps one day their discovery would pay the couple back for that which they'd stolen.

Now, having seen Father René, they approached the river at the top end of the Place du Port and stopped at the sight of German soldiers guarding the bridge. On their way north they had avoided crossing by the bridge as Frank had guessed that it would be heavily guarded and that to cross would require the showing of papers that they clearly did not have. Instead, they had followed the bank on the southern side until they had come across a small boat that they had crossed with, before casting it adrift.

"What do we do now?" Alec asked in a worried tone.

Frank looked about. Obviously the Germans were not only stopping people as they crossed the bridge but were interested in any traffic that was leaving or passing through the town. He thought of retracing their steps and trying to make their way out by the Grande Rue but discounted that. If there were guards here then it was just as likely that they were posted on all exit routes.

Across on the corner of the small square, at the western end, some workmen rebuilding a small section of walling had obviously just downed tools for a break in the café on the other side of the square. He pointed across. "You take the shovel and I'll take the broom... then walk with me as if we know what we're doing. Pretend we're road sweepers. I'll sweep the muck in the gutter and you pick it up and put it in piles on the edge as if it's ready to be picked up later." Alec looked far from convinced but, nevertheless, he followed Frank across and selected one of the shovels whilst Frank picked up a yard broom. Shouldering these, and all the while dreading the challenge, they sauntered across the square and on to the Rampe du Haut Quai, where they were thankfully out of sight of the café. They could see now that three soldiers guarded the end of the bridge, and as they watched two of them approached an elderly couple crossing on foot and demanded their papers, whilst the other one stood nonchalantly staring down the quai. Frank started to work the broom, pushing the fallen leaves and sand into small piles. "Pick them up and pile them on the side," he hissed at Alec, who was standing still as if transfixed by terror. He looked back at Frank and then back at the soldiers. "Go on... do it!" Frank demanded.

Alec bent down and scooped up the small pile. He stepped up onto the cobbled bank and dumped the muck before returning and repeating the process. For a full ten minutes they worked their way slowly along the road in the direction of the bridge, with Frank keeping up a stream of unanswered conversation with a silent Alec. At the bridge Frank looked up suddenly, as if noticing the soldiers for the first time. "Can I get behind you?" he asked.

The soldier looked at him, the blank look on his face betraying the fact that he had not understood a word that Frank had said. Frank indicated his broom and pointed to the space just behind the post, making sweeping motions. The soldier stared at him for a moment and then nodded. "Ja... ja," before stepping aside. Frank reached in behind him and gathered the debris that had accumulated in the crook and swept it out into the main pile.

He moved to the other side of the road and continued sweeping, moving down the slope. Behind him, an inwardly quaking Alec scooped up the pile lying almost at the feet of the German soldier and carried it across to the eastern side of the bridge, where he started a new heap. "That's it," Frank called out cheerfully in French. "Make another pile here." He banged the broom clean on the kerb. "And then we'll move on to the other side." Alec looked at him with a total lack of comprehension. Frank grinned back at him and banged his broom on the kerb once more. "Pile ici. Ici pile macky," he said with a fixed smile on his face. For a second Alec looked at him as if he'd taken leave of his senses, but then the penny dropped and he walked quickly to where Frank had been and shovelled the swept pile up and onto the pavement. Frank moved across the sloping road to the higher level and continued sweeping, working his way ever closer to the end of the cobbled street and the beginning of the sandy path that would lead them on to the Promenade du Chastaing. He made the last pile and sat down on the edge of the quai, his broom held between his open legs as he waited for his companion to catch up.

Alec came up to him, his face white, his hands shaking as he held the shovel. "Stay calm," Frank whispered. "Now, we're going to walk down this path. I want you to put the shovel over your shoulder and whistle as we walk... can you whistle? Alec nodded. "Good. When we get to just along there..." He pointed. "...there's a clearing in the woods with a bench set back. Walk into the clearing and sit on the bench... don't run, just walk normally. Understood?" Alec nodded again. "Right my friend, I think we deserve a rest," Frank said loudly in French.

He slung his broom over his shoulder and the two of them walked off down the path along the river's edge. Alec started to whistle 'The White Cliffs of Dover' until Frank dug him in the ribs, but, in his fear, the tune had been barely recognisable anyway. They walked as nonchalantly as they were able and without speaking, as at several places on the path fishermen crouched silently at the bottom of the bank, until they reached the clearing. With an inward sigh of relief they saw that the bench was unoccupied.

Frank sat down heavily, the broom across his knees, as Alec joined him. "My God Frank, are you mad? I could have touched that soldier. I could smell the bugger's breath!"

Frank smiled at his friend. "Yes, but it worked, didn't it? Thank God those workmen took a long break. Speaking of which, we'd better get going before they miss these tools."

Alec looked at Frank. "I do believe you're enjoying this in a funny sort of way."

Frank shook his head, his face serious. "Not at all. This is my home so it's not all as strange to me as it must be to you, but even so, imagine if invaders were on the streets of your home town... imagine your town filled with the same oppressive fear that we feel here." He swept his arm around in an arc. "Fear that drives people to betray others... that banishes all trust and defiles everything."

For a moment Alec sat quietly looking out from the trees and across the river. Then he clapped his friend on the shoulder. "Yes, you're right... I hadn't thought of it that way."

Frank smiled. "I do go on, don't I? But don't worry, we're going to beat the bastards and we're going to get back to Blighty. Now let's get going before these tools get missed and they come looking for them."

He stood and hurled the broom into the dense bushes and Alec did likewise with the shovel. Then they turned and made their way through the trees, keeping away from the promenade until they were well clear and approaching La Ronce. Here they stopped briefly and looked back towards the town and the bridge, with Frank remembering the last time he stood just here with Pierre and Alec, torn between feeling like a tourist and the fear that seemed to crowd in on him.

Frank put his hand on his shoulder. "Come, follow me and I'll show you where I used to play as a boy and then we'd better head off to where we're supposed to be meeting Father René."

***

"Who is it darling?" Violet called from the small kitchen.

"It's me," Jesse replied quietly.

"Oh, I thought I heard someone else."

"You did."

Violet bustled out of the kitchen, wiping her hands on a cloth. "Oh well, have I missed them... who was it?" She stopped, seeing Jesse's stricken face and the orange-coloured envelope in her hand. "Is it... Is it for..."

"It's for you Violet... a telegram," Jesse croaked, her hand shaking as she held the telegram out to her.

Silently Violet took it. She scanned the name on it as if refusing to believe it was really for her and then looked back into Jesse's eyes. Jesse nodded her silent affirmation. "Yes... yes... just a minute. Let me sit down first," Violet whispered.

She looked around as if seeking out the whereabouts of the sofa for the first time in a strange room and then crossed to it and sat on its edge, still holding the envelope.

Jesse sat down beside her and the two of them stared out of the window in silence for what seemed like an eternity before Violet finally slid open the envelope and held up the telegram. She dropped it unread into her lap and reached into her pocket for a handkerchief to clear her opaque, glazed eyes. "Dear Mrs Slater," she read out aloud. "I regret to inform you that your son, Frank Balfour... that your son Frank Balfour is missing in action..." Her voice failed and she let the hand holding the telegram slip back down to her lap. For a moment the two of them sat silent before she raised it once more and continued. "Any further information will be passed to you as soon as it is received."

Only the loud ticking of the clock on the mantle and the sound of a great tit calling in the hedge outside broke the long silence, before Jesse cleared her throat. "He's not dead, you know?"

Violet turned to her. "But it says..."

"I know what it says... but he's alive. I knew it before and I know it now."

Violet stared at the old woman, her lips quivering, her eyes wide and questioning, striving to believe. "Are you... are you sure?"

"As sure as I am of anything."

"Then where is he?"

Jesse took hold of Violet's hands and held them tight. "I can't tell you that... I can only tell you that I don't think he's been harmed."

Violet scanned her face. "Oh I wish... I wish I could..."

"Then do so Violet. Do so," said Jesse, tugging at her hands. A half smile flicked across Violet's face before it crumpled and she fell into the older woman's arms, sobbing. Jesse just held her, patting her back, stroking her neck as if she were a child.

The back door burst open and George rushed in, followed by Ian. "Cor, you should see the crater them bombs made over the hill," George shouted. "If they'd've hit us we'd 'ave bin blown to smithereens." He stopped as Ian held him back.

"What's up mummy?" Ian asked quietly as George looked on puzzled.

Violet looked up into her son's face, seeing the gentle concern there, and beyond him his brother's expression, torn between question and annoyance that his exciting news was falling upon deaf ears. "It's Frank, he... he..."

"Is he dead?" George asked.

Ian flashed a look at him to silence him and then turned back to Violet. "What is it mummy?"

Violet smiled a wan smile of appreciation at her son and held out her hand for him to take. George moved beside the sofa, his face fixed expectantly on his mother's. Violet coughed to clear her throat. "I've had a telegram... there's a telegram..."

"Where... can I see it plea...?" cried George, before being silenced by his brother's look of disapproval.

Violet shook her head as Jesse reached out to restrain the boy.

"He's missing in action," she managed to blurt out.

George sucked in his breath and his eyes opened wider. His mouth started to work and he started to speak, but once more his brother cut him short. "That means that he may have bailed out," he said quietly.

"He's safe somewhere... I can feel it," Jesse announced.

Ian looked at her for a moment and then reached out and put his hand on Violet's shoulder. "She's right Mummy. Jesse's always right about that sort of thing."

"I bet he's battling it out with hordes of Jerry soldiers... fighting for his life against all odds," said a clearly excited George.

Violet smiled and patted her son's knee. "Yes dear, and I expect he's winning, isn't he?"

"Yeah, he'll be killing them left, right and centre... leaving them dead all over the place. Wish I was there..." His voice tailed off as he drifted into his thoughts of derring-do. Ian looked at his brother for a moment. Then he turned to Violet and caught her eye, his faint smile returning her understanding.

"Cup of tea, anyone?" Jesse asked as she rose from the sofa. Violet nodded. "Come on then George, you come and help me." She held out her hand for the boy to take and the two of them left the room.

For a moment Ian knelt beside his mother, but then, as the sounds of cups and saucers being assembled came from the kitchen, he moved up onto the sofa beside her.

He snuggled into her, his arm reaching across her lap to hold her tight, his head resting on her shoulder. "It'll be alright mummy," he whispered. "Jesse would know. He's alright... you'll see." Violet patted her son's arm and bent and kissed his head.

***

"So when can we go?" Frank asked. "We need to get away from here... we've been here for close on three weeks."

The maquisard they now knew as André stood in front of him, his face severe, his mouth set firm. "Well..."

"Your friend goes tonight," a voice interrupted. Frank looked up, seeking the source of the new voice in the gloom. A shape stepped forward into the light of the lantern and André stepped aside respectfully. "Your friend goes tonight and you stay."

"Stay?"

"Yes. We need you here." Frank searched the man's face for the truth. He registered the strange accent. Where was he from? Why did he so obviously command such respect from Andre, who he had assumed was the leader of the local Maquis? The man extended his hand and Frank took it reluctantly. "Lecroix. S.O.E., Royal Canadian Army," the man said in barely accented English. Alec looked up in surprise, but Lecroix switched back into French. "I understand you know this area pretty well."

"I live... I lived here before the Germans came and I escaped to England... that's where I want to go back to now. I don't want to stay here."

"You're ordered to stay here."

"What?"

"I've radioed England and your orders are to stay here and assist."

Frank bridled. "You... you did that without reference to me?"

The man bent closer, his face barely centimetres from Frank's. "Look Balfour," he hissed. "There's a war on here, and if your orders are to stay then you bloody well stay. Is that clear?" Frank stared up at the set face of Lecroix, holding the man's angry gaze. Then, as he watched, the anger seemed to die and Lecroix visibly relaxed and squatted beside him. "It's going to finish soon Frank." He looked around to make sure that they were not being overheard. All except André were out of earshot. André inclined his head, smiled and drew back beyond hearing distance. Lecroix put his lips close to Frank's ear.

"They're coming soon Frank," he whispered. "We need people on the ground who can liaise with non-French-speaking Yanks and the like."

"Yes, but I'm a flight engineer not a spy."

Lecroix grinned. "You were a soldier in the French Army, Frank... don't try and tell me any different."

Frank looked up into the determined face of the Canadian. "There is a German officer in Chateauneuf... he knows me."

"Then we'll kill him. If necessary, we'll kill him tonight."

"No! No, that's not the point." Frank swallowed hard. "He's my friend."

Lecroix's face went like thunder and he stood up. "Your friend!"

Frank rose too and stood his ground, aware of the man's rising fury. "Look, let me explain." He waited for Lecroix to nod his assent before continuing. "Gunther Schmidt. Leutnant Gunther Schmidt is his name. We were friends... best friends before the war." He noticed the expression of scorn that crossed the face of Lecroix and waved his hand as if to dismiss it. "No, listen. We were four friends... Pierre-Luc Cabel, who lives over between Saint-Martin- d'Abbas and Bouzy-la-Foret, myself... I lived partly in England but mostly here in the Chateau de Janvier... Marcel Fleisch and Gunther Schmidt. We were... well now the three of us are still friends."

"And the fourth? Is the fourth the Boche bastard?"

"No! No, the fourth is Marcel, but he's dead... killed by a sadistic bastard at the camp. He was Jewish you see... at the camp in Pithiviers." He noticed Lecroix's look of incredulity and, feeling powerless to stop himself trying to explain the seemingly unexplainable, he grabbed the man's arm for attention. "You must believe me," he whispered urgently. "Gunther risked everything in an attempt to save Marcel... and he helped me to escape to Spain and on to England."

There was a silence. Lecroix seemed to be thinking as he stared down at the floor. At length he called André over. "Do we know of a Boche officer called Gunther Schmidt?"

André shot a puzzled look at Frank and then turned back to face Lecroix. "He works in the kommandant's office as an adjutant... lives with a French whore in the Rue de Mouton."

"Annette... that'll be Annette. She's no whore. We rescued her from that swine Blondel when we tried to get Marcel."

André swung around to Frank, his expression open. "You know of Blondel?"

"Unfortunately, yes. He tortured and killed my friend Marcel Fleisch and God knows what he did to Annette before we took her from him. We knew him from school at Saint Benoit."

"Do you know where he is now?"

"In hell I hope."

"His body turned up recently in the Loire... well what was left of it."

Frank shook his head. "No... no, he was..." His face broke into a grin and he laughed out loud.

"What's so funny?"

Frank's eyes blazed. "Gunther said he'd kill him and he obviously did. Well good for him. I hope the bastard suffered."

There was silence as each man tried to digest and understand the import of this strange conversation, and then Lecroix spoke again. "It still means that this Boche is dangerous... unless he's prepared to help us directly."

Frank held his hand up. "No. He wouldn't do that. He helped me and he's probably helped Pierre-Luc but..."

"Pierre-Luc who?" André asked.

"Pierre-Luc Cabel. Why?"

"He's back. He got back yesterday from a labour camp in Germany. We're going to see him to persuade him not to go back when his leave's up."

Frank's heart leapt with joy. Pierre-Luc was nearby! "He'll tell you about Gunther, I'm sure."

Lecroix broke in. "Listen Balfour, stop all this crap about Gunther this and Gunther that... he's Boche and as such he's our enemy... understood?"

Frank looked him straight in the eye. "He is my friend and I will not harm him. Any other bastard, but not him. I'll kill you a dozen Webers, but I'll not touch a hair on Gunther's head... nor he mine." His eyes blazed as he held the Canadian's unwavering stare.

For a moment he thought Lecroix was about to hit him, but then the stare softened slightly. "You know Weber then?"

Frank smiled derisively. "Oh I know Weber." He cocked his head to show the scars on his temple. "These are from him... plus the ones on my back." A cold chill ran through him and he shook his head. "If Weber's in town and Annette is with Gunther, then the two of them are in great danger."

Lecroix snorted and shook his head. "I can't believe I'm listening to this."

"Then don't... you're the one who wants me to stay and I'm telling you that for me that German is off the list. If you can't accept that, then I'll leave tonight with Alec."

For a moment there was a heavy silence. Then Lecroix turned around to face Frank directly, his face set, a slight twitching in his left cheek betraying the anger he felt. Slowly his face relaxed and he smiled again. He extended his hand to Frank, who took it. "Alright, it's a deal... but for you alone... understood?"

"Understood," Frank replied. "This war's going to be over one day you know, and we'll all have to learn to live with one another again."

Lecroix's brow furrowed. "Maybe. Maybe... though not the Webers of this world, I hope."

Frank grinned. "Definitely not the Webers."

"Welcome aboard Frank."

"Just one more thing," said Frank.

The Canadian frowned. "What?"

"Have you arranged for my family to be told I'm alright?"

Lecroix smiled. "Of course." He indicated Alec. "And his."

"Thanks," a relieved Frank replied.

***

Frank lay back against the trunk of the tree and stared up at the stars sprawled across the night sky, like pinholes letting in the light of heaven. An owl called from just behind him and its mate answered in a long, quavering hoot from two-hundred yards away to his right. He stared up into the night, listening intently for the hoped-for sound of an aircraft overhead. A torch flashed from the trees on the other side of the valley and Frank flashed a brief reply and settled back against the tree. He turned to a rustling sound and André joined him, squatting down on his haunches beside him. "Anything?" he whispered.

"Nothing."

A faint hum in the western sky alerted them both and they stood, staring up. Two flashes from across the valley. Frank flashed his torch twice, and further along the valley others flashed theirs.

"Ready?" André asked.

"Ready," Frank whispered. He reached down and retrieved a lantern and held it up as André lit it. It flickered and then shone out its red light. Across and down the valley, red, green and white lights flickered and then shone in straight lines.

They waited quietly as the hum grew louder and they searched the night sky for sight of the aircraft. Frank's heart leapt as the drone of the Halifax's engines became recognisable; a link with England that transported him back to East Kirkby and the companionship he had found there. All too clearly he could imagine the tension in the cockpit, the quiet order as the crew prepared to complete their mission, the carefully rehearsed instructions that each man would give and receive.

How was Alec getting on? By now he should be in Spain, adjusting to life in the camp. His thoughts turned to his other lost companions...

Giles, Tom, Jim, Dick and John. Were they all lost? Had none got out? What had happened in the aircraft in those seconds after he had left? Why hadn't they got out? Had any of them managed to escape?

The aircraft swooped around in a long, invisible arc, betrayed only by the heavy throb of its engines. For a moment the tone changed as it banked steeply, way out over the hill to commence its run between the lights in the forest. Frank scanned the horizon, unconsciously holding his breath as its dark form swept low over the valley, releasing its spawn of billowing white parachutes in a long, steady stream, which drifted down to earth in its wake.

There were shouts now. With all secrecy lost, the need for silence was replaced by the urgent requirement to gather in and spirit away the contents of the long canisters that bumped and dragged along the ground as Frank and his companions leapt down the valley sides.

Others were arriving now. Speedily, each canister was lifted aloft and carried away, back up the western side of the valley. Frank paused for breath and clapped his friend on the shoulder. "A good night's work, Andre?"

"It'll be a better one when what's just arrived is put to good use," he growled.

"Don't worry my friend," Frank replied, laughing. "The time is coming." He bent down and picked up the edge of the parachute and André did the same on the other side, tugging it free of the low scrub. They worked quietly in unison, folding and refolding, working towards each other until, at last, they had a tidy bundle, around which they wrapped the shrouds. "Will you take this?" Frank asked.

"Why? Are you not coming back to camp?"

"No. I thought I'd go and see Pierre- Luc. If I could cut through the forest I could reach his house in about an hour and..." He stopped short as André tugged his arm and pointed down the valley.

"Look."

Frank stared in the direction his companion was pointing. Along at the far end of the valley, where they knew the road lay, there were the lights of approaching vehicles. As they watched they stopped and then went out, to be replaced, moments later, by the piercing shaft of a high- intensity search light that swept along the valley. Frank ducked down beside André as the beam swept over them, turning night into day.

"Boche," André hissed.

Frank looked up the dark valley sides towards the tree line. The others would have reached there by now and would be able to disappear into the forest before any troops could clamber their way across the rough terrain between them and the road. Always supposing that all the Germans had arrived on the vehicles. If not... he shivered... then they could be waiting at the top. No, surely they couldn't have been. If they had, there would be gunfire by now. No, the Germans had arrived too late, probably alerted by the noise of the aircraft itself... although they might have been expecting it on a clear night such as this.

"I think they got away safely," Frank whispered to Andre. "But if we go the same way, we'll arrive at the top just as the Germans get there."

"I was thinking that myself."

"Come with me then," said Frank. "We'll both go to Pierre-Luc's. If we cut back up that side of the valley, keeping to the trees, we can see if there are any Germans on the Chatenoy road."

"If there are, then we're in real trouble, because that means it's an organised affair... which means..."

"...that we've been betrayed. Yes, I'd figured that one out. But I don't think so somehow. If they'd known all about it then they'd have been up there on the ridge before now to cut off our chaps."

"I hope you're right."

"So do I. Come on, let's get going."

"What about this?" said Andre, pointing down at the chute.

Frank looked down at the white bundle at their feet. "Leave it. It'll slow us down."

The search light swept across the valley and they ducked behind a low bush. They waited until it had passed before diving off along a barely discernible deer track that wound its way through the heather, back and up the valley sides. Behind them they could now hear the shouts of the soldiers as they stumbled up the valley in the dark, calling to each other.

Suddenly, from the ridge above and behind them, came the sound of automatic gunfire, which was returned by the soldiers on the valley floor. For several seconds the fire chattered into the night as the search light swung around, seeking its source. It picked out the ridge and held steady, illuminating the thick tree trunks behind which the maquisard crouched. Another burst from the trees and the light died.

André laughed. "That'll slow the bastards down." Frank grinned into the darkness and the two of them turned and made their way up the track.

About an hour-and-a-half later, the two of them, by now muddy, tired and dishevelled, arrived at Pierre-Luc's house. They lingered for a while in the dark, close to the outbuildings, scanning the farmhouse for any sign of danger. It seemed all clear, but André warned Frank to stay hidden whilst he crept up the path. A dog barked without warning from a compound at the other end of the yard and André froze as lights went on, locks were thrown and the door opened, throwing a shaft of light down the path to reveal him crouching there.

"Who's there?" came Monsieur Cabel's voice.

"André Rodot," André replied as he rose. "A friend."

"Friend? At this time of night?"

"I'm not alone," André called.

Another figure joined the man at the door. Taller and broader, still pulling at the pantaloons he had hastily grabbed. Frank stepped from his hiding place. "It's me, Pierre-Luc."

Pierre-Luc pushed past his father to stand in front as Madame

Cabel joined them, staring fearfully out into the darkness. "Who's me?" he called. "Do I know you?"

Frank joined André on the path. "You should do," he said, laughing.

"Frank? Frank, is that you?"

"As ever was," he said, running forward.

Pierre-Luc ran down the path to join him. For a split second the two friends stood in the half light examining each other, but then they embraced as the big man lifted Frank off his feet. He set him down and turned back to his parents, grabbing Frank's hand, pulling him towards the door. "Look who it is," he called to them. "It's Frank. Frank's back."

Monsieur and Madame Cabel left the house and joined them, embracing Frank in turn amid protestations of surprise and delight. A cough from André and a hand on his shoulder brought Frank back to reality. "Yes... yes, this is my... friend... André Rodot."

"Perhaps we'd better get inside," André said urgently. He stared meaningfully at Frank and Frank returned his look, the joy turning back into caution.

"Yes. Sorry. Look, we need to get inside. There's been... well let's go inside."

Monsieur Cabel took charge. "Yes, come inside. Come and have a drink and tell us what you're doing here in the middle of the night. Giselle, put the pan on and I'll fetch us something a little stronger."

The five of them trooped into the kitchen. Pierre-Luc shut the door and crashed the bolts back in place, whilst his mother bustled over to the range and slid the pan of water back on to boil. Frank sat at the long table and indicated for André to do the same as Pierre-Luc joined them, staring with undisguised joy at his friend.

Monsieur Cabel came in bearing a large bottle, which he held aloft as his wife ducked under his arm to go and fetch the milk. "Plum alcohol from our own plums," he proudly announced as he plonked the two bottles down on the table and turned back to the dresser for glasses.

"So what are you doing here?" Pierre-Luc asked.

"Pierre-Luc," his father admonished as he straightened up and turned back to the table, the glasses in his hand. "Surely you can see what they're doing here?"

Pierre-Luc looked blank and his father continued, looking directly at Frank. "Maquis?"

Frank nodded, and the older man's gaze switched to Andre, who returned his silent enquiry with a purse of his lips and a nod.

Monsieur Cabel turned to his son. "Fighting for France! As you should be, instead of working in Germany."

"I don't do so by choice," Pierre-Luc protested.

"He fought for France," said Frank. "He fought once and now..."

"...now he should do so again," Pierre-Luc interrupted. He turned to his father. "I wasn't going back, papa. I'd already made up my mind not to, but I didn't..."

"...you didn't know who to trust," said Frank quietly.

Pierre-Luc nodded. "That and the problem of..." He looked across the table at Andre.

"Gunther," said Frank. He too looked at André and then back at Pierre-Luc. "He knows," he said. "He doesn't fully understand but he knows. Look, I know how you feel. But the fact is that there's a war on and through no fault of our own we find ourselves on different sides. He's with the enemy, and even if, for us, he's not the enemy... well I've had to come to terms with it myself. That doesn't mean that just because... we can't just sit back and do nothing, any more than he can."

"But what if..."

"...what if we come up against him?"

"Yes."

"Then we have to face that situation when we get to it. I swore that I would never take up arms against our friend... he helped me escape. He helped Annette. By the way, did you know that they are still together?"

"Yes. Yes, I knew," he said, as his father poured a measure of plum brandy into each of the glasses. "I saw Annette when I was back last year. She was..."

"They've got a little baby now," said Madame Cabel. "Nearly two years old."

Frank whirled around and stared at her. "Gunther and Annette? They've got a child?"

"Yes. A little boy. Detaire... Ditre... something like..."

"Dieter?"

"Yes, that's it. Funny name."

Frank turned back to the table, his mind racing. "A baby? They had a baby... just as he did... had. And they'd called him Dieter, after the father Gunther had never known, whose murder Violet had witnessed in the Great War. My God, if my presence in France is discovered then suspicion will fall on Gunther immediately... and even if not, then the coming battle will put all their lives at risk." He shook his head slowly. There was nothing they could do except what they each had to do... and if it came to it... He looked up into Andre's eyes, and for the first time saw recognition and sympathy for his situation.

"So what brings you here on this particular night?" asked Monsieur Cabel.

Frank took a gulp of the fiery liquid. He rolled it around his tongue and swallowed, feeling the warmth spreading through his body. "There was..." He looked up at Andre. "There was a bit of trouble."

"There was a drop. A delivery from an aircraft tonight and the Boche surprised us," said Andre. Frank looked across at him, aware that by saying this much, the man was demonstrating his trust in not only him but his friends. André continued. "Frank was coming anyway, and as we were cut off, I decided to join him."

"Coffee?" asked Madame Cabel.

Four heads looked up from the table and three nodded assent. Monsieur Cabel shook his and refilled his glass with the brandy.

"When are you due to go back, Pierre-Luc?" André asked.

Pierre-Luc snorted his derision. "Three days ago." His father looked up quickly and his son inclined his head to him, raising his eyebrows and smiling. "I said I wasn't going back papa. I've already spoken to Father René and asked him to pass on a message." His father stared at him, his expression serious. Then he raised his glass in silent salutation and drank deeply. Madame Cabel put mugs of steaming hot coffee on the table and bent down to kiss her son's head, tousling his hair.

31st July 1944

The motor car swung through the massive gates and down the drive leading to the chateau entrance. Gunther craned his neck to see the full extent of the building, his mind a whirl of mixed emotions.

He noticed the hanging black, red and white banners of his country and was unable to suppress a frown. He lived with and was part of all that their fluttering forms symbolised. Yet here? Here it seemed so wrong. He shook his head slowly.

The great doors were wide open to the warmth of the summer's evening and, as the vehicle drew to a halt at the foot of the steps, Gunther reached forward for the door handle and then settled back slightly as the sentry stepped forward to open the door. He glanced across at Annette, sitting stiffly in her seat, her face drawn and pale.

"Alright?" he whispered.

She gritted her teeth and grimaced. "I'm petrified. What if anyone recognises me?"

Gunther put his hand reassuringly on her arm as the door swung open. "How can they? Nobody here knew you before and they all know about you and me... and about Dieter."

"Weber knows."

"Weber thinks he knows. But that's all. Honestly darling, look at you. How could he possibly... how could anyone possibly confuse you with the ragged creature I first met?"

"Weber can."

"Well, we'll just have to bluff it out. If we didn't come he'd probably suspect even more. We've no other choice, have we?"

She smiled weakly. "None really." She squeezed his thigh. "How do I look?"

"Ravishing," he replied, smiling broadly. A discreet cough from the sentry holding the door open reminded them that it was time to go.

"Ready?" She nodded and Gunther dismounted, returning the salute of the soldier standing at attention. He turned to assist Annette from the motor car and held her arm as she adjusted her long dress and prepared herself for the ordeal ahead. The motor car door slammed shut and she started at the sound. "Steady darling," he whispered. "Steady."

The vehicle drew away and the soldier stepped back three paces and stood again at attention. Annette held fast to Gunther's arm and looked up and away at the chateau, its windows now ablaze with light, music flooding into the evening air. "Is this Frank's?" she asked in wonder.

"Yes. Yes it is... was..."

Her eyes blazed and she tugged at his arm. "Is!"

He smiled in the face of her anger, torn between guilt and the recognition that it served to stiffen her resolve. "Alright, is."

"It's wonderful." Her lips played with a smile. "For a decadent Capitalist."

He dug her in the ribs and laughed. He went to say something but stopped short as a figure appeared on the top step, framed in the light. "Ah, welcome. Welcome to our... good Lord, is it? Yes it is. Gunther, you naughty boy. All this time and this is the first time you have been here. My goodness, but you look wonderful and..."

"Madame Dupont. How nice to see you again," said Gunther, smiling. He turned to Annette. "Darling, this is Madame Dupont. Madame Dupont, may I introduce you to Mademoiselle Bertheau?"

"Mademoiselle Bertheau, I've heard so much about you," said Nicole, bustling down the steps, her face wreathed in smiles.

"Madame... Madame Dupont." Annette looked at Gunther. "So you know each other then?" she asked, knowing the answer full well, but wishing to hear it from this woman's lips.

"Know each other? Why of course we know each other. Gunther's been coming here since he was a little boy... when his dear mother was alive." She beamed at Gunther and reached up to cup his cheeks in her hands. "I owe a lot to dear Gunther, and now at last I can say thank you for restoring the chateau to its rightful family." She turned back to Annette. "Has he not told you how the Englishman who usurped our inheritance was finally put paid to by him? Surely he has?" Annette shook her head. "No? Well, he did and it makes you both doubly welcome in my home. Do come in my dears and let me introduce you to some old and dear friends."

Annette smiled as best she could amid the tide of revulsion she felt for this woman. Nicole took her arm and led her up the steps, reaching back to take Gunther's hand. "Come on you two. Come in and have a good time... ah, there you are Henri. Look who has come to see us."

Gunther looked up. Henri stood just inside the door, his face twitchy, a smile flickering on and off in nervous anticipation. Gunther extended his hand and Henri put his forward, seeming unable to decide between a handshake or a formal salute. Nicole's expression betrayed her disdain for her weak and vacillating husband. Gunther gripped his hand and shook it, turning to indicate Annette. "My... my companion and fiancée, Mademoiselle Annette Bertheau," he said briskly, reaching out to pull Annette forward. He straightened up and looked the man in the eye. "We live together in a house on the Rue du Mouton and we have a little boy, Dieter."

"Oh how lovely," trilled Nicole. "You must bring the little darling to see us. Mustn't they Henri?"

Henri muttered a nervous "Yes dear" and then turned as another figure approached.

Gunther stared at Jean-Claude's face as he came up to them. He searched for a friendly response. Here was the man who had guided him all those years ago. The man who had held him close when his mother had... when she had died on the... For a moment his gaze swept past the man and he imagined the lawns and the lake. But then his eyes refocused and he looked directly into his old friend's eyes.

Jean-Claude stopped just in front of the group and stood, his eyes fixed firmly in the distance, displaying no hint of recognition. "Jean-Claude?" Nicole said lightly. "Jean-Claude, don't you remember Monsieur... Leutnant Schmidt... Gunther? It's Gunther, who used to play here. Surely, man, you remember Gunther? And this is his friend, Mademoiselle Bertheau. Isn't it wonderful to see him again?"

Jean-Claude's face remained impassive, his eyes fixed on the middle distance. Gunther glanced at Nicole, seeing the anger rising on her face. "How are you Jean-Claude?" he said quietly. "Marie? Is she well?"

Jean-Claude's eyes focused on Gunther, observing the pleading in the young man's demeanour, feeling the power that, in that single moment, he had over this enemy. "We are both well enough," he replied.

"Good. Good. Well, we'll probably see you again," said Gunther, relieved that he had got some sort of response. He turned to Nicole. "So, where do we go? Who's here tonight?"

Nicole turned from her critical observation of Jean-Claude. For a moment she seemed not to register what Gunther had asked, but then her face resumed its hostess smile and she gripped Gunther and Annette by the arm and guided them across the hall and through the double doors. She paused briefly at the entrance to the main drawing room, waiting for effect.

All eyes swivelled towards them enquiringly, and the level of conversation died to almost a whisper. Nicole stepped forward, her arms raised in an encompassing gesture. "Mesdames et monsieurs. Damen und herren!" She turned, her arms sweeping down to indicate the couple framed in the doorway as Gunther's hand stole across and grabbed Annette's. "An old friend. A very welcome friend. Leutnant Gunther Schmidt and his friend, Mademoiselle... Mademoiselle..." Her brow furrowed.

"Bertheau," Gunther volunteered in a whisper.

"Mademoiselle Bertheau! Of course. How silly of me." She grabbed

Gunther's arm and pulled him forward, tearing him free from the startled Annette as she led him across the room to a group of his fellow officers, who turned as he approached and raised their glasses to him. Annette took a hesitant step forward. Gunther shot a glance back at her, but then lost sight of her as he was swallowed up in the group.

"She does rather take things over, doesn't she?" said a quiet voice beside Annette. She turned, grateful for the prop it offered. Henri stood nervously beside her, his eyes fixed on his wife, who, having deposited Gunther, was even now sweeping back across the room to another adoring group of men.

"Well, she certainly seems the perfect hostess," Annette replied, "but..."

"...but she seems to have left you high and dry," interjected Henri. "Well let's see. Do you know anyone here?"

Annette looked around at the sea of uniformed men and the scattering of elegantly dressed women. "No. No, I'm..." Her voice failed as she caught sight of Weber standing just off to the right, his head cocked as he pretended to listen to the officer standing beside him whilst he stared straight at her. Their eyes met and she involuntarily sucked in her breath.

Henri noticed her reaction, mistaking it for welcome recognition. "Ah. Herr Weber. You know Herr Weber?"

"No, it's..."

"Well come on then. Come with me." He gripped her upper arm and guided her across the room to Weber, who shook off the other man's conversation with a flick of his hand and turned to face them as they arrived.

Annette felt powerless to resist the gentle yet insistent force that propelled her towards this magnetically evil man. She stopped barely half a metre in front of him as Henri released her and stood aside.

Through a rising fog of terror, Annette heard Henri saying her name and was aware of its repetition on Weber's thin lips. Almost in slow motion, she took in the cruel patrician features, the cold grey eyes that reached into her soul as the corners of his mouth turned up in the semblance of a smile. She heard the click of his booted heels and the sharp sound seemed to summon other sounds from around the room, which until that moment had been muted. "You are well?" he asked in his thin, nasal voice.

Annette opened her mouth to speak but no sound came. She shut it again and swallowed hard, forcing her face into a smile, resisting the urge to turn and run. She coughed and covered her mouth with her hand as a shield, behind which she regained her composure. "Why yes. Herr Weber, isn't it? We met in the street outside our house before you left for Russia."

"We did indeed mademoiselle, although not for the first time I fancy."

She laughed lightly, the laugh sounding brittle to her ears as she effected a look of faint surprise. "Why no, Herr Weber. You must be mistaken."

"I am very rarely mistaken mademoiselle and I hope, with information I am expecting, to be able to prove that to you very soon."

Annette swallowed hard, trying not to betray the rising panic that threatened to engulf her. "Information? What sort of information would that be, Herr Weber?" she forced herself to ask, her voice sounding vulnerable, even to her.

"Information that..." He stopped, irritated, as an officer approached, his face wreathed in smiles, which failed to recognise the hostility in Weber's face as he turned to the newcomer.

"Herr Weber, guten abend," he said, clicking his heels and saluting.

"Leutnant Fronnel, guten abend," Weber replied, with little enthusiasm. He indicated Annette with a casual sweep of his arm. "Die dame spricht kein Deutsch. This is mademoiselle." He turned to Annette, his eyes boring into hers. "Mademoiselle..."

"...Bertheau," said Fronnel. "I know. We've met." He turned and looked around the room. "Where's Gunther?"

Relief flooded through every pore of Annette's being and she couldn't help the broad smile that cascaded onto her face as she clutched Fronnel's arm and turned him around and away from Weber. "I think... I think he's over there. Yes. There he is. And how are you?" she asked lightly, desperate to retain his attention.

"Fine. Fine." He turned to address Weber. "A little worried over the news from the north perhaps."

Weber wrinkled his nose. "That, Leutnant Fronnel, is not news, it is malicious gossip."

"Oh no. No, I'm afraid I have it on good authority that they've broken out of the Cherbourg peninsula..."

Weber raised his hand to silence the man. "Ich denke," he said menacingly, "Leutnant Fronnel, dass ein Deutscher offizier nicht am verbreiten von lügen helfen soll... speziell unter ..." He turned to Annette's questioning look and then faced the man directly. "... speziell unter ausländern."

Fronnel's smile faded in the glare of the Gestapo officer's cold fury. He swallowed and coughed. His eyes switched guiltily from Weber's hard face to Annette's and back again. "Ja, ja, sie haben recht Herr Weber. I'm sure I must be mistaken."

Weber switched back to French. "You will, of course, have heard that the uprising in Vercors has been crushed?"

"Yes. Yes indeed. I had heard that," said Fronnel, uncomfortably.

"Well then. Far better, if you must gossip, that you talk of positive things, don't you think?"

Fronnel looked into Weber's face, wondering just how long and how far this humiliation would go on. He opened his mouth to speak but was silenced by Annette's tug on his sleeve as Gunther approached, the smile on his face belying the question in his eyes as he searched Annette's face for clues.

"Ah, Leutnant Schmidt," said Weber as Gunther stopped in front of them, nodding curtly. "There you are. I was just telling the young lady that I am still certain that we have met before."

Gunther frowned and Annette waved her hand in an admonishing gesture. She leant forward. "Really, Herr Weber. You are naughty. Playing with us like this."

Weber's eyes blazed. "I assure you mademoiselle...!"

"...and I assure you, Herr Weber," Gunther barked, "that if you persist in these insinuations, I will have no alternative but to take up the matter with the kommandant. Veistenen sie mich?!"

All around them the sound of the raised voices caused a lull in the conversation, a pregnant silence that was gradually filled by the low buzz of whispered voices. Fronnel backed away from the three of them and attached himself to another group, who accepted him with enquiring looks. Annette's blood froze as Weber drew himself to his full height and faced Gunther, who stood square to him looking down at the smaller man, his face set firm. For what seemed like an eternity, but in reality was only seconds, they held each other's fierce gaze and she dreaded the next words from either man.

A gong sounded and Nicole appeared in the centre of the room, her arms spread wide in dramatic fashion as she turned full circle to all the guests. "Mesdames et monsieurs. Damen und herren. We have a buffet supper tonight. If you'd all like to make your way through those doors, you can help yourselves to food, after which we have some very special entertainment for you."

Amid the rising hum of expectancy and eager conversation, Annette seized the opportunity to grab Gunther's arm and steer him around and away from Weber, back towards the hallway. "Quick," she hissed as soon as they were out of the other man's hearing. "I don't know how much more of this I can take. Where's the toilet?"

Gunther pointed to the hallway. "Out here... come on, I'll show you." He led her out through the doors and across to the huge staircase. "Up here," he whispered, going ahead of her.

Annette followed slowly. Suddenly the tension of the last few minutes seemed to crash in on her. A tingling sensation ran through her limbs and she started to shake. She swayed and gripped the banister, sinking almost to her knees. Gunther ran back down to her. "There. I've got you," he murmured as he supported her.

"I'm sorry Gunther," she breathed.

"Sorry? What for?"

"For being weak."

He hauled her to her feet and held her tight. "You're not weak. You're strong... stronger than me. You faced up to him perfectly well until I got there. I'm proud of you."

"But he knows Gunther. He knows and he's going to prove it. He said so."

"How?"

"He says he's got information coming which will prove it."

Gunther looked around. He noted the familiar surroundings; the comforting curve of the magnificent staircase, the sweep of the softly rounded railings that he knew would lead up to the first landing and the portrait of Armand. His eyes searched for it. It was gone, and in its place the cold eyes of the Fuehrer, a man he had once admired, looked down on them, daring them to continue their climb.

He gripped Annette. "Come on darling. We mustn't be seen like this. Not after all that has been said in there."

Annette stood straight and looked around. She took a deep breath, her palm flat to her bosom. Slowly, reason replaced terror and she stared about in wonder. "This hallway is nearly as big as the house I grew up in," she gasped.

"That's my girl, said Gunther warmly as he recognised the courage flowing back into her. He led her up the stairs, quickly now, keen to be alone and out of sight for just a while. They reached the first floor and Annette drew her breath in sharply as they glimpsed the long, wide corridor leading across the whole of the front of the chateau. "My God, it looks as if... how many doors are there? How many rooms? Oh please show me around, Gunther."

"Another time. Another time, Annette. For now we really must be getting back or we shall be missed."

Her face dropped. "Back down. I don't know if I can... he's still there and..."

"...and he won't trouble you again this evening, I promise. Besides, there's the entertainment and that, I'm sure, will keep them all occupied, including Herr Weber."

"Why, what sort of entertainment is it?" she asked as they stopped outside a door that seemed the same as all of the others.

He pointed at it. "Here."

"Here?"

"The toilet. Don't be long."

"You didn't say what the entertainment was."

A boyish grin crossed his face as he smiled back at her. "Ladies... well, you know."

Annette affected an innocent look of surprise. "Know? What should I know, Gunther darling?"

He grinned openly. "Hurry up. I'll meet you at the top of the stairs in a few minutes."

Her face registered alarm. "Why, where are you going?"

"Same as you. I need one too."

"Then come in here," she said, grabbing his arm. "Please Gunther, don't leave me alone again."

For a moment he hesitated, but then he gave in and the two of them slipped into the toilet together. Minutes later the two of them sidled out again, Annette peeking out first to make sure the coast was clear and then quickly pulling Gunther after her. They stood adjusting their dress. "Ready?" he whispered.

"Ready," she replied.

They walked hand in hand down the corridor and on down the staircase, aware, as they reached the bottom, of the sound of loud music and cheering coming from the drawing room.

For a moment they paused outside the double doors and then

Gunther put his hand to the knob. Annette grabbed his sleeve. "Why did we come here Gunther?"

He grimaced. "Because... because I just got fed up with... no, that's not the right words. I felt that sooner or later we had to be seen and accepted as a proper couple."

"By these people?"

Gunther shook his head. "I was wrong and I'm sorry." He let go of the door handle. "I'm sorry. We'll go now."

Annette put her own hand to the knob. "We can't. If we go now then Weber will think that we've got something to hide... and all of the others too."

"Alright. We'll go in for a bit and then we'll slip out as soon as we can and get off. If anybody says anything afterwards I'll tell them..." He smiled. "...that as a good Catholic girl, what was on offer was not to your taste."

Annette grinned. "Agreed. But first, let's have a little look, eh?" She pushed the door open and recoiled slightly as the noise hit them. The room was in semi darkness apart from a bright orange light shining down on some sort of makeshift stage at one end, around which the cheering crowd of men and women was gathered.

They edged forward to stand at the back of the throng, Gunther clutching Annette around her waist from behind as she strained on tiptoe to see what was going on. Two girls... well women really, but made up to look like little girls, right down to the blonde hair tied in pigtails, lay on a couch dressed in nothing but see-through nighties. Seemingly oblivious to their audience and their surroundings, they caressed and kissed each other, reaching down between each other's legs to the accompaniment of loud cheers of encouragement.

Annette turned to look up at Gunther's face and half smiled, noting with some concern the flushed look of excitement, which he did his very best to hide. She wagged her finger. Gunther smiled guiltily down at her, bending to put his mouth to her ear. "Do you want to go?"

"Yes please but... just a minute," she said, pushing his face away gently. She looked around the room at the audience, their eager faces caught in the light from the stage. Where was Weber? She searched for him and found him near the front, his aquiline features accentuated even further in the glare of the spotlights. A shiver ran through her as she watched, fascinated and repelled at the naked lust in his eyes. Even at that distance she could see the concentration on his set mouth, the tiny beads of perspiration that lined his top lip and stood out on his brow.

There was a loud banging sound and a spotlight swivelled to the rear of the stage. On the couch the two girls sat up, feigning surprise and terror, their legs crossed demurely, their hands clasped in supplication. A large dark-haired woman dressed in a long black fur coat, her lips carmine red, her eyes ringed with ochre, strode forward onto the stage. She stood facing the hushed audience, her legs wide apart, the coat falling open to reveal thigh-length boots and the fact that she wore nothing underneath. Nothing except a high black basque adorned with red, which pushed up her enormous cleavage to outrageous proportions.

"Was ist hier los?" she demanded in a thrilling contralto voice that rang through the room. "Sind diese mädchen ungezogen?"

"Ja," came the almost universal response from the audience.

"Ja! Ja!" called a lone voice, and even without looking Annette knew who had called out. She leant forward to look at Weber's face, her eyes wide with revulsion at the naked thoughts displayed on his features.

"Was sollen wir tun?" the woman called out to the audience, who shouted back in an unintelligible howl of primeval emotion that seemed to rise up and fill the room.

"Here we are madame," came a woman's voice, speaking French from the crowd, that reached over the noise as she stepped forward and up onto the stage. Gunther's brow furrowed as he recognised Nicole and he shook his head in disbelief as she handed the woman a long, curved cane. She turned to face the audience as the woman flexed the stick, orchestrating the animal passions coming up from the floor. "They should be punished," she cried.

"They should be punished," the crowd roared back.

Nicole licked her lips and searched amongst them. She picked out Gunther. "Gunther. Gunther darling. Leutnant Schmidt, you'll help us punish these naughty girls, won't you?"

Gunther felt the blood drain from his face, the anger rising in his breast. He shook his head from side to side in exaggerated refusal. "No," he cried. "Not me. This has gone far enough!"

The crowd roared its disappointment, turning to Gunther, who stood there adamantly shaking his head, Annette by his side holding on tightly.

Nicole smiled slowly, shaking her head. "Is there nobody here who's willing to help?"

"Here madame!" came the almost inevitable reply from Weber, or so it seemed to Annette.

Nicole smiled broadly and reached down to help him onto the stage. She held his hand and raised it in the air. "A true gentleman," she called as she turned and placed his hand in the outstretched hand of the woman, who, having thrown off her coat, stood swishing the cane through the air. A chair was handed up onto the stage as Nicole dismounted and the woman guided Weber to it and sat him down, sideways on to the audience.

She strode across the stage and stood in front of the two girls huddling close to each other on the couch, beckoning one of them to come forward. For a moment the two shrank back, seemingly unwilling to submit themselves. But then, at the howling insistence of the mob, one of them tremulously raised her hand. The woman grasped it and she was hauled to her feet and dragged across the stage to the seated Weber, who reached up and pulled her down across his knee, her naked buttocks revealed to the crowd.

Annette tugged at Gunther's sleeve and he looked down at her white face, as if recovering from a dream. "Gunther," she pleaded. "Take me away from here, please."

He nodded and took her arm, guiding her back through the throng, who pressed forward, impervious to the departing couple, intent on getting a better view, grateful for the space they had vacated.

They reached the doors as the first cane stroke fell and the girl screamed out in a mixture of genuine and feigned pain. Annette turned the handle and slipped through, followed by Gunther, who shut the door and leant back heavily on it. From behind it they could still hear the sounds of the beating and the audience's synchronised reaction, and Annette put her hands to her ears to drown it out.

Gunther reached out to her and led her across the hallway. "I'm so sorry," he soothed. I thought it would be a striptease. I had no idea. Come on, we'll slip out through the kitchen. I know the way."

"Those poor girls," Annette wailed.

Gunther shook his head. "I think they knew what they were being paid for," he muttered.

Annette's eyes blazed. She stopped dead and turned to Gunther. "So that makes it alright, does it? You think that because circumstance, war and poverty bring them to that shame, it makes it alright? Do you?"

"No. But..."

"...but nothing. Do you not realise that that was what Blondel did? His little games, he called them. Little games..." She shook her head and the tears sprang to her eyes. "Oh why did you bring me here?"

"I'm sorry... so sorry Annette. I just... I'm sorry." He reached forward and clasped her shaking body to his, rocking her gently as she cried freely. At length she seemed to calm down, and he held her away and reached into his jacket pocket for a handkerchief, with which he dried her eyes, wiping her cheeks clean of the running mascara as best he could. "Alright?" he whispered. She nodded and he led her across the hallway and down the passage by the foot of the stairs.

"That couch was the one. My mother told me she was dying as

she sat on that couch. And now they use it for a sex show," he said through gritted teeth. "One more thing before we go."

"Oh Gunther, what? Please can we just go?"

He seemed to take no notice of her and instead continued to guide her down the darkened passageway, stopping at a set of stairs leading down to a door. He took her hand and led her down, stopping briefly at the bottom to knock.

There was no answer and none was really expected, so he pushed open the door and stepped through into the light, pulling Annette in with him. Marie straightened up from the sink and turned as they entered, the shock registering on her face. Jean-Claude put down his newspaper and rose from the bench by the table, hastily crossing the room to stand by his wife.

For a moment there was complete silence as Gunther pushed the door shut and stepped forward into the kitchen, holding Annette in front. The door hit the jamb and bounced back, slightly ajar as the latch fell.

"Hallo Marie," Gunther said quietly. "How are you?"

Marie raised her wet hands to her face, wringing them in obvious distress. "Oh Monsieur Gunther we..."

"We are well enough Leutnant Schmidt," Jean-Claude interrupted firmly, "and guests are not allowed in the kitchen."

"Is that all I am?" asked Gunther quietly.

Jean-Claude's eyes blazed and he stepped forward menacingly, his fist clenched, his mouth working violently. "No! That is not all you are! You are Monsieur Frank's murderer and I do not wish to have you anywhere near me or my wife."

"He is not!" Annette cried. Jean-Claude stopped in his tracks, his fist raised, his gaze switching to Annette's tear- and mascara-stained face. The fist lowered but the scowl remained. "He did not kill Frank. He saved him," Annette said firmly.

Marie lowered her hands from her mouth. Jean-Claude turned to look back at her, astonishment and disbelief written all over his face.

He turned back to Gunther, enquiringly, his stance still threatening. "You killed the master. You killed Monsieur Frank," he challenged.

Gunther looked across at him. He took Annette's hand and led her to the bench and sat her down under the incredulous gaze of the old couple, who now seemed rooted to the spot. "I did not kill Frank," he said quietly. "Frank is still alive and in England."

"But..." Jean-Claude spluttered, "we were told..."

"...that I had shot him in the river. So I did. But I shot to miss and, later on... now you know why his body was never found... later on we met and I arranged for him to escape to England."

There was a long silence, which was eventually broken by a derisive snort from Jean-Claude. "Pah, you're just trying to cover up your own guilt. We know he was killed. They told us. That is why we now have Monsieur and Madame Dupont running this house as a... as a brothel."

Jean-Claude lowered his head in shame and Marie covered her face with her hands.

"You can ask Pierre-Luc, said Annette quietly from the bench, and all eyes turned to her.

Marie lowered her hands from her stricken face. "Pierre-Luc? You know Pierre-Luc?

Annette stood and crossed to stand with her, taking her hands. "Yes I do. And you can ask him. He helped Gunther and Frank when they rescued me."

"Rubbish!" Jean-Claude exploded. "Don't listen to them Marie... a collaborator harlot and a killer. We don't have to listen to them."

"I want to hear," said Marie firmly. "Let me listen to their story and then we can make up our own minds."

"Well I'll not listen!" Jean-Claude stormed as he made towards the door.

"Stop!" Marie called. "Please stop, Jean-Claude."

He turned back to face his wife, his face troubled, the anger melting and uncertain in the unexpected command of her voice.

Gunther took a pace into the centre of the kitchen and reached out his hand to Jean-Claude. "Jean-Claude, you were the one who held me when my mother died. She is buried out there in the grounds of this chateau and I swear by her grave and by her memory that we are telling the truth."

Jean-Claude stood stock still, the workings of his mind showing clearly on his face and the tears started into his eyes. His hands dropped to his sides, useless in his despair and bewilderment. Annette left Marie's side and crossed to him, picking up his rough hand and guiding him silently to the bench, where she sat down with him.

Gunther crossed the room, motioning Marie to follow. He sat down opposite Jean-Claude and leant forward, speaking softly but firmly as Marie stood at the head of the table, her hands clasped together beneath her chin. "I heard that Frank was hiding in the farmhouse at Le Mesnil," Gunther began. "I went there and arrested him. But whilst we were alone we planned that he would make a break for it at the river and that I would pretend to shoot him..."

"We heard that's what you did. We heard you'd shot him. Madame Dupont told us that you'd shot him."

"She was supposed to think that. You were all supposed to think that," Gunther smiled. "After all, it was her own dear husband, Henri, that betrayed Frank in the first place."

"Monsieur Dupont?" Jean-Claude gasped.

Gunther nodded. "Urged on by Nicole, I wouldn't wonder. I took the call. That's how I knew. That's how I managed to be the one who went out to arrest him."

Marie lowered her hands. "So he's alive then?"

"Yes, and in England as far as I know," said Gunther quietly. He stared at the older couple in turn. "Did you really believe that I would kill my best friend in cold blood?"

Marie looked at him for a moment. Then her face crumpled and she burst into tears. Gunther rose and guided her sobbing form down and onto the bench, where he held her, his arm around her shoulder as she leant into him. Across the table Jean-Claude shook his head in a mixture of disbelief and wonder. Annette saw the doubt still lurking in his mind and reached across to grasp his hand. He tried to withdraw it, but she clung to it and he let it rest. "He's told you the truth," she whispered softly. "And there's more. There's Marcel and through him... me."

They both turned to look at her, enquiring. "What of Marcel? Is he safe in England as well?"

Annette shook her head sorrowfully. "No, Blondel killed..."

"Blondel? Serge Blondel from Saint Benoit?"

Annette nodded. "He ran the camp near Pithiviers. The one for Jews. He killed Marcel."

"And I killed Blondel for it," said Gunther quietly, as their eyes turned to him.

Jean-Claude observed the younger man for a moment and then turned to Annette. "And how do you come into this story?"

Annette lowered her voice and leant forward. "I am Jewish." Marie sucked in her breath and looked around fearfully, but Annette continued. "I met Frank when we were both detained by Weber, and later, for a short while, we were both at the camp before he was sent away..."

"When Frank escaped from somewhere north of Paris," Gunther interrupted, "he came back here and, after the episode in the river, we went... him, me and Pierre-Luc, to try and rescue Marcel."

"They were too late. But they rescued me instead," said Annette, "and I've lived with Gunther ever since. We have a little baby boy called Dieter."

"Dieter," gasped Marie. "Wasn't that the name of your father... the one who... oh I'd love to see him." Jean-Claude coughed and shook his head, but Marie waved his cautionary advice away. "I know Jean-Claude. But really. They could hardly make all of this up, could they? And you said yourself that you could never have believed it of

Monsieur Gunther." She reached across the table and took his hand, squeezing it gently.

Jean-Claude looked into his wife's eyes and held her unwavering look. Then he nodded almost imperceptibly and turned to Gunther, who smiled back at him.

The four of them lapsed into silence, looking up at each other occasionally, seemingly content to let the passion of the last few minutes die down, until Annette broke into their thoughts. "We are still in trouble."

The older couple turned to her, concern written all over their faces as she continued. "Weber knows who I really am. He says he can prove it and..."

"Then you must get away... hide," said Jean-Claude, urgently.

"And where would that leave Gunther?" she countered.

Jean-Claude shook his head. "In no worse a situation than if he's caught sheltering an escaped Jewess."

"Exactly," said Gunther. He turned to Annette. "I've made up my mind. You need to get away and I'm going to arrange it."

"But surely I can hide around here," Annette complained. "At Pierre-Luc's or... oh, I don't know."

Gunther shook his head. "No, that wouldn't do. Better that you're well away from here... well away from Weber. Besides, if you stay around here we'd be putting our friends in danger."

Marie looked across at Annette. "He's right my dear... for your sake and for the baby's."

Annette stared back at her and then dropped her gaze and nodded assent. "Oh when will it be over?"

"Soon enough I think," said Jean-Claude. He looked at Gunther. "This can't be easy for you?"

Gunther smiled. "It never was... but as you say, it'll be over one way or another soon enough." He stood. "Now I think that we really must go. I'd rather be gone when Nicole finds out that we've slipped away from her little show."

Annette joined him. For a moment the older couple sat still, looking at each other. Then they stood and followed Gunther and Annette to the back door, where they waited as if to bid honoured guests goodbye. Gunther held out his hand to Jean-Claude and the older man took it. But then he pulled him close and embraced him. Marie smiled and clasped Annette in her arms.

For several seconds the two couples stood like that before releasing each other to swap partners. At length, Gunther stood back and retrieved Annette from Jean-Claude's embrace. "We must go," he said in a choked voice. "Thank you for listening to me... for believing in me. I've wanted to tell you the truth for so long."

"Thank you for giving us back so much," said Marie. Gunther looked puzzled and Marie explained. "You've given us back Monsieur Frank and..."

"...you've given us back yourself," Jean-Claude interrupted.

Gunther smiled broadly. He reached for the door handle and guided Annette through and out. Then he turned one last time and winked at his old friends before firmly closing the door.

Across the other side of the kitchen, the other door closed silently and Nicole hurried away up the passageway, a slow, sly smile on her face.

***

Annette reached up over the child's head and pulled the door shut. She smiled at Dieter as she picked up her bag and helped him climb slowly down the steps to the street. "There's a clever boy... steady now. Mummy's got you," she said as the child stumbled and slipped sideways before recovering his balance. "No need to hurry. We're just going across to Father René's house to meet Marie. You'll like her. I know you will."

The blonde child looked up into his mother's face and grinned, gurgling his delight, as much in recognition of her happiness as any understanding of what she was talking about. His little legs pumped in double time and he lost his balance once more, swinging round in her grasp. Annette put down the bag and swept him into her arms, hugging him to herself.

A passer-by looked at the pair of them and smiled. Then, recognising who she was, scowled and shook her head, muttering "whore" under her breath as she hurried away. Annette caught the word and her mood changed immediately. She swung the child onto her hip, leant down to pick up the bag and crossed the street to the priest's house. She knocked and it was opened almost immediately by a beaming Marie, with Father René standing just behind her.

"Oh here you are," Marie said excitedly, "and the little mite with you. Oh, he's so beautiful!"

Annette stepped quickly through the door, her face serious. "Best if we're not seen together," she said quietly. Father René and Marie's smiles changed to concern. "Not everybody approves of me around here... on both sides. I've just been called a whore."

Marie dropped her hands from the child's shoulders, her face stricken. She looked at the priest and then back at Annette. "And I was one of them," she said quietly. "I judged you badly, just as I judged poor Gunther for a crime he did not commit and..." She glanced once more at the priest, then the baby, and then back to look Annette directly in the eye. "...and I'm sorry."

Annette put Dieter down and he turned and grabbed her skirt with both hands, looking up at her and obliquely across at the priest and the strange woman standing beside him. "War. It is the war that is the culprit... not you. Not me. Not even that woman in the street just now," she whispered softly.

The child plucked up the courage to turn and face Marie whilst still holding on to his mother's skirt. Marie knelt down and held out her hands to him. "He's beautiful," she breathed again. The child looked up at his mother and then let go of her skirt and stumbled alone into her embrace. Marie held him, rocking on her heels as she buried her face in his hair. She picked him up and stood. "He's so beautiful," she murmured. "So beautiful."

Father René placed his arm around Marie's shoulder. "I am so happy you are reconciled... that I have been able to..." He looked around the room as if to make sure they were not overheard and then shook his head in disbelief. How deep had the oppression become when a priest was afraid to speak in his own house? How much further would the ratchet of sinister despair be turned? "I have told Marie the full story," he said.

"Not that I didn't believe you," Marie added hurriedly. "We were so happy after you left the other night. So happy and so... well you know..."

"I know," said Annette. "And after the war, when I get back, I want to see lots and lots of you all... and when the Nazis are finally defeated, I want you to show me that wonderful chateau."

"Do you know when you're going and where?" Father René asked.

"No. Gunther says that he hopes I can leave at the weekend. But with all that's been going on... well he's a bit busy at the moment."

"Fighting the war," said Marie. "He's still fighting for the Germans, isn't he? How could he do that?"

"Because he has to and he doesn't actually fight... he's more in... well, it's more like he's in local government really. And what good would it do for us all if he was imprisoned as a traitor?"

"He has no choice," said Father René sternly. "But if the rumours we hear from the north and west are true, his position may become even more difficult."

"That's why he has to get Dieter and me away from here... from any association with him, so that we don't get tangled up in whatever he has to do," said Annette wearily. "Sometimes I wish that I hadn't fallen in love with him. But then..."

"You can't help who you fall in love with," said Marie.

Annette laughed sardonically. "Tell that to the woman in the street. Tell that to Weber. We're damned, whatever we do."

"Not in this house and not by us," the priest said firmly.

"But that's just the point, isn't it? You know. Pierre-Luc knows and now Marie and Jean-Claude know. And by you knowing we are in danger... and so are you."

"This little mite is no danger to anyone," said Marie, hugging the child. "But he looks thirsty and I don't doubt that we could all do with a drink of something." She looked at the priest. "Coffee?"

Father René grimaced. "Ah well, I've got the coffee but I'm afraid I've forgotten the milk... and I have to leave now... I have to be at the church."

"I'll go and get some," said Annette. "Give me your churn and I'll nip up to the market."

"Are you sure?"

"Of course I'm sure. I haven't been in hiding, you know. What would be the point? Until I actually leave we're carrying on as normal. In any event, if Weber wants to find me he knows where I live." Father René shrugged his shoulders and went into the tiny kitchen, returning with the churn.

"I'll stay and put the pan on," said Marie. "Would you like me to look after the child or would you prefer to keep him with you?"

"I'd be quicker on my own. Do you mind?"

"I'll walk with you as far as the church," said Father René.

Annette chucked Dieter under the chin and the child automatically reached up for her. "You stay here with Marie whilst mummy goes for some milk," she soothed. "Mummy won't be long."

The child's bottom lip pouted and trembled. Marie noticed and swung him aside, blowing raspberries into the soft flesh of his neck. The child giggled and Marie jerked her head at the door, indicating for Annette to leave. "There we are," she crooned. "Now what have we got in here?" She carried the child into the small kitchen and reached up to the cupboard. "Has Father René got any biscuits in here?" She heard the front door close and blew into his neck once more. The child giggled and she hugged him close.

Outside, Annette adjusted her dress. "Will she be alright with him?"

"Of course she will," said the priest. "She may not have had children of her own but she's cared for a few in her time, including Frank and Gunther."

They set off up the street towards the church. "Why did she not have any?"

Father René shook his head. "I don't know. Not by choice I think... I think that maybe God..." He smiled. "I think that it just didn't happen, that's all."

They reached the end of the street and he handed the churn to her. "Take care my child," he counselled.

"I'll be alright," she replied. "See you later." She turned right and headed down the main street towards the new market. For a moment the priest watched after her, but then he crossed the road and entered the church.

Annette paused outside the boulangerie and peered inside. They had some tarts. She would get some on the way back. 'No, I'll get them now,' she thought.

"Guten morgen, Mademoiselle Winklesdorf," said a cold voice.

She swung round, aware, even as she did so, that by reacting to the name she was betraying herself.

Her blood froze as she confirmed the presence of Weber, standing on the edge of the pavement beside the open door of a large motor car. "I... I... you are mistaken, Herr Weber," she stuttered. "My name is Bertheau... Annette Bertheau."

A cruel smile played on his lips and he indicated the open door of the vehicle. "I don't think so Jewess. I told you I don't make mistakes."

Blind panic overtook her and she dropped the churn, which clattered to the ground, rolled across the pavement and into the gutter. "No... no... you're wrong... I need. Where's Gunther? Gunther will tell you..."

"I'm sure he will," said Weber, the thin smile still on his lips. "I'm sure he will... just as I'm sure I will not believe him." He reached forward and gripped her arm.

"No wait. Wait please!" she pleaded as his grip tightened and he dragged her towards the open door. She twisted in his grasp and threw her hands in the air, screaming "Help me! Help me please!" He spun her around roughly and swiped his gloved hand across her face. She stumbled, crying now in incoherent terror as he swung her around and literally hurled her through and into the well of the motor car. Quickly, he brushed his coat down and slipped in, pulling the door shut as the car slipped away, its rear wheel crushing the churn as it lay in the gutter.

12th August 1944

Frank shifted his weight and shuffled his chest into the hard earth, trying to dislodge a stone that was digging into his ribs. He reached up and pulled the bracken fronds into an arch above him and carefully arranged the foliage in front.

"Are you alright?" came a voice from barely a metre away to his right.

"Yes I'm fine. Just a stone. You?"

"Bit nervous I suppose. Wondering how I let you talk me into all this."

Frank laughed softly. "Go on Pierre-Luc. You know you're loving every minute of it."

"Oh yes. Sleeping in a huge hole in the ground with dozens of sweaty men. Never bathing properly from one week to the next. Hiding from everybody... yes, I must admit, it's been fun really."

"Well, we get home to your house every so often and you've got to admit that it must be better than the work camp in Germany."

"Don't you believe it. We were three Frenchmen for every hundred Russian women."

"What? You're kidding?"

"No word of a lie. And all of them young and healthy."

"Who got the third?"

"Who's counting at those odds."

"Quiet there you two," a voice hissed from over beyond Pierre-Luc. "I think they're coming."

Frank edged forward on his elbows, taking care to keep his rifle muzzle low and hidden. He parted the fronds and peered along the verge towards the crossroads off to his left. A group of small houses clustered around the crossing. No sign of life came from them other than the lazy flapping of washing on the lines. Those who lived there would have been told to make themselves scarce. 'Pray God they don't get caught up in reprisals,' Frank thought. 'Too many times in the past, whenever they had struck out at the Germans, the result had been that innocent civilians had been made to suffer on their account. No wonder the Maquis, as an organisation, found so little support amongst the general public simply trying to survive.'

His gaze travelled back along the road to the barn opposite, one half of it filled with bales of sweet hay, the other half empty, its stockade fences open to let the cattle graze in the dry, summer pasture. Now they gathered by the hedge to the road, herded there as cover. For behind them, hidden in the hay and behind their brimming troughs, lay men like himself: men intent on causing mayhem.

The sound of heavy lorries, their engines straining at the slight incline, came from his left and Frank ducked back beneath his cover and peered through it and ahead to his right. There, at the second crossroads, he could make out the figure of a man, hidden from the view of the oncoming traffic, a red flag held aloft.

This was it! Meaningful combat at last, after all these months of useless skirmish. This time they had a worthwhile goal. The approaching lorries carried Panzer tanks, hurrying north to try to cut off the Allied advance from the Cherbourg peninsula as Patton's 3rd Army swung out, arcing south towards them in a long curve towards Paris. They had to stop these tanks reaching their destination.

He kept his head as flat to the ground as he could whilst searching out of the corner of his eye for the first of the approaching transporters. A motorcycle and sidecar with a mounted machine gun came first, driving in the centre of the road, its outrider swinging the gun from side to side in lazy anticipation. Across at the second crossroads, Frank glimpsed the fall of the red flag and witnessed the man running back up the road to the small feed shed on the corner.

The motorcycle approached the crossroads, its riders oblivious to the lorry that now sped down the side road in their direction. Too late, the outrider swung his machine gun sideways, firing wildly as if to repel its crazy advance. The lorry struck the sidecar, throwing it up, spilling its hapless occupants as it swerved deliberately sideways, depositing its load of loosely stacked lumber across the carriageway like giant matches tumbled from a box.

Even as it raced off, followed by gunfire from the cab of the leading lorry, the small shed exploded with a thunderous roar, scattering the terrified cattle and spraying stones and shrapnel into the flank of the vehicle. Gunfire erupted from the barn, raining down on the convoy, joined by fire from Frank's side of the road. Frank raised himself as far as he dared, firing down into the tyres of the carriers as men scurried out and took up positions beneath the tracks of the tanks.

Across to the left, as the tail of the convoy ground to a halt just north of the first crossroads, a tractor and trailer, loaded with bales of straw, pulled out from the road on Frank's side. It swerved violently, spilling the bales onto the road and then stopped, blocking off any retreat. The driver leapt from the cab and ran, making for the houses, desperately trying to keep the bales between him and the enemy. Suddenly he raised his arms in the air and crashed lifeless on the tarmac.

Now the full fury of the ambush was joined with fire exchanged in both directions. In front of him, Frank heard and felt the bullets thudding into the carefully camouflaged sandbags. Beside him, now calling wildly, Pierre-Luc rained fire down on the scattering German soldiers as they scrambled to escape the withering crossfire.

The last lorry, a troop carrier, tried desperately to reverse through the tractor and trailer. The unit folded in on itself, preventing its escape, and soldiers leapt from beneath its canvas to take up firing positions, their backs to the houses, from which more maquisard now ran to crouch behind the bales of fallen straw, pouring fire into their exposed rear. Panic now overtook the trapped Germans, who, deprived of cover, scattered to either side of the road, only to be cut down by the merciless fire from the fighters on the bank and within the barn.

Gradually, as the outward fire from the convoy dwindled,

maquisard stood up all along the road to take careful aim at both helpless men and machinery, and as all return fire ceased, Frank stood and jumped down the bank to the road, his rifle held ready, every sense alert. Beside him, Pierre-Luc strode forward purposefully, his face set and resolute, his rifle held at his hip.

Off to their right a young soldier, his helmet lost, broke free from behind the huge wheels of a transporter and ran towards the forest behind them, his eyes wide with terror, his hands held high in the air. Pierre-Luc let him pass, watched as he scrambled up the bank and then, almost as if it was an afterthought, pulled the trigger. The boy threw his hands in the air and let out a long drawn-out cry of despair as he slid back down the bank to lie in a whimpering heap on the verge. Pierre-Luc turned away as if he'd done no more than swat a fly, but Frank's gaze hovered between his friend's face and the dying soldier. He shivered. Pierre-Luc was the gentlest man he knew. Yet here... here in this carnage, he had no pity. He glanced across to the right as another German broke cover and crouched, taking careful aim. "To your right!" Frank yelled as he fired over his head, even as Pierre-Luc instinctively ducked.

The kneeling figure crumpled forward, his shot going harmlessly into the road, his rifle slipping from his hands as he clutched his chest, a foaming rush of red spewing from his open mouth. "Thanks my friend," said Pierre-Luc grinning, and the two of them ran forward and crouched against the giant wheels, their backs to each other.

Now from the forest, men rose and ran forward carrying rucksacks. Whooping and hollering, they surrounded the stricken vehicles as the first fighters withdrew. Quickly they took out their charges and fixed them to axles and tracks, setting timers and calling out the times as they completed each one.

"Well that was fun, wasn't it?" said Pierre-Luc, grinning.

Frank grinned back at him. "It was certainly worthwhile."

"Two minutes!" André yelled down from the back of a transporter, waving his arms above his head.

Frank raised himself from his knees and stood, his back to the vehicle. Pierre-Luc stepped away and turned back to Frank, smiling. Frank watched as the smile faded and died. His mouth opened to form words, but none came as he fought to bring his rifle to his shoulder and searched for the trigger, pointing frantically above Frank's head.

Behind Frank, a German, who had been lying as if dead beneath the tank, swung a heavy jack at his head, his face wreathed in blind hatred. The bullets from Pierre-Luc's rifle tore into him, flinging him backwards, his hands opening to release the bar almost at the moment it connected with Frank's head.

Pierre-Luc stood back as both enemy and friend crumpled to the ground at his feet. He threw aside his weapon and clawed at the German's uniform, flinging him clear of Frank. He dropped to his knees, cradling his friend's head in his arms, feeling the sticky gash that tore across his scalp.

"Is he dead?" André shouted as he ran from behind the vehicle. "If he's dead, leave him. This lot's about to blow!"

"He's not dead!" Pierre-Luc cried. "There's a pulse in his temple. He's unconscious!"

André bent down to take a look. He felt his neck. "Yes you're right. Quick now, for God's sake, or we'll all go up with this lot!" Pierre-Luc slung his rifle across his shoulder and grabbed Frank's arm, hauling him to his feet as André retrieved his rifle and grabbed the other arm. Between the two of them they dragged him, his feet dangling uselessly, his head hanging down. "Hurry!" André screamed as they reached the edge of the metalled road and scrambled up the bank with their burden, to the relative safety of the trees.

Behind them the first of the charges, at the rear of the convoy, blew. Even as they breasted the rise and threw themselves forward, flat on the ground, with Frank between them, the ripple of explosions ran down the whole line of vehicles, sending shards of metal and rubber to rain down upon them. Pierre-Luc covered Frank's lifeless body with his own, his hands crossed over his own head as he prayed not to be hit.

As peace reigned again he gingerly raised his head, feeling down his body for any sign of damage. Beside him, André did the same.

"You alright?"

"Yes I think so. Bloody miracle."

André got up on his knees and reached for his rifle. He hesitated and listened intently, his ear cocked back towards the road. "Company," he hissed. "And if I'm not mistaken, bad company. Quick, pick him up and let's get out of here."

They took an arm each and half dragged, half carried Frank, pushing their way through the bushes, which seemed to constantly entangle his limp form. "It's no good," Pierre-Luc panted when they had covered no more than twenty metres. "This is too slow. You take my rifle and I'll carry Frank across my shoulders. If I make for over there, I can run down the driveway to that chateau, past the stable block and back to the forest while you cover me. When I'm clear, make your own way."

"Done," said Andre, dropping Frank's arm and reaching across for Pierre-Luc's rifle. Where will you head?"

"I'll drop him off at my house and then make my way back to camp."

"Alright. Let's go." Pierre-Luc slung Frank across his shoulders and the two of them ran through the forest for about fifty metres until they reached the driveway, where Pierre-Luc paused, his great chest heaving from the exertion. "You carry on. I'll cover you," André whispered. Pierre-Luc, speechless, hefted Frank's body and lumbered on up the driveway.

André waited until he was safe and had gone behind the buildings before he too turned and ran up the drive. Rifle fire and spurts of gravel forced him to zig-zag, but he made the corner of the building in time to see Pierre-Luc disappearing into the undergrowth. Those two certainly were friends. You could envy any man the love they had for one another. He peered around the corner and down the driveway. Two soldiers were running towards him. He knelt, took careful aim at the first one, gently squeezed the trigger and fired. The man fell in a heap, and the other one dived for cover on the right. André let off two more rounds at where he imagined the soldier to be and then turned and headed in the opposite direction and the cover of the forest.

13th August 1944

"**M**y God, there are Germans in the front!" screamed Madame Cabel.

Pierre-Luc's father rushed through from the back, crashing through the kitchen, scattering chairs as he pushed forward to peer out of the window as his wife backed away, her hands held to her mouth, her eyes wide with terror. "You're right. Oh shit!" He wheeled around. "Go up to Frank and warn him... tell him to..." He turned back to the window. "Wait! There's only one. I can only see one of the bastards. There doesn't even seem to be a driver." He turned to his wife. "See if there's anyone at the back."

Madame Cabel ran to the door and then looked at her husband. "But what if..."

"Just look and tell me!" he yelled. "And quick!"

She bustled through into the scullery and he heard the grate of the back door as she pulled it open. He concentrated on the lone uniformed figure walking steadily up the drive. He flexed his hands. A weapon. He needed some sort of weapon. If the German was truly alone they could overpower him... but no... What would they do with the body? What would they do with the vehicle parked outside their gate?

Madame Cabel came back into the kitchen. "Nobody out there," she whispered, bending down automatically to pick up a fallen chair.

The knocker crashed.

The soldier was actually knocking politely on the door and had stood back waiting for a reply. Monsieur Cabel peered through the window, his face hidden by the heavy curtain. The man was taking off his cap, was smoothing over his hair. "It's... it's Gunther," he hissed.

"Gunther?"

"Yes, Gunther. The one who used to be their friend."

Madame Cabel wrung her hands. "But he..."

"I know but..."

"Pierre-Luc? Has he come to tell us?" Her hands dropped to her sides. "Open the door. Ask him what he wants. Don't let him in."

The knocker sounded again, this time louder and with more urgency. Monsieur Cabel nodded to his wife and motioned for her to stay where she was, out of sight. He reached up and slid back the top bolts, bent down to the lower bolts and then turned the knob.

"Monsieur Cabel," Gunther almost cried out as the door opened a crack and the older man peered out. "It's me, Gunther. I need to talk to Pierre-Luc."

"He's away in Germany," Monsieur Cabel growled. "You should know that."

"I know he's home," said Gunther, his voice high, almost panic-stricken. "I heard that he didn't report back."

"Well he's not here," Pierre-Luc's father said impatiently, pushing the door shut.

Gunther leapt forward, pushing his arm through the door. He screamed involuntarily as the heavy door pushed against it, the full weight of the man behind it. "No! No! Please Monsieur Cabel," he yelled. "I need help!"

"Take your arm away from the door Gunther," Monsieur Cabel said between gritted teeth, "or I'll break it, I swear."

"Then break it. But please..." He cried out from the pain in his arm. "Please Monsieur Cabel, I need help. They've got Annette!"

The staircase door opened and Frank stepped into the kitchen, his head swathed in bandages. "What's happening?" he asked urgently.

"Go back upstairs please Monsieur Frank," Madame Cabel whispered. "It's..."

"It's that Gunther," panted Monsieur Cabel. "He's alone but..."

"Let him in."

"What?"

"Let him in."

Monsieur Cabel stared at Frank as if he'd gone mad, inadvertently relaxing his pressure on the door. "No Monsieur Frank, he's..."

Gunther retrieved his arm and applied his full weight to the door, pushing Monsieur Cabel back as he fell into the room. He stood bent double with pain and exertion, holding his forearm. Frank stood stock still. Madame Cabel backed away to the scullery door and stood half in, half out, her hands held to her mouth as if to stop herself screaming. Monsieur Cabel recovered himself and grabbed a heavy pan, brandishing it above his head as he advanced on Gunther.

"Wait!" Frank called, holding his hand up. Monsieur Cabel paused behind the doubled-up figure, his weapon poised to strike.

"I need help," Gunther moaned. "Please. I need help. They've got Annette."

"Gunther," said Frank quietly. "Gunther, it's me."

"Frank?" Gunther straightened up slightly, turning towards the voice. Monsieur Cabel made a threatening gesture, but this time his wife called out for him to stop. She crossed the room and took the heavy pan from him. "Frank! It is you," said Gunther as he stood erect, still clutching his arm.

"Yes it's me, as you see," said Frank smiling. He opened his arms and the two of them embraced, hugging each other tight before Gunther stepped back as the pain shot through his arm. "God, I think you've broken it," he called across to Monsieur Cabel.

"Serves you..."

Frank held up his hand to silence him. "Come on Monsieur Cabel. It's Gunther. Our friend."

"That was a long while ago and a lot's happened since. He's a German officer and as such..."

"Not for much longer," Gunther interrupted with a bitter laugh.

Frank's eyes whirled back to his friend. "Why? What's happened? What was that...?"

"They've taken... Weber's taken Annette. They'll be looking for me now as well."

"What?"

Gunther looked straight at his friend, his eyes filled with anguish, the tears welling in them. "He's got her Frank. That sadistic swine's got Annette and he knows my part in your escape and hers."

"Where?"

"The chateau."

"The chateau?"

"Yes, your home. He's holed up there. Jean-Claude... I didn't know where they were, you see. I got back and Father René and Marie..."

"Father René and Marie? Has he got them too?"

For a moment Gunther looked at him, trying to understand what he was asking. Then the penny dropped and he shook his head. "No... no, I'm not explaining it properly."

"Sit down here," said Madame Cabel, ignoring the warning looks from her suspicious husband. "You too, Monsieur Frank."

Gunther half turned to look at his old friend's mother, the warmth of her concern bringing a slight smile to his face, even if it could not reach into the terror he felt in his heart. He turned to Frank, and for the first time noticed the bandages on his head. "You're injured Frank. What happened? How did you...?"

Frank smiled. "A bit of a run-in with your lot yesterday, I'm afraid," he said as he sat down.

Across the room, Pierre-Luc's father sucked in his breath and shook his head.

Frank looked across at him and smiled. "It's alright Monsieur Cabel. I have a feeling that we're all on the same side in this room." He turned back to Gunther and pulled a face.

"You were... yes, you were at Chicamour yesterday," said Gunther incredulously. Frank nodded and Gunther continued. "How? If you... how long have you been here?"

"Since March. I crashed south of here in the Sologne. Our aircraft... we were on a bombing raid. I joined the RAF when I got back to England."

"But why didn't you tell me? Why didn't you let me know you were here?"

"Because Gunther, you are... well after all you are still a German officer and I..."

"You're in the Maquis."

Frank stared at his friend, his gaze unwavering. He nodded and Gunther returned his nod in silent understanding. "It would have compromised us both," Frank explained. "It was better that I kept away from you and..."

"Annette! That's why I've come," said Gunther, rising from his seat to pace the room, his head held in his hands to shut out the terror that threatened to engulf him.

"Weber's taken Annette. He took her from the street just after she'd left Father René."

"What about the child?" Madame Cabel asked. "Did they take the child?"

Gunther stared across at her. He shook his head slowly, the tears jumping once more into his eyes. "No. Marie was looking after Dieter at Father René's house... she'd only gone to get some milk... he'd run out and..."

"Where's the child now?" Frank asked firmly.

Gunther turned back to him. "Marie... Jean-Claude came to tell me that Weber had Annette at the chateau and..." He swallowed. "They're safe. He and Marie have taken the child to her sister's house in Gien. They're going to stay there until..."

"Until the end?" Gunther nodded. Frank reached up for his friend's arm and pulled him back down to his seat. "You know the end's coming, don't you?"

Gunther nodded again, his posture submissive, but then his head shot up again. "But that won't help Annette, will it? He grabbed Frank on both shoulders. "The Madonna! We could get in by the Madonna!"

Monsieur Cabel crossed to them. "You can't go in there alone, just the two of you. It'd be suicide."

Frank seemed to take no notice and continued to stare into Gunther's eyes. "The Madonna," he said quietly.

Monsieur Cabel threw his hands in the air in exasperation. "What's all this about a Madonna?"

Frank smiled. He looked up from his friend's face to the older man. "It's... well it's a way into the chateau that we know. We could get in without being seen."

Madame Cabel joined them, concern written on her face. "Are you sure you're well enough?"

Frank fingered his head. "I think so." He touched the wound and winced. "Nothing broken except the skin."

"The double vision? Has that gone?"

He laughed. "Well, there's only one Gunther here at least."

"If there'd been two we would have had to kill them," said Monsieur Cabel. Gunther smiled a self-deprecating smile.

"Pity really," said Frank. "I'd like to kill two Webers."

"You're going to kill Weber?" said Monsieur Cabel, aghast. "If you do that..."

"No, I'm going to kill Weber if I can," said Gunther quietly, as all eyes turned to him. He returned each stare with a curt nod.

"What about your arm?" Madame Cabel asked, reaching forward to touch it. "Take your jacket off. Let's have a look at it."

"In fact, take off that whole bloody uniform," said Frank. "It making me nervous."

"Me too," said Monsieur Cabel.

"It's the last thing you should be wearing tonight."

Gunther took off the jacket and laid it aside, holding up his arm to Madame Cabel. "No. No," he said. The uniform could come in handy if we're stopped. We'll need the car to get close and for our escape. We should drive as close as we can get and then hide it somewhere."

"Nothing broken," Madame Cabel announced. "Just badly bruised, I think."

Gunther looked up at her husband, who shrugged his shoulders and looked away. He turned back to Frank. "Tonight then? Are you sure you're fit?"

Frank reached across to pat his friend's shoulder. "I'll be fine. What time is it?"

"Four o'clock. Why?"

"It's dark around half past nine. We'll go at eleven."

Gunther looked up. "Can't we go before... we don't know. He could be doing anything to her."

"And he'll have a lot longer to do it if we fail," said Frank quietly. "No, we'll wait until eleven. When we get in we'll wait until it's quiet. It's Sunday night, so Nicole won't be having any of these parties I've been hearing about."

Gunther shuddered at the memory. "We went to one. It was disgusting. If we are to lose this war it will be, in large part, due to the decadence of our people."

"And the fact that you were wrong to start it in the first place," Monsieur Cabel growled.

For a moment the two men glared at each other, each one daring the other to argue. Then Gunther nodded. "That too," he whispered. "That too."

Frank touched his friend's arm. "So Jean-Claude told you that Annette was at the chateau?"

"Yes. He knew Marie was at Father René's house seeing Annette, and when he saw her brought to the chateau, he thought that maybe something had happened to Marie. So he ran all the way into town and found her safe with the child. She didn't know where Annette had disappeared to."

"When did you find out?"

I've been away in Vierzon organising... well it doesn't matter now. I was trying to arrange for Annette and Dieter to get away to the south. I got back this morning and there was nobody at home. So I went over the road and there they all were. They'd spent the night in the priest's house."

"Did he tell you I was here?"

"Did he know?"

"Of course. He was the first person I... we contacted when we got here."

Gunther smiled. "He didn't tell me. I came here to find Pierre-Luc." He swung round to face Monsieur and Madame Cabel. "I had a report about Pierre-Luc's failure to report back... it came through to my office and I intercepted it. I was going to come and see him anyway to warn him... not to arrest him. Is he coming back?"

The couple did not reply and Gunther turned back to Frank, who shook his head. "Don't ask Gunther. He saw the look of concern on his friend's face. "Oh no, I didn't mean... he's safe. But... what you don't know... it's best if you don't ask."

Gunther heaved a sigh of relief. "Oh good. I thought for a moment... I thought..." He nodded his head. "I understand. If... when we get Annette I'll be a fugitive. Can your people hide us?"

"Yes, we can hide you," Frank said seriously. "But as a prisoner of war in a situation where we don't usually take prisoners, they may want you to give certain information... to betray your people."

Gunther sat still for a moment, seeming to contemplate his boots. He coughed. "Well I suppose that my people, as you call them, have betrayed me. The Webers of this world... no, that's not true. We've all betrayed ourselves. He lapsed into silence again and then said, "When we've got her, I shall surrender to you."

Frank nodded his agreement. "Do you have any weapons?"

Gunther patted his holster. "Just this. That's all. You?"

Frank looked up at Monsieur Cabel. "Is my rifle anywhere?"

Gunther smiled at the sight of the man's panic-stricken face, realising that despite all that had gone on and been said, he still didn't trust him.

"It's... err hidden. I'll show you later."

"Rabbit stew anyone?" said Madame Cabel. I've got a rabbit stew in the oven and some roast potatoes. Anyone interested?"

For a moment, the sheer domesticity of this innocent question drove all of the dark thoughts from the young men's minds and they were back in their youth.

They smiled knowingly at each other; the smiles of two friends who knew no boundaries in that friendship and recognised no division of loyalties. They responded in unison, and for a short while the terror was broken.

***

"How many guards were there when you came?" Frank whispered as he got out of the car.

"I don't know. Two at the main gate. Two more at the farm gate and one at the door. I never got to see how many were out the back."

"Chances are that if there are any at the back, they're on the top patio."

"If they are, they won't be able to see us," said Gunther as he got out of the car and shut the door as quietly as he could.

"Exactly."

"There may be guards in the grounds though," said Gunther. "Weber wouldn't leave himself exposed. Do you think this thing's hidden well enough here?" He chucked his cap into the back seat.

They had parked the motor car under a tree, just up a short driveway, leading into a hedged field. If they stood back, its camouflage rendered it almost invisible in the darkness. "Cover the glass bits over so there's no reflection," Frank said, bending into the hedge to break off some foliage and jamming it in the bumper. Gunther did the same on his side, until they were both satisfied. "Where did you put the keys?"

"In my pocket. Why?"

"Put them on the top of the front wheel." He sensed rather than saw his friend's quizzical stare. "In case only one of us comes back."

There was a moment's silence before Gunther took out the keys and placed them on top of the tyre. "If... if it's not me... if I don't get back..."

"Plan for the worst and aim for the best," said Frank lightly.

"I know, but if I don't make it you'll..."

"We'll both make it."

"I love her you see... I love her so much... and Dieter."

"I know."

"If anything happens, you will look after Annette won't you... and Dieter?"

"Nothing's going to happen and yes I will."

In the darkness, Gunther smiled. He linked arms with his friend for a moment before they crept down the lane side by side. "I'm sorry. Bit nervous. I'm afraid... frightened for her," he whispered as they walked. "I'm the soldier, I know, but I don't normally do this for real. The last time was when we freed Annette."

Frank laughed. "I'd never really planned to do any of this either. I thought I'd got away from it all. There I was, happy in my bomber, and then... boom... I'm back down here."

"Why didn't they ship you back? You mentioned 'we' in the kitchen. What happened to the others?"

"Only one. None of the others got out. He was passed down to Spain."

"Why didn't you go with him?"

Frank stopped and turned face to face with his friend, his hands on his hips. "So you are a spy after all."

"Me? What? No. No, I was just..."

Frank hugged him. "Oh Gunther, I was only joking. God you're touchy."

"I'm not. It's just that... well Monsieur Cabel seemed to distrust me, despite everything that was said."

"Monsieur Cabel, like all Frenchmen who have had to live under occupation, has become cynical... suspicious. You would be too if you lived under the same threat... amid constant fear of reprisal."

Gunther bridled a little. "But I do! And, for me, the threat has come true. Hasn't it?"

Frank shook his head and looked at the ground, his hands held out in a submissive gesture. "I'm sorry. Yes, you're right. It can't have been easy for you. But we're going to put it right, just as we did when we got Annette out last time." He looked up. "By the way, was it you that killed Blondel?"

"I said I would."

"Well let's hope we can do the same with Weber. Now let's get a move on. We've work to do."

They turned and made their way along the narrow lane, keeping close to the edge in the shadows of the overhanging trees, until they came alongside a rising stone wall. Behind this, they knew, lay the woodland at the rear of the chateau, which in turn would give way to the far edge of the lake.

"We'll go on up here," Frank whispered, "and through and down to the cemetery. Then we can sneak along the long wall and dive across to the lower patio."

Gunther put his foot in a crack in the stone and reached up for a hand-hold. He hauled himself up and sat astride the wall. "Hand me up your rifle," he called down softly. Frank slipped the small torch he was carrying into his pocket and passed the rifle up. Gunther slipped it down the other side and then reached down to grab Frank's hand and pull him up. The two jumped down on the other side and leant against the wall. "You lead the way," Gunther whispered.

Frank looked his friend up and down. "Your buttons and insignia, they're glinting in the moonlight."

Gunther looked down and then quickly stripped off his cross belt and jacket, turning it inside out and draping it across a branch. "We can pick it up on the way back... we might need it to get through to Gien."

He shivered and Frank assumed that he was cold. "Put the bloody jacket back on if you're cold."

"I'm not cold. I'm bloody terrified..."

"So am I," said Frank quietly, "but if we're going to help Annette then we've got to..."

"I know, I'm sorry... I didn't mean. It's not just for myself... it's for Annette." He grabbed Frank's arm. "What if...? What...? Do you think she's alright Frank, really?"

Frank shook his head slowly. "I don't know Gunther... I just know that we have to try... and I know that if we just stay here talking about it then..."

"I'm sorry. Come on. You lead," said Gunther.

They turned and made their way up under the dark canopy of the large beech trees that had grown there for generations, flitting furtively from smooth trunk to trunk, brushing aside the low branches that spread like many-fingered hands, bearing foppish leaves that softly painted their faces as they passed. Beneath their feet the leaf litter rustled softly, deadening the sound of their progress to that of the soft murmur of a summer's breeze.

Frank breasted the rise first and reached back to haul Gunther to the summit of the long horseshoe ridge, where they stood together for a moment to catch their breath. Before them the ground ran down again, leading to the lower lawns and the lake, which they could see stretched out before them, shimmering in the moonlight. To their left the ridge ran on and down into the darkness that ended at the high yew hedge surrounding the small cemetery, and before that, they knew, was the dew pond in which, as small boys together, they'd caught newts and tadpoles.

"Ready?" whispered Frank.

"Ready," Gunther replied.

They slipped down the hill, keeping to the shadows. As the trees gave way to open ground, they paused for a moment to look around. Away to their right, the dark shapes of the outbuildings showed against the night sky and beyond that the chateau stood proud against the dark, its tall windows casting their light into the night.

Before them, across about thirty metres of open grass, the long dark shape of the cemetery hedge beckoned them, and with a murmured "Go" from Frank, the two of them set off across the void, keeping low, Frank's rifle held at the ready, Gunther fumbling for his pistol in its holster. Frank reached the hedge first and threw himself into its welcome shadow, crouching against it as Gunther arrived. "Alright?"

"Yes," Gunther replied. "It's really no different from the games we used to play, is it?"

Frank smiled to himself and tugged at his friend's sleeve. "Yes, if you forget that they... and we've got real bullets this time."

Gunther shook his head. "As if I could." He looked along the hedge and then turned briefly to Frank. "Do you... would you mind if we went in a moment? I..."

Frank reached forward to his friend's face and cupped his chin, pinching it and tugging it almost playfully. "No, I'll come with you, but not for long mind you."

Gunther moved along the hedge, followed by Frank. They felt their way to the corner and around to where they knew the entrance would be, an arched gap in the carefully manicured growth. They slipped in and stood still for a moment, taking in the serenity of that silent world of the dead. Gunther looked up and across to where he knew Gisela's grave lay and, holstering his weapon, he moved quietly forward to stand at one end, staring down at the thick slab that marked his mother's passing.

The tears sprang unbidden to his eyes and he reached up and tapped his breast, feeling for the pocket that had been left behind in his folded jacket. He glanced across the graveyard to where Frank stood, head bowed at Armand's grave. For a moment Frank seemed to be saying something to the silent earth, but then, as Gunther watched, he turned and went across to Philippe's spot and stood as if acting as a messenger.

Gunther looked down again at his mother's grave and wiped his eyes dry. "Auf wiedersehen mutti," he whispered to the headstone as Frank joined him, resting his hand on his shoulder.

"If... if... I want..."

"I know," Frank said quietly. "I know... me too." He squeezed Gunther's shoulder and let his hand drop.

Gunther turned to his friend. For what seemed like ages, the two of them stood examining each other in the half light, drinking in every detail of the well-remembered face before them. Then Gunther opened his arms and the two of them embraced silently, rocking slightly as they hugged.

At length, Frank pushed himself free. "Come on. We've work to do," he said grimly.

Gunther nodded and the two of them walked to the arch. With just the briefest of backward glances, they set off along the hedge base to the corner, where they crouched in the last remaining safety of its shadow. Frank looked across to the beginnings of the complex. Nearest to them was the small end extension of the main barn and, beyond that, the main milking parlour and calf sheds, which in turn gave way to Jean-Claude and Marie's now deserted quarters and the huge towered entrance.

If necessary they could escape this way, via the kitchens, but for now they needed to skirt the main buildings.

With a silent signal, Frank set off and the two of them crossed the last open space to the gate and then along the edge of the buildings, taking care to keep within the shadows as much as possible. With all the lights on in the chateau, nobody in there could see what was going on outside. Still they couldn't be too careful. If just one enemy soldier was outside on the top patio, then they would be clearly visible. They reached the end of the long tongue of outbuildings at the corner of the main chateau and crouched there for a moment to draw breath.

Again, almost by telepathy, they set off along the wall, moving down now as the ground fell before them and the top patio rose above them. At the corner they paused again, before creeping forward along the lower patio in the direction of the wide stone balustrades and the steps curving between the two levels. At the bench that they knew would be there, just behind the wisteria-covered arbour, they slipped into the small grotto set back into the main wall and stared at the white marble visage of the Madonna in its arched setting.

Frank took off his rifle and handed it to Gunther. Then he grasped the rose-shaped knobs on each side of the statue and pushed hard against the wall. Nothing happened.

"What's wrong?" Gunther whispered.

"It won't move."

"What do you mean it won't move... do you want me to try?"

"No, you've hurt your arm. I'll do it." Frank pushed harder, trying not to grunt in the process. "It's probably just a bit stiff... probably just dirt... yes, it's moving... it's going..." He continued to push and now, even in the darkness, Gunther could see that the figure of the Madonna was sliding in and away out of sight.

"Come in," Frank breathed, and the two of them pushed the heavy stone door shut again.

"Will we be able to open it again from in here?" Gunther whispered, starting in alarm as even his lowered voice echoed back at him.

"Yes, I think so... we didn't turn anything, did we? It just moves on its rails, doesn't it?"

"I think so," said Gunther nervously. "Try it now. We don't want to be trapped."

Frank pulled hard on the handle on the inside of the door. It opened, grating slightly on the dirt that had accumulated in the bottom rail. He pushed it shut again and then knelt and flicked the channel clean. "Yes it's alright. It moves quite easily," he assured his friend as he reached into his pocket for the torch. He lit it and shone it back along the passageway. "Just as I remember," he said quietly. "Now do we go all the way through to the staircase, or do we branch off and come up in the scullery?"

"I think we should go to the scullery, sneak through the kitchen and up the small staircase," said Gunther.

"But that puts us on this side of the chateau and I bet he's got her..." Frank stopped and faced Gunther, pointing the torch in his face.

Gunther blinked in the light and shook his head almost sorrowfully. "It's alright, I know... I know he's probably got her in his room... I'm not stupid. I know what he's like. Don't forget I've seen him in action."

Frank nodded. "Come on then. At least his lusts will mean that she's probably still here and in one piece." He turned and led the way, the two of them padding softly down the long tunnel, following the beam of the torch. They reached the flight of steps that they knew led up to the secret doorway in the back of the main staircase in the hall. Here the passageway turned left and narrowed, and before long gave way to a set of spiral steps which led directly upwards to a stone slab in the scullery floor.

"Here, let me go first," said Gunther, pushing past Frank. "You shine the torch on me when I get to the top."

Frank stood back briefly and then followed his friend around the winding staircase until Gunther stopped and he bumped into him. He shone the torch up and beyond Gunther. The stone slab that they both knew needed to be lifted straight if it was to clear the hole was just above Gunther's head. "Can you manage?" Frank whispered.

"Course I can manage," replied Gunther. "I always did before, didn't I? It was you that got stuck."

Frank laughed lightly at the memory, despite the tenseness of their situation. "Do you remember how poor old Marie never knew how we got into the kitchen all those times?"

"Or why we'd suddenly arrive from the scullery."

"She must have guessed."

"I don't think so... apart from that time when she left that bucket of dirty water in there and it went everywhere when I lifted the slab."

The moment of lightness passed and the two of them settled down to the serious business of exiting the tunnel. "Alright then, let's do it," said Frank firmly, "...and take care. We don't know who's in the kitchen. It can't be Marie."

"Shine the torch on the slab as I lift," said Gunther, moving up the stairs to put his shoulders squarely beneath it. "When it starts to move, turn it off and hold your breath." He took a few deep breaths and then pushed up on the slab, taking care not to let it bind on its setting. Frank flicked off the torch, and for a few seconds they were in total darkness before the stone moved up and a chink of light shone around its rim. Gunther stopped pushing and waited, listening intently for any signs of life in the room above. None could be heard. At least the scullery itself was clear, even if the kitchen was probably occupied.

He pushed up some more and then reached up to grab the front edge of the slab as he peered directly out at floor level. The sounds of a man humming to himself as he worked away at the stove out on the opposite wall of the kitchen came to him and he ducked slightly down. "There's at least one man working in the kitchen," he hissed through closed teeth.

"Be bloody careful with the slab then," Frank breathed back.

Gunther raised himself again, reaching up to grip the edge of the slab as it cleared the floor. Frank pocketed the torch and placed his rifle carefully against the wall before almost climbing up Gunther's back to stand behind him on the same step. He reached up and gripped the opposite edge of the slab and the two of them slowly turned, their arms outstretched, quivering with the strain, and placed it silently on the floor. Frank bent down and retrieved his rifle whilst Gunther raised himself from the hole and crouched down as he unholstered his pistol. He peered through the cracked door into the kitchen and then turned back to Frank as he cleared the trap.

He held up two fingers, then one, and gestured in an arc, making a stirring motion to indicate one man cooking at the range. Frank nodded his understanding and then looked quizzically at his friend for details of the other man. Gunther held his elbows away from himself and then brought them down, to indicate sitting. Again Frank nodded his understanding. He gripped his rifle and stepped clear of the hole to stand beside him.

Gunther waited until Frank was clear before pushing the door open. The soldier sitting at the table turned and his mouth fell open as Gunther stepped into the room, his pistol levelled at him in silent menace. Gunther jerked the weapon and the man stood, raising his hands, as the other man remained oblivious to their presence.

"Guten abend," said Gunther in a low, menacing tone. The cook swung around at the sound of his voice. "Guten..." he stammered, before a hissed "Stille!" and a meaningful jerk of the gun silenced him.

For a moment they stood stock still, staring at the single intruder, but then, as Frank entered the room, his rifle levelled straight at them, the two men exchanged frightened glances and slowly raised their hands above their heads. "That drawer over there," Frank indicated to Gunther. "If it's still as I remember it, you'll find kitchen rags in there, and in the one next to it you'll find string."

Gunther circled the room, continuing to face the two soldiers, with his pistol trained all the while on them. He reached behind and pulled the drawers open, feeling about within them. For a split second he turned and looked into the drawers, but equally quickly he turned back to cover the two men as he withdrew the rags and a large ball of twine.

"Stuff their mouths with the rag," Frank ordered. "I'll cover them."

Gunther handed Frank the pistol and stepped forward, motioning the two men to turn around. He reached up and stuffed first one and then the other one's mouth with the rags. "Bind the string around their faces to stop them spitting it out," said Frank. Gunther quickly wound the string about the poor men's faces and tied it tight behind each of their necks, cutting the loose ends with a knife from the range.

Frank stepped forward. He leant his rifle against the table, keeping the pistol levelled at the two men. "In dort," he barked softly at the two terrified men, indicating the scullery he had just stepped from. The two soldiers needed no further urging and quickly made their way around the table and into the scullery, with Frank close behind them, prodding them forward and up against the wall. "Bind their hands and feet Gunther," he commanded, "and then bind them together, front to front."

Gunther roughly pulled first one and then the other man's hands behind their backs and tied them tight. Then he bent down and just as quickly tied their feet, before Frank stepped forward and the two of them manhandled their captives together. "Wind it all around them and then tie it off," whispered Frank urgently, "then we'd better get going."

Gunther whipped the string around and around the two, by now helpless, men and then finally, when he was completely satisfied that there was no slack, he tied it off and cut free the remainder of the ball.

Frank and he then picked up the two men and carried them bodily to the open trap, where they lowered them, none too gently, into the void before replacing the slab and scuffing the floor to remove all sign of it ever having been moved. "They'll die in there," Gunther hissed.

"Maybe," said Frank, "but what else can we do?"

"Nothing," said Gunther sadly. He shut the scullery door and Frank crossed to the door to the hallway. For a second Gunther stared at the scullery door, uncertainty written all over his face, but then, on a cough from Frank, he joined him. Frank handed him back his gun and gently opened the kitchen door.

In front of them were the five steps leading straight up from the kitchen level to that of the main hallway. Pulling the door closed behind them, they crept forward on hands and knees to kneel, their heads at floor level as they listened out for signs of danger.

To their right the hallway narrowed, and from their vantage point they could clearly see the small wooden door that opened on to the servant's staircase, leading up to all levels of the building and down to the wine cellars. To their left the hallway widened into the grand entrance hall, with the main staircase sweeping up to the first floor. Beyond that, slightly forward of the start of the stairs and offset from it was the dining room, from which they could faintly hear a low hum of male conversation interspersed with the tinkling laughter of Nicole, still playing the perfect hostess.

Frank jerked his head to the right. Gunther nodded and crept across and down the hallway to the door as Frank covered him. He reached it and waved Frank across to join him. Gently they eased up the latch and slipped through, silently closing it behind them. "Phew," said Frank. "Quick, we'd better get up there as quick as possible. We don't know who uses this, and if we're caught here we're trapped."

As quickly as they could they ran up the steep flights, two steps at a time, until they gained the first floor. Gunther reached it first and put his hand on the latch just as Frank arrived. "Just a second," he panted. "Let me get my breath or I'll sound like a steam engine on the landing." He clutched his head, lifting the woollen hat he was wearing, fingering the bandages below.

"Are you alright?"

"Yes... bit of a headache. He grimaced slightly. "Sorry... I'm alright. Right, quiet now, let's get going," he whispered.

Gunther eased the latch up and opened the door, standing aside for Frank to slip through and then following him. Frank pointed down the long landing and raised his thumb. Gunther nodded and the two of them crept slowly forward, moving from door to door as they made their way towards the gallery.

They froze at one door as they heard sounds coming from within the room, and for a moment the two of them remained flattened against the wall, steeling themselves to go on. Frank glanced at

Gunther, who returned his look with a meaningful nod of his head and a jerked signal to carry on.

They drew ever nearer the gallery and the open well to the ground floor, hearing, as they crept, the faint sounds coming from the dining room below. Suddenly the door to the room where they had heard sounds opened and a soldier, his head bent as he buttoned his jacket, came out and turned left in the direction of the small staircase, humming tunelessly. Frank felt the fear rush through his limbs as he stared, as if in a nightmare, at the receding figure of the soldier. Surely he could hear his heart thumping. He certainly could feel it thundering through the constricting veins in his temple, forcing the pain back into his wounded head.

Even as he watched, the figure of the enemy reached the doorway to the staircase they had climbed and disappeared through it. For what seemed like ages Frank continued to stare at the door, but then, almost reluctantly, he swung his gaze back to Gunther's pale face, staring wide-eyed and straight ahead as he held himself flat against the wall.

The door slammed shut to a loud greeting, obviously given to some other soldier already on the staircase. For a moment the two companions thought that their discovery was only a matter of seconds away, before the receding sounds of the men's voices told them that the other party must have been coming down the stairs from above rather than travelling up to their certain discovery.

Frank sucked in his breath and closed his eyes momentarily. "Alright?" Gunther breathed in his ear.

Frank blew out and nodded his head, raising his eyebrows in a gesture of pure amazement that they had got away with it. Then he turned and continued along, seizing hold of the balustrading and working his way around the stairwell, followed by Gunther.

Ahead now were the double doors of the main bedroom, the bedroom that Frank had hurriedly left when he had come here with Pierre at the beginning of the nightmare. Armand's and Violet's bedroom as was. Then his bedroom and now, almost certainly, Weber's.

Gunther held him back. "I hope you're right and she's in there."

"I hope so too," Frank breathed back, "otherwise I don't fancy searching every room. Do you?"

Gunther shook his head. They stopped outside the doors and Frank put his ear to one of them and listened intently as Gunther kept watch back along the landing. "Anything?" he whispered.

Frank shook his head, motioning silence. He reached for the door handle and slowly turned it. The door opened, and he held it open for a moment before slipping through and then reaching back to pull Gunther inside. He pushed the door shut, holding the latch open until the two doors met and then slowly letting the handle turn back.

For a few moments they stood just inside the door, staring forward into the dark at the great canopied shape that they knew was the bed. "Annette," Frank whispered. "Annette, are you here?"

A low murmur, almost a whimper, came from the direction of the bed, and before Frank could stop him, Gunther rushed forward. Frank followed more slowly, his rifle held in readiness. But, as Gunther reached the bed, Frank could tell by his reaction that it was, indeed, Annette and that they were alone.

He moved forward to find Gunther cradling a bound Annette in his lap as he sat on the edge of the bed. She was bound hand and foot and dressed in the rumpled clothes that she had been wearing when she was taken.

"Untie her," he urged. "We've got to get going." Gunther stared up at him, seeming not to comprehend exactly what he meant. "Here, let me," said Frank impatiently. He reached down and fumbled with the crudely tied knots at the girl's feet, as Gunther finally seemed to realise what was required and gently turned Annette over to untie her hands as she murmured his name.

"Has he... has he hurt you?" he whispered urgently into her ear. She turned her face back towards him, her eyes shining, the pain visible even in the dark, her face set confirming his worst fears. "I'll kill him," hissed Gunther, rising from the bed.

"And just what would that achieve tonight?" said Frank in an exasperated tone. "Just how would that free Annette?"

"Frank? Frank, is that you?" Annette whispered incredulously from the bed as she rolled over, struggling to shake the feeling back into her lifeless limbs.

"Yes, it's me," Frank whispered. "Can you walk?"

"I can't feel my legs... yes I can now... is that really you Frank?" She winced in pain as the blood flowed back into her limbs. Her eyes flew open wide and she gasped, "Dieter! Is he safe?"

"He's safe," Gunther soothed. "He's with Marie in Gien. We're taking you there."

"Rub her arms. I'll rub her legs," Frank ordered. "Quick, we've got to get going!" The two men vigorously rubbed Annette's arms and legs, pulling her into a sitting position on the bed and placing her feet on the floor. "Can you stand? Try and stand," Frank begged. "Come on Annette, we've got to get going."

"Leave her a moment, please Frank," pleaded Gunther.

"No. Frank's right. We've got to get out... help me to stand," said Annette, reaching her bruised and painful arms up for each of them to take. They lifted gently and she stood gingerly, swaying slightly as the pins and needles rushed through her legs and the feeling flowed back into her feet.

"Alright now?" Gunther asked gently.

"Yes," she replied, a little uncertainly.

"Right," said Frank, "now listen Annette, we've got to go downstairs. We'll help you, but we must be quiet. Understood? We've got to go down the main stairs. That's the quickest way, and that takes us near the door to the dining room."

"Why can't we go out the way we came?" Gunther interrupted.

"Because I reckon that that staircase is the one the soldiers use and we're much more likely to get caught there... especially if we're moving slowly. Besides, we need to go out through the staircase panelling because we've blocked the scullery exit," said Frank.

"Damn. Why did we do that? It's too dangerous to go down the main staircase," moaned Gunther.

"And how much more dangerous would it have been if somebody had come into the kitchen and found our two friends?" said Frank quietly.

Gunther thought for a moment then nodded his head. "Yes. Yes, I'm sorry, you're right... but it is dangerous nevertheless."

Annette looked from one to the other. "Are you two going to argue all night, or are we going to escape?"

Frank smiled and put his arm around her shoulders, playfully reaching across with his other hand to punch Gunther. Gunther grinned back. "Sorry Frank. Nerves I suppose... let's get going, shall we?"

The two of them lifted Annette to her feet and then Frank went across to the door and opened it, listening out. He waved them forward and slipped out of the door and across to the landing, peering down over the handrail as he held his hand out to halt the others at the door. He listened to the sounds for a moment and then, deciding that they were the normal ones of a dinner conversation, waved the others across.

He turned as they joined him and slipped his arm about Annette's waist to link in with Gunther as the two of them half carried the girl along the landing to the top step, where they paused. Annette looked, wide-eyed, into first Gunther's and then Frank's face, seeing, in both, the resolution and the fear as they steeled themselves for the task ahead.

Gunther relaxed his grip on her waist and fumbled with his holster to withdraw his pistol. He pointed to himself and held one finger up to signal that he was going first. Frank nodded, shouldering his rifle and seizing Annette around the waist.

Gunther crept down the staircase, his body crouched, taking one step at a time in a sort of sideways crab movement. He kept his eyes fixed on the half open dining room doors.

At last he paused and waved Frank down. Frank tugged gently at Annette and the two of them started down the stairs, with Frank letting her go one step at a time as he supported her before he joined her and repeated the process.

Gunther reached the half landing and flattened himself against the wall, looking up at Frank and Annette as they painfully and ever so silently made their way towards him. The heartbeat in his chest and his very breathing seemed to echo all around him. His eyes flicked back to the dining room doors and he sucked in his breath as they swung fully open and a figure appeared, framed in the light, its back to them. His hand flew up to stay Frank's descent and he levelled the gun and took aim.

"I won't be a moment," came Nicole's voice. "I'll just see what's keeping them." She turned and bustled off down the passageway in the direction of the kitchen. Frank, Gunther and Annette froze in their respective positions, their eyes wide with terror.

The sound of the kitchen door slamming shut and the tapping of her shoes on the stairs as she ran up the flight to the passageway alerted them to Nicole's return and Gunther pushed himself back against the panelled wall.

She swept down the corridor, humming tunelessly to herself, and went straight into the dining room, pushing the doors partially shut behind her. "Nobody there!" they heard her say.

For a moment they were certain that there would be a general exodus from the room and that their discovery was therefore certain, but then the sounds of dining and the clinking of glasses resumed. Gunther shot a look up at Frank and signalled him to follow. Then he crept quickly down to the bottom newel and stood holding on to it, one foot on the bullnose, the other on the floor as he waited for them to catch up.

Frank and Annette joined him at the bottom and he grabbed

Annette's arm, pushing and pulling her along the edge of the staircase. They drew level with the dining room door and all instinctively turned and flattened themselves against the wall as they crabbed past, their eyes fixed on the light.

They reached the end of the staircase panelling and Frank pulled Annette into the shade, leaning her up against the wall with a finger to her lips, commanding silence as Gunther half crouched on the corner, his gun trained at the dining room. Frank felt for the carved rose emblem he knew would be there and turned it slowly, pushing the secret door inwards and feeling in his pocket for the torch.

He reached back for Annette's hand to guide her around the corner of the staircase to the top of the steps, almost exactly as Henri swung the dining room door open and stepped into the hall. For a moment there was a stunned silence as he and Gunther regarded each other, but then Henri turned, his hands flew up and he shouted out Gunther's name, as the sounds of chairs being thrown backwards came from within the room.

"Go!" Gunther hissed to Frank and Annette, hidden behind the staircase. "Go! I'll hold them."

Henri, who, apart from turning around, had seemed rooted to the spot in the light of the open door, now wheeled around and began shouting out and pointing. Gunther crouched and fired, the shot echoing through the chateau. Henri crumpled face down in the doorway. In a flash, before Frank could react differently, Gunther whipped around and pushed him and Annette through the secret door, pulling it closed before they could recover themselves, and turned the rose back to lock it. For a moment he regarded the panelling, his mind working clearly despite the awful pressure. 'No... nobody would know... They would think he was alone... until it was too late.' He turned back and crouched down, taking careful aim at the dining room door.

"Soldaten! Achtung! Achtung!" came Weber's voice, screaming from the dining room. Gunther whirled around on one knee. The kitchen! He could get... he heard the kitchen door open and watched with dismay as soldiers bundled through and positioned themselves in the small stairwell, with him clearly in their sights. He waved his gun in their general direction and then spun back again as Weber and another officer appeared at each jamb of the dining room door, their pistols forbidding his retreat.

For a moment there was complete quiet, before Gunther let out a deep sigh of resignation. His head dropped, his gun pointed uselessly to the floor, and he stood slowly and tossed it out into the hallway. Slowly the soldiers in the well stood up, their rifles pointing directly at his chest. Weber stepped forward, a cruel smile on his face. "Guten abend, Leutnant Schmidt," he sneered. His expression changed to acute distaste as Nicole screamed and pushed past him to throw herself sobbing on to Henri's lifeless corpse. He stepped across them, his face a mask of disdain. "Sind sie allein?" he demanded.

"Wie sie sehen," said Gunther, holding his hands in the air. He had to make him believe that he was alone to give Frank and Annette time to get away. "Bin ich vollkommen allein."

"Fassen sie ihn und bringen sie ihn her," Weber barked, flicking his fingers towards Gunther, who gasped in pain as two soldiers obeyed the command and his arms were roughly pulled behind him as he was frogmarched into the blazing light of the dining room.

Weber bent down to Nicole and hauled her unceremoniously to her feet. "You! You go upstairs and see if the Jewess is still there," he ordered. Nicole looked at him, fear and grief written in equal measure on her face. "Go!" Weber screamed into her face. She nodded mutely, then turned and ran upstairs.

"Nett, dass sie gekommen sind, Leutnant Schmidt," said Weber, pointedly and slyly, as he picked up his fallen chair and resumed his seat.

He sat and picked up his fork to toy with the remaining food on his plate, clearly having lost his appetite. "Es tut mir leid, dass die mahlzeit bienahe beendet ist." He turned at the sound of running feet on the staircase and stared at the open door as a clearly distraught and exhausted Nicole almost fell through.

She stood, her hands on her hips, her head bent low as she struggled for breath. "Gone," she mumbled.

"What?!" yelled Weber.

Nicole raised her head and looked him straight in the eye. "She's gone. She's escaped!"

Weber wheeled around, realising now that Gunther must have had an accomplice. He stood, scattering his chair once more, and crossed to Gunther, swiping him across the face and then back again. "Wo ist sie?" he screamed, his face contorted with rage. "Wer ist mit ihnen?"

Gunther simply smiled through his broken and bleeding mouth.

Weber spun around to the soldiers. "Finden sie sie!" he yelled, waving his arms in all directions as he commanded them to search. He turned back to Gunther. "Und sie, sie werden den tag, an dem sie geboren wurden bedauern." He pointed at him. "Nehmen sie ihn fest und sperren sie ihn ein, dann kommen sie mit mir!" he commanded, and the two soldiers holding Gunther proceeded to bind his arms behind him. He wheeled around as another guard entered the room, running. "Woher kommen sie?"

"Vom hinten rum," the overawed soldier replied.

"Hat sonst noch jemand diesen weg genommen?"

"Nein, Herr Weber. Das hätte ich gesehen."

Weber turned to the other soldiers, gesticulating wildly towards the kitchens. "Sie kamen von der küche?"

"Ja, Herr Weber."

"Dann müssen sie vorne rausgegangen sein. Schnell, folgen sie mir!" he yelled, rushing from the room in the direction of the front entrance doors.

Even as Weber reached for the handle, Frank, with an exhausted Annette in tow, was scooting across the last open piece of ground for the sanctity of the yew hedge. He reached it and virtually hurled the poor girl into its base as he collapsed on to his knees, panting for breath. For a while there was silence except for their laboured breath, but then as lights came on all around the chateau, he rose, still clutching his chest with one hand whilst reaching out his other for her. "We have to keep going," he panted. "They must've realised you're gone."

"I can't," she wailed. "I can't go on any more."

"You must," he said, hauling her roughly to her feet. "Gunther and I didn't come here just to leave you."

The mention of his name brought the horror of Gunther's certain capture back to her mind and she stood a little uncertainly and stared back at the chateau. "Can't we do anything for him?" she pleaded.

"No. I'll need some help for that one. We'll get you to safety and then I'll go and fetch help... he'll be alright," he said as he grabbed her hand and practically dragged her along the side of the hedge. "He's a German officer and they'll want to court martial him or something, rather than just shoot him... now quick, we must hurry."

He led the way up the hill, pulling the exhausted Annette behind him as she stumbled on every tree root, her feet dragging through the leaf debris. Several times she fell over sideways, painfully wrenching her arm in the process as he refused to let go. "You're hurting me Frank!" she cried.

"I'm sorry Annette, but please... if we're caught it's... well he'll kill us. You know that, don't you?"

"He'll kill Gunther," she wailed. "Oh Frank, we can't just leave him." The enormity of the tragedy crashed in on her and she tore away from him and stumbled back down the hill, calling out Gunther's name. Frank turned in disbelief. He threw down his rifle and tore after her, bringing her to the ground with a flying rugby tackle, the two of them rolling over and over on the ground as he struggled to contain her hands and pin her to the floor.

"Annette!" he almost shouted. "Annette, listen to me... Gunther knew what he was doing when he shut that panel... he did it to save you. Don't throw that away... don't let it all be for nothing."

"But Gunther... he..."

"Dieter! Think of Dieter... please Annette... think!"

She looked up at his face, her eyes wide with terror, her mouth open as if to speak. Gradually, as he stared down into her well-remembered face, the features began to crumple, the mouth closed into a tight and quivering line and the eyes narrowed as the tears flowed from them. "Frank... oh Frank, I'm so frightened... that man... he... he... oh Frank..."

"There, there," Frank soothed. He rolled off her and cradled her head in his arms, stroking her face. Behind them, the floodlights on the patio came on and he whirled around. That meant that they were going to search the back, but it also meant that those within the light would be blind to the inky blackness of the night beyond... until, that is, they came out with the light behind them or they turned the search lights on. He stood, reaching down for her hands as he did so, and hauled her to her feet. "Quick, we've got to get back up the hill beneath the trees... they're coming."

Annette cast an eye back down the hill and across to the chateau, realisation of their dire position finally dawning on her. She turned back to Frank. "Quick, help me."

Frank needed no further urging. He grabbed her arm and pushed and pulled her up the hill to the tree line, reaching it even as the long probing arcs of the search lights reached across the grounds.

They stumbled on through the woods, each now silent except for their laboured breath. Up to and over the summit they ran. Down through the spreading trees to the edge of the wall, where Frank dug his heels in to prevent himself falling and turned as Annette fell into his arms. He stood and held her back, passing her across himself to park her against a tree. "Here, wait here and I'll get down and catch you!"

Annette brushed against Gunther's uniform, her hands encountering the unexpected material as it lay across the branch where he had draped it. She screamed out in terror and Frank leapt back up and stifled her mouth with his hand. He let go and she pointed in terror. He turned and retrieved the jacket. "It's Gunther's... he left it here. It's alright, calm down and take it. We've got to get away!"

He turned around and crabbed down the wall to the lane. "Throw me the jacket," he commanded, catching it and sweeping it to the ground as she did so. "Now come on, turn around and come down as I did."

She grabbed the top copings and lowered herself over the edge, frantically struggling for a foothold as her body slid over the rough stones. "Let go," he shouted. "Let go, I'll catch you!"

Annette held on for a moment longer, then she released her grip and fell backwards into his arms. He stumbled as her weight crashed into him and fell sprawling backwards onto the rough tarmac, with her on top. For a moment the two of them lay there in the road, their breath coming in painful gasps, but then, through the still of the night air, from the direction of the chateau, came the sound of whistles blowing and dogs barking. Quickly, without ceremony, he rolled her off him and dragged her to her feet, grabbing Gunther's jacket as he pulled her up the lane to the hidden vehicle. "Get in!" he almost screamed as they finally got there. "Get in!"

"Where are you going!" she cried as he ran past the door and ducked out of sight in front of the vehicle.

"The key!" he shouted as he reappeared and jumped into the driving seat, flinging Gunther's jacket onto the back seat. He reached forward and started the car, crunching the gears into reverse and pulling out of the gateway.

He winced and shook his head. 'Calm down Frank,' he told himself... 'calm down.' He drew a deep breath. Annette shot a worried glance across at him.

Gently now, he eased the vehicle into forward gear and let the clutch out, keeping the engine noise as low as possible as they rolled on down the lane towards the hamlet.

They approached the junction and he applied the brakes slowly.

They squealed slightly and he let the pressure off the pedal and coasted around the corner before heading off in the direction of Saint Benoit.

As they cleared the last houses and crossed the open fields towards the main road, Annette heaved a sigh of relief, but then Frank suddenly pulled in to the side of the road. For a moment he sat still, his hands on the gear shift, the engine idling. "What's the matter?" she asked in alarm as he turned off the ignition. "Why aren't we going?"

He looked across at her. "Sorry... I was just thinking... we have to get to Gien. That's where Marie has taken Dieter." He glanced back at the rear seat as if thinking something through, then he quickly stood up and reached back for the jacket, stepping out of the vehicle to put it on. "Can you see his cap? He threw it in the back."

Annette reached back, feeling about in the well. She found it and brought it out. "Here."

Frank took the hat, put it in his lap and gently removed the dark woollen cap he was wearing. For the first time Annette saw that he was injured and reached out to touch the bandages. "You're hurt," she whispered.

"It's nothing much," he said. "Just a bump on the head." He put Gunther's cap on. "How do I look?"

"Like a Boche officer, from the waist up."

Frank got back into the driving seat. "Right... Look, I'm sorry, I panicked a bit back there but..." He listened out in all directions. "No sound of any pursuit... they must still think we're in the chateau grounds. Now listen, I'm sorry for what's happened, but now... if we're to get to Gien, we have to try and be calm. Understood? We've got to drive without attracting any undue attention or we're finished. Is that clear?" Annette nodded.

"Good girl," he said as cheerily as he could muster. "Let's go then. Let's go and find Dieter and then I've got to get back to camp to try and organise some help for Gunther."

Annette put her hand on his arm. "Thank you Frank," she said quietly.

He reached across and cupped her face in his hand. "It'll be alright Annette. We'll get you to Gien and then I'll find Gunther... I promise."

"I know you will Frank," she said softly. "I know you will, but..."

"No buts," he said firmly. "I'll find him... I have to." He smiled with as much conviction as he could muster... an empty smile, he knew. It matched the void that was opening up within him as a terrible dread crept across him, forcing its darkness into his very soul. He shook his head as the shivers ran through him. Then he reached forward, started the engine, flicked on the lights and slipped the car into gear.

14th August 1944

Pierre-Luc bent down and took hold of the rough canvas bag, waiting as his companion did likewise with the other end. He didn't know the name of the young man lying dead and still within the bag, but he had seen him around in the weeks leading up to the ambush and he had heard him cry out from his terrible wounds over the previous nights.

The memory of the boy's cheerful face, his laughing dark eyes and wavy, overlong hair, seemed to hover before Pierre-Luc's eyes as the two men took the strain and gently lowered the shroud into the soft, moist earth. For a moment the two of them stood, heads bowed in silent contemplation, but then with a loud sigh Pierre-Luc turned and picked up the shovel. He took a large scoop of the mushroom-fragrant earth and emptied it down onto the canvas. His companion did likewise, and the two of them worked mechanically together to fill the void.

Beside them, other men performed the same grim task for the other eight men who had perished in the ambush. How quickly the euphoria of success had turned into the bitter truth of these losses. Even as they had walked tall from the trees and strode back into the camp, they had all heard the cries of the dying, the low moaning of men who knew that their lives were hopeless and that death lurked around every shadow.

Thank God that Frank was alright. He should be back this morning... he had expected him back the previous evening but he had not shown up. 'Lazy bastard... probably too busy tucking into my mother's cooking,' he thought with a smile.

An older maquisard stepped forward and handed Pierre-Luc a rough cross made from two lengths of branch tied together. "Put this in the earth," he grumbled.

"No name?" Pierre-Luc asked.

"No name," the man confirmed. "No name, no information, no reprisals."

Pierre-Luc nodded his understanding. He bent down to push the cross into the disturbed earth, his thoughts lingering on the buried face of the man below.

The sound of an engine caused him to straighten up suddenly and then crouch down, staring through the trees to the road about twenty metres away.

"Who is it?" the old man hissed in his ear. "Ours?"

"No, it's Boche."

"What are they doing here at this time of the morning?" his fellow grave-digger whispered, as he too crouched down beside them.

"Search me," said Pierre-Luc. "I'd just feel happier if we had a gun between us."

"Me too," his companion murmured.

A forest guard, who had stopped off on his way to work and lingered with them, crept across to them, keeping low. "What are they doing?" he asked.

Pierre-Luc raised his head as far as he dared and peered through the scant undergrowth. "I don't know... they're driving slowly... I think they're lost."

"God I wish we had guns instead of shovels," groaned the older man, "then I'd give them lost!"

Pierre-Luc held his hand out palm down, fingers spread, for the man to be quiet. He crept forward on his belly, looking down the road at the departing lorry, from the back of which he could clearly see the pale faces of soldiers in full combat gear. Suddenly the vehicle stopped. He half raised himself from the ground, preparing for flight, but then flattened himself back again as it executed an almost lazy three-point turn and headed back down, past them, in the direction of the Route des Bordes. Relief flooded through him at the thought that they were truly lost... a relief which was just as quickly replaced by a creeping coldness as he watched the lorry stop again about eight-hundred metres on down the road. The tailgate dropped and soldiers dismounted silently. As if to some prearranged plan, some took up defensive positions in the road whilst others moved swiftly to piles of lumber stacked up on the side of the roadway, hauling it into the middle of the carriageway. Yet more leapt from the vehicle and proceeded to file, at both right angles, into the forest.

Pierre-Luc wriggled backwards towards his friends, cursing silently as his clothing rucked up his torso. He spun around on the earth and crawled back to the graves. "It's planned!" he warned. It's us they're after!"

"What?" said the older man. "What do you mean?"

"They're making a barricade on the road and others are fanning out from it," Pierre-Luc whispered.

"What time is it?" the man asked.

"Just after eight o'clock... why?"

"Jesus Christ! There's a lorry due to go to Lorris. They'll run straight into them!"

Pierre-Luc grimaced. He cocked his ear and caught the sound of another lorry coming down the other road, from the direction of the Carrefour de Joinville. "Is that them?" he whispered.

"No... that must be more Boche, but... oh God, they'll be coming along at any minute."

"We've got to warn them," Pierre-Luc hissed.

"I'll do it," volunteered the forest guard. "My bicycle is hidden in the undergrowth back there... which road will they take?"

"They'll probably be coming up Chat Sauvage, heading for the main road," whispered the older man.

"Right then, I'd better go now and try to head them off," said the forester, sliding backwards and then crouching as he slipped from tree to tree.

"Take care," Pierre-Luc called quietly after him.

The forest guard turned back and grinned at him, his white teeth showing clearly against the dark burnt hue of his skin. He opened his arms in a Gallic gesture. "But I am supposed to be here... it's my job."

Pierre-Luc grinned back and waved him away before turning back to look through the trees at the enemy. "What are we going to do?" he whispered to the older man.

"Stay hidden here is all I can think of for the moment," he replied.

Pierre-Luc cocked his ear again. "I can still hear engine noise from the Carrefour de Joinville," he said quietly. "Do you think we should take a look?"

"We can't all go lumbering through the forest looking for Boche," said the man, a note halfway between disdain and despair in his voice.

"No we can't," said Pierre-Luc, realising that if they were going to do anything at all, he would have to start making decisions himself. "But someone can stay here and keep an eye on those chaps at the barricade whilst the rest of you make it back to the houses back at the Carrefour d'Orleans and I go off in that direction..." He pointed in the direction of the Route de Chat Sauvage. "...to see what's happening. We know that they're on the Route des Bordes, that they're here and that they're at Joinville. That's two sides of a triangle, and if they're coming at us from the other directions then we may well be trapped."

The other men looked at Pierre-Luc with frightened faces. The older man stared into his eyes with open hostility, as if to forbid him to summon up these terrible possibilities. For a while the two men held each other's gaze, but then the older man's wavered and he lowered his head and nodded. He turned to one of the burial party. "You stay here and keep a watch on those men... dig yourself in, there's Boche in the forest as well as on the road. You lot come with me... and you..." He tapped Pierre-Luc on the shoulder. "...you follow the guard and then report back to the houses."

Pierre-Luc nodded his acceptance of his own suggestions. He turned and wriggled away, up the slight rise and behind a huge oak tree, slipping over its gnarled roots and back down out of sight of the others. He paused, listening out for signs of other life. To the north he could still hear engine noise at the Carrefour de Joinville. 'Good,' he thought, 'they had not moved.' To the south he could hear the slight rustling of his erstwhile companions as they filed off through the forest, back towards the houses.

The houses! The wounded men from Chicamour were in there. If the Germans came up any of the other roads then they would be trapped for certain.

A cold dread crept through him... a really bad feeling which threatened to banish all rational thought. He shook himself. 'Stop it! Stop it! Pull yourself together,' he commanded himself. Where were those other Germans? They had filed out into the forest at right angles. That meant that one lot would have gone back behind him in the direction of the Route des Bordes, and that the others would be away off to his left. If the vehicles he could hear at the Carrefour de Joinville remained stationary, that meant that...

'Quick!' he told himself. 'Get to the road.' He stood, paused for a moment to look at head height through the dense trees and, having satisfied himself that all was clear, strode off along the narrow deer track.

He passed the broken patch of bracken where the forest guard had hidden his bicycle. Good, he had done as he was bidden... brave man. A shot! A single shot from up ahead made him drop to his knees. Another shot. He dropped to his belly and slid forward through the bracken, cursing silently as, at the edge of the trees, near the road, it gave way to tangled brambles which snagged at his clothing and tore into his flesh.

A large old tree leaning at an angle of about forty-five degrees gave him cover from the road and he crawled up to it and peered over its twisted trunk, parting the thin shoots which sprang vertically from it in a vain effort at normal growth. To his left he could see along the road, and to his horror there was another barricade. If they had filed out from that one at right angles then, whilst some of them were heading away from him, others would, even now, be shutting the gate behind him as they joined their comrades from the other barricade.

A helmet appeared over the top of the barricade. He watched as it raised itself, revealing the pale face of a young soldier, his features otherwise indistinguishable at that distance. A long stick... no a gun, was extended, resting on the top log. The face lowered itself, taking careful aim down the road. Pierre-Luc followed its direction and was dismayed to see a familiar vehicle approaching from the direction of the Carrefour d'Orleans.

The lorry! Surely they could see? They must see. Could they not see the barricade? Could they not see the... Then something caught his eye. He squinted as, from the ditch, a figure raised itself on to its knees, waving one hand in the air. The forest guard! The man stood, picking up his bicycle, leaning heavily on the handlebars, his right leg stretched out at a peculiar angle. The front wheel, crumpled and broken, meant that the frame refused to take his weight and the handlebars twisted as he fell, forcing them into his stomach. Once more he raised himself from the wreckage, his voice raised, thin-sounding in the morning air, his arms waving above his head like those of a drowning man seeking air.

The sharp crack of the rifle presaged the final collapse of the forester, and almost simultaneously the brakes on the Maquis lorry made it squeal to a halt.

For a moment there was a silence, within which Pierre-Luc raised himself from his crouched position, no longer aware or even caring about concealment. He could see the white faces of the two occupants of the cab as they stared out and along the road. Andre... it was Andre. 'Get out Andre! Get out!' he shouted in his head. 'That's right!... that's right,' he silently congratulated the men, who now spilled out from the back of the lorry.

Now there was rifle fire from behind him and several of the men fell to the ground.

Oblivious to his own safety, Pierre-Luc ran down the bank waving his arms, pointing in the direction of the forest on the other side of the road. "Go that way!" he screamed. "Go that way! They're behind us on the Route des Bordes. Go north!"

Some of the men looked at him as he ran towards them and changed direction to the other side of the road, but others continued to run into the trees on his side, caring little for anything else other than the immediate sanctuary they offered. The engine of the lorry revved up and it lurched backwards, almost as Pierre-Luc drew level with it, turning away from him and across the road in the first part of a three-point turn. André leant out of the window. "Got to warn the main camp!" he screamed as the lorry jumped forward, forcing Pierre-Luc to reel back, even as a bullet tore past him and thudded into its sidegate.

"But they'll be up ahead..." Pierre-Luc shouted uselessly.

He stopped, aware, at last, that he was standing in full view of the soldiers at the barricade behind him. Aware that, but for the fact that the soldiers were taking aim at the larger target of the lorry, he was next in their sights. He dropped to one knee, swerved and dashed into the trees on the side of the road he had come from. 'Damn!' he screamed to himself as he made their cover. "Damn!" he cried out loud as he realised that he had made the very same error of judgement which he had tried to warn the others of. He spun around in his tracks and went back to the edge of the forest to stare out and along at the German barricade. Across the road the forest beckoned. A distance of no more than fifteen metres, but for all the world it could have been the same as that to the Moon. For the road was now clear of all obstructions, other than the fallen bodies of the forest guard and the maquisard who hadn't made it to the trees. But to cross it would be suicide.

He turned and made his way through the trees, towards the Carrefour d'Orleans, keeping the road on his left. Off to his right he could hear gunfire and, behind him, the sound of yet more. Poor buggers, they had obviously run straight into the Germans he had first seen. He'd tried to warn them but they hadn't understood. A simple trip to Lorris for supplies had turned into a disaster. Pray God André made it to the main camp... he could bring help... maybe even weapons, so that they could at least go down fighting. 'Not one of the men he had seen jumping from the lorry had been armed... they wouldn't have been, would they?' he thought. If they were going into town, then the last thing they'd have wanted to be caught with was guns.

Would there be weapons at the houses?

Yes, surely there would. There must be.

Mustn't there?

He reached the back fence of the forester's cottage and vaulted it lightly, aware that on landing he was exposed on the open lawn. Quickly he ran across to the back door and banged upon it.

"Who is it?" came a voice from inside.

"Pierre-Luc," he replied urgently. "I was with the burial party. Let me in quick."

There was the sound of bolts being drawn. A key turned in the lock and the door was pulled open. "In. Quick!" a gruff voice commanded and Pierre-Luc, needing no further urging, slipped through the door, even as it slammed shut again. He leant against the wall breathing heavily, his eyes adjusting to the gloom within the heavily shuttered house.

"You made it then," said the old man.

Pierre-Luc nodded. "I made it. Did you see Andre?"

"I saw him... couldn't stop him when he went by the first time. And then when he went by the second... where was he going?"

Pierre-Luc stood away from the wall, his hands on his hips. He sucked in air and then let it out slowly before answering. "He said he was going to the main camp to warn them... he may bring help."

"Help? All he'll bring is more Germans... they're on the other roads, you know."

"Are they? How do you know?"

"We heard them... saw them as we got here first of all. Then heard them shooting at the lorry as it went by... I reckon they got him."

"Shit," said Pierre-Luc. "Shit, shit, shit!" A discreet cough made him turn from the older man to observe a young dark-haired woman, standing in the shadows, wearing a white apron, now covered in stains which, even in the half light, he knew bore blood from the injured that she tended in this house. "I'm sorry mademoiselle," he said quietly.

"No matter," she said with a slight grin, wiping her hands on the apron. She brushed past him and through into the other room.

Pierre-Luc turned from her and looked at the older man. "How many are we?"

"Eighteen. Fifteen that were here already, including the girl, and an old woman, you, me, and young Raymond who was in the forest with us."

"What happened to the rest?"

The man shrugged his shoulders. "Two went the other way towards the Route des Bordes. The rest carried on heading out towards the Carrefour... what's the one off in that direction?" He pointed over his shoulder.

"Saint Michel."

"Yes, Saint Michel. That's how we first knew that the Germans were there as... well, they got them."

Pierre-Luc sighed and shook his head. "We're trapped then... until they come from the main camp."

"They'll not come."

"They will. They will," repeated Pierre-Luc. "Soon as they hear what's going on they'll attack. We've got to hold them off until they get here, that's all."

The older man laughed now, a low rumbling laugh that rose as he clutched his chest and finished with him coughing up years of accumulated tobacco tar.

Pierre-Luc waited until the man raised his flushed face.

"What's so funny?"

Grimacing, the man shook his head. "It's not funny really... apart from... well apart from the fact that we've nothing to hold them off with."

"Nothing?"

"Not a thing."

"Christ... there are sixteen of us then... plus the women?"

"And ten of those are wounded already... some of them in a pretty bad way too."

Pierre-Luc rubbed his chin, thinking. "We need to get out there and post sentinels."

"What for?"

Pierre-Luc looked at him sternly. "Now look here, I know it's pretty bloody hopeless, but we still need some warning of what they're up to. They don't know we're unarmed and we don't know what their intentions are, do we? Do we?"

The old man's face took on a sheepish expression as, not for the first time that day, he was admonished by the earnest young man standing before him. He nodded his head slowly, biting his lip. "Alright. You're right. You take one other man... the one who came in with me, and position yourselves under the Sequoia. You can see all ways from there." He turned and called back into the house. "Raymond!"

A muffled reply preceded the figure in the doorway and Pierre-Luc recognised the young man who had partnered him on the burial party. "Yes. What do you want?"

"I want you to look lively and to go with..." He looked at Pierre-Luc expectantly.

"Pierre-Luc."

"Go with Pierre-Luc here and keep watch from the Sequoia."

"The what?"

The older man sighed. "The bloody great tree in the middle of the carrefour."

The young maquisard looked at him, shaking his head in disbelief. "Out there? Without weapons? Are you mad?"

"No, he's not mad, and if we see any sign of anything we'll get straight back in here, I promise," said Pierre-Luc softly. "It's just important that we know what we're up against and just as important that when help comes we're ready."

"Help? What help?" said the man dejectedly. "We're trapped here and you know it."

"He knows nothing of the sort," the older man interrupted. "There's people that have got through to warn the main camp and they'll come... mark my words." He looked directly past the young boy at Pierre-Luc, holding his gaze this time, begging confirmation of his lie.

Pierre-Luc nodded his head sagely. "Yes it's true... André has gone to raise the alarm... we need to get out there, so that when they come we're ready."

The young maquisard looked at Pierre-Luc as if seeking the truth. Pierre-Luc held his look and the boy turned to the older man, who merely nodded his head. Raymond rolled his top lip and shook his head. "Come on then... but one sign of the Boche and we're back in. Agreed?"

"Agreed," said Pierre-Luc. He turned to the older maquisard. "Watch out for our signal," he said, and put two fingers between his lips and blew softly. "Two whistles like this and we're coming in. Make sure the door's ready and make sure you're ready to bolt it after we're in."

"Understood," the other man said quietly. He moved across to the door and drew the bolts, pulling the door open. "Good luck," he whispered as they slipped out.

For a moment the two men stood just outside the door, Raymond longing for the apparent safety of the house, Pierre-Luc glad to be back in the open again, however unsafe. He had felt like a rat in a trap inside. At least out here he could see what was happening, and to an extent was in control of his own destiny. "Come on," he said quietly. He turned and led the way around the house. At the corner they paused, looking each way down the road before scooting off across the carriageway onto the long grass of the roundabout itself to crouch beside the tree.

Raymond scuttled around the other side but Pierre-Luc stayed, looking up the Route de Chat Sauvage to where he could clearly see, about six-hundred metres away, the barricade from which the fire had mown down the forest guard. He turned and looked along the Route des Bordes, only to be greeted by a similar sight, backed up by three or four troop lorries. "Anything?" he called around the tree, noticing, as he did, that at least one armoured car was parked on each of the other roads in his field of vision. "About eight-hundred metres on both roads," came the reply. "We're finished. They've come to get us this time, make no mistake."

"Keep down and keep watch," Pierre-Luc commanded. "If you see any movement in our direction then we'll go back in. What time is it?"

"I don't know," the younger man replied. "I don't carry a watch... I reckon it's about nine o'clock. Why?"

"Oh nothing," said Pierre-Luc, "Just interested." 'Just interested,' he thought. Where was Frank? He should have been here by now, but thank God he wasn't. At least he was outside the cordon that was inexorably tightening around them.

***

Less than seven kilometres away, Frank entered the forest, cycling along the road from Bouzy. Nine o'clock and already the day promised warmth, yet in his heart there lay a cold dread. Gunther was in terrible danger, even supposing he was still alive. How foolish, yet how brave of him to shut the panel like that. Unless he told them, the enemy would have no idea how they had escaped... that is, unless the two men in the passage below the scullery had escaped. No, they couldn't have done. 'Though, if they were still trapped, they could be there 'til doomsday, poor buggers,' he thought. A twinge of guilt hit him, but he shrugged it off. What else could they have done? Nothing. And now he had to get help, if not from other members of the Maquis then at least from Pierre-Luc... he couldn't just leave Gunther there... always supposing he was still there, still alive. God what a mess.

At least Annette was safe and reunited with Dieter, even if he had lost an entire night's sleep getting her to Gien. Dawn had been breaking as the milk lorry that had smuggled him back as far as Saint-Martin-d'Abbat had dropped him off. The sun had been well up when he had finally knocked on Monsieur and Madame Cabel's door to borrow the bicycle.

The trees arched over the road, shielding him from the sun's rays and bringing with them a cool freshness which had previously always lifted his heart. Not now. Now the cool reflected his own feelings and only served to reinforce his fears. What would Weber have done with Gunther? Handed him in? Tortured him? Shot him on the spot? What had he got to gain? The Allies were only days away, sweeping all before them. Le Mans yesterday, Monsieur Cabel had said. What was the point in Weber continuing his lost cause? Couldn't he see that the end was in sight? Frank sighed heavily, swerving as he did so to avoid a pothole, the wheels of the bicycle scrunching on the gravel, flicking small stones away into the grass. No, Weber would never see things that way. For him the war was only a part of the whole, a means to an end, which no reasonable man could ever foresee.

'You're going too fast,' he told himself. 'Slow down.' He looked ahead as he approached the junction with the main road to Lorris. The Lorris road?! 'Is this where I was going?,' he thought. 'Damn, I was going to the Etang des Bois, I should have turned right at Chateaubriand.' He thought again. 'No wait, Pierre-Luc might be at the Carrefour d'Orléans. If he wasn't, then they'd know where he was.'

Suddenly, he skidded to a halt about twenty metres from the main road. Ahead, lined up all along the metalled road, he could see lines of German trucks, their engines running, the canvas at the backs raised in the rising heat of the day to reveal their full occupancy of uniformed soldiers. Frank stood stock still, praying as he straddled the ancient bicycle that his noisy halt had not been detected. Gently he lifted his leg over the crossbar and wheeled the bike to the side of the road, leaning it up against the bank before slipping quietly up it himself and under the cover of the trees. What was going on? There must be twenty lorries within his view and... 'my God,' he thought in rising panic, 'they must be after us! Pierre-Luc was in there. But then, no,' he thought, 'he might be at the houses at the Etang des Bois. What was going on?'

He crept closer to the main road, keeping low in the dense undergrowth, inching forward centimetre by centimetre until he had a clear view. Ambulances! They had ambulances. That meant they were expecting casualties. A whistle sounded and an open-topped car, very like the one he had used and abandoned the night before, drove slowly past the line of trucks amid shouted orders. Hordes of troops disembarked from the trucks and lined up at the forest edge, facing away from where he lay. A second whistle blew and the soldiers mounted the bank and entered the forest, keeping in line.

Frank watched until they were out of sight. What to do? He had to warn someone at the main camp, but to do so would mean skirting around the forest almost in the wake of the advancing Germans. He pushed himself back, taking care not to disturb the cover until he was several metres away from the forest edge. Then he turned and crawled on his hands and knees for almost the same distance before finally rising to his feet and making his way as quietly as possible back to the bicycle.

He paused at the top of the bank and peered both ways down the road. No sign of any Germans on this side of the main road. Silently he slipped down the bank and lifted the bicycle, turning it around to face the other way. A last glance back over his shoulder at the road and he was off, pedalling furiously in the direction he had come from.

'Where to now?' he thought wildly. 'God, two friends in trouble now and me cut off from doing anything useful... no proper papers... no weapon.' Weapon! There would be guns at the forester's house at the Etang des Bois. If he could get there and warn them, then they could get someone else to telephone ahead to warn someone to alert the main camps, assuming the main camps themselves were not already discovered. No, they couldn't be, not without someone betraying them and... 'my God, have we been betrayed?' Was anyone captured at Chicamour? Surely everyone alive was carried off from the battle... He had been... or had that been Pierre-Luc saving a friend? No. No, it was standard procedure.

Almost without thinking he reached the Carrefour de Chateaubriand and turned right, heading north-west in the direction of the Etang d'Orleans. His mind raced with the fears and uncertainties that the night before and the morning had brought about. He raised his head from his desperate pedalling and glanced ahead. God almighty! More Germans at the 'T' junction! He pulled on the brake handle and was appalled at the screeching sound that the old pads gave out as they bit into the rusty wheel rims.

A soldier, who had been looking the other way, turned around and stared back up the road at Frank standing still, astride his bicycle, torn between flight and a desire to complete his errand. "Halt!" he shouted, slinging his rifle from his shoulder and bringing it around to point at Frank. "Halt!"

Frank's heart jumped into his mouth. The man was barely thirty metres away, and even as he watched, another, and then another, appeared in view and took similar aim at him. Frantically he searched about for an escape from his exposed position. A narrow track led off to the left! He spun the wheel and mounted the saddle in one swift movement, not realising that he had swung the wheel too far before pushing down on the pedal. The bicycle somersaulted, tipping him forward and over, ripping the metal grip down his torso even as his ears registered the crackle of the rifles.

The bullets tore through the air where he had stood moments before. In a blind panic he grabbed at the bicycle and scrabbled across the rough road, dragging it after him. His feet reached the grass and he jerked the bicycle around onto the footpath and slung his leg over the saddle, preparing to pedal off into the trees. He pushed down hard and then cried out as something seemed to thump him in the shoulder, toppling him to the ground, one leg trapped within the frame.

He could clearly hear the shouts of the soldiers as they prepared to run up the gravel road towards him. He rolled over and almost screamed out from the pain in his shoulder, reaching up and feeling the stickiness of the blood oozing from the wound. 'God, I'm hit,' he thought with perfect clarity. 'Get away! a voice screamed in his head. Get away!'

He rolled away from the bicycle and stood, his right arm hanging useless at his side. Sounds now, running feet and shouts from barely twenty metres away... out of sight, thank God. He mounted the saddle and, holding tightly to the handlebars with his one good hand, pushed down hard on the pedals, pushing again and again until he felt the momentum bringing with it the balance he so prayed for. His legs pumped up and down, up and down as his eyes fixed themselves on the winding footpath ahead, a narrow ribbon of dirt no more than twenty centimetres wide cursed with bumps and fallen branches, which he crunched through in his blind haste.

"Halt! Halt!" came the cries of his pursuers at the road, but he kept on pumping at the pedals. Shots and more shots rang through the forest and sent showers of broken leaves and bark down around him. He braced himself for the jolt he knew must come, but it never came. Instead, the footpath turned slightly to the left and its very narrowness obscured him from the kneeling soldiers.

Frank looked down at his chest, seeing the spreading stain of red from his upper breast and feeling the creeping numbness that seemed to follow its path. He shook his head as waves of giddiness rushed over him and the path before him seemed to divide and then divide again, until he was unsure which fork he was supposed to be following. A bush seemed to rear up in front of him and then again at either side, and he turned from it and slid down from the saddle, seeing the bicycle continuing on its crazy course without him as he fell to the ground. He raised his head in time to see it crash through a stand of tall grass and plop into a small pond. A blanket of duckweed opened up to receive it and then closed in, hiding it.

His eyes closed and his body sought refuge in sleep, even as his brain warned him that he must stay awake. He must seek cover before his pursuers arrived. He forced his eyes open and, rolling over, struggled to his knees. "Don't stare at the bloody ground," he shouted to himself. "Look up! Look up!"

He jerked his chin up and swung his head around wildly, seeking sanctuary, willing his weakened body not to fall. A tree! A fallen tree lay beside the path, just down from it. He placed his knuckle on the ground and pushed hard until he was kneeling upright. 'Got to stand. Got to stand!' he told himself. Then, leaning sideways, he brought his right foot forward then pushed down and straightened his leg to stand. Bent forward, he began swaying wildly from side to side until he grabbed an overhead branch and steadied himself.

Now he fixed his eyes on the tree, reaching across himself to cradle his useless arm. He gritted his teeth and forced himself to walk forward, across the path and into the grass. The ground dropped and he lost his footing and fell and rolled the rest of the way, coming to a halt with a painful bump against the body of the fallen tree. Waves of pain and nausea raced through him, but he raised himself to his knees once more and crawled along its length. 'Got to hide! Got to hide,' he kept saying to himself as he rounded its shattered end. It was hollow! Thank God it was hollow! He crept within its shell, feeling the softness of its internal decay, burrowing, animal-like, in his blind desire to be hidden within its warm darkness. Now he could sleep. Now he could seek refuge and healing in the dreams that beckoned him. He pulled his body into a foetal position, unwittingly dragging his legs out of sight, and closed his eyes.

***

Pierre-Luc raised himself from his prone position in the grass at the sound of gunfire. Some poor bugger was in trouble. Probably one or more of the chaps that had run off into the forest.

"Did you hear that?" Raymond whispered.

"Yes. It's quite some way away... beyond the Lorris road, I think."

Raymond shuffled around the tree to lie beside Pierre-Luc. "I expect they'll come for us soon."

"I expect so. They must know by now," responded Pierre-Luc.

"Who?"

"The chaps at the main camp."

Raymond snorted a laugh. "I didn't mean them. I meant the Boche! I expect they're nearly ready to take us now. They must realise we're sitting ducks."

Pierre-Luc just grimaced to himself. He raised his head and stared down the road at the barricades. Was it his imagination or were there more soldiers there? "Anything happening on your side?" he added.

Raymond slid around the tree, keeping low to the ground. "No. Nothing that I can... wait a minute, there is... some sort of... well it's got a huge sort of mast on it."

"That'll be a radio van," Pierre-Luc mused to himself, as much as in reply. "They'll be waiting until everything is ready and co-ordinated before they strike."

"I reckon we should get out of here," said Raymond, his voice showing the first signs of panic.

Pierre-Luc fixed his gaze on the road. His eyes narrowed as the logs from the barricade were removed and tossed aside into the undergrowth.

More vehicles moved up. Soldiers in full combat gear milled around them, forming themselves up into groups, whilst others seemed to spread out and disappear into the trees.

"They're coming," he said quietly. "Time to go."

Raymond stood up and, almost as if he sensed his action, Pierre-Luc spun around, hissing for him to keep low.

The boy seemed to take no notice. He stepped from the shadow of the tree trunk and stood, almost nonchalantly, in full view. Pierre-Luc rose to his knees and pulled him back down, covering his body, pinning him to the floor. "What the hell are you doing?" he hissed. Raymond looked up at him, his eyes wide open with fear and panic. Pierre-Luc held his gaze, gently stroking the boy's face.

"Come on Raymond," he soothed. "Come on now. Let's get back inside."

Suddenly the eyes of the young man narrowed and blinked. Tears appeared in the corners and trickled slowly down his cheeks. "We're going to be caught, aren't we?" he whispered through quivering lips. "They'll kill us all."

"No," Pierre-Luc soothed. "Someone will have warned the main camp by now... and even if we do have to surrender then the Americans are already in Le Mans. The Germans will have to think of their own safety soon."

The boy stared up into Pierre-Luc's face, searching for reassurance. Pierre-Luc smiled. "Come on. Let's get back inside..." From the direction of the Route des Bordes came the sound of rifle fire and the heavier, chattering thump of machine gun fire. "Come on!" he said more urgently, swinging around and crouching against the tree trunk.

Raymond raised himself on his elbows, looking nervously down the road. He rolled over on his stomach and then crouched. "Now?"

Pierre-Luc nodded. "Yes, you go first and I'll follow. Don't stop and remember to weave." He put his fingers to his lips and blew hard twice. "Right... go!" he shouted.

Raymond raised himself from his knees and sprinted in a direct line towards the houses. "Weave!" Pierre-Luc screamed, but too late as a bullet tore into the young boy's body and he fell, sprawled out on the gravel road. For a split second he lay still, but then he raised himself on his elbows and began crawling, toad-like across the rough stones.

Pierre-Luc crossed himself briefly and then dashed from the tree, weaving his way across the open space. He reached the boy, and in one movement scooped him up and dragged him across to the grass and on to the corner of the house. Here he paused for a moment to catch his breath before finally rushing around the back and through the open door, where hands reached out to pull him through and others took away his burden, pulling the two of them clear of the door before it was hastily slammed shut and the bolts thrown.

He leant against the wall breathing heavily, his eyes shut. "What's the situation?" He opened his eyes. The older man stood in front of him, his expression questioning, urgent. Beside him a young boy leant heavily on a makeshift crutch, the nurse holding on to his arm. Pierre-Luc shook his head silently. The old man nodded, mumbled something to himself and then turned and made his way back into the main body of the house.

Pierre-Luc looked into the eyes of the young couple, seeing there the pleading for hope that he knew he could not give. "Can't we make a run for it... into the forest?" the young man asked.

"No. They've got every road covered and there are more of them in every segment of the forest around."

"What will they do?" said the nurse, and for the first time Pierre-Luc saw how pretty she was. Dark curling hair bobbed around her shoulders. Her elegantly arched eyebrows framed dark eyes that, despite the lack of sleep, still glowed bright in the half light.

Pierre-Luc pushed himself off the wall. He put his hand on her shoulder. "They'll wait a while. They don't know what we've got here... don't know that we're unarmed. That'll give the others time to muster help."

"And what if they don't come?" said the young man. "What then?"

"They will," said Pierre-Luc firmly. "Sooner or later they'll come and..."

"...and that'll be too late, won't it?" the young man interjected bitterly.

Pierre-Luc looked at him, his emotions torn between anger and understanding. He too felt the hopelessness of their situation, but there was no sense... nothing to gain by a general panic. "We've got work to do," he muttered, pushing past and into the main room. He stopped, looking around in the gloom. Men lay on makeshift beds on the floor, and as he stood there the nurse guided the young man on the crutches back into the room and sat him down before crossing to stand beside him. She looked up at him. "Ten wounded?" Pierre-Luc asked rhetorically.

"Eleven now," she replied.

"How bad are they?"

"Six of the ones who were here already are very ill... one with a lung shot. The rest... limbs."

The older man rose from the floor where he had been kneeling beside Raymond. He stood in front of Pierre-Luc, and to his unspoken question simply shook his head silently. The nurse clutched her hand to her mouth.

Pierre-Luc jerked his head back at the prone figure of Raymond on the floor. "We'd better get him out of here," he said quietly. The older man nodded and the two of them crossed to each end of the body, picked it up, and carried it across the room towards the back scullery.

Suddenly, just as the nurse held the door open for them to pass through, a young man stood up on the other side of the room, screaming. "Yes! Yes, and we'll all be dead soon, won't we?!"

Pierre-Luc and the other man froze, hearing the panic in his voice, fearing the contagion that they knew could follow. "Keep calm please men," he said. "We have got to stay calm."

"Calm?!" shouted a voice from the centre of the floor. "Calm? You want us to stay calm... what, like sheep at the abattoir?" A form rose up, leaning heavily on a crutch, and Pierre-Luc recognised the young man he had spoken to in the rear hall. "And just what do you think that would achieve?!" He turned and addressed the room in general. "I say that we should get out of here and get into the forest."

"Me too," said the first man who had spoken.

Pierre-Luc looked along the body of Raymond at the older man. The two of them nodded imperceptibly to one another and put down the body. The man turned around to face the room, pointing down at Raymond. "He was outside," he said quietly. "He went outside to keep watch and look what happened to him." He pointed directly at the two men who now stood beside each other. "Do you want to end up like him?" There was a silence in the room as each person contemplated the man's words, before he turned around, bent down, and picked up the body.

In silence they shuffled through and placed it against the wall of the scullery. Pierre-Luc straightened up. "Phew, that was close. Well done... I'm sorry, I don't know your name."

"Maurice," replied the man, extending his hand.

"Pierre-Luc Cabel," Pierre-Luc said, warmly shaking the older man's hand.

He turned as figures obscured the door to the main room and the first man who had spoken came through, followed by the man on crutches and one other.

"We want to go," he said firmly.

"Go?" asked Pierre-Luc. "Where?"

"Out of here. Listen, we can sneak out the back and over the fence into the forest."

"I've told you, there's Germans all through the woods," said Pierre-Luc, the exasperation rising in his voice. "You'll not get a hundred metres, if that."

"We're going," said the second man in a tone of voice that brooked no argument.

Pierre-Luc looked at them and then at Maurice. Maurice shrugged his shoulders. "How many of you?"

"Us three. Robert doesn't want to go."

"Robert's the sensible one," said Pierre-Luc bitterly.

The man on the crutch shook his head. "Whoever's the sensible one... seems to me we've got two choices. We stay here and wait for them to kill us or we go out there and try... and..." His voice lowered. "Then even if they kill us, we'll have tried." He fixed his eyes on Pierre-Luc.

Pierre-Luc held his gaze for a while. Then he nodded. "You're right. If that's what you want to do then go ahead, but those chaps in there... they can't go anywhere. And me? I'm for staying."

"Me too," affirmed Maurice. The young man reached forward and clasped his arm. Maurice smiled wanly.

"Well then," said the other man behind. "Let's get on with it then if we're going. Can you make it on that crutch?"

The wounded man looked down. "I'll use this as far as the back fence, then, once we get to the forest, it'll be no use... besides, we'll be better off crawling anyway."

Pierre-Luc crossed to the door and gently and as quietly as possible, so as not to draw attention from either inside or outside the house, drew the bolts. He pulled the door open, letting the daylight flood into the room, and winced as it illuminated the tortured dead face of Raymond lying against the wall. The man on the crutches hobbled into the doorway and extended his hand. "Good luck," he said quietly.

"Good luck yourself," said Pierre-Luc, shaking the young man's hand earnestly. "Take care, and if... if you get through, try to send help."

"I will," the man replied. He turned to Maurice and shook his hand, then left silently, making for the rear fence and the trees. One by one the other two made their farewells and, as the last of them cleared the door, they gently shut it and pushed the bolts home.

"Do you fancy a cigarette?" said Maurice, turning from the door into the store room. "There's a whole load of stolen German ones in here."

"I don't smoke," replied Pierre-Luc.

"So what?" the older man retorted.

Pierre-Luc smiled and shook his head. "Yes, what the hell," he said as he clapped his arm around the other man's shoulder.

***

Frank awoke with a start. He raised his head, banging it hard against the soft rotten wood of the interior of the trunk, showering wood dust down his neck and dislodging his hat and the bandages, which fell down in front of his eyes. He brushed them aside. 'Where am I?', he thought for a moment, and then the memory of his escape came rushing back to him, and with it the pain that seared through his shoulder.

'How long have I been here?' He straightened his legs and looked down his body. 'Daylight! Full sunlight. Have I been here all night? No, it must be late morning,' he reasoned.

He turned over on his stomach and cried out as his shoulder knocked against a harder piece of timber, sending shock waves down his arm.

'Quiet!' he ordered himself. 'You don't know if they're still out there hunting for you.'

Gingerly he wriggled his torso backwards and out of the trunk until he lay in the sunlight. 'What time was it? Damn it, why hadn't he worn his watch?'

Wait... he had turned off the Route de Chateaubriand in the direction of the Carrefour du Clocher. That meant that the path he was on was heading roughly west. He looked up into the sky, searching for the sun through the trees. Yes there it was, virtually at right angles to the path. God, that meant he'd been in the tree trunk for over three hours... it must be between twelve o'clock and one. Christ! And the Germans had had all that time to consolidate their positions.

Had they moved yet? He cocked his ear, listening for sounds of battle. None were to be heard.

He jerked himself upright and leant against the fallen tree, wincing in pain as his right arm flopped useless by his side. 'Got to get help,' he thought. 'Got to get help.' He pushed down with his legs, pushing hard against the tree, forcing himself up its rough bark until he stood, swaying slightly, leaning against it. His head reeled and his vision swam. 'Where are they all? Where have they gone? Why had his friends left... no they didn't... stop it Frank! Stop it! Don't let your mind play tricks on you,' he told himself.

He looked around. The grass seemed to be fairly undisturbed. No sign of active pursuit. If they had come this far looking for him, then they had missed him and given up the search. Probably thought he had got away on the bicycle. The bicycle! It was in the pond! 'No... no, I can't get that out of there,' he thought. 'Anyway, I doubt I could ride it now.' Best on foot. Best go slowly and carefully in the direction he had been going. It can't be more than a kilometre to the first houses on the outskirts of Bouzy. André Leconte's house... well his father's house. His father would be there and he would help him and send word to... yes, that's it.

He pushed himself away from the tree and staggered up the slight rise to the footpath, where he paused for a moment to re-orientate himself before setting off, his eyes fixed firmly on the route ahead, his legs moving in automatic sequence as he concentrated his every effort.

He reached the carrefour and paused at the barrier before entering the open space, listening out for any signs of danger.

Gunfire! He could hear it clearly now. It seemed to be ringing all through the forest from... from behind him. Sounded like... as if it was coming from the other side of the Lorris Road. No... yes it was! It seemed as if that whole section of the forest was being shot up. He turned around slowly, listening out. Yes, all behind him. 'My God, I've got to get help.' He committed himself to the open space, throwing caution to the wind as he shambled along the wider road, muttering to himself in his increasing delirium and panic, the tears flowing down his face.

***

As the sounds of gunfire rattled and screamed through the forest, those trapped in the houses turned their pale and frightened faces to each other. Some crouched down on the dusty floor. Others flattened themselves against the walls seeking shelter, and Pierre-Luc rushed across to the shuttered window and peered out through the crack.

"What can you see?" whispered Maurice.

"I don't know. Can't really see anything..."

He raised his head and looked up, listening all around. "Seems as if they're shooting up the whole forest... seems to be coming from all around."

"What do you reckon's going on?"

Pierre-Luc shook his head. "I think they're... it's as if they've decided to kill anything that's moving out there."

Maurice shook his head sadly. "Those boys haven't got a chance."

Pierre-Luc put his hand on the older man's shoulder and pulled him closer, whispering in his ear. "They'll take us next... they must know we're defenceless."

Maurice pulled back and nodded, his face serious. "I know. I know... well they might as well get on with it, because I couldn't stand another four hours of this."

Pierre-Luc grimaced. "It could be preferable you know."

"Maybe," Maurice mused. He started at the sounds of vehicles on the road outside.

Pierre-Luc put his eye to the crack and then pulled back quickly. "Everybody down on the floor!" he screamed, diving to the ground himself and pulling Maurice with him. All others in the room did likewise except two men, who rushed out into the back scullery and lay down beside the body of Raymond.

"What's there?" Maurice whispered.

"Machine gun lorries... three of them at least, mobile guns and God knows how many men."

"Boche?" asked a young man, his head swathed in bandages, his voice betraying the almost useless hope in the question.

"Boche," Pierre-Luc confirmed. "Keep your head down now."

A whistle blew outside, and at its signal a massive barrage of rifle and machine gun fire tore into the house, shattering the windows and shutters, sending shards of glass howling around the room as bullets spattered off the thick plaster.

A stretcher case screamed out loud as a ricocheting missile tore into his already wounded leg. Pierre-Luc buried his head in his arms, trying to ward off the evil that now seemed to enter every pore of his body. A panic-stricken man crawled over him, burying himself against him, seeking shelter against his body, burrowing beneath him.

And then there was silence. Complete silence, broken only by the soft pattering of the plaster and dust that fell in a gentle rain on their prone figures.

"What do we do?" Maurice whispered to Pierre-Luc. "We can't..."

"We can't take any more of that. And if they turn the heavy guns on us then we'll be blown to bits or burnt alive," he replied.

"I don't want to be burnt alive!" the body beside Pierre-Luc screamed. "I can't, I can't..."

His voice was stifled by Pierre-Luc's hand over his mouth. "Everybody keep calm!" he called. "Listen, we've got to surrender. It's our only hope. Anyone got something I can use as a white flag?"

"I have," said the girl from the floor in the middle of the room. She raised herself and crawled across to him, taking off her apron as she did so. She handed it to him with a nervous smile. "Here you are."

Pierre-Luc took it, caressing her shaking hand as he did so. "Thank you," he whispered. He turned, clutching the apron, crossed to the window and forced the garment through the broken shutters, waving it frantically, oblivious to the glass that cut into his forearm.

A whistle sounded. He braced himself for the next barrage but none came. Gently he raised his head above the cill. Armed soldiers rose up from every quarter, their rifles pointed straight at the house as they formed up in an impenetrable line. An officer stepped forward holding a loud hailer. "You will all stand up!" he shouted in French. "Leave your weapons on the floor!" Pierre-Luc laughed silently to himself. "Come out one by one, hands in the air."

Pierre-Luc turned to the room and then put his face to the hole in the shutter. "There are people in here who cannot walk. We have wounded in here."

There was a short silence from outside as the officer obviously consulted with his fellows. Then, "How many are you?"

"We are three able-bodied men, two women and nine wounded... six of whom cannot walk."

"Is that all of you?"

"Yes... apart from one dead."

"Any weapons?"

"We are unarmed."

There was a silence, during which time they could all imagine and regret the amusement and relief this information must have given their enemies.

The loud hailer barked again. "All who can walk will come out, one by one, with their hands up!"

Pierre-Luc turned back into the room. Pale, drawn and frightened faces greeted him. He smiled thinly and shook his head. "This is it, I'm afraid. Help the walking wounded to their feet." He turned to Maurice. "Open the door," he said quietly. Maurice nodded and went through. Pierre-Luc could hear the bolts being drawn and the door being pulled open.

"Aufraus. 'raus," came the calls from outside as, one by one, Pierre-Luc helped the wounded to their feet and guided them to the door where Maurice stood, ushering them through. A line of soldiers had formed on either side of the path, and as the men hobbled and made their way down between them they were chivvied, jeered and spat at.

An older woman, unseen by Pierre-Luc until this moment, rose from the shadows, her lined and weather-beaten face set in resignation.

"Alright mother?" Pierre-Luc whispered, cupping his hand on her shoulder. She turned to him, nodded and then turned away and marched through the door, her head held high.

The young nurse hesitated beside him, her lip trembling, her hands clasped in front, shaking. Pierre-Luc bent down and held her tight, tipping her face up to kiss her on the forehead. "Courage," he whispered. "What's your name, pretty one?"

"Margot."

"Well Margot... for France..."

"For France," she muttered almost inaudibly. He guided her through the door, wincing at the catcalls and whistles that greeted her in the afternoon sunshine.

He looked at Maurice and smiled. "For France, my friend."

"For France," the old man replied firmly, before turning and marching through the door.

Pierre-Luc turned back to the main room. "Good luck lads," he called to the six lying prone and silent on the floor. He took a deep breath, turned and walked into the sunshine.

For a second he was blinded by the light, but then a sharp blow in his side made him practically double up. Another blow. "Hande hoch! Hande hoch!" He turned to his attackers, fear and puzzlement written large on his face. "Arms in the air," a soldier shouted in French. He turned to thank the translator, but another brutal cuff sent him spinning away down the gauntlet of jeering soldiers, around the side of the house, onto the open road and across to the grass of the carrefour, to join his compatriots huddling beneath the tree.

Maurice ushered him into the centre of the group. "What do you think they'll do now?" he asked nervously.

Pierre-Luc shook his head. "I don't know." He smiled as a pale-faced Margot appeared beside the older man, her expression displaying the fear she felt, together with the comfort she so obviously gained from being near him. "Alright Margot?" he whispered. Maurice looked at her and then back at Pierre-Luc, a sad smile playing on his lips.

A cry distracted their attention, and they all turned as the wounded were carried from the house and brought across the road to be deposited, none too carefully, on the grass.

Margot flashed a look of concern at Pierre-Luc before rushing across and kneeling beside the man who had cried out. Pierre-Luc joined her. "Is he alright?"

She looked up at him, tears welling in her eyes, her head gently shaking from side to side. She stood and whispered in his ear. "He's lung shot and the movement..." She knelt down quickly and, taking her skirt in her hand, sponged the pink foam that dribbled from the corners of his mouth. "There, there Jacques," she soothed. "Lie still now. Lie still." Pierre-Luc put his hand on her shoulder and squeezed it gently. She flashed a look of gratitude at him and then bent to her task.

Maurice came over to him and tugged him on the arm, pointing across the road to the soldiers. "They seem to be waiting for something."

"Orders, I expect... or someone else... more senior... to know it's safe for him to come now..." He stopped as two officers detached themselves from the main body and swaggered across to the middle of the road to stand with their hands on their hips.

The one on the right raised his hand and lazily indicated the two mobile machine gun lorries on the other side of the carrefour. The prisoners followed his indication and fell silent. The officer snapped his fingers again. A group of soldiers ran forward onto the grass, and by pushing and shoving with their rifles, separated the walking men and two women from the rest of the group lying on the ground, forcing them into a line with Pierre-Luc at the head.

There was a moment's silence as captives and captors alike stood weighing each other up. Then the officer on the right, an SS Major by his insignia, raised his arm again and pointed at Pierre-Luc. The soldiers stepped forward and jabbed their rifle muzzles at him, forcing him out of the line and across, to stand in front of them.

"Papers?"

Pierre-Luc reached into his upper coat pocket. The two officers stiffened visibly but continued to stare at him, their hands still resting on their hips. The soldiers on each side of him readied their weapons, alert for any threat. Pierre-Luc smiled slightly. "Something funny monsieur?" the officer asked languidly, his voice full of barely concealed menace.

Pierre-Luc removed his hand from his jacket and held the papers out. "I said we were unarmed," he said quietly, "and we are." The soldier on his left snatched the papers and handed them to the officer, who opened them up and read them slowly, looking up from time to time. "You are a deserter," he stated. "These papers clearly indicate that you are required for work in Germany and yet you have not gone. Why not?"

"I was unwell... I..."

Fury erupted in the man's eyes and he swiped Pierre-Luc across the face. "You are a saboteur... a member of the resistance!" he screamed. His eyes flicked up and the soldier on Pierre-Luc's right swung his rifle, butt first, into his lower back, forcing him to the ground to kneel, panting for breath at the officer's feet, his senses reeling from the pain.

"No... no..." he stammered through clenched lips.

"No?! Then what?" sneered the other officer.

"I was... I was walking in the woods... taking an early morning walk... when I saw you all and I was frightened... I..." The rifle butt fell once more, this time in the small of his back, and he straightened up with the pain, his face jerking skywards to be greeted by the sneering grin of the officer.

"You are Pierre-Luc Cabel," the man screamed down at him. "You are a member of the resistance and you took part in the ambush and murder of soldiers of the German Reich on the 12th of August at Chicamour!"

"No! No!" Pierre-Luc hissed through clenched teeth. "I was walking in the forest..."

Again the blow fell. "Where is the main camp?! Where?!"

"I was walking in the forest..."

The officer bent down and seized Pierre-Luc's chin in his gloved hand, forcing his face up as he bent close to him. "Tell us where the main camp is. Show us and we will be lenient," he whispered. "Otherwise..."

"I was walking in the forest..." The rifle butt smashed into the side of his head and he fell senseless in the dirt.

He awoke with his head in Margot's lap as she gently sponged the blood from his cracked jaw. He went to speak but the words didn't form properly through lips that were swollen and bruised. He raised his hand to touch her and winced at a pain in his finger. "Careful," she soothed.

"How long?" he hissed through clenched lips.

"Half an hour... maybe a bit longer. Hush, pretend you've fainted, they're questioning the others one by one... torturing the poor things more like. Close your eyes."

"What time is it?"

"Just after two o'clock. Careful, they're coming back over." She looked up as two soldiers, backed up by a group of about ten more, crossed the road, supporting the practically senseless figure of a young maquisard. They threw him forward, laughing as he drunkenly lurched around, spun and then crumpled to the ground.

"Help me up please," said Pierre-Luc. Margot stood and then helped him to his feet, where he stood, swaying slightly. "What did they do to my hand?" he asked incredulously, trying to flex his fingers.

"Your ring."

His eyes flew open. "My ring...?" His eyes closed as a wave of pain ran through his head and he clenched his teeth to withstand it. "What did they want with...?"

"They've taken all jewellery... all mine..." She turned her head, lifting her hair to let him see the torn earlobes. "All papers... everything. They've... look."

He turned and followed her gaze. A soldier walked to the centre of the road carrying a cardboard box. He placed it on the ground and then knelt down in front of it. Pierre-Luc turned, puzzled eyes, to Margot. "Our papers," she whispered.

He turned back to see the smoke rising as the soldier stood and put away his matches, poking the box with his boot as the flames took hold and the blackened flakes of paper rose into the warm air. A cold, dark feeling of dread swept over Pierre-Luc and he shivered involuntarily.

He looked across at Maurice, sitting on the grass, and the older man returned his stare with a meaningful nod of his head. Margot slipped up against Pierre-Luc and he put his arm around her shoulder. She jumped as one of the machine guns suddenly swung around and fired off blindly into the forest, joined shortly afterwards by the other one firing in the opposite direction. Pierre-Luc swung her around to face him and cuddled her trembling body close.

The guns stopped firing and a kind of tense peace resumed. The captives stood in loose groups surrounded by the masses of German soldiers, who had now been provided with food and drink, which they noisily consumed, flinging the empty beer bottles far into the forest or smashing them against the walls of the houses.

"Do you think they're going to feed us?" asked a young maquisard, sporting a black eye. "I'm dying of thirst."

Pierre-Luc caught Maurice's look. He smiled weakly. "Yes, I should think so... when they've had their fill." The young man nodded and moved away.

'What are they waiting for?' Pierre-Luc thought.

As if in answer to his question, a staff car hove in sight from the direction of Bordes. It approached the carrefour and swung right around in front of the watchful prisoners, giving them ample opportunity to identify the chilling sight of Herr Weber sitting in the back, his gaze fixed firmly ahead. The car pulled up beside the two officers, who saluted the Gestapo officer as he dismounted, clicking their heels before turning to indicate the prisoners and updating him on all that had transpired during the day.

For a long while the three men stood talking and laughing, whilst on the other side of the road the prisoners waited, their fears aroused, dread rising in every breast.

The noise of another approaching vehicle distracted their attention and they turned to see a van coming into view along the dusty road. Weber indicated its arrival with a wave of his hand and the two officers and he stepped forward as it pulled up in front of the houses.

Two soldiers pulled open the doors as Weber stood behind the van, a cruel, triumphant smile on his thin lips. Orders were barked and two black-cowled figures, their hands bound in front of them, dismounted with difficulty and stood, heads bowed in the sunlight.

"Priests?" whispered Maurice.

"Abbé Jordan and another," Pierre-Luc replied, craning his neck to get a better view.

"Has he betrayed us? Do you think?"

"No," said Pierre-Luc firmly. "No, not him... never. Besides, he's a prisoner."

Weber walked slowly up to one of the cowled figures. He stood in front of the man and spoke quietly to him, his words inaudible to the other prisoners. The cowled head looked up and Weber spat into it, giving Pierre-Luc a glimpse of blonde hair beneath.

His brow furrowed. "What's the matter?" Margot asked as she felt him stiffen.

He looked down at her. "Nothing... just..." He gently disengaged her hand from his arm. "I'll.." He touched Maurice's arm. "I'll just see if I... wait there a moment."

He turned and worked his way over the lines of wounded, lying with their heads to the tree. The three other wounded men sitting on the grass at the road edge moved slightly as he made his way past them to the edge of their group, staring across the road, seeking to see the face beneath the cowl. Could it be? Was that... no...

A whistle blew and the soldiers suddenly fanned out from their positions on the road side, their rifles held at the ready as they spread into a semi-circle on the house side of the carrefour. Instinctively Pierre-Luc turned around to look in the other direction, only to be greeted by the sight of the machine guns, cocked and ready as their operators swung them from side to side.

He turned back as Weber walked across the road, with the two officers behind him, their pistols drawn and ready. He tried to move... tried to go back across the grass to re-join Margot and Maurice, but his feet seemed reluctant amid a steady tide of horror that seemed to rise up and engulf him. Weber stopped at the verge. He pointed down, with his left hand, at the three wounded lying on his right of the tree and then waved some soldiers forward.

Gunther stole a look at the man standing beside him, dressed, as he was, in priest's garb. The Abbé returned his glance with a soft, resigned smile, which did nothing to take away the terror which he now felt... a terror which seemed to drain all will from him... to strike him dumb.

Annette! Was she safe? Weber had railed and shouted all night trying to get him to tell him where she was. He couldn't have found her... otherwise he wouldn't keep asking. Frank had got her clear... and... and Weber had no idea how it'd been done. It had never occurred to him that there was another way in and out of the chateau. She was safe! She was safe and she would be with Dieter. Thank God!

He watched, almost dispassionately, as the soldiers divided the pathetic group on the carrefour into two groups of seven, herding the walking to each end of the grass, carrying the disabled and depositing them brutally at the road edge. He scanned the group on the right. Two women... one young and pretty. She reached her hand up and called across to... to a man... was that?... oh God no! No! No!... make it not... Pierre-Luc, the great ox. What was he doing here? Why?

Tears rolled down his face as he saw his friend return the wave of the young girl. He turned as one of the officers approached, grabbed the arm of the priest and pulled him across to the little group. What were they doing? The older man was being separated and made to kneel on the ground. A shot! A single shot and he just crumpled forward on the ground, twitching slightly.

Black horror rose up in him as one by one the others were taken slightly apart and shot in similar fashion. The girl cried out in fear, begging and pleading with the men pushing her down to the ground, her eyes wide in her pale face, her mouth open in terror as she refused to look down... refused to submit the back of her neck to the executioner's bullet. They shot her in the forehead and he watched as her expression faded and her arms flew up... as her lovely body crashed awkwardly to the ground. Beside and behind him the soldiers giggled and laughed like schoolboys watching others scoring at a coconut shy. Gunther closed his eyes, trying to blot out the scene.

A cry arose! He opened his eyes. A man had broken free and was running down the road. A great roar came from the throats of the audience as the machine gun swung around and chattered loudly. Twenty metres of futile freedom gained, the man threw up his arms and fell face down on the road, his body jerking as each new bullet tore into him.

Silence. Oh God make them stop, Gunther cried to himself. A single shot and the priest's body folded forward. Rough hands reached down and dragged it into the pile of bodies. Cans... drums of diesel were opened and their contents poured over the still-warm objects that only minutes before had been human beings. The fire was lit and the ghastly pyre was enveloped in flames as the perpetrators withdrew and crossed to the other side of the carrefour.

Gunther stared at the other group. Three lying down, one desperately trying to prop himself up on shattered arms... four standing, three of them bandaged and one... one proud and defiant now. His friend Pierre-Luc.

He watched as the grim process was repeated. He took a stumbling step towards his friend as the big man was forced to his knees by a blow to his head and the pistol was made ready. Pierre-Luc raised his head and stared out at the forest. His mouth opened and the words, cracked yet defiant, rang out, "For France!"

"Allemanceterre!" Gunther screamed.

A smile... almost a whoop of defiant joy. "Alleman..." The shot cut short Pierre-Luc's last word... broke off his last joyful thought. His body fell forward into the dirt.

Gunther lowered his head and wept openly. Was this why Weber had brought him here? Was this how he wished to make him. Weber appeared in front of him.

"So you know... sorry..." He smiled. "...knew that man? Well that tells us something, doesn't it? And now... now you can spend eternity with your friends." He flicked his fingers and indicated Gunther.

Two soldiers grabbed each of his arms and propelled him across the road. For a second he looked down at his fallen friend before he felt himself pushed down to his knees.

A strange calm seemed to come over him. This was it. The fight was over.

Annette. He concentrated on the memory of her face... the warmth of her body... the scent of her being. 'Take care of them for me Frank,' he prayed. 'Frank... my best friend... take care.' Senses heightened... had birds ever sung that loud? Did grass crushed beneath his knees always smell this good? His nose wrinkled... did death always...? He felt the cold muzzle against his exposed neck as the cowl was wrenched back.

For a split second his brain tried to accommodate the intrusion, before his mind fled into dark oblivion and his body fell forward to the earth.

20th August 1944

"I want to go with you."

"Don't be silly Frank," said Lecroix, "you're not well. That was a pretty bad wound... not to mention the one you already had to your head."

"I've got to go with you," said Frank, rising stiffly from the bed and putting his feet to the floor. "This is my fight as much as yours... more really because Pierre-Luc was my friend and he has Gunther."

"Gunther. There you go again. Gunther... Leutnant Gunther Schmidt of the German army... Frank, we can't go around trying to rescue renegade German officers."

"We can... well I can, and I will," said Frank, fishing with his feet for his boots.

He connected with them and forced his feet into them. "Could you do up my laces for me?" he asked.

"No... no I won't Frank. Listen, you can't go... Weber is holed up in a chateau just outside town with about twenty others... we've got to..."

"Which chateau?"

Lecroix looked at him, seeing the urgency in his face. He went to answer, then changed his mind, shaking his head. "Look, it doesn't matter which..."

"Chateau de Janvier."

Lecroix looked up. "Yes well... how did you know?"

"I own that chateau... it's my home... that's where Gunther was captured when he and I went to free Annette. If Weber's there then chances are, so is Gunther."

"Well, if he is then we'll get him as..."

"And how many lives will you lose trying to storm the chateau?"

Lecroix began to look annoyed. "Frank, there's nothing you can do or say..."

"I know a secret way into the chateau which will let you come up in several places inside. You'll come up behind any barricades they have up, and if you're quiet you'll creep up on them unawares."

Lecroix looked interested. He sat down on the bed beside Frank. "Alright, I'm listening," he said.

"You'll take me?"

"No! No, look Frank..."

Frank clutched the Canadian's arm. "I have to go!" he hissed. "Let me get you in there and then let me look for my friend... and Weber."

Lecroix smiled. "Weber's mine."

Frank laughed now. "Only if you find the bastard first."

Lecroix laughed with him. "It's a deal." He clapped Frank on the shoulder and Frank winced with the pain, but kept his composure through gritted teeth. Lecroix noticed and shook his head, smiling. "Sorry. Now tell me about this way in."

"Do my laces up first," said Frank firmly. Lecroix bent and did up Frank's shoelaces and then stood expectantly. "Alright, I'll tell you on the way," said Frank.

Lecroix shook his head from side to side. "Come on then, let's go." He turned to lead the way out.

Frank called him back. "We'll need torches."

"Torches? Frank, where are you taking us? It's broad daylight."

"Nevertheless, we'll need torches."

"Then you shall have torches," said Lecroix. He turned and issued instructions to a man just outside the door, who bustled off and came back with three torches. "Do they work?" Lecroix asked. The man tested all three, one by one. Lecroix grunted his satisfaction and turned and led the way out of the house. Frank followed slowly and climbed into the van beside him as he started the engine.

Twenty minutes later they turned off the main road and onto the small road leading through to Le Mesnil. "It's amazing," Frank observed.

"What?" said Lecroix as he drove past the old barn and turned right at the crossroads towards the chateau.

"It's amazing that... it's an amazing feeling to be able to drive about almost openly..."

"There's still a lot of them around you know."

"I know but... how far off do you say the Americans are?"

"They'll be here by this afternoon... that's why we've got to hurry."

Frank pointed to the gate on the left. "That's where we parked up the other night. If you go just past and along the end of that wall there's another gate and we can go in that way."

His instructions tailed off as an armed figure stepped from the gateway and waved them down.

"Oh... there's Alain," Lecroix said as he slid the window open. "Where are the rest of your men?"

"They're covering the front," replied Alain. "The Boche have barricaded the doors to the chateau with sandbags... our men are out by the main gates and below the rear patio."

"Any in the yard by the farm buildings?" asked Frank.

"No, but we've got both entrances covered from the lane and from the... there's a small cemetery just down here." He pointed behind him.

"Yes I know... my family are buried there," said Frank quietly.

"Oh... oh yes. Yes, I'm sorry... but..."

"...but it's the perfect place to cover the yard from," said Frank. "It's alright Alain, I understand. We should go in this way," he said, touching Lecroix on the arm. "They can cover us through to the rear patio."

"Is that where we need to go?" asked Lecroix. Frank nodded and Lecroix turned the van into the gateway and got out. Frank followed him and Lecroix opened the rear door for the four other chaps in the back.

"What's happening?" said Alain. "We could be here all week at this rate. We need heavy guns." He looked at Frank. "Begging your pardon Frank... they've barricaded themselves in there good and proper and it's nearly impossible for us to make a move."

Lecroix pointed at Frank. "He knows a way in."

Alain looked at Frank in wonder. "A way in? Well if that's the case then... I thought we'd have to wait for the Americans and then the bloody swines would give themselves up and claim prisoner of war status."

"Some of the ordinary soldiers might still do so. But not Weber," said Lecroix coldly. "He's ours... and the other officers who carried out the massacre. We have our own justice for them."

"But not Gunther," Frank said quietly.

Lecroix turned to him. For a moment he stared at Frank, then he smiled. "Not Leutnant Gunther Schmidt. If he's there, no harm is to befall him."

Frank closed his eyes briefly and nodded his appreciation.

Alain looked at Frank and then back at Lecroix. "I understand," he said.

Lecroix turned back to Frank. "Well Frank, let's get in there shall we?" They moved off down the track and alongside the great barn until they got to the yew hedge surrounding the cemetery. "How many of you here?" asked Lecroix.

"Five here... plus me and you six," Alain replied.

"And behind the chateau?"

"Twenty... mostly on the steps covering the patio doors."

Lecroix turned back to Frank. "What do you think?"

"How many out the front?" Frank asked Alain.

"About thirty I think... some came from the river."

Frank thought for a moment. "Right," he said. "Send one man to the front and tell him to tell them to start firing at the front doors in..." He looked at his watch. "...in exactly half an hour from now. Tell them to keep up the firing for a full fifteen minutes..." He looked at Lecroix. "That'll give us time to get over there, pick up half the men on the steps and get in."

"Are you sure?" asked Lecroix.

I'm sure," Frank replied. "Gunther and I have done it enough times... including the other night. Leave three men here to cover us and... well let's go!"

"You sure you're fit enough?"

Frank smiled at the Canadian. "I'm sure... if I'd lost both legs I'd roll there for this one."

"I don't doubt it," said Lecroix. He turned to the men standing just inside the cemetery hedge. "You, you and you stay here and cover us. Don't fire unless there's firing. If we can get across unnoticed then all well and good." He turned to the rest and singled one man out. "You go around to the front and tell them to commence firing for fifteen minutes in exactly..." He looked at his watch. "I make it just coming up to ten o'clock." He looked up expectantly at the man, who looked at his own watch and nodded affirmatively. "At exactly half past ten. Clear?"

"Clear," the man replied.

Lecroix turned to Alain. "You, Alain. You can help me with this invalid." He turned to Frank, smiling, and Frank returned his look with an incline of his head and a grimace. "The rest of you follow me along this wall and around to the rear patio..." He turned back to Frank and linked his arms around his waist as Alain did the same on the other side. "Just until we get around there... then you're on your own," he said quietly.

"Understood," Frank said. "Let's go then."

The group of them ran along the wall, keeping as close as they could to the overhanging building, looking nervously up from time to time at the high-level windows in the end of the chateau that looked straight at them. A figure appeared briefly in one, but ducked back out of sight without making any aggressive move. "I reckon they're just trying to sit it out until the Yanks come," Lecroix hissed. "Otherwise they'd be firing at us now." He spoke too soon, for even before he had finished the sentence a window was flung open and a rifle poked through.

They flattened themselves against the wall. The rifle fired and a shower of plaster and stone spattered around them. A series of shots from the cemetery and the window was rapidly pulled shut. "Phew, that was close Alain," Lecroix whispered.

"Too close," Frank agreed. "Quick, let's get to the end, where we'll be out of sight."

The group picked up again and ran, doubled up, along to the end wall of the chateau, where they paused for a moment to recover their breath before making their way down the hill, keeping their backs to the wall around to the lower patio.

Two men stepped from the alcove beside the steps. For a split second they made as if to challenge, but then they recognised their leader. "Thierry," Lecroix growled. "Alright?"

Thierry shook his head. "Alright if you mean are we all safe. But we can't get any further in. If we try to move up onto the top patio they'll just pick us off one by one."

Lecroix pointed at Frank, now slumped against the wall, breathing heavily. "That's why he's here."

Thierry looked at Frank and then back at Lecroix. "Him? What can he do?"

Frank pushed himself off the wall and stood free. He took a deep breath and then waved Lecroix across. "Get three of the men to stay on the steps," he said quietly. "Tell them to start firing as soon as they hear the chaps at the front begin... the rest come with us."

"Come with us where?" said Lecroix, a slight note of exasperation creeping into his voice. Frank turned and indicated the alcove and the Madonna.

"Grab those two knobs on either side and push in," he said. Lecroix looked at where he was pointing and then back at Frank. "Go on," Frank urged.

Alain brushed past Lecroix and grabbed the Madonna, pushing inwards as the others crowded around him, trying to see what was happening. The figure moved and revealed the opening. All fell silent as Alain stood back and Lecroix stepped forward and peered in. He looked from the darkness to Frank and smiled and then snapped his fingers at Thierry. "Get your men... all except three, as Frank said. Get them down here now." Thierry nodded his head and turned. "And tell them to stop firing fifteen minutes after they begin at the front," Lecroix called.

They waited as Thierry rounded up the men and brought them back down off the steps. "Torches!" Lecroix called. They were handed through to him and he switched them on, handing one to Frank, one to Alain and one to Thierry. He indicated the tunnel entrance with a sweep of his hand and inclined his head in invitation to Frank. "What now?"

Frank bent a section of a hydrangea bush growing from the carefully manicured sand of the pathway. He brushed a patch smooth and then quickly stripped the leaves from the stem and crouched painfully down. Lecroix followed him and the rest gathered around. Swiftly, Frank drew a rough map in the sand. "The tunnel runs straight in from here, and then about halfway through the building it splits just here. One section goes to a stone trapdoor in the scullery, next door to the kitchen... the other goes straight on and ends up at a secret... well a panel at the end of the main staircase..."

"What do you suggest?"

Frank thought for a moment. "The passageway to the scullery will be blocked by two bodies... Well, they may still be alive. Gunther and I stuffed the poor buggers down there the other night. We need to get them out if we're to go in that way, and the best thing is for us to go in from both entrances at the same time, two minutes after the shooting."

"Can we make it?"

Frank stood, assisted by Lecroix. "Yes, easily. Now, when we come up in the main hall, we'll be facing down that way." He pointed to the left. "The corridor will go on, and just along on the left is a small staircase behind a door, which leads up through all the floors. Down five steps, just on the right of where we'll come up, is the door to the kitchen... so that's where the others will be coming in from. If we come up and turn right, we'll be behind any defences at the front door and also those at these patio doors up there." He pointed back over his head at the top patio.

Lecroix looked concerned. "Yes, but all of that presupposes that they'll all be on the ground floor when we know, because they've just been firing at us as we came across, that they're upstairs as well."

"Exactly," said Frank, "that's why we need to split into three groups. One to go through to the scullery... the other two to go in through the panel in the staircase, with one section holding the ground floor from the foot of the main staircase, whilst the others get upstairs as soon as they can using the secondary staircase."

Lecroix looked around the group of men. "Right, you all heard that. Now we've only got... Christ! We've only got twenty minutes until they start firing..."

"Plus the fifteen that they'll be firing for," Frank reminded him. "If we're making our final preparations during all of that it'll cover up any noise we make and, besides, they'll be too busy to notice us."

Lecroix looked relieved. He nodded. "Right, Frank will lead the way. We'll split into three groups. My group and Alain's group will go to the main staircase, with Alain's group going up using the other stairs. Thierry, your group will clear the other passageway and come up in the kitchen." He turned to Frank. "Is that in the front of the building?"

"Yes."

"And does it cover the yard?"

"Yes, and the way into it." He turned to Thierry. "Your tunnel ends in a spiral staircase leading straight up to a stone slab that you have to lift. That leads into the scullery and to the kitchen. The Germans... the ones I told you about, are tied together on that staircase and you'll have to move them before you can lift the slab."

Thierry laughed. He reached into his jacket and withdrew a wicked-looking knife, which he brandished in front of Frank. "We'll remove them," he drawled cruelly, "even if we have to cut them into little pieces to get them out."

Frank grimaced in distaste and Lecroix turned to Thierry. "You make sure when you're in that there's no Boche in the yard who can come through to us and then, as soon as you can, make your way in to where we'll be. Understood?" Thierry nodded and Lecroix turned from him. "Right, weapons ready? Good. Keep up close to each other, keep quiet, and listen for instructions. Understood?"

The men replied with nods and grunts and Lecroix turned and followed Frank into the cool of the tunnel. For a full ten minutes they padded along the dusty stone floors in silence, each man concentrating on keeping his distance from his companion in front and the light of the torches flickering around the tunnel walls.

Frank forced himself to set the right pace, aware that they must reach the tunnels' ends by the time the firing began so that they would have time to prepare themselves before bursting in. He bumped against the tunnel wall and recoiled from the pain that shot through his shoulder, stopping in his tracks. Behind him, Lecroix stopped and half turned as the man immediately behind him bumped into him and the whole line of men ground to a halt, muttering and cursing.

"What's happening?" Alain called in a whisper, holding his torch up high and shining it down the line of stalled men.

Lecroix turned, shielding his eyes from the glare. "Nothing. Wait a moment." He turned back to Frank. "Alright Frank?" Frank's head swam and he lowered the torch, its beam shining at the ground. Lecroix took it from him. "I said you weren't well enough for this Frank," he hissed through clenched teeth. "I should have... You could jeopardise this whole thing."

"I'll be alright," Frank said, willing himself to stand upright while reaching out for the torch.

Lecroix shone the torch at him and Frank, despite the glare that made him want to drop his gaze, held steady, staring into the light in the direction he knew Lecroix would be examining him from. He reached out for the torch. "Not far now to the junction." There was a moment's hesitation before Lecroix handed him back the torch. "Thank you," Frank mumbled before turning and making his way along the tunnel. The others followed as before for about another ten metres before once again Frank stopped, holding his torch up high in his good hand.

"What now?" came the muffled question from behind.

"This is the split. That's the tunnel that leads to the scullery," Frank said, pointing the beam of his torch down the branch. The beam seemed to divide in front of him and his senses swam. He slumped against the curved wall of the tunnel and slid down to the floor.

"This is as far as you go Frank... and that's an order," said Lecroix, taking the torch from Frank's practically nerveless fingers. "Wait down here and..."

Frank raised his head despairingly. "You need... the panel. There's a handle on the right. Turn it and the door opens inwards. The trap door. That's got to be lifted straight up, otherwise it'll bind." Lecroix nodded his understanding. "Leave me a gun please," Frank continued.

"Why? What good will it do?"

Frank made as if to rise. "I could cover this tunnel. What if one of the Boche tries to escape this way after you're through?"

For a second Lecroix considered the possibility, then he lifted the flap on his hip holster and withdrew a pistol. He handed it to Frank and then turned. "Pass the word back that this is where we divide. Thierry and his group take this route... the first two groups follow me straight ahead," said Lecroix. He tapped Frank on the shoulder. "Thank you Frank. Now rest here and let us do our work." He turned. "Good luck men," he called softly. "Let's nail the bastards."

Frank pulled his feet in and pushed himself up the wall of the tunnel as the column of men swept past him, apologising whenever one of them inadvertently knocked into him. The gloom gave way to the torch held by Alain, who paused momentarily as he drew abreast of him before continuing on. Ten more men stumbled past him with returned murmurs of identification before Thierry's torch lit the junction. "Is this it?" he asked briefly.

"Yes," Frank replied.

Thierry looked quickly along the main tunnel at the receding lights of the other two torches. He turned. "Right men, we're this way... hurry now, we've only got a few minutes." He led the way off down the branch and Frank allowed himself to slip back down the tunnel wall and sit on the floor in the darkness. He cocked his ear, listening for sounds of his companions. They must be at the end by now. Even now they would be climbing the straight flight of stairs to the back of the secret panel. He sighed. They would get Weber and he would never get the chance to see him die... to tell him that Pierre-Luc... His thoughts were interrupted. Faintly at first and then louder came the sound of the barrage as it started, first at the front and then from the rear. Louder rifle fire... followed by return fire from within the chateau. 'Good, they would be so busy firing out that they would never suspect where their real danger lurked,' he thought. 'Gunther would know that any attack, any rescue, would come from the tunnel. He quite obviously hadn't given the secret away, otherwise...'

Then an odd noise diverted his attention. Someone was coming down the tunnel! He could clearly hear the sound of heavy boots on the stone and a strange dragging sound, coupled with a low... singing? Was someone singing?

He peered into the pitch darkness, fear and horror rising in equal measure as the strange sounds came closer. His nose wrinkled as an acrid smell came to him, the smell of fear, urine and sweat. It got stronger and he sensed, as much as felt, the imminent arrival of whatever... whoever this was, even before whatever it was bumped into him in the dark. The singing stopped and Frank felt himself face to face in the darkness with what was obviously one of the German soldiers he and Gunther had tied up. The man was now, clearly, completely mad. The singing started again and the man moved forward, brushing past Frank in the narrow confines. Frank's hands travelled unwittingly down and across the man's tunic, feeling the leather straps, the buttons, the gash... and the warm entrails that flowed from the slash in his lower tunic. Thierry had been as good as his word, it seemed, but this poor demented creature seemed oblivious to anything.

Even as the man stumbled past him to his imminent and agonising death, Frank's feet were swept away from him by the body of the second man as it jerked past, tethered to one leg of the dying man. Frank fell heavily, cushioned by the stiff body, his face millimetres from that of the dead German, feeling the stubble that grazed his cheek. A tug forced his weight full down, and a long, low, rattling moan issued from the corpse's lips. Horrified, Frank struggled and wriggled off in a rising tide of revulsion, even as the body jerked forward and continued its slow journey.

For a moment he lay on the floor of the tunnel, panting with a mixture of terror and pain. 'Got to get up,' he thought. 'Get up and get to the end. I can't stay down here in the dark.' He sat up and felt about for the pistol that he had dropped in his fright, searching the dusty floor with his palms held open. His hand connected with the cold, hard metal of the barrel and he gratefully picked up the weapon and cradled it to his chest like some rediscovered treasure.

He got to his knees and then rose unsteadily to his feet, breathing deeply. 'Which way was it? Yes that way... it was that way,' he thought.

Above him the guns still sounded as he made his way slowly down the tunnel, and in front of him, as he approached the place where the stairs would rise up, he became aware of the dim light given off by the torches of his companions, waiting there for the barrage to stop. He reached the foot of the stairs, even as he realised that above him the gunfire had changed and that all he could hear was the dwindling sound of outgoing fire.

A shout warned of the attack and light flooded down the stairs as the panel was burst open and the men poured out into the main hallway above. Shots and cries of alarm carried down to Frank, waiting at the foot of the stairs. Summoning up the strength to mount them, he put his foot on the first step. This was it. He had to be there when Weber was caught... had to see his face when he realised that he had come to rescue Gunther.

Gunther! Would Weber use him as a hostage? Would he kill him just out of spite? He had to get there. Fear and anger flooded strength back into his veins and he mounted the stairs, the pistol held before him. He reached the top and paused before entering the hallway. No gunfire?! Why was it all so quiet?

He stepped from beneath the staircase, his pistol held ready, and then lowered it at the sight that befell him.

Rows of German soldiers stood facing the end walls of the hallway, their hands in the air in surrender, whilst about them and behind them his companion maquisard busied themselves with checking them, none too gently, for weapons. Two officers stepped from the dining room, their hands held aloft, their faces pale with the knowledge of what was about to befall them, yet still retaining that air of disdain they had so long cultivated when dealing with or addressing Frenchmen.

"We are prisoners of war and we claim our rights under the..." one of them haughtily began demanding before his words were cut short by a rifle butt thumping into the back of his neck. He stumbled and nearly fell, but recovered himself just in time.

"Prisoners of war!" growled Lecroix. "Were they prisoners of war, the men and women that you shot in cold blood at the Carrefour d'Orleans?"

The second officer half turned. "We... it was orders. We were under orders. We had no choice in the matter. It was Herr Weber," he stammered.

"Weber!" Frank interjected. "Where is Weber?"

"I thought I told you..." Lecroix started to yell, but Frank, standing in front of the officers, had seen their eyes flick towards the stairs at the question.

"He's upstairs!" Frank cried. "Got to get him." He turned and made for the foot of the stairs.

"No Frank! Leave him to Alain. He's up there already," Lecroix called over the heads of the two German officers. "They'll bring him down."

"But if he's got Gunther..." Frank stepped forward to within a metre of the two officers, one holding his neck, his head bowed, the other staring defiantly at him. He raised his pistol and pointed it between the man's eyes. "Where has he got Gunther?"

The man's brow furrowed and his eyes took on a questioning expression. "Gunther?"

"Yes, Leutnant Gunther Schmidt. Where is he?"

The faintest flicker of a smile crossed the man's face before he drew himself erect. "The traitor Schmidt was executed with the other criminals in the forest."

Frank stood open-mouthed. His head rang and the words of the man seemed to repeat and repeat in his brain. No... no, it couldn't be. Gunther was upstairs. Weber had him there. "You lie," Lecroix shouted, and the man turned as Frank recovered sense enough to shout himself.

"No! You're lying!"

"No German soldiers were amongst those murdered at the carrefour," Lecroix stated coldly.

The officer smiled openly now. He turned to Frank's stricken face and laughed. A deep, cruel laugh which welled up and shook his frame. Lecroix swiped the barrel of his rifle across the man's neck and he stumbled forward, almost crashing into Frank, who just managed to step aside as he fell to the floor. He looked up from the ground, the smile still playing on his face despite the obvious pain that he felt from the blow. Frank stared down at him with loathing. How could he just smile as he told these lies? "You're lying!" he almost screamed at the fallen man. He looked from him to Lecroix. "Did you see Gunther or any Germans amongst the dead?"

Lecroix shook his head. The officer struggled to his feet, brushing dirt, both real and imaginary, from his tunic. Frank turned back to him and the man looked him squarely in the eye. "No, but there were two priests, were there not?" Frank's eyes flicked beyond him to Lecroix, who nodded confirmation. The officer noted the gesture. "One of them was the traitor Schmidt... no longer worthy of being called an officer of the German Reich... a Jew lover and a traitor who..." His words were cut short by the shot from Frank's pistol that ripped through his temple and exploded out from the back of his head, scattering brains and blood in a wide arc that ran across the wall and over the other officer.

For a moment Lecroix stood there, but then even as the second officer turned to him beseeching, he swung his rifle around and fired. The man stood swaying slightly, staring at him, a puzzled expression on his face, before he slowly crumpled forward and fell dead to the floor.

Frank stood looking down at what had, moments before, been two human beings... before he and Lecroix had extinguished their hateful lives. He felt no remorse for his actions, no pity for the broken corpses. They had killed Pierre-Luc... Gunther... all of those poor souls who had surrendered, unarmed at the Carrefour d'Orleans, even if it had been at Weber's...

Weber! Where was Weber? He looked up at Lecroix. "Where's Weber?" he mouthed. Upstairs! He was upstairs. The officers had said as much before their death! He turned and looked up the wide flight, his pistol held in anticipation. Men appeared at the balustrading, calling down and pointing back along the gallery, out of sight from those below. Frank stepped forward. "Weber?"

"He's gone down the other staircase!" Alain shouted from above. "The bastard hid in a cupboard until we were past and then ran back... he'll be coming out in a minute... we'll go in from up here!"

Frank wheeled around, all sense of pain and fatigue now forgotten. Weber was here. His friend's murderer was within metres of where he stood and he was going to kill him. Cold rage took over as he turned and made his way towards the door to the secondary staircase, his pistol levelled at it in expectation.

"Careful Frank!" called Lecroix. "Wait for me a moment."

Frank took no notice. He continued walking towards the door as Lecroix joined him. He reached the door and stood silently waiting. Lecroix levelled his rifle and the two of them waited in silence, oblivious to all that was going on around them as maquisard chivvied their captives out of the front doors and onto the front lawns.

The door burst open and Frank raised his pistol to fire. "Hold your fire!" Alain screamed, pulling the door shut again. "It's me!"

Alain? Alain?! Then where...? Frank darted forward as Alain once more pushed the door open. "Where is he!" he screamed.

"I don't know, a clearly shaken Alain said. "He must have gone on down... where does the staircase go on to?"

"To the wine cellars, but there's no way out from there," Frank mused.

"We need to get him out from there then," Lecroix said quietly. "I'll lead the way and you follow Frank... if you're up to it."

A grim smile crossed Frank's resolute face. "Let's get it done," he said.

Lecroix nodded. "Follow me then," he turned to Alain. "Alain, you help the others get those Boche out and see if you can identify which ones were at the carrefour." Alain nodded and turned back towards the main doors. Lecroix opened the small door and stepped through. He looked down and then back up to where a maquisard was perched on the landing above. "Alright Guy?"

"Alright," came the reply.

"You stay there and keep watch," Lecroix ordered. He glanced at Frank. "Ready?"

"Ready," Frank said.

Lecroix started down the stairs, his rifle held before him. Frank followed, his pistol gripped tightly in his hand as they wound their way down the narrow flight until Frank put his hand out and held Lecroix back. "That's the bottom around the next turn... we'll be in his sights."

Lecroix looked up at Frank and nodded his understanding. He put his finger to his lip, commanding silence, and crept on down.

"Ah, good morning gentlemen," came the echoing but unmistakable voice of Weber. "Oh monsieur... I beg your pardon, Mr Balfour. How nice to see you again."

Frank's blood boiled and he went to brush past Lecroix, but the stronger man held him back.

Weber stood in the aisle, his hand in his jacket pocket near his breast.

"Take out the gun!" Lecroix ordered, "...and throw it on the floor five metres in front of you. Any false move and I'll drop you before..."

Weber smiled. "Gun? I have no gun gentlemen... but I do have this." He withdrew his hand from his jacket and held up a grenade. "The pin is out gentlemen, and this..." He swept his other hand in an arc around him. "This is ammunition... explosives... grenades like this one. So much more useful than wine, don't you think... so much more practicable."

Lecroix lowered his rifle a little, but Frank stepped forward and levelled his pistol at the German's head. "No Frank!" Lecroix warned, putting his hand out and taking hold of Frank's arm. "If that goes off..."

"If this goes off, the entire chateau and all of us go off with it," added Weber coldly. "Now gentlemen, let us go from this dark and dreary place and see if we can't come to some suitable arrangement."

"Suitable arrangement!" hissed Frank. "You killed Gunther, you swine."

Weber smiled. "Gunther? Gunther? Oh you mean Schmidt. Leutnant Gunther Schmidt." He smiled. "The late Leutnant Gunther

Schmidt. Yes, I had him killed... along with all his fellow criminals. He deserved no better."

"He was my friend!" Frank yelled back at him. "Him and Pierre-Luc... they were... you bastard!"

Weber stood still, the grenade still held aloft. He tutted, shaking his head. "Now now, Mr Balfour, this is war, you know. You really shouldn't get so emotional about it..."

"They were my friends too," growled Lecroix. "Those men and women you so cruelly murdered in the forest."

"War! They were killed in the proper execution of a war," Weber insisted. Lecroix went to reply, but Weber waved his free hand in a dismissive gesture. "I've got neither the time nor the inclination to carry on this pointless argument," he said impatiently. "You," he pointed at Lecroix. "You, over there." He indicated an aisle of ammunition boxes to the right. Lecroix moved slowly towards them and Frank made as if to follow. "Not you Balfour! You lead the way up the stairs and tell your friends to make way, otherwise, if they don't, then one false move and the two of us will go to heaven together."

In spite of the situation, Frank couldn't help a bitter laugh. "Heaven! Do you imagine for one moment that if there is a heaven, a swine like you will get there?"

Weber looked a tiny bit nonplussed for a moment, but then recovered his composure.

"I've no time for an argument on theology either," he said thinly. "Come now, we've wasted enough time down here... lead the way." He jerked the grenade-carrying arm at the staircase. Frank glanced over at Lecroix and the Canadian nodded his assent and inclined his head to the stairs. Frank turned and made his way back up, with Weber following on behind. Lecroix joined in, keeping five steps back.

The man Lecroix had addressed as Guy showed himself. He looked past Frank to Weber and then back at Frank. "He's got a primed grenade," Frank said, matter-of-factly. "You go ahead and then let us through." Guy nodded, opened the door and stepped into the hallway. Frank followed and then turned, his pistol held ready as first Weber and then Lecroix stepped from the small door.

"What now?" asked Lecroix, sidling past and around Weber to join Frank. "You can't go on holding that or even threaten us all with it outside, can you?"

Weber looked into his eyes. "No. I can't. And I therefore surrender to you Mr Balfour as, I believe, a British officer, and I expect to be..." His voice tailed off as his eyes went beyond the two men in front of him and took in the sight of the dead officers and the long arc of gore across the wall. His gaze flicked up to meet the cold hatred in the other men's eyes. He stared deep within them, his brow furrowing slightly as he recognised the abyss of his own demise. He nodded, almost imperceptibly in acceptance.

Frank and Lecroix stood silent, watching the workings of the man's mind show on his face. He backed away slightly, towards the door they had all just stepped through. They realised what he was doing, but too late. Weber swung with one easy motion and flung the grenade at them before turning to the door.

In almost slow motion Frank raised his pistol and shot, catching the fleeing man in the back, sending him sprawling through the open door to tumble down the cellar stairs and out of sight, even as Lecroix threw away his rifle and dived on the grenade to catch it with one hand and fling it after Weber in a long curve.

"Get out! Get out!" Lecroix screamed. Frank turned, dropping his gun, and started to run. His legs felt like lead and he pushed and pumped them, willing them to go faster as Lecroix screamed "Out! Out! Out!"

A crump from below turned into a roar that seemed to just grow and grow, and a section of the wall around the staircase blew out in a hail of splintered wood and dust that sent the two men sprawling, face down, on the floor and blew them like tumbling litter in the wind, along the hallway, to crash into the dining room wall.

Frank winced in agony as his injured shoulder smashed against the masonry. He raised his head and stared into the face of Lecroix, a white mask studded with the shards of a thousand pieces of wood rooted in small, spreading stains of red. His eyes blinked, the lashes coated with white powder, and his mouth worked, still screaming the one word, "Out!"

The two of them raised themselves on all fours and wheeled around to the beckoning light of the open doors, their legs pushing their bodies up like runners at the start of a race. They pushed off and cleared the corner, even as a second huge blast tore through the building, smashing white-hot air into the wall they had just left, its force ejecting all before it and blowing the two men like corks from a bottle to tumble and roll out and down onto the driveway.

As he rolled, Frank saw the fire rushing from the building's windows; then the men on the lawn, friend and foe alike, scattered like nine pins. An animal instinct took hold and he scrabbled in the rough stones, forcing himself forward by any means, away from the building, whilst beside him Lecroix did the same.

They reached the low wall bounding the steps down to the lower garden, previously the old moat, and tumbled down them in freefall as the chateau behind them seemed, to those still looking, to expand as if breathing in heavily. Walls bulged outwards and then settled back in place for a split second. Then a third huge roar went up and the whole roof appeared to lift slightly and then simply disintegrate as a Roman candle of multi-coloured fire shot heavenwards, carrying flaming spears which rained down on the terrified men and the surrounding buildings.

The air seemed to solidify and the sound seemed to roll around in each man's heads, scrambling all rational thought. Frank's eyes fixed on the stone step he lay upon and he examined its every detail, noting the etched lines of lichen... the intricate patterning and overlay of colours... decades of slow growth.

As the red mist clouded his vision, a hand touched his shoulder and he turned wild eyes to this intrusion. Why was anyone interrupting his reverie? "Are you alright Frank?"

Thoughts tumbled around in Frank's head. "Frank? Is that who I am? Alright? Lecroix? Yes, it's Lecroix. Why is blood dripping from his eyes? Why...?" He raised his head and sat up painfully, turning on the step to look beyond Lecroix to the chateau.

The heat from the fire struck his face and he raised his arm to shield his eyes. The whole main building already seemed an empty, burning shell... a vast oven in which all of his memories... all of his childhood was being reduced to ashes and hurled skywards. A crash, and the building seemed to shudder as the top floor collapsed down onto the first and the combined weight of the two, sinking as a whole, operated like some giant bellows, pumping ash and super-heated air from every orifice.

He stood slowly, mounting the steps, his gaze fixed on the inferno that was now Weber's funeral pyre. He turned to look at Lecroix, who returned his look with a sorrowful shaking of his head. "I'm sorry Frank..."

"It's best... it was defiled... now it's..." He paused and turned as a fresh roar sounded to the right and the main farm buildings, stacked with hay and straw, much of which he, himself, had helped to put there, burst into flames. All would soon be gone. A crash, and the front wall of the main chateau seemed to simply fold inwards, and the rest of the walls followed as if they were a box that had outlasted its use and was busy storing itself for another time.

Hot ash and dust rained around them, igniting small grass fires against the outer walls. The assembled men began to separate out into their respective roles of captor and captive, filing silently through the gates and out onto the road. "Time to go Frank," Lecroix whispered, touching his arm.

"What?" Frank asked.

"Time to go Frank... there's nothing more to do here... the others will see to these Boche and I need to get back to town. The Americans will be here soon. You could help, they'll need translators... if you're well enough."

Well enough... well enough. 'Am I well enough?' Frank thought. Intense weariness seemed to flow through him. He turned away from the questioning eyes of Lecroix and looked at the remains of his life, crackling like some huge bonfire, its pall of dark smoke rising high into the clear August skies. Pain shot through his arm and he winced and gripped his shoulder, bowing his head. Lecroix moved close and put his arm around his waist. "Here, I've got you," he soothed. "I think perhaps you've done enough for today, my friend."

Frank looked up at him, noting the kindness and respect in the man's eyes that seemed to replace the usual cold aloofness of authority. Everything was changing. Soon the war would be over for this part of France... maybe soon for all the world. The Americans... he would like to see the moment... "Can I come with you just to..."

"Savour the moment?" interrupted Lecroix. "You sure can Frank... Come on now, let's go."

Frank took one last look at the blazing ruins. Then he straightened up, and with Lecroix holding just his elbow, he turned and marched out of the gates and along the road towards where they had left their vehicle. As they passed, both friend and foe seemed to recognise his loss, respectfully falling silent as the two men approached, with those who didn't know of his connection being told of it by their nearest neighbour, whether French or German.

At the point where the road curved around the outside wall of the great barn, they had to step to the outer side to avoid the intense heat being given off by the stones as the mortar crumbled, powdered and spat. Frank stared resolutely ahead, concentrating on reaching his destination.

They approached the gate and crossed the road, with Lecroix rushing forward to open the door for him. Frank took his seat and stared ahead through the windscreen.

Lecroix took the driving seat, reversed out and, without a backward glance from either man, they drove slowly off in the direction they had come from and back towards Chateauneuf.

The journey into town was conducted in total silence. Frank stared ahead, his mind blank with dismay. All gone! All lost forever... the chateau... all that Armand had really loved... all gone. The fellowship, Gunther, Pierre-Luc and Marcel... Philippe... all that he had cherished...

They approached the new market and drew to a halt before a swirling crowd of men, women and children, waving flags and carrying flowers as they sang and laughed.

In their midst was a tank. The vehicle was garlanded with flowers as smiling American soldiers reached down to the sea of outstretched hands.

"It's nearly over Frank," Lecroix said.

Frank looked at him and shook his head. "Over for this town maybe, but..."

"...but nothing Frank. Yes there's more to go, but this is the beginning of the end... Paris by the end of the month, at least. Home for you, I shouldn't doubt."

'Home,' Frank thought. 'Home? Where is home?' He closed his eyes and the towering walls of the chateau rose up in his mind's eye before crumbling in flames before him. He shook his head and the rolling green hills of Devon flashed before him. Lizzie was there with James... and George. Kent? No, Kent had never been his home, even if Jesse was there with Violet and the boys... he had felt at home but never... it had never been his home. Here was his home, in this smiling town that he had known so long... that he had grown up in, where he had..."

His thoughts were interrupted. "Look at that!" Lecroix shouted, pointing off to the right. "They don't take long, do they?"

Frank followed the direction of Lecroix's pointing finger.

Away at the other end of the market, a jeering crowd of men and women pushed and prodded a trio of shaven-headed women, who stumbled wide-eyed from iron pillar to iron pillar seeking some kind of sanctuary, only to be forced from it and driven on.

One of the women broke and ran off left, her hands outstretched to someone in the crowd... beseeching. Frank stared. Was that Marie? It looked like Marie. Yes it was, he realised as she stepped forward, a small child in her arms. Why was Marie...? Frank looked on incredulously. Who was the shaven-headed woman begging her for help? It couldn't be..." "Oh my God! Annette!" he cried, flinging open the vehicle's door.

A woman, her face contorted with hatred, grabbed Annette by the arm and swung her back into the crowd. She turned, triumphant, in Frank's direction as he started to run, a cruel smile on her face, which froze as he approached. Nicole! Of all... He raised his hand to shout her name, but she turned and darted back into the mob.

"Annette, it's me, Frank!" he called from about twenty metres away. "Leave her alone!"

The frightened girl's eyes swivelled towards him, wide with terror yet narrowing as she struggled to recognise and believe it was truly him. "Frank!" she screamed, reaching out towards him. "Fran..." Her voice was cut short as her outstretched hand was grabbed and she was swung violently against the fluted iron of the stanchion. Her head cracked against the dull metal and her eyes glazed over before her knees buckled and she slipped sideways, cracking her head with a terrible sound on the sharp edge of the kerb, just as Frank reached her.

He sank to one knee, cradling her head in his arms, feeling the sticky blood oozing from the gash in the back of her skull. "Annette," he soothed. "Annette it's me, Frank... you're safe now. Her eyes flickered open.

"Frank. Is it truly you?"

"Yes. Yes it's me, Annette... you're safe now." She smiled. Her eyes closed and she appeared to fall asleep in his arms. Lecroix arrived, pushing back the crowd with his rifle, demanding respect, subduing the beast within the mob, who backed away grudgingly, unwilling to be deprived of their victim.

Annette's eyes opened again, a strange, sleepy look in them. She spoke as if in a dream. "Gunther?"

Frank's eyes filled, but he held her clouded gaze. "Gunther's alright... he'll be along in a moment..." Marie approached, the child in her arms... Gunther's child, no doubt of it with his blonde hair and clear grey eyes. "Here's..."

"Dieter," Marie whispered.

"Here's Dieter," said Frank quietly, taking the little boy from Marie and holding him close to his mother. The child's chubby little arms reached out and Annette smiled weakly.

"Take care of him Frank," she whispered. "Make sure... I loved him... tell him..." Her eyes flickered and rolled upwards and her head slipped sideways.

"Maman," the little boy wailed, but Frank held him tight. A hand clutched his shoulder and he turned to see Lecroix looking down at him, concern and pity written large on his face.

"Annette," Frank whispered. "She was the girl, the Jewish girl I told you of, that we rescued from Pithiviers. Gunther and she... this is Gunther's child, Dieter." He stood slowly, still cradling the child.

Marie stepped forward, her eyes streaming tears."Is she...?"

Frank nodded and she buried her head in her hands, sobbing.

He lowered the child to the ground and turned on the mob, searching amongst and within them for Nicole. She was nowhere to be seen.

The faces that surrounded him were many that he knew, but here... here they were strangers. He searched amongst them for one who he knew for certain had resisted, one that had actively helped in the struggle against the Germans... there was not one. All were involved in a macabre role in expiation of their own guilt... each one assuming at last, in the freedom granted by the resistance of men and women they had decried, the role of judge and jury.

He held their gazes, one by one, daring comment, willing argument. None came and eyes were lowered in silence as their attention shifted. "That's it!" he cried, flinging his arms open. "Good job. Well done... another Boche collaborator dead... another lover killed, another child..." He turned and indicated Dieter as Marie leant forward and took the child's hand. "...orphaned. Feel good, does it? Feels good? You know nothing. She..." He pointed to Annette's body. "...she fought her way through life, survived the concentration camp at Pithiviers... lived as a Jewess... oh yes, she was Jewish... didn't you know that?... lived under the shadow of fear that you and your kind encouraged..." He stopped, unable to continue... afraid that he might go on and say more than was warranted.

The crowd melted away, leaving the other two shaven-headed girls standing, unsure of what they were to do. Lecroix jerked his head at them to disappear and they both picked up their heels and ran, their white heads displaying their shame.

Frank turned to Marie. "Are you alright? Where's Jean-Claude?"

Marie looked up at him with frightened eyes, realisation dawning on her. Her hand rose to her lips and she screwed up her face in anguish. "He's at the factory, Monsieur Frank. He heard there were some who were going there for Leclerc and he..."

"How long ago?!" Frank demanded, grabbing her shoulder roughly and shaking her. "I'm sorry Marie." He let go of the frightened woman. "How long?"

"A few minutes ago... I was going too... but then I saw Annette and..."

"Take care of the boy... go to Father René's house, I'll be back... don't go to the... the chateau has gone..." Her face showed disbelief and horror. "Go to the priest's house and wait there for me." She nodded and Frank turned to Lecroix. "Get the van quick!"

Lecroix opened his mouth to say something, but the look on Frank's face brooked no argument and he turned and ran back to the van.

Marie bent down by Annette, shielding and cradling the boy from the direct sight of his mother's body. "We can't just leave her here," she wailed softly.

"Tell Father René," Frank said quietly, wiping the tears from his face. "He'll come and get her." The van pulled up, the door swinging open. "Quick Marie, get to the priest... take care of her," Frank urged. She nodded and he got into the passenger seat, pulling the door shut as Lecroix pulled away.

"Where are we going?"

Frank pointed ahead. "Left at the end."

The van screeched around the corner and raced along behind the market, with Frank directing Lecroix, urging him on to greater speed. "Where exactly are we going Frank?" Lecroix demanded, gripping the steering wheel as they swung right with the thin tyres wailing on the tarmac. "If we're not careful, we'll be picked off as escaping Boche."

"My factory," Frank answered, wincing as the motion threw him against the side of the vehicle. "I've lost my home... I don't want to lose my livelihood as well."

"Christ!" Lecroix swore as they swung into the Avenue du Gatinais and rumbled over the rail tracks. "I seem to have given up fighting the main war to fight your private one."

Frank smiled weakly across at him. "Turn right here!" he called, pointing down into the industrial area. "Told you to send me home with Alec, didn't I?" he said, as Lecroix grinned ruefully. "Here... there... behind that crowd, those gates... bloody hell, what are they doing?"

In front of them, a crowd of angry men stood hurling missiles across and over the huge iron gates, whilst beyond them Leclerc and a very frightened-looking Jean-Claude pleaded in vain for calm.

Two men broke from the mob and ran at the gates, scrambling up the vertical railings, cheered on by their fellows.

Lecroix swore as he pulled up, taking in the situation in one glance. He dismounted and ran around to help Frank out. "Stop!"

Frank shouted as he struggled from the van, trying to make himself heard above the din. "Stop it please!" One or two at the rear of the crowd turned around and swore at him, shouting at him to mind his own business before turning back to cheer at the men now reaching the top of the gates.

A shot rang out and the noise died, as all turned to observe Lecroix standing, his legs planted apart, the rifle that had fired into the air now pointed directly at the men on the gate.

"Get down now!" he called. "You all know who I am, who this is." He pointed to Frank. Now get down and disperse from here now!"

"Why should we?" snarled a burly man with a cap pulled low on his brow and a cigarette dangling from a blackened lip. He lurched forward, pointing back at the factory. "They're traitors... collaborators. That's no more than a German arms factory and he," he gestured back, "Leclerc is no more than a bloody Boche himself."

"That is my factory!" said Frank loudly. "None of you has the right..."

"The right? The right?! You talk about right. We've had to work in that place whilst you... you and your like have..."

"...have fought the Germans!" Lecroix interrupted.

The man sneered and lurched closer to Lecroix, who could now smell the drink on his breath. "Fought the Germans? What, from his estates in England." He laughed out loud and swung around, inviting his fellows and indicating Frank. "These bloody bosses are all the same... all as bad as the bloody Germans, if you ask me." He sneered and adopted a whining, cringing tone. "Did he take tea with Mr Churchill whilst we slaved here?" He straightened up and spat on the ground, growling. "Bloody plutocrats." A nervous ripple of laughter ran around the mob.

Lecroix held up his hand. "From the air as a British flyer and here, since March, with us in the forest." He swept his hand in an arc across the face of the mob. "How many of you were at Chicamour? How many of you were in the forest on Sunday?" He pointed to Frank.

"He was, and not an hour ago we were still fighting... whilst you..." He pointed directly at the drunken man. "...you were drinking and waiting until all was safe for you to come out and be heroes."

For a moment there was silence, but then an angry buzz started and the men on the gate made the last haul to perch atop the gates. Lecroix fired again and, as the sound of the shot died away, silence fell on the crowd. "Disperse, or the next shot will be the last sound one of you will hear!" he shouted.

He stood firm, his rifle held at the hip, pointing directly into the mass of bodies. Frank joined him and stood beside him, wishing that he too had a weapon. Gradually, grudgingly, the men backed away and started to retreat back down the road and across the rail tracks, towards the station yard. The two men on the gate swung down and joined their friends, standing for a moment in muttering groups before sidling off, leaving only the man in the cap standing defiant in front of Frank and Lecroix.

"Time to go home," Lecroix said quietly. The man looked around and, seeing that he was deserted, swore and spat once more on the ground before turning and walking off unsteadily, forcing his way through a gap in the wire and across the tracks towards town.

Frank breathed a sigh of relief. "Phew, that was close," he whispered. "Thank you. I owe you."

Lecroix smiled. "It's nothing... besides, I couldn't let you lose your livelihood, could I?"

Frank grinned at his companion and new-found friend. He held out his hand and Lecroix took it and shook it warmly.

"Monsieur Frank... is that you, Monsieur Frank," Leclerc called out.

Frank turned and walked forward to the gates. "As you see, Monsieur Leclerc. It is me."

Leclerc raised his hands to his mouth and stared at him in disbelief. "My God... it is... you are not... I saw you... I saw you..."

"Monsieur Frank, did you see Marie?" Jean-Claude interrupted. "I think they may have got Annette."

A cloud crossed Frank's face and his gaze dropped. He shook his head. "Yes, I saw Marie and... and Annette. They killed her."

Jean-Claude's eyes widened in horror. "Marie? They killed... who...?"

"No!" cried Frank, raising his hands, alarmed at the misinterpretation of his words. "No, not Marie... they killed Annette!"

Relief flooded over the older man's face, to be replaced almost as quickly by a look of genuine concern and grief. "Oh no. Oh no, the poor girl... the poor girl."

Frank stood silent for a moment. Lecroix moved forward. "Best open these gates and come with us," he said quietly.

Leclerc bustled forward now. "Yes. Yes, we're coming monsieur..." He looked at the resolute face of the Maquis commander and quailed slightly, turning flustered to Frank. "I did it for... there was little else I could do, Monsieur Frank... you know that the factory is all that has ever been important to me and... well it's all here for you, Monsieur Frank... I didn't do it for myself you understand... I..."

"I understand Monsieur Leclerc," said Frank softly. "I understand and I..."

"Will you... will they forgive me?" the frightened man stammered.

Frank looked at his old mentor and shook his head. "Will you forgive yourself?" he said quietly.

The old man looked into his eyes, held his gaze for a moment and then dropped his head, shaking it ruefully. Jean-Claude clapped him on the back and he flinched at the touch. "Come on," he said. "Get those gates open and let's go and find my Marie."

EPILOGUE
August 1946

A tern hovered briefly in the pale sky before dropping into the water, to rise again in a splash of silver and continue its lazy, flapping progress down the river.

Frank shielded his eyes from the glare and shifted his hip on the coarse sand. A twinge of pain made him wince and he rolled over to lie on the other elbow, gripping his shoulder and rubbing it gently.

"Mind you, don't get your shoes wet Dieter," he called to the small blonde boy playing with the loose-limbed black puppy by the water's edge.

The boy turned and waved before picking up a piece of driftwood and hurling it out into the water. The dog ran to the edge but stopped, looking back expectantly at the boy. "Go on Cashew," the boy shouted.

The dog stepped, hesitantly at first, into the water, but then at the continued and excited urging of the boy breasted the stream and swam powerfully out to the slow-moving stick. Frank smiled. The puppy was certainly doing the boy good and had brought him out of himself.

He sat and drew his knees up, gripping them and resting his chin on them as he stared out at the river. What would Gunther... Annette have thought of the boy? Would they have been pleased? He'd taken him to England as a tiny boy barely four months after poor Annette's stupid death. Violet had begged him to leave him with her after he had been released from his RAF service and sent back to France.

'Was it selfish of me,' he thought? 'Should I have...?' Funny, by having this small boy with him it felt... well it felt almost as if... but no, nothing could bring Gunther back. Not him, not any of them. All gone.

It hadn't been fair on the boy. He'd had to go to Paris several times before he was finally out of uniform forever... last May... barely a month after the terrible news of the death of darling Jesse. He'd wanted to go to England as soon as he heard, but it would have been too late... even the funeral was over by the time he got back and got the letter. Poor darling Jesse... hard to imagine that she was not still there in her little cottage just as she always had been... the start and the ending of every trip to England he'd ever made.

"Look Frank," cried Dieter. "Look how far he's gone!"

Frank looked up quickly in alarm. The puppy was indeed quite far out, still swimming bravely towards the swirling stick, now gripped by the current. He stood and hurriedly stripped off his trousers, kicking his shoes loose. He waded into the water, calling the dog's name, and at nearly waist high grabbed the struggling creature's collar and turned it back to the beach.

"Don't throw any more sticks here Dieter," he shouted as he reached the shoreline. "Go further up there, opposite the island. The current's too strong here."

The boy didn't reply as such, but instead picked up a stick and ran off down the sand in the direction of the island, followed by the barking dog. Frank smiled. He seemed happy enough. Marie had been wonderful with him, even if at her age the antics of the small boy did tend to leave her exhausted.

He'd be four soon. 'Good God! His birthday was in a week's time. Better get him something special,' he thought. 'Four... I was four when Violet first brought me here.' He bent down to pick up his trousers and started putting them back on before thinking the better of it and laying them out on the sand. He sat and lay back, his hands clasped behind his head.

Two... the boy had been two when he'd been orphaned. 'How well I know,' he considered. 'Well, I wasn't orphaned,' he thought. But... Frank shook his head at the memory, both real and imagined, of loneliness... emptiness... that awful void in the pit of the stomach.

He'd known that same feeling again when he had looked once more on the charred ruins of the chateau. "We can rebuild it," they'd all said. "You can build another chateau just as nice... maybe even nicer..." Build a chateau even nicer? How could you rebuild the memories? Could a new building ever bring back his friends? Could it... would it ever satisfy Armand? Could it take away the evil presence of Weber, whose earthly being was forever scattered in its midst?

No. Nothing could ever bring any of that back... nothing could ever replace the chateau of his boyhood... his manhood. He half smiled to himself and shook his head at the memory.

He'd sold the mineral rights of the grounds to a sand and gravel company. A wry smile played on his lips. The company was headed up by the very same man who had once tried to sack his factory on the day of liberation. They'd already all but obliterated all evidence of the chateau's existence. The whole area was fast being turned into a vast lake beside the river, which in the next few months would join and become one with the old lake that had lain at the bottom of the lawns. All that now remained was the small island that the cemetery had become, its banks forever shored up and fortified by the iron-strong roots of the yew hedge.

Gunther and Annette... well Annette and some of the ash-blackened earth he had managed to painfully scrape from the funeral pyre at the execution site in the forest, lay there as he had promised. He couldn't retrieve Gunther's whole body. He had been too late for that. In some way, part of his friends must be there... the rest... the rest lay in those lonely graves in the forest, Pierre-Luc's named, Gunther's marked as unknown, his body burnt beyond... And then there was the letter... he had buried the letter with them. Tears stung his eyes. In Gunther's jacket, which Marie had handed to him, there was the letter from Gisela... a private letter... a letter of farewell from a mother to a son but a letter, nonetheless, that had dictated and guided Gunther's actions. "Promise me that you will never take up arms against our friends," she had written... and he had kept that last farewell all those years in the pocket closest to his heart. Frank closed his eyes and forced himself to think of something else.

James! Florrie had sent him a photograph of his son, taken on his second birthday in the arms of... The familiar knot grew in his stomach and he compartmentalised the thought and memory of Lizzie, as if saving it for later. James would be three next month.

Violet had written recently... well back in May, that Lizzie's husband, George, was ill with some sort of lung infection. Apparently he was pretty ill... poor George. Poor George? Cuckolded as he was, his existence was one of warmth and love. He had Lizzie, Kate, Florrie and... and James.

Dieter's laugh rang out across the beach and he turned over and rested on one elbow to watch the boy and the dog playing with another boy.

Who was that other small boy? He seemed to be about a year younger than Dieter. He shaded his eyes with his hand and squinted along the sand.

A shadow fell over him, stretching across his prone body and pointing off in the direction of the two boys.

"Hallo Frank," said a woman's voice in English. He turned over and stared up at the figure, the features shaded, hidden by the glare of the sun in his eyes. The woman squatted down to his level and he gasped and rolled over, fumbling for his trousers. A hand stretched out and grabbed them, flinging them aloft as she rose and stepped back.

"Lizzie?" he stammered. "Is that you?"

"It most certainly is, Frank Balfour." She waved his trousers over her head and pointed with her other hand at his near nakedness. "Have you been expecting me?"

He stood, looking around, expecting to see others. "Shhh... where's George... are they with you? You should have..."

"I'm alone Frank... apart from James."

"But why? What's happened, why are you...?"

Lizzie lowered the trousers. Her voice dropped. "George is dead, Frank. He died..."

"Died? But... but... Violet said he was ill, but..."

She turned and he followed so that the sun was out of his eyes. "Are you not pleased to see me, Frank?" she whispered.

He shook his head in disbelief. She misinterpreted the movement and he saw the lowering of her eyes and the droop in her proud bearing. He put his hand out to her to put right the mistake. "No... I mean yes! Yes, I'm pleased... I'm bloody delighted... oh Lizzie!" He opened his arms and she stepped into his embrace, her mouth seeking his through her tears, as a blind puppy seeks its mother's milk.

For an age they embraced, murmuring softly as they swung gently in each other's arms. Then a small hand tugged at her skirt. They parted and looked down at James' enquiring face, looking up at them.

"Mummy this is Deetah," he said, looking at Frank. "Why hasn't this man got his trousers on?"

Lizzie giggled and stepped away from Frank, handing him his trousers as she bent down to cup the small boy's face in her hands. "This is Frank, darling... the one we came to see. The man I told you about."

"Is he going to be my new daddy?"

Lizzie cast an embarrassed glance back over her shoulder at Frank as he pulled up his trousers and buckled his belt. He smiled back down at her, raising his eyebrows in mock admonishment. "Well..." she began.

"Yes," said Frank firmly, and now it was her turn to look questioningly at him. He smiled down at her as she stood holding the boy's hand. "Yes," Frank repeated, "if she'll share me with a mistress called France."

Lizzie smiled. She let go of the boy's hand and stepped once more into Frank's embrace. "And if he'll share me with a heaven called Devon."

Frank inclined his head and raised his eyebrows. "They say travel enlightens the mind."

"They do indeed," she murmured as he once more put his lips to hers. James looked at Dieter as he arrived and the two of them grimaced in disgust, before running off together along the sand.

Frank held Lizzie in his arms, unwilling to break the spell... the magic of the moment, yet unable, also, to hold back the questions tumbling around in his mind. "What did you say to them at home... Florrie... Kate?"

"They told me to come."

"Both of them?"

"Both of them."

His eyes narrowed. "Does she know?"

"Kate?"

"Yes."

Lizzie's face was calm and serious. "I was going to tell her but..."

"...you couldn't do it?"

Lizzie shook her head. "She told me." She looked across at the boys playing in the sand with the dog. "She always knew... she just never said... until..."

He held her tight and rocked her in his arms. For what seemed an eternity they stayed like that until he released her and retrieved his shoes, slipping them on. "Come on," he said. "Let's get home and get something to eat. When did you arrive? You must be starving."

She laughed lightly. "It's alright, Marie gave us something... we'll last."

"You should have said you were coming."

"And spoil the surprise?"

He shook his head in wonder. "Come on boys. Back to the house now," he called. The two of them stood up, brushing the sand from each other. Dieter crossed to Frank and looked up expectantly. Frank tousled his hair. "Go on," he said softly. "You go ahead and show James." The boy smiled then turned and rushed off up the beach, followed by James and the puppy.

Frank watched them go, one taller with the startlingly blonde hair, the other shorter but thicker set, following his new-found hero.

"Ca commence encore," he whispered to himself.

THE END

The Author

The story within *Sing to Silent Stones* (Volumes One and Two) is largely fictional, but it does, nevertheless, incorporate very many true tales from David Snell's, and his wife Linda's, family.

Both of David's parents were wartime pilots in the RAF and he and his brother, Peter, spent much of their childhood on RAF bases in the UK and the Far East, where the talk often revolved around the war and flying. Peter became a pilot but unfortunately died, aged 38, doing aerobatics in his own Second World War Harvard. David has spent a lifetime in the property/building industry and is a well-known writer and speaker on the subject of self-building.

Without prejudice to his parents, the phrases 'The only good German is a dead one' and 'The Frogs are hopeless at fighting' were a constant theme. But David always questioned these assumptions. He is a lifelong anti-war campaigner.

David's interests revolve around history and bird-watching. He has been married to Linda for 47 years and he has three children and three grandchildren.

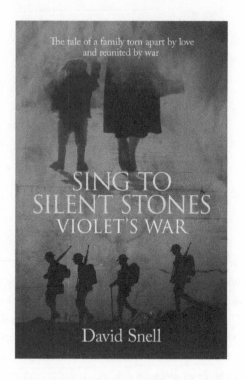